MF

W9-BJI-382

"What's going on?"

Hazel demanded an explanation for his evacuation order. "I know there's no fire. I heard the dispatcher say she was sending a unit. Who's coming?"

"The bomb squad," Burke answered.

"A bomb? I thought it was just another... I hadn't gotten a letter this week. I'd hoped Aaron would stop once his parole officer spoke with him. You think he sent a bomb to my clinic?"

"Gunny alerted there was an explosive. His nose is never wrong. I need you outside, too. Gunny and I have to clear the building."

"But...that's what the bomb squad is for, right? Shouldn't you have backup?"

"Go. It's what we do." He reached out to cup her cheek in his hand. "But I need you to be safe before I can go to work."

She nodded. Then she reached up and covered his hand with hers. "I'll see you outside," she vowed, as if her will could guarantee that they'd be reunited.

MISSION: K-9 RESCUE

USA TODAY Bestselling Author

JULIE MILLER
and
DANICA WINTERS

2 Thrilling Stories
K-9 Protector and *K-9 Recovery*

If you purchased this book without a cover you should be aware that this book is stolen property. It was reported as "unsold and destroyed" to the publisher, and neither the author nor the publisher has received any payment for this "stripped book."

⊕HARLEQUIN®

Recycling programs
for this product may
not exist in your area.

ISBN-13: 978-1-335-43000-7

Mission: K-9 Rescue

Copyright © 2022 by Harlequin Enterprises ULC

K-9 Protector
First published in 2020. This edition published in 2022.
Copyright © 2020 by Julie Miller

K-9 Recovery
First published in 2021. This edition published in 2022.
Copyright © 2021 by Danica Winters

All rights reserved. No part of this book may be used or reproduced in any manner whatsoever without written permission except in the case of brief quotations embodied in critical articles and reviews.

This is a work of fiction. Names, characters, places and incidents are either the product of the author's imagination or are used fictitiously. Any resemblance to actual persons, living or dead, businesses, companies, events or locales is entirely coincidental.

For questions and comments about the quality of this book, please contact us at CustomerService@Harlequin.com.

Harlequin Enterprises ULC
22 Adelaide St. West, 41st Floor
Toronto, Ontario M5H 4E3, Canada
www.Harlequin.com

Printed in U.S.A.

CONTENTS

Julie Miller is an award-winning *USA TODAY* bestselling author of breathtaking romantic suspense—with a National Readers' Choice Award and a Daphne du Maurier Award, among other prizes. She has also earned an *RT Book Reviews* Career Achievement Award. For a complete list of her books, monthly newsletter and more, go to juliemiller.org.

K-9 PROTECTOR

Julie Miller

For Dr. Missy and the staff at Animal Medical Clinic
in Grand Island, NE.

You've taken such good care of many of our pets.
And you've supported us
when we've lost our furry loved ones. Thank you.

Chapter 1

"He was totally flirting with you, Mom."

Dr. Hazel Cooper startled as her older daughter opened the door to the examination room. She crumpled the disturbing note she'd been reading in her fist and stuffed it into the pocket of her scrubs jacket before fixing a smile on her face and turning around. "You mean Sergeant Burke? I was up to my elbows in dead ear mites and cleaning goop. He brought Gunny in so I could clean his ears and make sure the medication is clearing up the yeast infection he had. He helped me hold the dog and we discussed updating Gunny's leptospirosis vaccine. None of that is flirting."

Ashley Cooper pulled on a pair of sterile gloves before sweeping the pile of soiled gauze and cotton swabs off the stainless steel table into the trash. "I was here to hold the dog. Burke didn't have to."

"Gunny is his boy. Burke is a hands-on kind of owner."

"I can tell he's *hands-on*," Ashley teased. "When Burke moved around the table, he brushed against you. By the way, *you* didn't move away."

Hazel shook her head at that silly reasoning. "Practicality. Not evidence. I wanted to show him that the infection had cleared up."

"Methinks she doth protest too much." Ashley pulled aside the blinds on the exam room's window, giving Hazel a clear view of the parking lot and the man in the black KCPD uniform loading his Czech shepherd, Gunny, into the back of his K-9 unit truck. "He's a bachelor, right? I bet all kinds of women are throwing themselves at him. And yet he brings his dog here to trade quips and rub shoulders with you."

Jedediah Burke opened the back door and issued a sharp command, and the black-and-tan brindle dog, built like a sturdier German shepherd, jumped inside. The muscular dog was strong and moved his powerful body with a fluid grace. Not unlike his partner and handler. As commander of KCPD's K-9 unit, Burke oversaw the ongoing training of the twelve dogs and handlers working for the department, in addition to his own duties as a patrol officer. The material of Burke's fitted black T-shirt stretched tautly across his broad shoulders and tapered down to the thick leather utility belt at his waist and the gun holstered to the thigh of his black cargo pants.

She tamped down the little frissons of awareness that hummed inside her blood as Burke leaned into the truck, pulling other parts of his uniform taut across another well-defined part of his body. The man was fit and interesting and aging like a fine wine. And she really did appreciate a good merlot.

Hazel shook her head at the analogy that sprang to mind. Her daughter's fantasies must be rubbing off on her. She pulled the curtain and turned away from the window. Yes, Jedediah Burke was an attractive man, but she wasn't in the market for romance. Or whatever sort of relationship her daughter was imagining for her.

She'd done just fine without a man for sixteen years.

Many of those years had been difficult. All of them had been lonely. But after that blindingly stellar mistake she'd made in saying "I do" to her ex-husband, could she really trust herself to handle anything more than a few frissons of sexual awareness? Could she ever know a man well enough to give in to her hormones and risk her heart again?

"He's not a bachelor," Hazel corrected, needing to inject some logic and common sense into this conversation. "Burke is divorced." She disposed of the syringe in the sharps container and peeled off her gloves.

"What a coincidence. So are you." Ashley held up the trash can for Hazel to toss her gloves. "You have that in common. I bet that gives you plenty to talk about besides vet care and police work. Failed marriages. Broken hearts. Have you ever comforted each other? I bet he's good in the sack, too."

"Ashley Marie Cooper! I am not just your mother—

I'm your boss." She glanced toward the door, confirming it was closed and that no one was overhearing this mother-daughter conversation. "You will not be discussing me being in the sack with anyone. Especially here at work, where another employee could overhear."

"Did I mention you specifically?" she teased. "Or have you been thinking the same thing?"

"Give it a rest." Hazel pulled up the computer screen on the workstation beside the sink to update Gunny's records. "Sergeant Burke doesn't flirt. And neither do I."

Ashley was messing with the curtains again. "Then why is he coming back in here?"

"What?" Hazel spun around to look through the window. Burke was striding across the parking lot, jogging up the concrete steps to the clinic's front door.

"Got you. You just fluffed your hair."

Hazel pulled her fingers down to her side. "My bangs were in my eyes."

Ashley touched her mouth. "A little lip gloss wouldn't hurt, either. You should keep a tube in your pocket." She reached into the pocket of her own scrubs and pulled out a small compact of pink raspberry balm. "Here. Borrow mine."

Hazel backed away from the offer. "You should find a nice young man your own age and focus on him instead of creating a love life for me." She turned her attention back to the computer. "Burke and I work together. He runs KCPD's K-9 unit, and I manage the dogs' health concerns. We're friends. Colleagues. Period."

Ashley pulled the disinfectant spray from the cabinet beside Hazel and spritzed the examination table. "Then you are woefully out of practice in reading men. He was eyeing your butt when you bent over to pick up the cotton swab you dropped. When was the last time you went out on a date?"

"Why are we having this conversation?"

"Because you were just looking at his butt, too. Or is it the square jaw or those deep brown eyes you like?"

"Why are you sizing up Jedediah Burke's attributes? He's old enough to be your father."

"He's not old enough to be yours." Ashley came up beside Hazel and draped her arm around her shoulders. "Besides, hot is hot at any age."

Although Hazel absolutely loved having Ashley working with her at the clinic as a vet tech, they were going to have to set some ground rules about conversations getting too personal here at work. Especially around the rest of the staff, who might not be familiar with her daughters Ashley and Polly's lifelong quest to play matchmaker for their single mother ever since she divorced their father after he went to prison to serve a fifteen-year sentence.

Ashley and Polly had been children then, ages six and four. If only they knew the whole reason for that divorce—and why an eight-year sentence had been extended to fifteen. They'd already been traumatized enough, and Hazel had done everything in her power to protect them. There were some secrets that no child needed to know about her father.

Hazel turned and pressed a kiss to Ashley's cheek. "Just for that remark, you get to finish cleaning up in here. I believe Mrs. Stinson's corgis are waiting for me in room one."

"That's not all that's waiting out there."

A soft knock at the exam room door mercifully ended the conversation. Before Hazel could reach it, the door swung open and Jedediah Burke filled the door frame.

"Hey, Dr. Coop." His low-pitched drawl skittered across her eardrums and made various nerve endings prick to attention throughout her body. He removed his black KCPD ball cap in a politely deferential gesture that spoke to long-ignored feminine appreciations inside her. "One of your receptionists out front said you were still back here. That it was all right to come in."

Good grief, Ashley was right. He did have a square jaw, dusted by an intriguing mix of dark brown stubble salted with silver, which echoed the military-short cut that framed his handsome face.

Why had Ashley put these thoughts in her head? Not that a normal, healthy woman of any age wouldn't notice that Jedediah Burke was an attractive man. But she'd never allowed herself to react to the masculinity oozing from every pore and that air of natural authority he carried on those broad shoulders. And now she was…reacting. Former Army sergeant turned veteran KCPD cop Jedediah Burke was… Burke. A longtime acquaintance. A colleague. A friend.

He wasn't potential dating material any more than the author of those sickly personal letters she'd been receiving was.

Remembering the disturbing notes effectively put the kibosh on these uncomfortable feelings that had surfaced, allowing her to once again bury her attraction to Burke under a friendly facade. "That's fine." She could even get past the staring and offer him a genuine smile. "Did you forget something?"

"Two things. I think I left Gunny's chew toy in the exam room. That dog is all about play. If I lose his favorite toy, he won't work for me."

Ashley picked it up from beneath a chair and handed it to him. "Here."

"Thanks." He smiled and nodded before turning those whiskey-brown eyes back to Hazel. "Plus, I forgot to tell you that I'll be in training sessions with a couple of new recruits all morning tomorrow. The rest of my team and their dogs are coming in to have lunch before you run the monthly checkups on the canine crew. Ed's Barbecue is catering the meal as a thank-you for Pike Taylor and K-9 Hans stopping those teenagers who tried to rob him last month. You're welcome to join us."

"Ed's Barbecue?" She didn't need to fake her enthusiasm at the mention of her favorite hole-in-the-wall barbecue joint. "Are you getting the scalloped barbecue potatoes?"

Burke grinned. "Can't have the pulled pork without the potatoes."

"I can't pass those up." She'd walk an extra mile to keep the carbs from settling on her already round hips for a chance to indulge in Ed's creamy, yummy potato dish. "I'll get there are soon as I can tomorrow. Make sure you save me some."

"Will do. See you tomorrow." He put his hat back

on and tipped the brim of it to her and then to Ashley. "Dr. Coop. Ash."

"Burke." Ashley's squee of excitement burst from her lips the moment the door closed behind him. She threw her arms around Hazel and hugged her. "See? That's flirting. He asked you out to lunch."

"Down, girl." Hazel patted her daughter's arm before pulling away. "The men and women on his team and all their dogs will be there, too. Nothing says romance like routine checkups on slobbery canines and updating vaccinations."

Ashley rolled her green eyes toward the ceiling in a dramatic gesture. "You're killin' me here, Mom. Burke's a stud. And a nice guy. You two share interests and don't have any trouble communicating with each other. Isn't that what you want in a relationship?" Hazel returned to the computer to finish her updates. Ashley followed, her tone sounding more mature, less giddy. "You are an attractive, intelligent, funny, desirable woman who shouldn't be alone as much as you are. Dad hasn't been a part of our lives for sixteen years now. Yes, he's been out of prison for a few months—but we've made it abundantly clear that we don't need his kind of trouble in our lives anymore. Polly and I are grown-up now. You don't have to be the stalwart single mom who provides for us and protects us 24-7. It's okay to move on and fall in love again." She shrugged as though any kind of protest would be a nonstarter. "Polly and I agree— Jedediah Burke is a prime candidate for you to date. Or have a fling with."

"You dragged your sister into discussing my love

life?" Two years younger than Ashley, and a junior in nursing at Saint Luke's, Polly Cooper might be the quieter of her two daughters, but there was no denying that she could be just as stubborn about a cause as the outgoing Ashley. "Of course you have." With a weary sigh, she faced the younger version of herself. "First of all, I'm your mother and I love you both, and I will never *not* want to protect you in any way I can. Secondly, I know it's in good fun, but this matchmaking has to stop. If Burke gets wind of this conversation, it might embarrass him. Not to mention embarrass me if anyone else overhears this grand design you have for us."

There was another soft knock at the door, and for a split second Hazel held her breath, half expecting, perhaps half hoping, that Burke had come back for some reason.

Instead, Todd Mizner, another of the three vet techs who worked for her, stepped into the room, reminding her of just how busy the clinic could get this time of the afternoon. Todd was a few years older than Ashley and was attractive in a nerdy-professor kind of way, with his dark-rimmed glasses and longish hair that he pulled back into a ponytail. The young man was driven to achieve, commuting twice a week to Manhattan, Kansas, to pursue his DVM degree while holding down this job, and he had a real knack for handling animals. Her daughter could do worse than a hardworking cutie like Todd.

Hazel turned to give Ashley a meaningful glance. "Speaking of grand designs..."

But her daughter shook her blond ponytail down her

back, dismissing the matchmaking role reversal, and left the room.

Right. Much to Hazel's chagrin, Todd Mizner wasn't bad boy enough to suit Ashley's adventurous taste in men. Although Ashley had thankfully left her wild-child teenage years behind her, it was another lingering by-product in how the Cooper women dealt with the rest of the world after those long years of uncertainty surrounding Aaron Cooper's betrayal and the subsequent divorce, trial and incarceration.

"It's not so comfortable when the shoe's on the other foot, is it?" she called after Ashley before the door closed.

Todd joined Hazel at the counter while she printed off the notes for Gunny's file. "What was that about?"

"Nothing. Some girl talk."

He reached around her to click the computer mouse. "I've got the X-rays ready on that poodle with the herniated disk. Looks like there is a fracture in the pelvis."

"Oh, damn." That could mean surgery instead of the laser therapy she'd been planning on using to reduce the inflammation making the dog drag its right hind leg. She took her reading glasses from her chest pocket and waited for him to pull the film up on the screen.

Todd muttered a curse against her ear, reminding Hazel that he was standing right behind her. "This computer is doing its own thing again. I can't get the pictures I took to load."

Whether it was a problem with the software or the compatibility of the hardware, Hazel didn't know. And with patients waiting, she didn't have time to figure it out, either. "All right. I'll go look at the film in the X-ray room. You go on to exam three and sit with Maggie's owner. I know she's stressing about the accident. Make sure there's a box of tissues in the room and see if you can pull up the X-rays on the computer screen in there. I'll want to show her pictures to explain what's going on."

"Can't Ashley do that?"

"She's doing the prelim intake on Cassie and Reggie." Mrs. Stinson's corgis would have to wait until Hazel assessed the poodle's injuries and started treatment. "With the dog's age, Mrs. Miller may be thinking there's nothing we can do for Maggie. I don't want her alone in there." She tipped her chin up to Todd and smiled. "Go use some of that Mizner charm on her to keep her distracted until I can get there."

"But you promised I could scrub in on the next surgery. I want to be a part of the process from initial consult to seeing that dog walk again. Or fitting her for a wheelchair if therapy and surgery don't work."

Todd hadn't budged an inch from behind her, and when Hazel inhaled, her shoulder brushed against his chest. Squashing down an instant imprint of *eeuw* at the contact, Hazel stepped to the side, so she had room to turn and face him. She hadn't batted an eye when, as Ashley had pointed out, Burke had bumped into her. But even this accidental contact with the younger man felt somehow inappropriate. Maybe it was the stress of the long day. Or that awkward conversation with Ashley. Or maybe it was something else entirely that made her anxious to get on with her work. "We'll discuss it

later. The priority is the patient's care right now—and
that includes the owner as well as the pet."

"The more experience I get, the better. One of these
days soon, I'll be finishing my classwork and intern-
ing..." Todd rested his hand on the counter beside her,
his arm nearly circling around her as he winked. "Then
you and I can be full partners."

The message in that letter burned through her pocket
and seared her skin. *That* was what bothered her about
Todd's tendency to be overly familiar with her. She
gently pushed Todd back a step. "Personal space, Todd.
We've had this discussion, remember?"

Maybe not such a great catch for her daughter, after
all. Todd might be good with animals, but his people
skills could use a little work.

He stepped back even farther, putting his hands up
in mock surrender. "I don't mean anything by it, Dr.
Coop. You know I'm harmless. You're jumpy today for
some reason."

No. He was behaving in a way that she didn't appreciate. Not as a boss with her employee. Not as a woman
with a man young enough to be her son. Not as someone who'd been receiving anonymous letters that spoke
to a disturbing desire for a relationship. She pointed to
the door, reminding him that she was the boss here.
She didn't have to explain anything to a vet tech who
worked for her. "Exam room three."

"Yes, ma'am. Whatever you need." While Todd
headed across the lobby to the exam room on the opposite side, Hazel pushed through the swinging door
leading into the restricted area where she performed

surgery, stored meds and housed specialized equipment. She went straight to the X-ray room to see how poor little Maggie had fared after her fall down a flight of steps.

What she needed was time alone in the darkened room to clear her head. She pulled her glasses from her pocket to study the film. But the moment they touched the bridge of her nose, she thought of the letter and tugged them right back off.

She didn't need to pull out the letter to read it again. She knew every word by heart.

I've been watching you, Hazel.

Your bright green eyes are so intelligent, so pretty. Even when you wear your reading glasses, they shine and entice me. No man deserves you.

I want to be a part of your life. I want us to share everything.

I want you.

I want you.

I want you.

Hazel might not recognize flirting anymore—or maybe she subconsciously chose to ignore it. Her relationship skills might be rusty since her divorce and bankruptcy and the threats and humiliation that had filled her life during her husband Aaron's trial and for several years afterward.

But she'd been a different person then. Now she knew when something wasn't right. A man who wrote *I want you* a dozen times on a letter, and then refused to sign it or even include a return address, did not have her best interests at heart.

This letter, and eight more she had like it at home, told her she'd become someone's obsession.

The feeling of being watched, of being stalked, of feeling terrorized in the places she was supposed to feel safe felt a lot like...

She gasped at the knock outside the open door. "Todd, I said..."

"Whoa." Jedediah Burke filled her doorway again. His hands raised in apology did nothing to lessen the impact of his size dwarfing the tiny room. "Sorry about that. You were really concentrating. Everything okay?"

When Hazel realized she was clutching her hand over her racing heart, she immediately reached for her glasses again and put them on. With his eyes narrowed on her, she doubted she was fooling him. He'd startled her, and he knew it. Avoiding Burke's probing gaze, she studied the troubling results of the X-ray. "You can't seem to leave."

After a moment he nodded. "I forgot to tell you what time lunch was tomorrow. I know I could have texted, but I was already here." He stepped into the room, stopping beside her chair to glance at the X-ray. Unlike when Todd had invaded her personal space, she knew the strongest urge to turn and lean into him—especially when his hand settled gently on her shoulder. "Did something happen? Lose a patient?"

Damn it. The man smelled good, too. An enticing combination of spicy soap and the subtle musk of the early-October afternoon clinging to his skin that only intensified in the small confines of the X-ray room.

Hazel considered brushing off his concern and sending him on his way. Then her peripheral gaze landed on the brass KCPD badge clipped onto his belt. Burke represented help and safety in more ways than one. She'd known him for five years now. She could trust him with this. She tucked her glasses back into her jacket pocket and tilted her gaze up to his. "Could I ask you something? As a police officer?"

"Of course." He pulled away, the moment of compassion masked by his wary alertness.

She pulled the note from her pocket and spared a few moments to smooth it open against the tabletop before handing it to him. "Would you read this?" He'd probably think she was being paranoid. Or maybe he'd be angry that she hadn't reported the letters sooner. His chiseled expression grew grimmer with every line he skimmed.

"Is that normal?" she asked.

"Who's it from?"

She hesitated a beat before answering. "I don't know."

"Then no, it's not." He leaned against the door frame, facing her again. "Got a jilted boyfriend I need to worry about?"

The friend she knew might be teasing her to help her feel a little less worried, but the cop was waiting for an answer.

She'd asked for his opinion. She owed it to him to give him a clearer understanding as to why an innocuous note could rattle her this much. "At first, I thought my ex-husband, Aaron, was writing me again. You probably remember him from the news a few years back." Burke nodded but waited for her to continue. "He used to send me flowery garbage like that when we were dating. I told him I wasn't impressed, and he stopped. He always said he liked my directness—until he went to trial. Then he wasn't real keen on me telling the truth. The letters he used to write from prison were straight-out blame for testifying against him. Those were angry tirades. I stopped opening his mail and then had a judge stop them altogether. I asked him not to have any contact with me or the girls. There were too many threats back when the trial…back when Aaron was arrested. He ruined a lot of lives when he raided those retirement funds. I didn't need his vile messages on top of the threats we were getting from other victims."

"*Other* victims?" Oh, hell. He'd picked up on that rare slip of the tongue. "Were you a victim, too?"

She shook her head instead of answering the question. "I just meant I thought the obsessive language meant they were from my ex."

"You said *they*?" Burke repeated, holding up the letter. "You thought *they* were from your ex."

Damn. He didn't miss a trick. No sense avoiding the full truth with this veteran cop. "That's the ninth one I've gotten since the first one came on my birthday, August 5."

"Nine letters in nine weeks?"

"The first ones were pretty innocuous. But…he seems to get angrier or more frustrated with each letter."

Burke turned the paper over, inspecting it for identifying clues she knew he wouldn't find. "Did the envelope have a post office stamp?"

"Kansas City. But no return address."

"Is Aaron still in prison?"

Hazel shook her head. "He got out on parole the end of last year. The restraining order should prevent him from having contact with me or the girls. But then these started arriving. They're not exactly a threat, but they're…unsettling."

"Do you know where he is now?"

She stood when he handed back the letter. "Our lives have been a lot more peaceful without him. I didn't want to jinx anything by reaching out to him. Even through a third party."

"I'll look into it." Burke reached for her hand. But it wasn't a reassuring squeeze he offered so much as a warning. "But I'm guessing he's here in Kansas City."

Chapter 2

"Uh…huh…" Hazel drew out her response as she looked through her scope into Gunny's ear. "Everything's looking pink and perfect. No signs of the infection."

Burke mirrored her, scooting around to the other side of the examination table while she moved to inspect Gunny's other ear. Although he trusted that Gunny would maintain his stay command until he released him, Burke had volunteered to hold the big dog while Hazel gave the Czech shepherd a final all clear on his ear treatments. With all the exam rooms full and clients waiting in the lobby, it was clear that Friday afternoon at the clinic was a busy time for boarding drop-offs and medical appointments. Letting Burke stay here to help not only freed up a member of her staff to work with another patient but also gave him a few minutes of privacy he needed to update Hazel on what he'd found out about her ex-husband and the letters.

There was one particularly disturbing item he'd discovered in Aaron Cooper's arrest record. While the cop in him wanted to dig into the details, the man in him wasn't sure how he'd handle what he might find. Besides, Hazel was a private person, and if she had chosen not to mention the incident in the five years they'd known each other, then he wasn't going to bring it up. Not yet, anyway. He understood about divorce and betrayal, and that the injured party did whatever she or he had to in order to move on with their lives.

But if push came to shove and there really was a credible threat here, or he had any inclination that history was going to repeat itself, then privacy be damned. He'd demand the whole truth from Hazel in order to mount the comprehensive security detail she might require. And if she still wouldn't share, he knew other ways to get the specifics he needed. But he wouldn't like going behind her back, and neither would she.

Burke scrubbed a hand over Gunny's brown-and-black head, more to keep the dog from falling asleep than to prevent him from acting up while he lay on the table and let Hazel check him out. His nostrils flared with a calming breath as he edited any emotion from his tone. She'd asked him to do this favor as a professional, not as the man who was finding it harder every day to respect the boundaries she put up between them. "I talked to Aaron's parole officer and notified Officer Kranitz about the letters. He'll ask your ex about them.

If Kranitz thinks Aaron is responsible for sending them, he'll remind him about the restraining order. After that, another letter arrives and he's back in jail."

Hazel peered into the scope and nodded. "That can't prevent him from giving the letters to someone else to mail for him. Even at the worst of the lawsuits and legal proceedings, he always managed to have a couple of pals who seemed willing to do his bidding. Still don't know if he paid them to be his allies or relied on his rather convincing charm. One thing Aaron always excelled at was making deals."

Damn. Not one blink to reveal just what her ex-husband had been capable of, and what she must have gone through at his hand. Instead, she straightened and smiled up at him. "This ear is looking great, too. I'd say your partner is fit for duty."

No details today. Burke wasn't going to push, because he had a feeling Hazel would retreat to that unspoken distance between them that he'd worked patiently to overcome. He didn't want any of the closeness they'd settled into in this relationship, which was something more than friendship, yet something less than what he truly wanted, to erode.

"Good." He moved his hand along Gunny's fur to pet his flank as Hazel took over scratching around the dog's ears. He grinned at the way Gunny turned his head into her palm, savoring her touch. He ignored the sucker punch of jealousy he felt and ordered the dog up to a sit. "You're gettin' soft, big guy. I need to get you back to more than just training sessions."

Hazel set the scope on the counter behind her and

came back to rub her hands around Gunny's jowls. "Don't you listen to the mean ol' sergeant," she teased. "You're as tough as any cop on the force."

"Don't encourage him," Burke teased right back. "He's already got a big ego I have to keep in check."

Now the examination was done, and they were standing around spoiling his working K-9 instead of all three of them getting back to work. If Hazel hadn't shown him those creepy letters she'd been receiving and asked him to help her reclaim some peace of mind by finding out where they were coming from, he'd have no reason to be here at all.

While he couldn't say for certain who was sending her the anonymous notes, he had done everything he could to give her that peace of mind. "Your building downtown seems secure with the parking gate and coded entry system. While I don't like that wall of windows at the front of your condo where anybody and his brother could look in on you if they're in a high enough location, at least you're not on the ground floor. Plus, they've done a good job installing locks on the front door and fire escape windows."

"A refurbished historic building has structural limitations. I saved long and hard to buy that place. Plus, it's only a few blocks' drive from the clinic. At least it's in a good neighborhood near the library, hotels and convention center."

Burke nodded. No place was truly safe if someone was determined to get to her. And the fact that the perp had said he was watching her made him think he knew exactly where she lived. Or worked. Or both. "I also talked to hospital police regarding Polly and the potential threats. They'll do what they can to keep an eye on things there. Polly and Ashley's apartment has good security, too." His fingers stilled in Gunny's fur beside the KCPD vest the dog wore. "I've also got Aaron's current address. If the harassment doesn't stop and you want Gunny and me to pay him a personal visit, I will."

Her hands stilled as well, and her cheeks went pale. "I hope it doesn't come to that. You've been very thorough."

"How else would I do my job?"

Hazel reached across the dog to squeeze his forearm. Every nerve ending in his body zeroed in on the skin-on-skin caress. "Thank you."

"You're welcome."

He was tall enough that he could lean across the table and kiss her if he wanted. And damn, he wanted to. He wanted to ask her out, too, as evidenced by that half-assed attempt to invite her to lunch last week. There was something about Hazel Cooper that made him stupid like a teenager again. Probably because he hadn't wanted a woman the way he wanted her for a long time. She made him laugh. She got his dry humor. She was a smart woman and damn good at her job, and, despite trying to camouflage them in those scrubs and jeans, she had just about the sweetest curves he'd ever seen. And though he suspected that tomboyish pixie cut of hair was all about convenience, the silvery blond bangs drew his attention to her pretty green eyes, and the short length highlighted the elegant column of her neck—a whole stretch of creamy skin he'd like to nuzzle his lips against and taste with his tongue.

But he respected her unspoken wish to keep a friendly professional relationship between them. Besides, his ex-wife, Shannon, had burned him badly enough that he'd choose a woman whose friendship and loyalty he could trust without question over satisfying any itch he had to find out what Hazel's skin tasted like. Pity he couldn't find a friendship like this and a lover in the same woman. He might not be such a crusty, out-of-practice horndog around Dr. Coop if that was the case.

It took a slurp of Gunny's tongue across Hazel's jaw to break the standing-and-staring spell that had possessed him for a few seconds. Burke wisely shrugged off her touch and pulled away as she laughed. "Sorry about that. I guess he's done. Gunny, down. Good boy."

He petted Gunny's flanks, buying himself a few seconds to set his game face back in place. He should *not* be jealous that his dog had kissed Hazel before he had.

Hazel scratched Gunny near his tail before turning away to the counter to open a cookie jar filled with green chews. "Want a treat?" Gunny's tail thumped against Burke's leg in anticipation of his reward. "Who's the best patient ever? That's right, Gunny. It's you." Hazel held up her hand, giving the dog a command. "Sit. Good boy. Here you go." He liked that she respected the dog's training and didn't simply spoil him with treats and petting, although his K-9 partner had no problem being a hand-fed couch potato when his vest was off and he was off duty. Hazel rubbed Gunny around the ears one last time before opening the door onto the hallway that led to the lobby. Burke was pleased, too, that the dog's ears were no longer sensitive to the touch and itching like crazy. Dr. Coop did good work. She smiled. "Come on, you two. I'll walk you out."

Gunny automatically heeled, noticing the people, pets and displays of food and treats and other supplies around them, without showing much interest or taking his focus off Burke as they followed Hazel to the front counter. The big dog paused once to touch noses and match tail wags with Cleo, the three-legged, one-eyed miniature schnauzer who trotted around the counter to greet him. Hazel brought the smaller senior dog to work with her every day, where she lounged in her own bed beside the reception staff or worked as something of a goodwill ambassador around the veterinary clinic. Cleo had earned the strands of white showing in her gray muzzle, and she made it her business to greet favorite customers and new patients. Gunny was definitely on Cleo's favorites list. If Burke was given to fanciful imaginings, he'd think Gunny and Cleo had a bit of a crush on each other, judging by the way they rubbed against each other and made quick work of the whole tail-sniffing scenario.

Hazel Cooper, however, *was* prone to fanciful imaginings with the animals she worked with. As Cleo danced between her legs and batted at Gunny, encouraging him to play, Hazel reached down to pet the schnauzer's flank. "That's right, your boyfriend's here."

"Cleo does know she's fixed, doesn't she?" Burke

teased. "Her flirting's not going to do her any good. Nothing's going to happen between these two."

"A girl can still look, can't she?"

When Hazel straightened, her gaze traveled up his stomach, chest and jaw to meet his. A flare of heat passed between them, and Burke's mouth went dry. Well, hell. What kind of mixed signal was that? The good doctor had checked him out. So it was okay for her to look, too? But she still wanted him to keep things professional and friendly between them? Maybe the rules of dating had changed too much since he'd last taken the plunge and he had no business even considering acting upon the connection the two of them shared.

Whatever spark she'd felt, she either dutifully ignored it or else it fizzled out. Hazel leaned over the counter to speak to the receptionist at her computer. "Go ahead and send today's bill to the police department," she instructed, before tilting her gaze up to his again. Burke liked that about her, too—that she made direct eye contact with him and didn't mince words. At six feet two, he figured he was about eight inches taller than she was, but the veterinarian never let that deter her from meeting his gaze, no matter how close they stood. "I don't need to see Gunny again until his next checkup or shots are due. Just be sure to keep his ears clean. And if he starts shaking his head or scratching again, you can use more of that medicated ointment I gave you. Call me, of course, if that doesn't take care of it."

"Will do." He was out of excuses for hanging around the vet clinic and Dr. Coop. Gunny had a clean bill of health. He'd stretched out on the floor and Cleo had propped her two front paws on his back, as though standing tall on her big buddy's shoulders made her a big dog, too. But even though Gunny was enjoying the pseudo-massage of the other dog walking on him, Burke was on the clock. And he had nothing left to report on the background investigation he'd done on Hazel's ex-husband. He pulled his KCPD ball cap from his back pocket and adjusted it over his closely cropped hair. "Better get back to work. I'll keep you posted if I find out anything more about—" he glanced around at all the people in the front waiting area "—that matter we discussed."

"Thank you," she mouthed, no doubt appreciating his discretion about keeping her private affairs private. "See you next time." Burke nodded. She pursed her lips together and made a noisy kissing sound to get her dog's attention. "Cleo, come."

After a tumble onto her back leg, Cleo quickly righted herself and trotted over to her mistress to be petted. Then Hazel picked up the stack of mail the receptionist set on the counter for her and started sorting through the letters, a couple of magazines and a padded mailer. Burke had turned to the door and pulled Gunny into a heeling position when he heard the soft gasp behind him.

"Dr. Coop?" He turned to see the lighter envelopes floating to the floor alongside the small package Hazel had dropped. "Hazel?" Her panicked gaze darted up to his when he used her first name. What the hell? He glanced down at the mess around her feet, searching for one that looked like a threat. "Did you get another letter?"

With a curt nod to him and a forced smile for everyone else in the room, she shook off her momentary panic and squatted down to gather up the envelopes and magazines. "Maybe. I don't know. There's no return address on that package, and the label is typed. Like the others. But there haven't been any packages before." Like Cleo, Gunny was curious why his favorite doctor was down at his level. The dogs sniffed at Hazel, sniffed the scattered mail…and then Gunny sat. "The others have gone to my home address. This is the first one to come here." Burke's concern that some anonymous turd had upset Hazel again morphed into something far graver when Gunny tipped his long brown snout up to him. Ah, hell. "Maybe it's nothing. Not everybody puts a return address—"

"Don't touch another thing." He grasped Hazel by the arm and lifted her to her feet, placing her behind him as he backed away from the counter. He scooped Cleo up with one hand and put her in Hazel's arms when the smaller dog tried to sniff the package, too.

"What are you doing?"

Burke pulled out his badge and held it up to identify himself to the entire room in a clear, concise voice. "I need everyone's attention. I'm Sergeant Jedediah Burke, KCPD." He swiveled his gaze to include everyone in the lobby. "I need everyone to stay exactly where you are. Does everybody have control of their animals? Don't. Move."

Hazel hugged Cleo to her chest. "Burke?"

"That includes you. Stay put. Don't let the dog down." He nudged her back another step before clipping his badge back onto his belt and leading Gunny out the double glass doors.

When he came back in with the dog, he was aware of fearful stares, questioning looks and a nervous laugh from behind the counter. But nobody spoke, nobody questioned his orders as he let Gunny nose his way around the shelves of dog food, a cat meowing in its carrier, then along the edge of the front counter and back to the pile of mail on the floor.

Gunny alerted again when he reached the padded envelope, sitting back on his haunches and tilting his nose up to Burke.

Burke swore. He slipped Gunny's chew toy reward between his teeth and pulled him away from the envelope, praising him for doing his job.

Gunny's nose was as reliable as clockwork.

Hazel's love letters had just taken a very sinister, very deadly turn.

He pulled his radio off his belt and summoned Dispatch before looking down into Hazel's worried expression. He couldn't spare more than a glance to reassure her he hadn't completely gone off his gourd because he needed to act.

"I need everybody—people, animals—to evacuate the building ASAP." He swiveled his gaze to include every staff member and client in the lobby. "I want you all at least twenty yards away, in the front parking lot. Turn off your phones. Do not send a text. Do not call anyone." He looked to Hazel again because he knew he could rely on her to keep her head and get the job done, even if she was frightened. "I'll need a head count to make sure everyone is where they should be."

"Of course." She waved the three receptionists out of their seats while Burke positioned himself to block-ade the padded envelope, so that no one would acciden-tally step on it as they hurried to do their boss's bidding. "Linda. Get on the headset, get the staff out of the back rooms. Tell everyone I want them in the parking lot. Get the animals we're boarding on leashes and put them in the kennel runs out back. Todd." She pointed to the swinging door as the young man came out of an exami-nation room. "Get the two dogs we neutered this morn-ing out of Recovery. Ashley—"

"I'll take care of the customers out here, Mom." Ha-zel's daughter didn't hesitate to do her mother's bid-ding, but fear was clearly stamped on her face when she stopped in front of Burke and asked, "What's going on?"

"It's just a precaution," Burke answered, nodding toward the exit and urging her to keep moving. "Call it a fire drill."

"There's a fire?" she whispered. "The alarm didn't go off."

Hazel pressed Cleo into Ashley's arms and turned her to the front door. "It's okay, sweetie. Just do as Burke says. I'll go through the exam rooms."

Ashley nodded, then held out her arm to escort one of their elderly clients to the parking lot, where custom-ers, patients and staff were gathering. Hazel opened the doors to each examination room and led the pets and people into the lobby.

"Twenty yards out," Burke reminded Todd as the young man hurried by with the dogs from the recovery room.

Todd spared a worried glance for Hazel as she stepped back from the double doors at the front vestibule. "Dr. Coop, you coming?"

"I'll be right there." Hazel peered through the glass, counting her staff members and assuring their safety before she turned around and came back to find Burke relaying details to the dispatcher. Normally he would have used his cell phone, but he couldn't risk using a wireless signal until he knew more.

"What's going on?" she demanded the moment he signed off. She needed an explanation to fit his evacuation order and calm the panic caused by the sudden mass exodus. "I know there's no fire. I heard the dispatcher say she was sending a unit. Who's coming?"

"The bomb squad."

Her eyes widened before dropping her gaze to the unmarked package. "A bomb? I thought it was just another... I hadn't gotten a letter this week. I'd hoped Aaron would stop once his parole officer spoke with him. Did that just piss him off?" He could tell she was hoping he'd say this was a false alarm when she tilted her face back to his. "You think he sent a bomb to my clinic? With all these people? These innocent animals?"

Burke reached down to rub Gunny's head. "Gunny alerted there was an explosive. That nose of his is never wrong." Taking Hazel by the elbow, he escorted her to the vestibule. He wished he could tell her there was nothing to worry about, that it was okay to smile and erase the fear he read in her eyes. "I need you outside, too. Gunny and I have to clear the building."

"But…" She planted her feet and refused to leave. "That's what the bomb squad is for, right? Shouldn't you have backup?" She splayed her hand at the middle of his chest. His heart leaped against her urgent touch. "Or body armor?"

"Go. It's what we do." He cupped her cheek and jaw in his hand. "But I need you to be safe before I can go to work. I need you to be in charge out there."

She nodded. Then, with those green eyes tilted up to his, she covered his hand with hers. "I'll see you outside," she vowed, as if her will could guarantee that they'd be reunited.

Bombs didn't come with any kind of guarantee. He'd seen far too many of them when his Army unit had been deployed to the Middle East. He'd seen more than he'd ever imagined stateside now that he wore this uniform. The volatility of the explosives Gunny had been trained to detect meant, by their very nature, there were no guarantees he could give.

He traded a curt nod before opening the door and sending her out.

Burke watched her join Ashley and that ponytailed vet tech before he felt the eager tension radiating up Gunny's lead into his hand. The dog thought bomb detections and building searches were a sport that would end with a tug-of-war game with his favorite toy if he successfully found his target. But Burke knew just how serious this job could be.

Backup was en route. But KCFD and the bomb squad couldn't do a damn thing to help unless he could tell them that there were no other explosives, no other potential casualties on-site, no perp lying in wait to take out a first responder. Their job was to make sure it was safe to enter the building to deal with whatever was in the package that some pervert had sent Hazel.

"Gunny, *voran*!" Burke tugged on Gunny's leash and gave him the search command in German. "Come on, boy. Let's go to work."

Chapter 3

"Lookin' good, Shadow." Hazel checked the incision on the black Lab she'd neutered that morning, adjusted the E-collar around her neck and petted her chest before closing the door to her kennel.

The big dog yawned and laid her head down on the cushion inside the kennel, relaxing as though she'd come for a day at the spa instead of a desexing operation and a bomb threat. Hazel wished she could slough off the stress of the day so easily. With the fire department and police cars that had blocked traffic around the clinic gone, and no one left from the bomb squad here except for Burke's friend Justin Grant, she should be breathing a sigh of relief. All but one of her clients had rescheduled appointments and left once the police had deemed it safe to move their vehicles out of the parking lot. The animals she was responsible for were all safe. The members of her staff, although understandably shaken by the threat, had gone back to their duties, like the professionals they were, to finish out the workday as soon as the first responders had informed them it was safe to come back inside the building.

But *safe* was a relative term.

Hazel couldn't help thinking that the vial of C-4 pellets and a trigger mechanism wrapped in a bunch of colorful unconnected wires were meant to do more than scare her. Why would a man who'd write love letters—no matter how unnervingly obsessive they were—send her a package of bomb parts? Did he think being afraid would make her turn to him for comfort? Was he angry because she hadn't responded the way he wanted to his professions of love and desire? Not that she could respond one way or another to a man who refused to identify himself. And if the package had come from Aaron, was he still so angry with her that he'd send what could only be construed as a death threat?

Sixteen years ago he hadn't been so courteous to give her that kind of warning.

For a few nightmarish seconds, Hazel's breath locked up in her chest as she relived flashes of memory from that horrific night when Aaron had done what he thought was necessary to stop her from testifying against him.

Even though there were no words, there was a message for her in that package.

If only she knew what it meant, and who had sent it, she could devise coping and security strategies—she could turn his name over to KCPD and move on with the useful, contented life she'd created for herself and her daughters. She'd dealt with death threats against her and her daughters before, years ago when Aaron's crimes had been discovered, and the people who'd trusted him had lost everything. Hell, she'd dealt with Aaron, who'd been even more frightening. But how did she equate *I want you* with the promise of violence and death?

What had she ever done that was so horribly wrong that someone wanted to do this to her? Again.

Hazel pushed to her feet. She hugged her arms around her waist and leaned against the frame of the kennel wall, closing her eyes for a few moments to take in the familiar sounds and smells of her clinic. From Shadow's nasal breathing to the rustle and vocalizations of the other animals settling into their kennels for the evening, from the stringent tang of antiseptic cleanser used on her equipment to the more earthy scents of the animals themselves—this was her world, her safe zone, the place where she felt most at home. She was the authority here, in charge of her own schedule, her own destiny. She was surrounded by her daughter and friends and work she loved. Being here helped to center her and call up the strength that would get her through this nightmare of being the focus of someone's dangerously obsessive attention.

She inhaled deeply, intending to release a calming breath, when the air around her changed its scent. She opened her eyes a split second before Todd Mizner reached for her and pulled her lightly against his chest.

The younger man's supportive hug startled more

than it comforted. "You okay, Dr. Coop? That was a big scare, wasn't it?"

If she hadn't felt the trembling through his arms, she might have chastised him for the unwelcome contact. But Todd was probably as rattled by the idea of a bomb threat as she'd been. Like some men, maybe he wouldn't admit his fear, but he took comfort by helping someone else deal with hers. Instead of pushing him away, she settled her hands at his waist and let him hang on to her for a few seconds before stepping back. "I'm fine, Todd. Thanks for checking. Fortunately, no one was hurt. We've reopened for business. I think we'll be fine."

He adjusted his glasses on his nose before frowning at her response. "We've all got your back here. You know that, right?"

"I know that, Todd. Thank you." She squeezed his arm and patted it just like she had the dog and moved on to the next kennel to check her patient there. "Are the staff doing okay?" she asked. "How are you holding up?"

"I'm not the one that package was addressed to." He reached in beside her to adjust the dog's E-collar while she inspected the sutures, brushing his shoulder against hers. Although she often made accidental contact with the vet techs when they were working together with an animal, Todd's next words made her think she needed to have a conversation with him about the difference between *friendly* and *too friendly* when it came to his interactions with the female staff here at the clinic. "You know, if you want to go get a glass of wine or something to unwind and let the tension go after work, I'd be happy to take you someplace."

"Todd—"

When she started to refuse, he put his hands up in surrender, retreating a step to give her the space he must have just realized he'd invaded again. "A bunch of us could go. Celebrate life and all that after our close call this afternoon."

Hazel shut the kennel door before answering. "No, thank you. If you and some of the others want to celebrate, that's great. I love hearing that you all are supporting each other. But I think I'll be heading straight home once this day is over. I'm exhausted."

"You sure?" His disappointment in her refusal to join him, or them, was evident for a few seconds before he rallied with a smile. "Maybe another time."

She made a point of checking her watch instead of replying to the open-ended invitation. "You'd better get those dogs we're boarding out for their last run before we close up shop."

"Anything you say, boss lady."

After Todd left to do her bidding, Hazel went through her office and the workrooms in the back to grab her purse, turn off lights and close the doors that connected to each exam room. Maybe there hadn't been anything all that unusual about Todd's concern for her. By the time she reached the reception area, her staff had all the computers shut down, and the appointment schedule and prescription orders ready for the next morning. One by one they gave her a hug and wished her goodnight, repeating Todd's invitation to join them for a celebration-slash-commiseration drink. Hazel thanked them all, commended them for keeping their heads in a crisis and ordered them to have some fun.

The sky was gray with twilight and the air smelled of ozone ahead of the promised storm by the time she hooked Cleo to her leash, locked the front doors and headed down the ramp to her truck. Two other trucks remained in the parking lot, both with the distinctive black-and-white markings that identified them as KCPD vehicles. Her gaze instantly went to the broad-shouldered man leaning back against the K-9 truck with his arms crossed over his wide chest in an easy, deceptively relaxed stance. Burke was in the middle of a conversation with the senior officer from the bomb squad she'd met earlier, Justin Grant. Clearly, the two men were friends, judging by the laughter they shared. Justin was younger—blond, slightly taller than Burke, and built like a lanky distance runner. Of course, most men seemed slighter standing next to Burke's muscular build.

Hazel's eyes widened as the surprising observation popped into her head, and she hurried Cleo over to a grassy patch in the landscaping around the parking lot for the dog to take care of business before the drive home. What was she doing? Comparing other men against Burke's standard? Officer Grant was a handsome man, but she had barely noticed him once she'd caught sight of Burke. She wasn't naive enough to deny that she was attracted to Burke on some subconscious level—any healthy woman would be. But when had her conscious thoughts become so attuned to the rugged police sergeant?

Once Burke caught sight of her and Cleo, he straightened away from the truck and smiled. Maybe that was what the distraction was—Burke's attention always seemed to shift to her whenever they were in the same space together. That could explain her hyperawareness of him. Why wouldn't she be equally aware of a man whose focus was concentrated on her?

That was all this was—alert cop, polite man, a few errant hormones appreciating the attention after so many years on her own—and the last years before that with Aaron, when she'd been reduced to invisibility one day, verbal whipping dog the next and, ultimately, the target of his desperation. She and Burke had shared a special friendship from the time when she'd first started working with him and the other K-9 officers at KCPD. He respected her. He was a calm presence. Sometimes he even made her laugh. Her self-preserving guard was a little off after those love letters and the events of today, making her thoughts a little scattered, her instincts a little sharper. There was no need to worry that she might be developing different, deeper feelings for him. Tomorrow she'd wake up with her strength and survival instincts intact, and she could push those feelings into the background, where she needed them to stay.

"Cleo, come." With the dog down to fumes now after staking out several spots, Hazel calmed her off-kilter thoughts and walked past her truck to join the two men. Cleo darted ahead of her, eager to investigate them, or perhaps catching Gunny's scent as the big dog lounged in his air-conditioned kennel in the back seat of Burke's truck. Cleo sniffed Officer Grant's shoes before propping her two front paws against Burke's knee, wobbling on her back leg and wagging her stump of a tail. "Easy, girl," she said.

"Dr. Coop." Justin Grant chuckled as he nodded a greeting, amused by the dog's favoritism. "Who's this little diva?"

"Cleo. She was hit by a car and left by the side of the road. She was with us in recovery for a long time, and since no one claimed her, my staff adopted her and made her the clinic mascot. I get the honor of chauffeuring her home for the evenings. And she has a crazy crush on this big galoot."

"You got everything locked up?" Burke asked. He knelt to scratch Cleo around the ears, easing the schnauzer's manic energy with his deep voice and large hands. "She probably smells Gunny on me. Makes me a hit with all the furry ladies." He talked to the dog, working his trainer magic. "Chill, little one. Gunny worked hard all afternoon and needs his rest. Maybe you can play with him tomorrow. That's a good girl."

By the time he was done talking, the three-legged dog had rolled onto her side and was panting while Burke rubbed her tummy. Some of the tension inside Hazel eased, too, hearing that soothing, low-pitched voice. She'd probably be panting, too, if he whispered little praises to her and stroked her skin like that.

Hazel quickly turned away as a different sort of tension seized her. Where were these sexual thoughts coming from? Why was she allowing herself to react to

Burke in a way she never had before? Once Ashley had put those thoughts about flirting and feelings into her head, she hadn't been able to compartmentalize her emotions the way she usually did. She really needed to find out who was behind these threats and get the normalcy of her familiar, predictable life back.

Studiously ignoring the man kneeling beside her and indulging her spoiled dog, Hazel tilted her chin to Justin. "You're certain it's safe to resume business as usual tomorrow morning?"

"Yes, ma'am." The younger officer seemed unaware of the embarrassment heating her cheeks, or else he was too polite to mention it. "Our search teams found nothing you need to worry about except for that envelope."

"An envelope filled with bomb-making parts," she clarified, still in a bit of shock that something so dangerous had traveled through the mail and ended up in her place of work, where she, her daughter and so many of her friends were.

"In this case, parts are just parts," Justin assured her. "Nothing was rigged to detonate. C-4 requires an electric charge through a triggering device like a blasting cap or detonator cord. The small explosion triggers the larger one. As unsettling as receiving a gift like that might be, nothing was going to happen. Even if you struck a match to it, it would burn, not explode. All the same, we've got the C-4 secured, and the envelope is on its way to the evidence locker."

"Nobody sends explosives through the mail for no reason." Burke pushed to his feet beside her, his shoulders filling up her peripheral vision, making a mockery of her efforts to ignore her awareness of him. "This perp has broken the law just by putting that package in a mail slot and lying about its contents. That's a big risk to take."

Justin nodded his agreement. "The sender may be an expert in explosives who knew the device wouldn't work, and this was either a gag or a warning of some kind. Probably the latter, given those letters you mentioned."

Hazel shivered, feeling the electricity in the air dotting her skin with goose bumps. She was swallowed up by the cold front being pushed ahead of the pending storm, and she hugged her arms around her waist, wishing she had more than her scrubs on to keep her warm. "Someone thinks this is funny?"

She shouldn't have been surprised to feel Burke's arm slide around her shoulders or his hand rubbing up and down her arm. "From the perp's perspective, not yours. Maybe he wants you to know how serious his feelings are for you. Or he's hoping you'll be scared enough to turn to him for comfort."

She was equally surprised at how easy it was to lean against Burke's warmth and strength as the unsettling chill consumed her. "The man doesn't even have the guts to tell me who he is. Does he really believe that threatening me is going to make me ignore the ick factor of those letters and fall in love with him?"

"Another possibility is that he's a novice who has no clue what he's messing with and didn't realize that the contents couldn't go off." Justin shook his head, as though he liked that possibility even less. "I hate to think that he'll keep trying until he gets it right."

"Don't worry, Doc." Burke squeezed her shoulders a little tighter. "Gunny and I are at your service whenever you need us."

She squeezed his hand where it rested on her shoulder. "Cleo and I appreciate it. Thanks." At the mention of her name, the little dog got to her feet and danced around her legs. She wished she could share the old girl's enthusiasm for this conversation. "So you think he'll try again?" Hazel asked the younger man.

"If he's already escalated from letter writing to threats like that, then yeah, as long as he has access to the right equipment, I doubt this is a onetime thing."

Hazel lifted her chin at the grim pronouncement. Sixteen years ago, at the height of her ex-husband's trial, she'd been bombarded with hate mail, anonymous phone calls and threats against her and her daughters—as if she was guilty by association for the way Aaron had destroyed so many lives. If only they'd known how thoroughly he'd destroyed hers, they might have felt sympathy rather than hate. But other than being jostled and spit on by a courthouse crowd, and her daughters being bullied at school—the last straw that had sealed her decision to testify against Aaron and finalize their divorce—none of those threats had ended in violence like this. Not the kind where people died. "He's trying to get my attention. He's probably too much of a coward to actually hurt me."

The two men exchanged a look as though her optimistic assertion was naive. But she wasn't about to explain to a man she'd just met why she had so little naivete left about the world—just a foolish hope that she'd already lived through the worst the world had to offer, and a belief that the future had to be better.

"I hope that's the case," Justin said. "In the meantime, I'll keep working the investigation from my end. See if I can find out where that C-4 came from. The guy has to have connections to construction jobs or the military—or the black market—in order to get his hands on that grade of explosive." He reached out to shake hands with Burke. "I'll keep you posted on what I find out."

Burke nodded his thanks. "Say hi to Emilia and the kids. When is number three due?"

"This summer."

"You know scientists found out what causes that, don't you?"

Justin grinned at the teasing. "Don't lecture me about making babies, old man. You know you love being JJ's godfather."

"I do. Tell him I'll bring Gunny by again sometime for the two of them to play."

"Will do." Justin looked to Hazel and extended his hand. "Dr. Coop. I'm sorry this happened."

"Thank you, Officer Grant."

"Justin." As they shook hands, he nodded toward Burke. "If you're hanging out with this guy, I imagine we'll be crossing paths again."

Although she didn't think that dealing with bomb threats and disturbing letters or even canine ear infections qualified as "hanging out," Hazel realized she had spent more time with Burke in the past week than she had over the past two months. Did Justin think there was something more going on between her and Burke, too? First, Ashley had claimed Burke was flirting with her. And now Justin had practically labeled them a couple. She'd better be careful. Leaning on Jedediah Burke could become a habit she wouldn't want to break. Did she imagine his hand tightening around her shoulder briefly before she decided it might be wiser to break contact and step away from him?

And why was that subtle pressure all it took to keep her snugged to his side?

Justin backed toward his truck. "You need anything else from me, give me a call."

"Roger that." Burke's arm was still around her shoulders as Justin drove out of the parking lot.

The breeze was picking up as Cleo tugged on the leash, apparently ready to do some more exploring if Hazel didn't offer her a comfortable place to nap and Burke wasn't going to be petting her anymore. The wind held an unexpected bite as she moved away from Burke's warmth to let the dog reach the grass. Was the chill she felt physical or mental or both? She rubbed her free hand up and down her arm and turned her face to the sky to see the layers of clouds darting by. The wind whipped her bangs across her eyes and lifted the short waves on top of her head. "Looks like we're going to get a storm."

Burke's sigh was a deep rumble through the air behind her. "Are we reduced to that now? Talking about the weather like a couple of acquaintances who barely know each other?" He stepped up beside her, his callused fingers a soothing caress as he brushed the hair out of her eyes. He repeated the same gentle stroke across her forehead and along her temple before cupping the side of her jaw and letting his fingers curve around the back of her neck. "Promise me one thing. You'll never be afraid to speak what's on your mind to me."

She nodded. "Same here. You've always been a straight shooter with me, and I don't want that to change."

His fingertips pulled against the tension at the nape of her neck. "Then, in the spirit of honesty…you look worn-out. You doin' okay?"

"Nothing that a good night's sleep and feeling safe again won't cure."

"Anything I can do to help?"

Hazel had closed her eyes against the heavenly massage, until she realized she was just as shamelessly addicted to his touch as Cleo had been. She blinked her eyes open to find Burke studying her expression, waiting for her answer. "I thought I'd have some answers by now—that this obsession would end, not escalate." She reached up to wrap her fingers around his wrist, stilling his kneading long enough to share an embarrassing truth. "What if I can't handle this? I'm not as young as I was when I had to deal with this kind of emotional chaos before. And it nearly broke me back then."

"You're not alone this time." He tugged against her neck, pulling her into his chest and winding his arms around her. "I assume you're referring to that mess with your ex?"

She nodded.

He might not know the details, but he knew enough to understand that she'd been put through hell and had survived. "Maybe you've traded some of those youthful energy reserves for life experience. You'll be smarter about dealing with this mess than you were the last one. And if you are intimating in any way, shape or form that you are over the hill, and not strong or vibrant or able to deal with what life's throwing at you right now, I'm going to have to pick a fight with you."

She huffed a laugh at the compliment. "Have I ever told you how good you are for my ego, Sergeant Burke?"

"Just being a straight shooter, ma'am."

The inner voice that reminded her to maintain a professional distance from the veteran cop grew weaker with every breath she took. She settled against him, soothed by the strong beat of his heart beneath her ear. Her arms snuck around his waist as he nestled his chin against the crown of her hair and surrounded her in his abundant heat. She flattened her hands against his strong back and admitted to the tingling she felt in the tips of her breasts as they responded to the friction of her body pressed against his. God, he felt good. Solid, masculine. He smelled even better. If she wasn't gun-shy about starting a relationship with him, she could see herself falling for Burke far too easily. If he could work such magic with his hands, she could only imagine how sexy and addictive his kisses would be. Would he be gentle? Authoritative? Some heady mix in between?

As for sex... Her experience with Aaron had been all about the bells and whistles after the initial bloom of young love had faded. Just like her trust, their physical relationship had deteriorated to mechanics and trying too hard and finally to disappointment and neglect. Other than her husband, she hadn't had any partners. She had a feeling that, like the man himself, getting physical with Burke would be straightforward. *I want you. I'll make it good. Let's do this.*

Her breasts weren't the only part of her stinging with wakening desire now. Fantasizing about Jedediah Burke, imagining something more between them, reminded Hazel that she was a sexual being who'd denied her needs for far too long. Her marriage had crumbled, and she'd gone into survivor mode. She'd concentrated on being a mother and father to her girls, as well as a successful business owner who could support them and their dreams. She'd found solace in her work and a purposeful way to atone for the damage Aaron had done to the world by helping the animals in her care. But somewhere along the way she'd forgotten what it felt like to be held by a man, to be desired by one, to want something that was just for her.

She parted her lips as the heat building inside her demanded an outlet. As restlessness replaced her fatigue, she shifted her cheek against Burke's shoulder. Even his beard stubble catching a few strands of her hair and tugging gently against her scalp felt like a caress, but she couldn't seem to make herself pull away from his embrace. She opened her eyes to focus on the KCPD logo on the side of his truck, reminding herself why she'd turned to Burke in the first place. "Haven't you already done enough today? If you hadn't been here, I might have opened that package."

But then he pressed a kiss to her temple. His arms tightened imperceptibly around her. "Just doin' my job, Doc."

Hazel shivered at the deep, husky tone, but not because she was chilled by the cooling weather. Her body was responding to the call of his. Were Ashley's observations right? Could this strong, kind man want something more between them, too?

"Haze…"

She leaned back against his arms and tipped her face up to his descending mouth. "Burke, I…"

A beep from her purse interrupted whatever mistake she'd been about to make. A text. She was equal parts relieved and disappointed as she pressed her palms against his shoulders and backed out of his arms. She needed a good friend more than she needed another failed relationship right now. And she didn't imagine the kiss that had almost happened would have resulted in anything else but a complication neither of them needed.

"Sorry." She reached into her purse to pull out her cell phone. "Just in case it's a patient emergency."

Burke turned away, scrubbing his palm over his jaw as she unlocked the screen. She wasn't sure if that was frustration or relief that left him rolling the tension from his neck and shoulders. Instead of worrying about his reaction to that almost kiss when she wasn't sure of what she herself was feeling, she pulled up the text.

She didn't recognize the number or name of any patient, but, needing the distraction, she opened it, anyway. It was an animated meme with a caption. She recognized the familiar shape of her younger daughter's red car and smiled for a moment, thinking Polly had sent her a funny message to cheer her up.

But the number wasn't Polly's. Hazel frowned in confusion. Confusion quickly gave way to a fear that hollowed out her stomach.

The words that accompanied the picture were neither her daughter's nor funny.

I'm coming for you and everything you care about.
    Don't make the mistake of thinking I'm not a threat, or that I'm not watching your every waking moment.
    You're mine.

The picture exploded with cartoonish fireworks that faded away to reveal the burned-out frame of an automobile.

"Burke..." A mama bear's anger blazed behind her eyes, making her dizzy for a moment. She swung around and held up the awful image. "Burke!"

She showed him the text and he cursed.

He double-checked the time stamp and cursed again, swiveling his gaze 360 degrees around the empty parking lot and light traffic on the street beyond. The strip mall across the street had cars near a restaurant and waiting in line at the drive-through bank. The graying sky reflected in all the windows, keeping her from seeing if anyone was spying on her from inside one of the shops. "He just now sent this. He's got eyes on you. Or he knows your schedule, knows your routine."

Hazel looked, too, but she didn't see anyone staring at her, no one sitting in his car and pointing at her, laughing at how easily he could get under her skin and upset her. "Polly owns a Kia just like that. I'm sure she drove it to work this morning. She's at Saint Luke's Hospital, working and taking classes." Hazel watched the message play again, willing for some sort of clue to appear and reveal her tormentor's identity. "Is he threatening my baby...?"

Whether she was ten years old or twenty-one, her younger daughter would always be her baby. And a sick message like this text did more to frighten Hazel than any anonymous love letter or vial of C-4 could.

Burke clamped his hand around her upper arm and pulled her to the passenger door of his truck. "Get in. Call Polly. We're going to the hospital."

"I can drive."

"No." He opened the door.

"No? She's my daughter. I have to—"

His big hands spanned her waist and he picked her up and set her inside. He bent down to pick up Cleo and plopped the dog onto her lap before she could climb back out. Then he blocked the open door, meeting her eye to eye. "You're angry right now. And you're scared for your child. I don't want you driving while you're on your phone and worried about her."

She had to look away from the intensity in those dark brown eyes. She didn't need to argue for her independence. He was making sense. She thanked him with a nod. "Good point."

He jogged around to get in behind the wheel and started the truck. "Give me the number again."

Hazel rattled off the caller's ID while Burke backed

out of the parking space and picked up his radio to call
Dispatch. Gunny sat up the moment his handler had
climbed into the truck and whined quietly in the back
as they pulled into traffic and picked up speed. Cleo
was on her feet, wanting to touch noses with the working dog through the grate separating them, but Hazel
wrapped her arms around the schnauzer to keep her
in her lap.

Burke identified himself and reported the text as a
bomb threat before warning Dispatch to alert the bomb
squad and KCFD. Then he recited the phone number
and asked her to run a trace on it. After he signed off, he
glanced at Hazel. "They'll put an investigator on tracking down that cell number, although I'm guessing it'll
be a burner phone." He reached out to rub his hand over
the top of Cleo's head. "Once we know Polly's okay—
and she will be okay—you and I are going downtown
and filing a full report on this harassment campaign."

"Thank you."

He slid his hand along Cleo's back until he caught
Hazel's hand and squeezed it. "You and your girls will
be safe, Doc. I promise." Returning both hands to the
wheel, he nodded toward her phone. "Call."

Hazel punched in her younger daughter's number
while the truck sped along Front Street toward downtown. A mist was spitting on the windshield now, and
Burke turned on the wipers, along with his flashing
lights and siren as they ran into rush hour traffic.

"Hey, Mom. What's up?"

It was a relief to hear Polly's voice. "Are you at the
hospital?"

"Where else would I be?" Polly asked. Hazel heard voices and laughter in the background, as though her daughter was safely surrounded by friends. "It's my long day. Classes. Work. My evening volunteer seminar starts in half an hour."

The clouds blinked with lightning, and thunder rumbled overhead, the coming storm adding to the urgency of the moment. "Don't leave the building," Hazel warned. "We're on our way to you."

"We?"

"Sergeant Burke is driving me."

"Ooh, yum." She heard Polly excuse herself from whomever she was with, and the background noise quieted. "Sergeant Hottie McHotterson, who loves dogs as much as you do? Whose broad shoulders fill out his uniform like a man half his age? That Sergeant Burke?"

Hazel groaned, glad she didn't have the call on speakerphone, but she couldn't keep her gaze from sliding across the cab of the truck to verify her daughter's observation. She tried to make her next breath a sigh of relief. If Polly could tease her about her dating life, or lack thereof, then she had to be fine. "You've been talking to your sister."

"There might have been some cahootenizing over a couple of glasses of wine last weekend. You do know we both like him, right, Mom? If you ever decide you want to date again, Sergeant Burke would be on our approved list."

She wasn't having this discussion again. She needed to focus on the problem at hand. "Did you drive your car to the hospital this morning?"

"Of course I did."

"Have you been outside since then?"

"No. I had classes. Went on rounds with Professor Owenson in the maternity ward. I saw the rain in the forecast, and it was clouding up, so I just grabbed a bite of dinner in the cafeteria instead of going back to the apartment." Good. Her daughters shared an apartment, and knowing Ashley had headed home after work, she was relieved to hear that her older daughter wouldn't accidentally run into the danger indicated by that text when she pulled into the parking lot behind their complex.

"Where is your car now?"

"In the west lot." Polly hesitated, no doubt picking up on the urgency in her voice. "Mom, is something wrong?"

"Stay inside the hospital. Do not go to your car for any reason."

Burke motioned for her to hold the phone up and put it on speaker. "Polly? Jedediah Burke here."

"Hey, Sarge. What's going on?"

"Do what your mom says, and contact hospital security to cordon off your car. Tell them not to touch anything. We'll be there in ten minutes." The rain was coming down in sheets now. Could he guarantee that? "First responders are on their way."

"Okay, now you're both scaring me," said Polly. Hazel recognized the tightness in her daughter's tone. "Does this have anything to do with the package Mom got in the mail today? Ashley texted me about it this afternoon."

"Possibly. I don't want to scare you, but I believe someone may have tampered with your car. At least with one that looks like yours."

"Tampered? What do you mean? Like someone let the air out of my tires?" Even over the noise of the storm and traffic, Hazel could hear her daughter's quickened breaths. "I'm heading down the Wornall Road hallway to the south windows. I parked aboveground today. I can see my car from… There it is. Right where I left it. I was here early enough to get a surface-level spot."

"Don't go to it," Hazel warned. "Stay inside until we get there."

"It's okay, Mom. I'm just look—" When Polly gasped and went silent, Hazel nearly screamed into the phone.

But like all the women in the Cooper family, she was a medical professional and knew that panicking wasn't going to help anyone. "Polly?"

"Sergeant? Mom? There's a guy in a black hoodie out there. He's walking around my car, looking in the windows." Polly's soft voice told Hazel her daughter was afraid. "I can't see his face. What's he doing out there with all this rain? Nobody else is—"

"Call security," Burke ordered. He raced through an intersection. Gunny whined with more excitement and Cleo barked.

"He's jogging away. He ran down the ramp into the parking garage. I can't see exactly where he went. I hear sirens—they're not ambulances. Maybe he heard them, too."

"Do what Burke says, sweetie. Contact security and stay inside. We'll be right there."

Hazel heard a muffled thump like thunder in the distance. Had the storm reached Saint Luke's, too?

"Oh, my God." She barely heard her daughter's whisper.

"Polly? Please tell me that was thunder."

Burke shook his head.

Hazel knew by the pace of her breathing that her daughter was running. "I'm on my way to the security desk now."

"You need to talk to me right now, young lady."

"I'm okay, Mom. But get here fast. My car just blew up."

Chapter 4

The rain was pouring by the time the Kansas City Fire Department had extinguished the flames of Polly's car, driving everyone but the crime scene technicians back inside the hospital. Cradling Cleo in her lap, Hazel sat in a chair in the carpeted lobby, absently petting Gunny, who dozed at her feet, eavesdropping on Burke, Justin Grant and a stone-faced firefighter named Matt Taylor, whom Hazel had learned was a younger brother to Pike Taylor, the K-9 officer who worked with Burke.

Once the police had finished interviewing her, Polly had insisted on checking in for the last half hour of her volunteer seminar. Hazel understood her need to stay focused on something other than the danger that had come far too close this evening. Plus, Polly had inherited Hazel's own workaholic tendencies and wanted to finish the job she'd promised to do. Her big sister, Ashley, had shown up minutes after Hazel and Burke had arrived, as worried about Polly as Hazel was. The two young women were so close. Polly had probably texted Ashley for moral support the moment she'd gotten off the phone with Hazel.

Although the stress of the day was wearing on her, Hazel felt better knowing her daughters were under the same roof as she was, and she could keep an eye on them both and know they were safe.

She'd relive those last few months with Aaron a hundred times before she'd let anyone hurt one of her daughters.

Cleo stirred in Hazel's lap, alert to every employee, patient or visitor who walked past. Unfazed by her own physical handicaps, it was almost as though the small dog was keeping watch over her mistress. Or maybe the one-eyed schnauzer was keeping watch over her big bruiser buddy, who panted quietly at Hazel's feet. Unless they were registered therapy animals, dogs, as a rule, weren't allowed inside the hospital. But no one seemed to mind the smell of wet dog on the premises tonight. Burke's Czech shepherd had done his job, alerting to the remnants of explosives inside the front wheel well of Polly's car, his sensitive nose picking up the scent even after the firefighters had soaked the vehicle with foam and the storm had set in while the first responders cleared the scene. With the help of three other bomb-sniffing dogs and their partners, Gunny and Burke had cleared every vehicle in the parking garage and the interior of Saint Luke's itself.

Polly's car had been specifically targeted. Matt Taylor said the fire had been contained to Polly's car, the fuel in her gas tank had accounted for most of the flames, and only minor damage had been inflicted on the nearby vehicles. And though the police and search dogs had determined there were no other explosives on the site to worry about, Hazel still worried.

Her *daughter* had been targeted.

Even now, hours after the initial explosion, knowing Polly hadn't been anywhere close to the bomb when it detonated, Hazel felt light-headed with an overwhelming dose of anger and fear.

If Polly hadn't had such a full day and hadn't decided to eat dinner at the hospital, she might have been in that car, stuck in rush hour traffic, when it exploded. Hazel's baby girl might be horribly injured or... Hazel fisted her fingers in Gunny's long, damp coat. She refused to even think the word.

Threatening *her* was one thing.

Going after her children was something else entirely.

The letters had been upsetting, yes—the bomb parts delivered to the clinic were unsettling. But even with seeking out Burke's help, she hadn't taken the whole stalking situation as seriously as she should have until today. Now her friends and employees and daughters had been drawn into this senseless terror campaign. Her protective mama-bear hackles were on high alert. She could no longer separate the threats from the rest of her life, praying they'd go away, hoping she could handle the situation herself. Now she intended to meet the enemy head-on—protect her daughters, protect her staff—identify the culprit and then sic Gunny and Burke and the rest of the KCPD on him.

Matt Taylor had shed his big reflective coat and helmet, and he stood with his hands propped at the waist of his insulated turnout pants. "If the explosive had been placed in the back near the gas tank, we'd be talking a different story. As it is, other than the shrapnel that dinged the neighboring cars, most of the damage came from the fuel burning. The gas tank never exploded."

Justin looked from Matt to Burke. "So again, either this guy doesn't know what he's doing with these explosives, or he's deliberately drawing this out—upping the stakes with each threat instead of going for maximum damage." His green-eyed gaze darted over to Hazel, indicating he knew she was listening in. Yes, the damage had been more than enough, considering they were talking about Polly's car. But she hoped that locking gazes with him indicated she wanted to hear the questions and answers they were discussing, even if the topic might upset her. "How did our perp know which vehicle to target? The DMV's not a public-access database."

"Because he's watching Hazel and her girls." Burke's chest expanded with an angry breath. "He's inserted himself into their lives somehow, even in a periphery way, so he can learn all he can about them—where they work, where they live, their routines, what they drive." He scrubbed his palm over the stubble shading his jaw. "I need to ferret this guy out. Find out why he's doing this to Hazel and put a stop to it."

"Look, what you and the dogs you train do is invaluable. But you're not a detective, old man," Justin cautioned him.

Burke's glare was part reprimand and all irritation at the reminder. But whether it was the job description or the nickname that he didn't find amusing, she couldn't tell. "If Gunny can find a bomb in a campus this size, then I can damn well find the perp who put it there." He shrugged some of the tension off his shoulders and made a concession. "I won't go cowboy on anybody. I'll keep Detectives Bellamy and Cartwright in the loop. As long as they do the same for me."

Cooper Bellamy and Seth Cartwright were the two detectives who'd come to Saint Luke's to take statements from her, Burke and Polly. Now that the CSIs had set up a protective tarp and fog lights around the shell of Polly's car, Bellamy and Cartwright were out in the rain, getting preliminary statements from the criminologists on the scene and meeting with the guards at the security gate in front of the hospital to see if any of them had glimpsed the man in the black hoodie and could provide a more detailed description of the guy or his vehicle.

Right now, with no traceable phone number, no return address on the letters, and no answers yet on where he'd obtained the bomb parts and explosives, Polly's description of an oversized man in a black hoodie and dark pants who disappeared inside the parking garage was the best they had to go on.

"Keep KCFD in the loop, too," Matt said, extending his hand to shake both Burke's and Justin's. "I'll get you the results from our arson investigator as soon as we know anything more concrete."

"Thanks, Matt."

Matt nodded to Hazel as he strode past. "Ma'am."

"Thank you, Mr. Taylor."

She followed him to the front doors with her gaze and saw the young firefighter exchange a look with her older daughter, Ashley. Although she didn't think they knew each other, Ashley gave him a friendly wave before he walked out into the rain and she returned to the animated conversation she was having on her cell phone.

Hazel's eyes narrowed at the observation. Could something as simple as a friendly wave she didn't remember be the cause of all this terror and destruction? Did some creep fancy himself in love with her because she'd smiled at him or been polite?

Hazel had made a point of not dating for years now. Aaron had given her plenty of reason to be wary of men she didn't know. But even if she had considered getting to know a new man in an intimate way, she hadn't. First, because her daughters had needed her and the stability of being home every night during and after Aaron's trial and the dissolution of their disastrous marriage. And more recently because those years of emotional self-preservation had become an ingrained habit. If she wasn't any better a judge of whom to trust and give her heart to than when she fell for Aaron Cooper, then what business did she have risking another relationship?

It was Survival 101. She didn't lead on any man who might be interested in her. She stated her rules, tried to let him down easy if he pushed for her to bend those rules and kept her heart at a safe distance.

Had she slipped somewhere? She had several platonic relationships with men—like Burke, clients, coworkers, friends. Had she missed a sign that one of them had deeper feelings for her? Had she subconsciously encouraged someone into thinking she cared for him with a wave or a smile or a thank-you?

He's inserted himself into their lives...

Burke's assertion clanged like a warning bell inside her head.

Who was Ashley talking to? Judging by her big smile and lively responses, it had to be a boyfriend—or someone she wanted to be her boyfriend. Did Hazel know whom her daughter was interested in now? She'd broken up with her last boyfriend because he'd gotten too serious too fast for her. And bless Ashley's outgoing, adventurous heart, she didn't have settling down to babies and white picket fences on her mind anytime soon. Ashley claimed they'd parted on good terms. But could a man who'd been talking marriage really be content to walk away after a breakup?

Hazel turned in her seat, looking in the opposite direction down the hallway leading to the employees' locker room. Polly's ponytail was curlier than Ashley's and a couple of shades darker, but just as easy to spot. She strolled down the hallway, sharing a conversation with an older man wearing tattered jeans and an ill-fitting Army jacket. They stopped before reaching the side exit to the employee parking lot and faced each other. His shaggy beard and faded ball cap on top of his longish gray hair led her to think he was one of the home-less patients her daughter worked with in her volunteer seminar. Polly had a big heart and a bone-deep drive to help anyone in need. Hazel had always been proud of Polly's calling to be of service to others.

But she startled Cleo with a silent jerk of protest when the man leaned over and hugged Polly. Hazel absentmindedly stroked the dog's head to apologize but wasn't feeling any calmer herself. She didn't know that man holding on to her younger daughter as though she was a lifeline. Not that she knew every patient, class-mate or teacher of Polly's. But would a man like that fancy himself in love simply because Polly had tended his wound or offered him a smile?

Did Hazel have any men like that or Ashley's phone friend in her life?

Was that how a stalker was born?

Identifying the man behind the letters and explosives meant starting with a single question. Hazel intended to spend some time on the computer tonight, reading through her patient files to refresh her memory about her clients and the salespeople and consultants she did business with. She'd urge Polly and Ashley to do the same with their circles of friends, coworkers and ac-quaintances. But for now, she was going to find out who that man was with Polly. Plus, it would give her an op-portunity to check in with her daughter to see how she was holding up after seeing her most expensive posses-sion and means of transportation be destroyed.

A warm hand folded over Hazel's shoulder, and she yelped louder than Cleo had.

"Easy." Burke quickly drew his hand away and retreated a step. "Didn't mean to startle you. You okay?"

"Sorry." She pulled her focus from her speculative thoughts long enough to reorient herself in the moment. She grounded herself in Burke's narrowed brown eyes and leaned to one side to see the rest of the lobby behind him. "Justin left?"

"Yeah. Detective Bellamy said they recovered more of the bomb parts and wanted him to examine them before they bagged everything up for the lab." She nodded, glad to have all these professionals working to help her now but wishing they had more answers for her. "Bellamy said they've put out a BOLO on the guy Polly described."

"An oversized man in a black hoodie and dark pants is pretty generic, isn't it?"

"It is. But it's a place to start." He must have read the doubt in her expression. And he couldn't miss her gaze darting between her daughters and following the homeless man as he left Polly and strolled around the lobby to the front doors. "Are the girls okay? That guy bothering them?"

"Young women. Not girls anymore." Had the homeless man's gaze brushed across Ashley's back as he walked out into the rain? "And no. Not that I could see. He was talking to Polly. Probably a patient. I guess I'm suspicious of everyone now."

"Everyone?" Burke prompted, perhaps wondering if he and the other cops and firefighters he'd been talking to were on that suspect list.

"I just wish I knew who was responsible..." Hazel

pushed to her feet, setting Cleo down on the carpet beside Gunny. She placed both leashes into Burke's hand. "Do you mind? I need to check on Polly. I can find out who that man is and get at least one question answered tonight."

"I'll keep an eye on Cleo." Burke tilted his head toward the effervescent blonde laughing into her phone. "I'll keep an eye her, too."

Burke's matter-of-fact promise kindled a warm ball of light inside her, chasing away the almost desperate feeling of helplessness that had left her on edge from the moment she'd dropped that package at the clinic. Did he have any idea how grateful she was for his steady presence and ability to take charge of a situation and get whatever action was needed done? He'd been strong when her own strength had faltered. Hazel knew she was lucky that he was a part of her life. She reached up and splayed her fingers against his chest, fingering the KCPD logo emblazoned there. Did she imagine the tremor that rippled across the skin and muscle beneath her hand? "I'm not sure how I would have gotten through today without you. Thank you."

He placed his hand over hers, holding it against the strong beat of his heart. "Just doin' my job."

She shook her head. "You've gone above and beyond the call of duty, Jedediah. How long have you been off the clock? And you're still here with me."

His dark brows arched above his eyes when she used his given name, and she realized she'd never called him that before. He'd always been the big boss of the K-9 unit, Burke. Or Sarge. Or Sergeant Burke.

She liked the rhythmic sound of his name on her tongue. "Is it okay if I call you that? Jedediah?"

"Yeah." His answer was a deep-pitched rumble that danced across all kinds of nerve endings and scattered her vows of friendship and keeping him arm's length from her heart. "Jedediah's good. Do I still have to call you Dr. Coop?"

Good gravy. This man could read the phone book or a grocery list in that voice, and her pulse would race a little faster.

"Of course not. Hazel's such an old-fashioned name, though—I almost always had a nickname. I was named after one of my grandmothers. I was always the only Hazel in class, surrounded by Lisas and Karens and Marys." She wiggled her fingers beneath his hand, tracing the *C* on his chest, idly speculating how a man in his fifties kept himself in such good shape. "I bet there weren't a lot of Jedediahs, either."

"You were unique. You still are."

Why did that sound more like a compliment than a commentary? Was he talking about more than her name? Was she?

How had this whole interchange become more than a thank-you? Could Ashley be right? Had she and Burke been flirting with each other? She had rules in place, damn it. Rules to protect her heart, to protect her family, to keep herself from making the same mistakes she'd made with Aaron. She needed structure. She needed boundaries. Was she falling for this man?

Hazel jerked her hand away, putting the brakes on that possibility. "Excuse me. I'm sorry." Though what, exactly, she was apologizing for, she wasn't certain. Was she leading him on? Making him think that a relationship could happen between them? Did Jedediah want that? Did she?

"Haze—"

But she shook her head, turned and hurried down the hallway after Polly. "I'm sorry."

Hazel clutched her shoulder bag to her chest and followed Polly to the employee locker room at the end of the hall. She did not want to be one of those women who used a man when she needed one, then set him aside. How would that be any different from the way Aaron had treated their marriage? She had no intention of stringing Jedediah along, letting him think he had a chance for something more with her when she couldn't guarantee that was what she wanted, too. Hurting him would be worse than never allowing a serious relationship to happen. Jedediah deserved better than that from her. And she needed to set a better example of an honest relationship for her daughters.

Vowing to have a serious conversation with Jedediah about her rules, once her nerves were a little less frayed by bombs and threats, Hazel caught the door to the locker room before it swung shut. She had her game face back on by the time she stepped inside—even if that air of cool, calm, we've-got-nothing-to-worry-about Mom face was only a facade.

Hazel spotted Polly heading down the center aisle alongside the bench that ran between the rows of lockers. "Knock, knock. Is it okay if I come in?"

Polly waved her into the room. "Sure, Mom."

Nodding to two staff members who were chatting at the front end of the bench, Hazel walked past them. Polly was standing at her open locker door when Hazel wound an arm around her and hugged her to her side. "Hey, young lady. How are you holding up?"

Polly's shoulders lifted with a heavy sigh. "Honestly?"

"Always."

Polly's green eyes darted over to meet hers. "I'm exhausted. This was already a long day without your troubles spilling over into my life." She reached around to share the hug, easing the stinging guilt from her words. "Sorry. That didn't come out right. I don't blame you for any of this. I've just been so worried about you that I didn't realize I needed to be worried about me, too." She smiled as she pulled away and went back to changing out of her scrubs into jeans and a T-shirt. "I'm not looking forward to spending my day off tomorrow dealing with insurance."

"I can help you if you need me to."

Polly tapped her chest with her thumb, asserting her independence. "Grown-up, Mom."

Hazel tapped her own chest, reminding her daughter that some things would never change. "Mother, Polly."

She sat on the bench while Polly exchanged her clogs for a pair of running shoes. She picked up her daughter's discarded scrubs and rolled them up. She wasn't sure what prompted her to dip her nose to the wrinkled bundle and sniff. She inhaled the subtle scents of Polly's shower gel, and the disinfectants and unguents she'd come into contact with throughout the day. Hazel frowned, though, when she realized those were the only scents she was picking up. Was it stereotyping of her to think that a man who lived on the streets would have transferred some sort of pungent odor to her daughter's clothes?

"Don't worry." Polly plucked the bundle from Hazel's hands and tucked them into her backpack. "Laundry is on my to-do list tonight."

"It's not that." Hazel asked the question that had been worrying her. "Now that I'm paranoid about all the men who encounter my family, I was wondering…who was that man who hugged you?"

"Russell?" Polly pulled her ponytail from the back of her T-shirt and studied her reflection in the small mirror inside her locker door. "He's one of the homeless guys my class is volunteering with. They come to the hospital and we practice routine medical care, or we assist the doctors or senior nurses if they have something more serious to deal with. Tonight gave Russell a dry place to go to get out of this rain, too. He's usually at the Yankee Hill Road shelter, but that's several blocks from here." She muttered a euphemistic curse. "I forgot to ask if he had money for the bus."

"At least it's not chilly tonight," Hazel pointed out. "If he gets wet, he won't catch a cold."

"I'm sure you're right." Polly reached onto the top shelf of her locker. "He reminds me of somebody's grandpa. He said he missed working with me tonight. By the time I got to the area where the group meets, the others were gone. But he waited for me. He heard what happened and could tell I was upset." She pulled out a small rectangle of cardboard and handed it to her. "He gave me this card. Isn't that sweet?"

Hazel supposed she didn't need to worry about a grandfatherly patient paying attention to her daughter. She was the one with the unwanted suitor who was proving to be a threat to them all. Besides, a man who had to resort to crayons and cutting off the front of another card to glue to a piece of cardboard probably didn't have the budget to purchase C-4 and pay for the postage her stalker had already spent on her.

Smiling fondly, Polly sat down to tie her shoes. "Even in Russell's circumstances, he was thinking of me."

Hazel turned the card over to read the message scrawled in three different colors of crayon. *Out of all the people in the world, you're the one I'm thinking of today. Sorry about your car. Russell D.*

"Out of all the people in the world, huh? Your father used to say gushy stuff like that to me when he wanted to apologize for whatever event he forgot or promise he had to break." A message that had usually been accompanied by flowers or a gift they couldn't afford. She'd have preferred a considerate heads-up beforehand if he wasn't going to be at one of Ashley's concerts or plays, or one of Polly's games.

Too many grand gestures and not enough substance and reliability had slowly eroded her trust in Aaron until the girls were the only reason she kept fighting for her marriage. In the end, she'd finally admitted there was nothing left to fight for. And after the night of the accident that was no accident... Leaving with Ashley and Polly had been the best way to protect them from the backlash of Aaron's crimes. Erasing Aaron from her life had been the only way to stop the hateful, then pleading letters from prison. By the time he'd accepted his fate and started writing to Ashley and Polly instead, the girls were too afraid or too disinterested to rebuild a relationship with their father.

Polly bumped her shoulder against hers, cajoling her out of those negative memories. "Hey. I know where your head's at. This isn't Dad we're talking about. Russell loses points for creativity, but I believe the sentiment is legit."

Hazel laced her fingers together with Polly's and squeezed her hand. "You're absolutely right. It's the thought that counts."

"I suppose it's hard to form bonds with people when you're in a situation like Russell's. But I think he looks forward to me checking his blood pressure every week." Polly returned the card to the top shelf of her locker. "That means I'm making a difference in someone's life, right?"

Smiling, Hazel rose to hug her to her side again. "You've been making a difference from the day you were born, sweetie. I don't think there's a puppy, bug or baby bird you didn't want to rescue when you were little."

Polly scrunched her face into a frown. "Funny. I'm not so keen on the bugs now."

"Can anyone join this party?" Ashley beamed a smile as Hazel leaned into her older daughter to include her in the group hug. "It's good to see you laughing again, Mom."

Hazel's mood had lightened considerably from the gloom and suspicion she'd come into the hospital with. "It feels good," she admitted. "Spending time with my two favorite people always makes me feel better. Are you sure you're both okay?"

"The Cooper women have weathered everything else life has thrown at us. We'll get through this, too. Cooper Power."

"Cooper Power," Polly echoed, trading a fist bump with her sister.

Hazel marveled at the bond these two shared. No matter what she accomplished in her life, she knew raising these two fine young women would always be her greatest achievement.

As Polly grabbed her jacket from her locker, Ashley pulled a business card from her purse. "It's not a new car, but I have a present for you, sis."

"A present?" Polly took the business card and flipped it over to read it.

"Sergeant Burke's card with all his numbers." Ashley pulled a second one from her purse to show she'd gotten one, too. "He said to call if we needed anything— whether he's on duty or at home. Even if we just need someone to walk us to our car at night, or we get a flat tire somewhere." She grinned at her sister. "Not that you're going to get a flat tire anytime soon."

"Way to rub it in, dork." Polly stuffed the card into her pocket. "That's awfully nice of the sergeant."

It was. Even without a word or a touch, Jedediah Burke was working his way past Hazel's defenses. His caring offer to her girls warmed her heart and gave her one more reason to toss aside her rules and embrace the possibility of a new relationship.

Ashley slipped her card back into her bag. "He said I could call him Burke. Most of his friends call him that."

"Is that right?" The daughters exchanged a meaningful look before Polly asked, "What do you call him, Mom?"

Apparently, she was going with *Jedediah* now. But somehow, sharing that—even with her daughters—felt like betraying some sort of intimate secret.

"Don't think I don't see what you two are up to. Burke is a good man. We owe him big-time for all the help he's given us. I'm touched that he would extend his protection to you, too."

"He's protecting you? Ooh." Ashley clapped her hands together. "Like a bodyguard? Or a boyfriend?"

Hazel groaned. "I came back here to see if you were all right. Clearly, you are, if you have time to worry about my love life."

"Or lack thereof," Ashley pointed out.

"Stop it." Hazel pointed a stern maternal finger at each of them. "I want you both to come stay with me. There's plenty of room at the condo. Keep us all together until this guy is caught and no one else can get hurt."

"Stay with you?" Ashley frowned before turning her head toward the locker room door as the two women who'd been chatting earlier opened it wide to leave, giving them all a glimpse of the muscular man waiting out in the hallway with two dogs at his side. Burke was leaning against the wall, studying something on his phone, somehow looking both tired and alert as he formed a protective wall between her little family and the outside world that wanted to hurt them. "What if you're entertaining guests?"

Hazel's eyes lingered on his weary expression as the door slowly closed on him. "One, I am not entertaining Burke or any other man. And two, you and Ashley will always come first, even if there was a man in my life."

She was still watching the last glimpse of Burke and wondering what he did to relax after long days like this, or who he leaned on when he needed a boost of support, when Polly squeezed her hand. "When are you going to put yourself first, Mom? Ashley and I are adults now. Don't use us as an excuse to not move on with your life and find happiness."

"Be smart and find it with *him*," Ashley urged. "Burke's a silver fox. You know what that means, don't you?"

"Yes, I know the term. I'm your mother, not dead."

Ashley grinned. "So, you *do* think he's hot."

That was a given.

"I liked it better when I could send you two to your room." Hazel shook her head, forcing herself to remember that the strength she'd imbued in her daughters was there for a reason. "All right. I'll try not to be so much of a mother hen. But don't forget that this guy is no joke. I want you two to look out for each other."

"We will," Polly promised.

"Keep a watchful eye out for anyone paying too much attention to you. Don't go anyplace by yourself. Lock your doors. You know the safety drill. Call me or the police if anything seems wrong to you. Whatever this man wants from me, I am not going to let it hurt my daughters."

Ashley hugged her taller sister to her side. "I'll keep an eye on her, Mom." She tilted her chin up to Polly. "I've got a date tonight with Joe. Maybe we can double. I'm sure he has a friend."

"No, thank you." Polly pulled away to heft her backpack onto her shoulder and close her locker. "I need to study."

"Who's Joe?" Hazel asked. She knew that wasn't the let's-get-married guy Ashley had dumped. The idea of a stranger entering their lives right now worried her. "That's who you were on the phone with?"

"Uh-huh. He's the guy I met a couple of Fridays ago when I went to Fontella's bachelorette party at The Pickle up by City Market."

"The Pickle?" Hazel frowned.

"It's a rooftop bar with pickleball courts. He's a bouncer there. I told you, didn't I?"

She knew about her college friend's wedding, but not the new boyfriend. "No, you didn't."

"He's cool, Mom," Polly volunteered. "I met him when he picked up Ash for the movie last weekend. He's got more tats than any guy I've ever met. But he was funny and super nice. Don't judge a book by its cover and all that."

Bouncer? Tats? Funny and nice? Her daughters really *had* grown up. "Do I get to meet this guy?"

"Do you mind if I invite him to the apartment, then?" Ashley asked Polly, pulling out her phone, ignoring Hazel's question. "We could order a couple of pizzas, and then Joe and I can watch a movie while you're in your room with your books and headphones being all nerdy."

Polly rolled her eyes before shrugging. "That sounds fine. Then none of us will be alone." She nodded toward the exit door, indicating the man waiting patiently on the other side. "Right, Mom?"

Hazel put her hands up in surrender before pulling each daughter in for a hug. "I guess I'm outvoted. Just be safe. And check in with me tomorrow if I don't see you so I know you're all right."

"We will. Love you." Ashley tightened the hug before pulling back and nodding toward the hallway. "Burke's tired. Hungry, too, I imagine." She gave Hazel a little nudge. "Go. Feed him. He needs some attention."

"He's a grown man." Hazel was arguing against the pull of empathy she'd just been feeling. "He can take care of himself."

Polly took a more logical approach to the relentless matchmaking. "He's been with you all day long. It's after nine o'clock and neither one of you have eaten dinner. Wouldn't that be a nice way to say thank you to him for being such a rock for us today?"

"It's what a good friend would do," Ashley added. She touched her lips. "Although, every man likes a little pretty. Some lip gloss wouldn't hurt."

"Enough with the lip gloss." Hazel tried to stare them down but quickly realized the tactic that had worked to silence an argument when they were children wasn't going to work tonight. Besides, they did have a point. "Fine. I do owe him for his help today." She reluctantly took the lip gloss Ashley offered and dabbed a little color and shine onto her dry lips before pushing it back into her daughter's hand. But she grabbed onto Ashley's fingers and squeezed, still determined they understood her point. "You two know you can't will a relationship to happen between Burke and me just because it amuses you or you think I'm going to wind up alone and living in your spare bedroom. I'm in a good place on my own. I'm happy with my life—except for that idiot who won't leave us alone. I'm more worried about our safety right now than about falling in love again."

"Did she say *falling in love*?" Polly pointed out to her sister.

"That's what I heard. She likes him. She just won't admit it." Ashley was grinning from ear to ear now. "I can see if Joe has a friend he could hook you up with, if that's more of the kind of guy you like."

Another bouncer with tats who was probably half her age? No, thanks.

Polly linked her arm through hers and turned her toward the door. "Mom…there's nothing wrong with being deliriously happy and falling in love again. If you find the right man. And I can't see any way that Sergeant Burke would be the mistake that Dad was."

But what if *she* was the mistake? What if *she* was the one with the rotten judgment who could be tricked into another unhealthy relationship?

Although their hearts were in the right place, her daughters didn't know every detail of the hell Aaron Cooper had put them through. But she did. They thought they were helping by pushing her toward Burke—and they wouldn't let it drop until she gave in and proved them wrong.

Hazel sighed in surrender and traded one more hug before pushing the door open and marching into the hallway. "Call me when you two get home." Burke immediately tucked his phone into his pocket and straightened away from the wall. Barely breaking stride, she grabbed his hand as she passed by and tugged him toward the lobby. "Come with me."

He ordered the dogs into step beside him before subtly changing his grip on hers, linking their fingers together in a more mutual grasp. "Everything okay?"

"If you call two buttinsky daughters who don't know when to mind their own business okay, then yes, everything's fine."

He halted, pulling her to a stop without releasing her hand. "Did I miss something?"

Hazel glanced up. She couldn't help but smile a reassurance to ease the questioning frown that lined his eyes. "Never mind. Unless you have a better offer, I'm taking you to dinner."

Chapter 5

A better offer? Burke had been waiting for an invitation from Hazel Cooper for a long time. And even though there'd been no declaration of affection, or even an admission that this crazy lust he felt was mutual, getting an invitation to the fourth-floor loft in Kansas City's downtown Library District that Hazel called home felt like taking their relationship to the next level.

By mutual agreement, dinner had ended up being takeout from a burger joint they'd passed on their way from the vet clinic, where she'd picked up her truck and he'd followed her home. He'd been lucky enough to find a place to park on the street a couple of blocks from her building after she'd parked in the gated garage on the street level of the renovated tool and die shop and warehouse. The short walk to join her at the caged-in entrance where she let him in gave Gunny time to do his business before they took the elevator up to the fourth floor.

With only two condos on each floor, Hazel's place felt open and roomy, especially with the wall of floor-to-ceiling windows facing the skyline to the west. He was surprised to see how much of the industrial design of the original building had been preserved in the open ductwork and stained brick walls from when the building had been a hub of manufacturing and commerce near the Missouri River. Although a pair of bedrooms and two bathrooms had been closed in with modern walls, the rest of the loft felt big enough for him to relax in.

Hazel kicked off her shoes the moment she stepped through the front door, fed Cleo and Gunny, and found an old blanket for his dog to sleep on beside the sofa where the smaller dog had curled up. Then she invited him to sit on one of the stools at the kitchen island while she pulled a couple of cold beers from the fridge and set out plates and cloth napkins to make the paper-wrapped sandwiches and fries feel like a real sit-down meal. They talked about the decidedly feminine touches of color and cushy furniture that softened the industrial vibe of the place, her older daughter's apparent obsession with lip gloss that seemed to be part of some joke he didn't understand and her concern about her younger daughter shopping for a new car.

Burke insisted she sit while he cleared the dishes and loaded the dishwasher, offering to go car shopping with Polly. They talked about the rain forcing him to change his training schedule with his officers and their dogs, Royals baseball and whether she preferred the scruffy look he was sporting at 11:00 p.m. to being clean-shaven like when he reported for his shift in the morning. They talked about any-and everything except the bombs, the love letters and the threat she was facing from her unknown stalker.

He decided he liked Hazel's lips, whether they were shiny with gloss, pursed in a bow as she sipped her beer, stretched out in a smile or moving with easy precision as she articulated her words. And though he enjoyed the feeling of intimacy that sharing comfortable spaces and late-night conversation with a beautiful woman gave him, he didn't like that she was avoiding the reason why he and Gunny were here in the first place. He'd always admired Hazel's strength—raising her daughters alone, running her business, caring for others and standing by that strict code of right and wrong she believed in.

But surely, she'd let go sometime. Hazel knew she didn't have to entertain him, right? She didn't have to laugh at his lame teasing or make sure he got that third scoop of ice cream in the sundaes she fixed for dessert. He'd given her apartment the once-over, checking the fire escape and window locks, ensuring the lock on her front door was properly installed, closing the sheer curtains across her living room windows to keep prying eyes from seeing in as she turned on the lights. His offer of security was a given. But he was also here to give her a safety net to drop her guard and give in to the fear and fatigue or whatever she must be feeling.

He closed the dishwasher and turned to face her across the island, catching a glimpse of the big yawn she tried to hide behind the caramel sauce she was licking off her spoon as she finished her sundae. He imagined the swipe of that tongue across his own lips and shifted at the instant stab of heat that tightened his groin and made his pulse race. Man, she had a beautiful mouth. It was getting harder and harder for him to ignore this longing, this sense of rightness he felt every time he spent even a moment with Hazel Cooper. He was 99 percent sure she felt it, too, given the darting glances he spied when she thought his back was turned. But damn that strength of hers. Even as he admired what made her so attractive, he cursed her ability to ignore the possibilities between them.

"Sorry," she apologized around the last bite of the homemade sauce. "It's not the company, I swear."

"Leave something for the dishwasher to do." Burke grinned as he reached across the island to pluck the spoon from her fingers and pick up the empty bowl. He rinsed them off and added them to the dishwasher, carefully choosing his words before he faced her again. "You *do* know that I'm here for you if you need help with anything. An ear to listen. A shoulder to lean on. Someone to watch the place while you crash for a few hours." He braced his hands on the granite countertop and leaned toward her. "You've been through a lot today. Trust me to have your back. Let me take care of you a little bit while you let down your hair and relax or do whatever you need to do to regroup."

She flicked at the silvery blond bangs that played up the mossy green color of her eyes. "What hair?"

Fine. Make a joke out of his caring. He'd better

leave before he argued that he admired how practical her super short hair was, and how it gave him a clear glimpse of the delicate shells of her ears that he wanted to touch and taste. Scrubbing his hand across his jaw, he pushed away from the counter and strode to the back of the couch, where he'd left his ball cap and Gunny's lead. "I guess that's my cue. You don't need me anymore, so I'd better get Gunny home." Even before he gave the command, the big dog was on his feet. "Gunny, *hier.*"

He plunked his hat onto his head and hooked Gunny's lead to his harness.

"Burke." Hazel's stool scudded across the wood planks of the floor. Her bare feet made no sound, but he inhaled the familiar tropical scent of coconut from her soap and shampoo before he heard her behind him. "Jedediah." His muscles jerked beneath the firm grip of her hand on his arm, asking him to stop. Her face was tipped up to his when he glanced down over the jut of his shoulder. Her eyes were weary and worried and sincere. "I'm sorry. I don't mean to make light of your feelings. I'm just not sure I'm prepared to deal with them. Or mine. Not tonight."

He curled his fingers over hers, holding her hand against his skin as he turned. "You don't have to apologize," he conceded. "There was a lot more conversation going on in my head than what came out. You and I are so close, Haze, I sometimes forget that you don't want the same thing between us that I do."

"That isn't necessarily true."

He narrowed his eyes, studying her as she paused for a moment. What exactly was she saying here? His nostrils flared as he drew in a deep breath, willing himself to be patient and let her speak when everything in him wanted to pounce on that ember of hope she'd just given him. He missed the touch of her hand when she released him to hug her arms around her middle. But her gaze stayed locked on his, and she didn't back away.

"Maybe I've been on my own for so long that I've forgotten how to open up and be in a relationship…" She shrugged, the gesture reminding him that, other than removing her shoes and socks, she still wore the scrubs she'd had on all day. She had to be running on fumes. And yet she was still going to push through her fatigue and finish this conversation. "I know *friendship* doesn't truly explain who we are to each other. But…" She shook her head and smiled without finishing that sentence. "Thank you for looking out for me today. For looking out for Ash and Polly—giving them your cards. It comforted them knowing there was someone they could depend on besides their mother—and that was a comfort to me."

"Sitz." Gunny dropped onto his haunches beside him, his tongue lolling out between his teeth as he waited patiently for a more interesting command. Burke fished into the pocket on his utility vest and handed Hazel a business card, as well. "Here." He slipped the card into her agile, unadorned hand, hating that he could get turned on by even the subtle movement of her fingers brushing against his. "Same promise I made to them. You call or text me anytime. Day or night. On duty or off. I will be there for you."

"I know. This makes me feel as safe as one of your

hugs. And trust me, I love those." She braced her hand against his shoulder and stretched up on tiptoes to kiss his cheek. "Thank you."

As she dropped back to her heels, she drew her fingertips across the scruff of his beard. His pulse beat wildly beneath the lingering caress along his jaw. She had to feel what her touch did to him. "I may change my mind about this scruff. There's just enough silver sprinkled there to remind me of a wolf." Her breath gusted against his neck, as if she was feeling the same rise in temperature he was. "Like the alpha wolf." She gently scraped her short nails against the nap of his stubble again, and the blood pounding through his veins charged straight to his groin. Her eyes narrowed as she processed an unexpected revelation. "You're the alpha of your KCPD pack, aren't you?"

You don't want the same thing between us that I do. That isn't necessarily true.

Yeah. She felt it, too.

How the hell was he supposed to remain some celibate saint of a hero when she touched him like this?

When her surprised gaze darted back to his, Burke lowered his head and pressed his mouth against hers. Although he half expected her to resist, her lips parted to welcome him. She flattened her palm against his cheek and jaw, moaning into his mouth as he gently claimed her. He sampled the shape and softness of her lush bottom lip with a stroke of his tongue before pulling it between his lips. Hazel gave a slight shake of her head. But, just as he hesitated, he realized she wasn't saying no to the kiss. Instead, she was rubbing her mouth against him, seeming to enjoy the texture of his alpha-wolf scruff against her tender skin, or whatever that silly metaphor meant to her. He translated the words into *I think you're irresistibly hot, too*, and let her kiss whatever she wanted, reveling in the same tinder-like friction kindling between them.

He felt her leaning into him, rising onto her toes to take this sensuous investigation to the next level. Burke brought his hands up to frame her face, his fingertips curling beneath those delicate ears to cup the nape of her neck.

She reached up to push his hat off and rubbed her hands against his hair. Burke smiled at her newfound fascination with exploring him and set out on a journey of his own, peppering kisses along her jaw until he found the warm beat of her pulse beneath her ear. Hazel tipped her head back, arching her neck to give him access to sup there. Her bare toes curled atop the instep of his boot and he felt the imprint of proud nipples pressing into his chest as she struggled to get closer. Burke obliged by sliding one hand down over the curve of her hip to cup her sweet, round bottom and lift her onto the desire straining behind his zipper. Her arms settled around his shoulders and she held on, twisting to bring her mouth back to his.

But he'd waited a damn long time for this kiss to happen, and he hadn't satisfied his fantasy of nibbling on her ear and running his teeth against the simple gold stud on her lobe, savoring the contrast between hard and soft that was symbolic of everything about her.

"How long have we been puttin' this off?" he

breathed against her ear, loving how she trembled beneath the whisper of air and brush of his lips. Her fingers clutched in the layers of cotton and mesh, digging into the skin and muscle underneath. He wished he'd taken the time to shed his utility vest or her shirt or both before starting this kiss. "I'm tired of pretending we don't want to taste each other—don't want to hold on to each other like—"

"Enough talking." She palmed his jaw in a desperate grasp. "Just—" He captured her mouth in another kiss, spearing his tongue between her lips, tasting sweet caramel and cool cream, and a flavor that was uniquely hers.

Her sigh of surrender told him he'd given her exactly what she wanted.

Burke fell back against the steel door, taking her full weight and loving every curve that flattened against his body, which had been starving for the feel of her. Her feet left the floor entirely as she tightened her arms around his shoulders and pulled herself into the next kiss.

The friction between their bodies created shockwaves that cascaded through him, triggering a snarling groan of need from deep in his chest. "God, how I've wanted you. How I wanted this."

"Do you know how many years have passed since I've been with someone…since I even let myself think about…kissing…" She might be out of practice, but she hadn't forgotten a damn thing about what turned him on. She was eager to touch, raking her fingers across his short hair, down the column of his neck, across his

shoulders. They bumped noses and stumbled as he re-
positioned her in his arms. She smiled and went right
back to dragging her teeth along his jawline. "It's been
so long since I… I don't remember how to satisfy this
itch that's screaming inside me." She laughed against
his mouth. "Much less yours. I might need a refresher
course."

"You'll get no complaints from me."

"But—"

"Enough talking," he teased. The tips of his fingers
caught in her hair as he framed her face between his
hands, guiding her mouth back to his. "It's okay, babe.
I want this, too. I can't believe this is finally—"

"Babe?" She broke off the kiss, going still in his
arms, repeating the single word as if it was a curse.
Hazel braced her hands against his shoulders and
blinked him into focus, as if she was coming to after
being lost in a dream. Maybe he'd been dreaming, too,
thinking that they'd turned a corner in their relationship.
Before he could even catch his breath, she released her
grip on him and slid her feet back to the floor.

"Guess I got a little carried away." He straightened
away from the door, drawing her back into his arms.
"Making out like a man half my age isn't usually my
style. Guess I've been savin' up." Despite the joke, he
silently vowed to dial it back a notch before he went too
far and scared her away.

But, apparently, he already had.

Hazel palmed his chest and pushed him back. "What
did you call me?"

Any illusion of dream time was done. Burke shook

his head, clearing the lingering confusion from his thoughts. "I don't know. *Babe?* I can do *honey* or *sweetheart* if you prefer—"

"No." She was vaguely staring at the middle of his chest where her hand rested, replaying the last couple of minutes in her head, too. "Don't call me that. Don't call me any of that."

At least she had the courtesy to struggle to soothe her erratic breathing, just like he was fighting to inhale a steady, normal breath. She couldn't lie and say that kiss hadn't affected her, too. "Okay. I won't…" He clasped her shoulders to rub his hands up and down her arms until he could think with his brain again. "We can go slow."

"Burke…" She shrugged off his grasp. Her gaze locked firmly onto his. "Jedediah. We have to stop. We aren't a pair of hormone-fueled teenagers. We're old enough to know better than to give in to our urges. We're both exhausted. We're not thinking straight."

"I am. I'm not second-guessin' any of this." He reached for her again, hoping to ease her doubts, but she strong-armed him out of her personal space.

"Stop."

"Because I called you *babe*?" Burke held both hands out in surrender, understanding her right to end any contact she wasn't comfortable with, even if he didn't fully understand why.

The faint lines beside her eyes deepened with an apology. "That's what Aaron called me."

Swearing one choice word, Burke rubbed his hand across his spiky hair. "How was I supposed to know?

I'm sorry I upset you." He could feel the short-circuited desire still sparking through his fingertips. But instead of reaching for her, he bent down to retrieve his KCPD ball cap from the floor beside Gunny. "Guess I ruined the moment, huh?"

Despite his fatigue, every muscle in him was tight with desire. That kiss had been pure heaven. And it had only primed the fuel burning inside him. He wanted more with Hazel Cooper. He wanted the right to kiss her every time he walked away from her. Hell. He didn't want to walk away. He wanted to stay the night. Feel those cute, naked toes running up his leg and her body melting into his as she surrendered to his kisses.

"I'm not blaming you. But it's the wake-up call I needed to remind myself that I have rules. I don't do relationships. I don't want to—not with you."

He heard that message like a slap across the face. He pulled his cap onto his head and reached for Gunny's leash. "That's clear enough."

Hazel's fingers fisted in his vest, stopping him from turning to the door. "Not because I'm not tempted to see where you and I might go…but…because I *am* tempted. I've ignored the attraction between us because I don't want to risk what we have. I don't want to lose you from my life."

Why did the possibility of everything she'd just admitted make her look so sad?

He captured her hand against his heart. "Let me get this straight—you're willing to throw away a chance at us becoming more than friends because you're scared it could be really incredible between us?"

"What if it isn't? I'll admit it—I haven't been with a man in years. And I miss that. But what if this is just chemistry that flares out once we give in and get it out of our system? Or we're two lonely people who are so desperate to make an intimate connection that we're jumping on feelings that aren't really there? Think how that could taint what we already have." She tapped his chest with every sentence. "What I know is real. What I know is good and special."

Real. Good. Special. Sounded like a perfect scenario to him. "The best marriages I know are when the man and woman are friends first. That doesn't mean there's no passion. No soul-deep connection that defies logic. All of that goes into a relationship."

"Marriage? That's quite a jump from our first kiss to exchanging rings." Hazel pulled away, finally putting some distance between them. "You've been divorced a long time, Burke. Are you sure you can do a serious committed relationship? That you even want that?"

Back to *Burke*, huh? Boy, when she pushed him away, she pushed hard. "After Shannon, I never found the right woman I could put that much faith in—until I met you. I've wanted you for years, and in all that time, until this past week, until tonight, you've kept me at arm's length. But I'm still here. I think that shows a pretty solid commitment." After a moment she nodded, at least giving him that. "You've been divorced a long time, too. Maybe you're the one who's afraid to commit."

"Guilty as charged. But I have my reasons."

"I know you do. But, Haze, when your heart's involved, there's always a risk. You're sure you're not just afraid of getting hurt?"

"Why? You gonna hurt me?" She tried to make it a joke, but neither of them laughed. "I know you wouldn't mean to. But the last time I followed my heart, I nearly died. I can't afford to be impulsive again."

"What?" Her marriage had dissolved years before the two of them had met. And though her ex-husband's crimes had been big news in Kansas City, he'd been on active duty back then, stationed overseas, and had never heard all the details. Once he'd gotten to know the woman Hazel was now, he hadn't cared who she or her ex had once been. In his recent research into her ex's criminal history, he'd seen the charge of attempted murder along with the fraud and embezzlement charges. But he had no idea who her husband's intended victim had been.

A cold feeling of dread crept down Burke's spine. "What do you mean *died*?"

Chapter 6

"It's a long story, and I'm too tired to get into all of it tonight." The chill Burke felt must be contagious. Hazel crossed to the back of the couch, where she'd shed her scrubs jacket and pulled it on over her T-shirt and jeans. "I stood by Aaron like a good wife when I found out how he'd cheated all those people out of their investments and retirement funds. Gave him the benefit of the doubt. Hoped someone else was responsible and he was the scapegoat who'd been falsely accused."

"I've heard he put you through hell," Burke conceded. "What does that have to do with us?"

She paced over to the curtains and pulled one aside to stare out into the moonless night dotted with the lights of downtown KC. "Even after Aaron was arrested and the DA was hounding me to testify against him, I did everything I could to make our marriage work. Ashley and Polly were six and four. They didn't understand what was going on around them—why friends suddenly stopped calling, why kids were mean to Ashley in school."

Burke swore. "I had no idea it was that bad."

"I did everything I could to try to keep things as normal as possible for them—to keep our family intact. I gave up my life savings, my self-worth, my happiness and any sense of security because I thought it was the right thing to do. I thought love was going to conquer all." Hazel released the curtain and faced him. "It didn't." She hugged herself around her middle, and every cell in his body begged for the right to cross the room and pull her into his arms to share his warmth and strength. "I've worked hard for a long time to regain everything I lost. I don't know if I'm willing to risk that again."

"You haven't regained everything," he pointed out sadly. "You don't trust your own judgment. You don't trust your heart."

Sad green eyes locked on to his, and she nodded her agreement. "I paid a heavy price for loving Aaron."

To keep himself by the door, Burke reached down to pet Gunny's flanks. Like him, the working dog was getting antsy about staying in place instead of taking action. But Hazel needed to talk. "We all make mistakes, Doc. Hell, I've made my share. We're allowed to learn from them and move on. Mistakes don't mean we don't get to be happy."

"I get the learning part. Most people's mistakes aren't as big as the one I made in marrying Aaron."

He vowed then and there to request Aaron Cooper's case file and court transcripts and read them down to the very last detail. He had a sick feeling there was still more to this story, and he wished Hazel trusted him enough to tell him the worst. But she was locking down tight, letting him know he wasn't getting the answers he needed tonight.

"You can't judge every man by your ex's standard. I'm not like him, and you know it. I would never ask you to change who you need to be. And I'd be pissed if you thought you had to." Gunny whined an empathetic protest and Cleo popped up on the back of the couch to see what was upsetting her friend. "I'm a patient man, but you keep making me work too hard, and I might quit trying."

Hazel scooped up the one-eyed schnauzer and hugged the dog to her chest as she joined him at the door again. "That makes it sound like I've been leading you on. I swear, that's not my intention. That's why I never should have kissed you."

"I know you don't want to hurt me. Don't add that guilt on top of everything else you're dealing with. Your honesty is one of those things that make me want to be with you. Still, it's not fair of me to push when you're vulnerable like this." He scrubbed his fingers around Cleo's ears, glad that Hazel would at least accept comfort from her dog if not from him. "If it makes any difference, you don't have the monopoly on being gun-shy about risking everything on a new relationship. Sticking with you is a risk for me, too. I don't relish failing again."

"You didn't fail," she said, and he couldn't miss how her expression changed to one of unflinching support the moment he shared his own weakness. "When we first became friends, you said your wife cheated on you while you were deployed. That's hardly your fault."

For him, for everyone else, Hazel was a warrior. Why couldn't she put that fight into her own happiness? Did she really believe they were destined to fail if they gave in to their deepest feelings?

"I guess our bond wasn't strong enough for Shannon to be without me 24-7. I must not inspire that kind of loyalty. Not with her—and apparently, not with you."

"Of course you do. Look at the men and women you work with, the dogs you train. Look at us. That loyalty—that unquestioning trust—those are the very things I don't want to jeopardize."

"You can have both—friendship *and* love." He gave up on petting the dog and brushed his fingertip along Hazel's jaw. "If you trust me to be your friend, then why can't you trust me to love you?"

"I won't risk my emotional security for a roll in the hay or a chance at temporary bliss when it all might end in heartache and you walking out of my life."

"Who says I'm offering you a roll in the hay?" he teased, despite the evidence that had pushed against the seam of his BDU a few minutes earlier.

"I'm cautious, not blind." Her gaze dropped briefly to his crotch. It was good to see her smile again. "Promise me one thing, no matter what happens between us. Never lie to me."

He smiled back. "Deal."

"And I promise to do my damnedest not to give you false hope. Not to hurt you."

To hell with tiptoeing around his feelings. He slipped his hand around to cup the back of her head. Ignoring the dog squished between them, he kissed her squarely on the mouth, stealing her gasp of surprise. He kissed her hard. Kissed her well. Kissed her until she understood he'd never tire of kissing that beautiful, responsive mouth, and pulled away. "*That's* chemistry. It isn't a bad place to start a relationship." He reached behind him to unlock the door. "I've been through a lot of life, Haze. I'm tough. I'm not going to break—or walk away when you need me—because of a few dings to my ego, or because we're in different places in our relationship. Loving you may not be as simple as a fairy tale, but that doesn't mean I'm going to stop."

"Burke—"

He pressed his fingertip to her lips, silencing any more protest. "Good night, Dr. Coop. Lock up behind me."

Burke skipped the elevator and took Gunny down the stairs, knowing they both needed to work off some of the energy pent up inside them. He opened the steel mesh door at the pedestrian exit to the parking garage and waited for it to close and automatically lock behind him before jogging across the street to the parking lot framed by a narrow grassy area and let the dog relieve himself.

While Gunny sniffed and staked out a couple of trees and shrubs in regular dog mode, Burke took note of the young couple arguing over the roof of their car in the parking lot. He dismissed their petty whining as no threat and glanced back at Hazel's building. He tilted his head to the bright lights behind the fourth-floor windows, wondering how his favorite veterinarian was coping with the aftermath of that intense conversation and make-out session, which he'd let get out of hand the moment she'd kissed him back. He shook his head and tugged on Gunny's leash to get them moving toward his truck. He couldn't tell if he was angry or hurt. Probably both. "You handled that well, Sarge. All those years of biding your time and you blow it all in one night."

After the rain they'd had earlier, he expected the night to be cool. Instead, a fog of humidity hung in the air, closing in around him.

What the hell did she mean when she said her marriage to Aaron Cooper had nearly killed her? Could the tragedy of that marriage have anything to do with the creepy love letters and bomb threats? Her ex had been out of prison for almost a year now. Were the threats punishment for divorcing him? And did she have any idea how badly he wanted to protect her from bombs and stalkers and a painful past that still haunted her?

He didn't suppose there was any way to hide his feelings for Hazel now—no way to step back from laying it all out there. He wasn't worried about salvaging his pride—he was old enough to have learned that there were things in life worth a lot more than a man's ego. But he was also old enough to know that love was a precious thing, and that trust was probably the greatest gift a person could give him…and Hazel had refused to trust his belief that they were meant to be together in every way. He was stumped on how to get her to take that leap of faith with him. And it nagged at him to think that maybe she'd be better off if he didn't even try.

But losing Hazel… The idea of never working side by side with her or trading dumb jokes or kissing her again gutted him.

He exchanged a nod with a trio of young men they passed on the sidewalk before halting at a traffic light. One of the preppie guys in the front waved to someone up the hill behind Burke and rushed on to meet their friend. The one in the hoodie following a few steps behind them ducked his head and hurried after his buddies.

Could Burke be happy with the status quo anymore?

His phone rang in his pocket as the light changed. He led Gunny around the standing water at the curb and pulled his cell from his utility vest. For a split second, his dark mood skyrocketed at the slim hope Hazel had changed her mind. He wisely cooled his jets, though, knowing that at this time of night, even though they were off the clock, it was probably a work call.

"And the night just gets worse," he muttered when he saw the number.

Gunny jerked against his lead, stopping halfway across the street to glance behind them. Burke figured the low-pitched growl was just the dog tracking where the three young men had gone—or maybe he was sensing Burke's response to the name on his cell screen.

His ex-wife, Shannon.

"Gunny, *fuss*." The dog fell into step beside him again. They reached the next curb before he answered the call. "What do you want?"

"Hello to you, too." Her familiar giggle, which he'd once found so charming, grated on his nerves.

If he wasn't a cop, trained to respond to anyone in need—even the woman who'd broken his heart as a younger man—he wouldn't have answered at all. "It's late, Shannon. Is there an emergency? Is Bill all right?"

"You're not at home."

How would she know that? Ah, hell. Instinctively, he glanced around the intersection, wondering if she'd had someone track down his location. Thankfully, there was no sign of her. Had she gone to his house? It was located far enough away on the outskirts of the city that he could have a big fenced-in yard and some mature trees where Gunny could play. A home that was nowhere near the pricey Ward Parkway neighborhood where Shannon and her husband lived. "Are you at my place?"

"I'm parked in your driveway. The lights are out and no one's home." Her breathy sigh, followed by a dramatic sniffle, told him she'd been crying. "I needed to see you."

Burke slowed his pace, feeling a tinge of concern. Maybe there *was* a problem. "Shannon?"

"Why do I have to hear through the grapevine that my husband was nearly killed by a bomb today?"

And poof. Any concern he felt vanished. Now he was just annoyed that she'd dropped by his house unannounced. Gunny tugged on his lead again, curious about something only a dog could see or smell in the shadows. Burke tugged right back, demanding the dog sit and stay beside him. Gunny never ignored a command unless he was off leash. Something had caught the dog's attention, and Burke had been his partner long enough not to ignore his partner's instincts.

He paused on the corner, turning a slow 360 to see if he could spot whatever had the dog's attention. A bar two blocks up had patrons spilling out onto the sidewalk with their drinks and smokes. The rock music was loud, but not illegally so. The arguing couple had driven off, and the trio of young men had disappeared. But they could have gone into the bar, turned a corner or gotten into their vehicle and left downtown. A little farther up the street, a city bus was brightly lit and picking up passengers near one of the big hotels.

Burke kept searching for anything or anyone that would put Gunny on alert. "Don't go all drama queen on me, Shannon. First, it's *ex*-husband, three times removed. Unless you've divorced Bill Bennett and I haven't read about it in the paper yet." The irony that her fourth husband was a divorce attorney wasn't lost on Burke. "And second, which bomb are you talking about?"

"Which…? There was more than one? You and that dog. Why can't you have a regular pet like everybody else?" He could picture her wiping away tears from her dark almond-shaped eyes now that she understood he wasn't swayed by them. "I'm talking about the bomb threat at the veterinary clinic. I saw the report on TV."

He'd been clearing the hospital when the evening

newscasts had aired. Maybe a reporter had caught him on camera. "A friend was sent a package at her work. Gunny identified the explosive and we cleared the building. It wasn't really a bomb. Just the parts to make one. I wasn't in any significant danger."

"Significant? But you were in *some* danger. I was right to be worried."

He was a cop. He'd been a soldier before that. The danger surrounding either job was a given. "Go home, Shannon. I'm not yours to worry about."

Although it had been years since he'd come home from a deployment to find her in bed with one of the attorneys she'd worked for as a paralegal, and the anger, heartbreak and blow to his pride had long since mellowed, her betrayal had left a mark that influenced how he approached relationships in the years since. That was probably why it had taken him so long to realize that Hazel was the only woman he wanted to be with, why he'd been content to let things simmer beneath the surface of their relationship...until tonight.

Burke suspected that, in her own way, Shannon truly had loved him, and maybe part of her still did, judging by the infrequent phone calls like this one. But the infatuation shared by high school sweethearts hadn't lasted. She hadn't been cut out to be a military wife. Even with access to support groups, being alone for extended periods of time, managing the day-to-day responsibilities of running a home, working a job and living a life on her own just weren't in her skill set. Even after he'd retired from the Army and Reserves, he doubted she would have done any better with the hours and dangers of him being a cop, even though he was on home soil.

"That's cold, Jed. You know my heart will always belong to you."

"Don't let Bill hear you say that." Since he hadn't spotted anything unusual to account for Gunny's restlessness, he headed on toward his truck. "I'd hate to be the cause of his own divorce."

"About that… You know I've matured since we were married. We were too young. *I* was too young. I didn't understand about commitment then. And I was so lonely. But now I—"

Beep.

"Hold on a second, I've got an incoming message."

Thank God. He'd been down this road with Shannon too many times before. She must have gotten into an argument with her current husband. Every time she hit a bump in the road with her latest relationship, she got these sentimental urges to call Burke to reconnect— expecting him to fix the issue, comfort her or, *ain't never gonna happen*, even take her back. Hell. Maybe she called all her exes looking for sympathy when the going got rough. He had no interest in a woman he couldn't trust. And knowing Shannon's affairs had led her from one husband to the next told him she wasn't going to change.

Burke pulled up the text and frowned. Hazel's name was at the top of the screen.

I need you. Bring Gunny.

A chill of apprehension trickled down his spine. Burke glanced up at the windows of the old tool and die building. Even from this distance, he could see that all the lights had gone out in Hazel's condo. Every lamp and overhead bulb had been blazing when he left.

"Fuss!" Burke was already moving, jogging, pulling Gunny into a loping run beside him. "Shannon, I have to go."

"Let me guess—work?"

"Goodbye."

"It's another woman, isn't it? You said *her* workplace. Are you seeing someone? It's that doggie doctor, isn't it?" Anger edged into her voice. "You told me she was one of the guys, Jed. She means more to you than that, doesn't she?"

Uh-uh. He wasn't going down that road with her. He wasn't the one who cheated, so she had no right to be jealous, and he wasn't about to feel guilty about answering a friend's call for help. "You should be talking to your husband about whatever's going on, not me. Bye."

"Jed, don't hang—"

He ended the call, texted back an On my way and stuffed the phone into his pocket before lengthening his stride to match Gunny's. In a matter of seconds, they were back at Hazel's building. But the cage that closed in the parking garage and pedestrian access stopped him like a brick wall. He didn't have a key card to swipe or pass code to punch into the access panel beside the door. The fact that there were no more texts to give him any idea of what was going on only ratcheted up his concern.

He quickly typed in Hazel's condo number and pressed the intercom button.

His blood pressure rose with every second of silence before he heard a quiet, hesitant voice. "Burke?"

"It's me, Haze. Are you all right? Let me in."

Gunny barked, adding his voice to the urgent request. The dog was probably picking up on the tension running down the lead from his partner's hand, but it was enough of a confirmation of their identity for Hazel to buzz them in. The lights were on inside, so this wasn't something as benign as a power outage. Hazel was hiding in the dark for a reason. After a quick glance around the lobby, looking for any signs of an intruder, they vaulted up the stairs and knocked on Hazel's door.

"Sergeant Burke, KCPD," he announced, warning anyone who might be a threat on the other side of that door. "Open up."

He heard a yip from Cleo and a muted cry a split second before the dead bolt turned and the door flew open.

Hazel walked straight into his chest, wound her arms around his waist and clung to him as though a tornado might blow her away if she didn't hang on tightly enough. Burke didn't mind the contact one bit. But standing out on the landing, exposed to potentially prying eyes, wasn't the place to do it. He hustled Gunny into the apartment, wrapped an arm around Hazel's trembling shoulders and pushed her inside, kicking the door shut behind him.

"Voran!" He ordered the dog to search the apartment while he held Hazel close and peered into the semidark-

ness over her head. The only light on in the whole place was the flashlight shining from her cell phone, which sat on the coffee table in front of the sofa. "Anyone here besides you and Cleo?"

Her fingers convulsed beneath his utility vest at the back of his shirt as she shook her head beneath his chin. "I'm sorry. First, I chase you away, and now I can't seem to let go."

"I said you could lean on me." But he needed to know what the problem was first. "What's happened? Why are the lights out?" He spied Gunny moving from one room to the next, with Cleo limping along in his shadow. Surely the small dog would have been making noise if there was someone in here besides his mistress. Gunny cleared the back bedroom and trotted down the hallway toward him to be rewarded with a toss of his ball on a rope. As both dogs took off after the toy, Burke leaned back against Hazel's grip to frame her jaw between his hands and tip her face up to his. Her skin was cool, her cheeks pale. He wanted to punch somebody for rattling her like this. "Haze, you gotta talk to me."

She bravely raised her gaze to his. "He called. Right after you left."

No need to explain who *he* was. "What did he say?"

"Come to the window."

"Tell me what he said first. Did he threaten you?"

"No. That's what he said. That's all he said." Nodding that she was all right enough for now, Hazel took his hand and led him to the curtains. *"Come to the window."*

When she started to open the edge of the first curtain, Burke pulled her behind him and peered outside over the street, parking lot and buildings. Even with the sky covered by clouds, with the streetlamps, the neon signs of the nearby bar and traffic lights, it was brighter outside than it was inside the condo. He saw the same variety of faceless people walking the street and going about their business that he'd seen from the sidewalk below. "What am I looking for?"

"Is he gone?" She tugged on his arm to get to the window. "I just saw... I'm not making this up."

"I know you're not."

"It was him." Hazel drifted away from the window. "In the parking lot across the street. I saw him. Everyone else was going somewhere. But he was just standing there. Looking up at me. His face was weird, like he had some sort of deformity."

"Do you know anyone like that?"

"No. I tried to get him to say something else. I wanted to know who he was, why he was doing this to me. All I could hear was him breathing. I hung up and texted you. Turned the lights out so he couldn't see me. But he already had."

"Can you describe anything else about him?"

"I couldn't judge his height from this angle, but kind of a beefy build. He had on a dark hoodie. Dark pants. Like the man Polly described at the hospital."

Burke swore, closing the curtain. The man following the preppie boys had worn dark blue pants and a hoodie. He hadn't been one of them. He was... "I saw him. Passed him on the street." Burke had been too distracted by frustration and self-recriminations to piece together what he'd observed earlier. "I never saw his face, but Gunny recognized him. Something about his smell must have been familiar. Or he still had trace explosives on him." Burke pulled the curtain shut with more force than was necessary. "I don't see him out there now."

"He looked right at me. Made a stupid little heart symbol over his chest. Like that would mean something to me. And then he gestured like...boom." She placed her hands on either side of her head, then quickly pulled them away, splaying her fingers. *Head blown.* An all-too-familiar gesture indicating an explosion—a threat meant for Hazel.

"Let me see your phone."

He followed her to the coffee table, where she turned off the flashlight app and pulled up the recent call list. He texted the number to Dispatch and requested a trace, although he'd bet money that the call had come from a burner phone. Then he headed to the door.

"How do I make this stop?" Hazel followed him to the door. "He knows where I live. He knows where I work, who my children are. He has my number..." She caught him by the arm and stopped him. "You're going after him?" The panic fled her voice when she realized his intent. "You said he was gone."

"I said I didn't see him." He squeezed her hand in a subtle reassurance as he pried it from his arm. He had a job to do. She seemed to understand that. Her eyes had lost that wild lack of focus and were trained on him as she nodded. He called Gunny to him and unhooked the shepherd's leash. *"Bleibe."*

"Stay?" Gunny sat squarely on his haunches beside Hazel. "Don't you need him?"

"No." He unsnapped his holster and rested his hand on the butt of his Glock. "He stays with you and protects you, in case this guy has already gotten into the building somehow. What's your entry code?" She gave him the number. "This door stays locked until I get back."

"What if he calls again?"

"Switch phones with me. If that bastard calls, he's going to talk to me."

Hazel handed over her cell and clutched his to her chest. She drifted closer to Gunny and buried her fingers in his fur. "Be careful."

"You, too."

The dead bolt slid into place behind him. Burke made a quick sweep through the building, startling one couple who were enjoying a good-night kiss on the top floor. No hoodie. And though the guy could have easily ditched it somewhere, these two weren't hiding their faces from him. And they both wore jeans. Burke's grim expression and curt command chased them into the apartment. The rest of the building and parking garage were clear of anyone who looked suspicious. Once outside, he moved through the parking lot across the street, checking vehicles and the spaces in between. He entered the bar for a quick once-over and gave the bouncer at the door a brief description of the perp. But there were too many possible suspects who fit the general description for him to make any useful identification. He checked down the street in the other direction. A block farther, and he'd be on an overpass crossing the interstate running through the north end of downtown KC. There was simply too much ground here for one man to cover. Whoever had been terrorizing Hazel was gone.

Burke was jogging back to Hazel's building when her phone beeped with a text. He eyed his surroundings and got no sense of anyone watching him before he pulled it up on the screen. It was a fuzzy picture of Hazel peeking out her window into the night.

Do I have your attention now? I don't expect you to answer. But I do expect you to listen. I want you to know that everything you have belongs to me.

FYI, your policeman and your dog can't stop me from taking what's rightfully mine.

"Hell." Burke ran the last block and typed in the code to enter the building.

By the time he was back at Hazel's, he was worn-out and angry and relieved to see her with color in her cheeks again as she locked the door behind him. He briefly considered trashing the text, so her healthy, confident look wouldn't disappear again. But the cop in him knew he needed to save it as evidence. Making a case against a stalker almost always relied on having a stack of circumstantial evidence that showed a pattern of harassment and escalating danger. Besides, he'd promised to always be honest with her.

"It's decaf." She handed him a mug of coffee she'd brewed while he'd been out. "I used your phone to call the girls. They're fine. They haven't seen anything suspicious at their place." The coffee smelled heavenly and reviving, but he set it aside to capture her gaze. "What is it? What did you find?"

"Nothing. He's gone, or he would have seen me reading this." He handed her the phone. "I doubt he would have kept silent about me interfering with his private conversation with you."

She read the text and went pale again. Without comment, she simply picked up his mug and carried it back to the kitchen, where she lingered at the counter with her back to him. She busied her hands by adding half-and-half to the mug and sipping on the hot brew herself.

"What does he want from me? Revenge? My undying devotion? Is he getting off on toying with me like this?" She stood at the refrigerator door as the flare of emotion ebbed and her shoulders sagged. "I can't tell if he thinks he loves me or he wants to hurt me."

"Maybe both. Obsession can change from one to the other pretty quickly."

She drank another sip of creamy coffee and abruptly changed the subject. "Someone named Shannon called while you were out. I saw her name. Isn't she your ex-wife? She left a voice mail. I hope it wasn't important."

"It wasn't."

Hazel set down her mug with a decisive thunk. "You're going to think I'm an absolute nutcase, but could you—"

"I'm staying."

She turned to find him draping his utility vest over the back of the couch. He knelt to remove Gunny's harness. He ruffled the dog's fur and sent him off to play with his rope ball. "The couch will do just fine."

Her smile told him he'd made the right decision. Not that he was giving her any choice.

"Good." She padded down the hallway and brought him a pillow and covers. She made up the sofa and fluffed the old blanket for Gunny. "I have the extra bedroom I keep for the girls. You could sleep on a real mattress."

Burke removed his gun, belt and badge, and set them on the coffee table within easy reach. "I want to be between you and anything that comes through that front door."

"Are you afraid he'll come back? That he can actually get into the building to get to me?"

"Aren't you?" He could see she was by the bleak shadows in her eyes. Burke took her gently by the shoulders and turned her toward her bedroom. She didn't protest as he dug into the tension cording her neck and followed right behind her. "It's been a long day for both of us. We have work tomorrow. Try to sleep. In the morning, we'll call Detectives Bellamy and Cartwright and fill them in on this latest incident."

She stopped at the bedroom doorway, and they shared a smile at Cleo pawing herself a nest in the middle of Hazel's blanket. "I seem to be saying it a lot lately, but…" Hazel turned and tilted her eyes to his. "Thank you."

"Go to bed, Doc."

"I haven't been scared like this for a long time."

"I know."

"I hate being scared. I'm used to handling whatever I need to on my own."

"I know that, too."

"I'm sorry about arguing with you earlier. It's not that I don't care—"

He silenced her with a finger over her lips. "That was a discussion, not an argument. An honest exchange of what we're thinking and feeling. People who trust like you and me can have those kinds of conversations. It helped me understand those ground rules of yours. It helps me be patient." When she didn't immediately turn in or protest his touch, Burke brushed her bangs across her forehead and cupped the side of her face. "You'll be okay, Doc. You're the strongest woman I know. Gunny and I are just here to back you up."

She considered his words, then stretched up on tiptoe to kiss the corner of his mouth. "Thank you for saying that. It helps me believe it. Good night, Jedediah."

After she closed the door and turned on a light inside, he checked the locks and windows one last time. Once the light had gone out beneath her door, he untied his boots and settled onto the couch, tucking his gun beneath the pillow.

They were back to *Jedediah*. He breathed a sigh that was part fatigue and part relief. He hadn't ruined everything by putting his feelings out on the table. Sure, he wanted more than a peck on the cheek, more than a closed door and distance between them.

But he knew Hazel was safe, and for now, that was enough.

Chapter 7

"*Hey, babe. I know I'm not supposed to contact you, but we need to talk. It's really important.*"

Hazel knew the first voice mail from her ex today by heart now. And the second. And the fifth.

Her phone vibrated in the pocket of her jeans, stealing her attention away from her current patient, telling her she'd just ignored call number six. How dare Aaron Cooper keep contacting her?

Having her stalker call her last night to taunt her had left her feeling vulnerable and afraid. Waking up to find Jedediah Burke sitting at her kitchen island, drinking from a fresh pot of coffee and reading the news on his phone like he was a normal part of a normal day had gone a long way toward restoring her equilibrium. Not only was Burke a familiar presence, but his strength and easy authority made her feel like there was nothing the world could throw at him that he couldn't handle. And that air of calm confidence made her feel like she could handle it, too.

But that equilibrium that had quickly been knocked off-kilter for a very different reason when she sat beside him with her own mug of coffee. She smelled freshly showered man, felt the warmth radiating off his body and filling the space between them, and found herself silently mourning the sexy salt-and-pepper scruff that had vanished from his clean-shaven jaw this morning.

Burke was one of her best friends.

He was also solid and hot and one hell of a kisser.

For a few minutes last night, she'd been a woman on fire in his arms, intimately aware of every sexy attribute the mature man possessed. Jedediah had done far more than make her feel safe. He'd made her feel desirable, hungry, eager to be alive. After all these years of denying herself, he made her want to be with a man again. It had been empowering to be the woman he couldn't resist. He said he loved her. But did she have it in her to love someone again?

The phone vibrating in her pocket was stark evidence of how wrong choices could ruin so many lives. She already had five messages on her phone today to remind her of those mistakes. The first message had been friendly, polite, even apologetic. But with each call Aaron sounded more and more irritated, more like the desperate, dangerous man he'd become before the divorce.

"Hazel. It's Aaron. Pick up. I have a right to see my

girls. You once said you forgave me for what I did to you. I know you won't believe me, but you still mean something to me. And I love my girls. I'm not the man I was sixteen years ago. Prison changed me. You need to let me be a dad to them."

There was a reason for the restraining order against her ex that had been in place for sixteen years. Once a man endangered her children, betrayed her trust and tried to kill her, she really didn't want to hear from him anymore.

A stalker with an explosive hobby.

Jedediah talking love and second chances.

Aaron harassing her with call after call today.

How had her safe, predictable life gotten turned completely upside down like this?

"Dr. Coop?" Todd Mizner's hand closed over her shoulder and Hazel startled. "Sorry. Everything okay?" he asked before pulling away.

She glanced up at the concern in his blue eyes and gave a brief jerk of her head. Time to focus on the problem right here in front of her.

She looked across the stainless-steel examination table into the unblinking scowl from her client, Wade Hanson. For an out-of-shape man who must be in his sixties or early seventies, wearing grungy workman's clothes that had seen better days, he still managed to look intimidating. He had every right to be upset by her lack of concentration on this long, rainy afternoon. The dog he'd brought in needed some serious attention, not a vet who was too distracted by her own problems to provide the care the alarmingly skinny cattle dog mix needed. Of course, Hanson's combative stance with his beefy arms crossed over his potbelly, and his jaw grinding away on the chaw of tobacco in his cheek, could have more to do with the suspicions she hadn't done a very good job of hiding.

"It's not good." She tilted her chin, catching Mr. Hanson studying her from beneath the brim of his soiled ball cap. He quickly shifted his gaze back to the skinny dog on the table while she moved the stethoscope and checked for gut sounds to confirm her initial diagnosis.

"You can fix her, though, right?" Hanson spoke without moving his jaw. Probably a good thing since she didn't want to see the tobacco juice staining his teeth. But he gave her the sense that he was a powder keg about to blow—an unsettling analogy considering recent events. Hazel wondered exactly where that anger seething beneath the surface was directed.

One last vibration on her phone told her Aaron had left another message. Ignoring both the pestering from her ex and the critical glare from Mr. Hanson, she finished her exam. Besides the dog being clearly overbred, she could see ribs and hip bones through the mutt's thin skin and spotted tan fur. A stray scrounging for food on the streets would have more body mass than this poor waif. She had no fever or obvious masses to indicate a serious illness. And Hazel didn't want to draw any blood to check for internal parasites until she'd gotten some intravenous fluids in her to increase her blood volume and stabilize her. "This is a working breed. Athena should be compact, muscular. She needs to be spayed, too. You should have brought her to me sooner." Maybe dropped a few bites of whatever had put that paunch on Hanson's belly to the floor for his pet. "Neglect like this doesn't happen overnight." Since the animal couldn't tell her what she'd suffered, Hazel had to ask the owner questions. "Has she been keeping food down?" She bristled when he didn't immediately answer. "Have you been feeding her?"

Wade scratched at his scraggly white beard and grumbled. "I didn't do it. Margery took her to piss me off. I just got Athena back from her."

Interesting deflection of her queries. Even a few days was too long for this dog to be suffering without basic care. "Your wife did this?"

"Ex-wife. Athena should have been mine when she left. But my selfish, vindictive—"

"I get the picture." Unfortunately, this wasn't the first time Hazel had seen a patient who'd been the victim of an unfriendly split. It wasn't the first time she'd defended the innocent pet who'd been either forgotten or used as a weapon to punish an ex. It was just as likely that Hanson was lying, and he'd taken the dog to spite his ex. Either way, she would see to it that Athena got the help she needed. Hazel set her stethoscope on the counter behind her and slid her arms beneath the dog's chest and rump to help her stand. "Todd. Priority one is to get some IV fluids in her."

Todd took the lightweight dog and cradled her against his chest. "You want me to try a half cup of food with her? See if she can keep it down?"

Hazel nodded. "No more than that. I'm guessing

she'll eat anything we put in front of her. But she won't be able to digest much."

Interesting that Mr. Hanson, who claimed to be so attached to the dog his wife had allegedly taken from him and abused, didn't pet Athena or even try to talk to her as Todd carried her from the room. Nothing suspicious about that. Right.

"How long have you had Athena?" Hazel asked, once the door closed behind Todd.

"I told you. Just a few days. Margery took her."

Hazel pulled her reading glasses from the collar of her T-shirt and picked up her clipboard to make a notation on the dog's chart. "How long did you have her before that? Did you get her as a puppy? Rescue her? Take her in as a stray?"

"She kept showing up at work, lookin' for handouts." Even when he finally uncrossed his arms, Mr. Hanson's stance still looked defensive. "I'm on a road crew. We're paving a gravel road out in east Jackson County. I figured somebody dumped her out in the country."

Sadly, that might be true. Perhaps he thought he'd done a good thing by helping the dog find a home. But not if he didn't know how to, or couldn't, give the dog proper care. "Is she current on her shots? Has Athena had any vaccinations you know of?"

He pulled off his cap and scratched his thinning white hair. "I dunno."

Not the answer she was hoping for. "Don't take this the wrong way, Mr. Hanson, but...can you afford to keep a dog? There are programs through several vet clinics I work with that provide food and basic equipment like leashes and bedding, even medical care, for pets whose owners need a little extra help. Would you like me to put you in contact with them?"

Muttering something under his breath, he plunked the hat back on top of his head and started to pace. "What's with the twenty questions? Can you help her or not?"

Unless they found evidence of an internal parasite or illness, this was an easy diagnosis. And she hated it. "Right now, we'll treat Athena for starvation and dehydration." She removed her glasses and hugged the clipboard to her chest as she met the resentful glance he tossed her across the table. Probably every woman was on his hit list now. She'd proceed cautiously, but this dog wasn't going back to Hanson or his wife, not until animal control had investigated the case and she knew exactly who was responsible for the dog's deplorable condition. "I'd like to keep Athena here for at least forty-eight hours, to keep her under observation and make sure she's getting the care she needs. When she's stronger, we'll get a complete blood count, urinalysis and biochemistry profile to find out if there are any underlying issues causing her malnourishment. I'll call you with my results, of course."

"You're taking my dog, aren't you?" he muttered, sliding his chaw into the opposite cheek. The subtle movement struck Hazel as a pressure valve the man used to contain his temper. "You're gonna get me in trouble with the law." He circled around the table to trail his dirty fingers across the counter, touching the handle of every drawer and cabinet along the way. "I told you, it was Margery who let her get like that."

Hazel turned to keep him in her sight as he moved behind her. "I don't have the authority to take your dog, Mr. Hanson. But if I can't find any evidence of a medical reason for her weight loss, then I will report your ex-wife for animal cruelty." She'd be putting his name on that report, too, as the registered owner.

"Do that." He stopped at the door to the lobby and squeezed the knob. "She took everything I had left. And that wasn't much. I'm just glad to get Athena back."

"Divorces can be hard. Even under the best of circumstances."

"Under the worst of circumstances, they're…" He faced her again, nodding toward the fingers she'd curled around her clipboard. "I see you ain't got no ring on your hand. You divorced, Dr. Cooper?"

Hazel curled her toes into her clogs, resisting the urge to back away from those icy gray eyes. "I am."

He splayed one hand on the metal table and the other on the countertop. He pressed a button on her computer keyboard, clearing the screen saver, before pushing down on the scale she used to weigh puppies, kittens and other small animals. The cradle bounced up and down as he released it. She respected a hardworking man and understood the grime that came with a construction job like his. But since this was a medical facility, there was a sterility factor she had to protect. When he reached toward the sharps disposal bin on the wall, she grabbed his wrist and stopped him. "Mr. Hanson, that's a potential biohazard. Some of this is expensive equipment, too. I ask you not to touch it."

"Yes, ma'am." She couldn't tell if that glimpse of yellowed teeth was a smile or a snarl. But he pulled away and crossed his arms over his gut again in that challenging stance he'd used earlier. "You have a successful business here, Dr. Cooper. Your ex pay for it?"

Hazel bristled at the question. "Excuse me?"

"Did you use his alimony to start your clinic?"

Alimony? That was a joke. When her marriage to Aaron had ended, there'd been nothing left to ask for. The simple answer was no, she'd started this clinic and paid off her student loans on her own dime. She didn't need anyone's help to be a good veterinarian and smart businesswoman. But Wade Hanson was practically a stranger. This was the first time she'd seen Athena as a patient. The dog was already three or four years old and hadn't been fixed or had her teeth cleaned. Other than this brief time they'd spent together in the exam room, she didn't know this man. He didn't need to know her history. "I'm here to take care of Athena—not tell you my life story." Since he wouldn't take the initiative to leave, she moved past him and opened the door for him. "I'll make sure she's eating and does her business before I send her home. Now, if you'll excuse me, I have another appointment."

"You never answered my question about starting this clinic."

"I don't intend to." Whatever prejudice he had against his ex-wife or divorced women, Hazel wasn't going to let him get away with the veiled insults. "You'll notice that it's *my* name over the door, Mr. Hanson."

He grunted a smug sound that seemed to indicate he hadn't really expected her to share the details of her divorce, or that he didn't believe she had become a success in her own right. If Wade Hanson wanted sympathy or someone to commiserate with over the bitterness he felt for his ex-wife, he'd have to make an appointment with a therapist.

"I get the message, Dr. Cooper." He stepped through the open door, turning back to her, and said, "But you get this message. I intend to keep my dog. No woman is going to take him away from me again. I'll call or stop by tomorrow to see how she's doing."

The inner door opened behind her, and Hazel didn't think she'd ever been so happy to see Todd walk into a room. The interruption finally got Hanson moving.

"You're welcome to do that," she answered, dredging up a smile she didn't feel before closing the door after Wade Hanson. Her shoulders sagged in a weary sigh before she straightened again to face Todd. "Did you get Athena situated?"

"She's handling the IV just fine," he reported. "And she wolfed down that pâté like it was going out of style." He opened the door a crack and peeked out into the lobby before closing it again. "Did you get a load of that guy? He was more interested in getting the dog away from his wife than in taking care of it himself. You gonna report him to animal control?"

She'd like to report him for animal cruelty, female

bashing, failure to bathe and creeping her out for no good reason.

Instead, she simply nodded, putting on her reading glasses again and pulling up Athena's patient file on the computer to transfer her notations from the clipboard. "Whether it was Wade Hanson or his wife who let the dog get into this condition, it doesn't matter. Someone needs to be held responsible."

"Hey. You okay?" If Todd had put a hand on her, she probably would have snapped. But maybe he was finally learning the rules of conduct she expected from him. "You look a little rattled. You worried Hanson is going to retaliate if he loses his dog?"

She was worried about a lot of things lately. But she wasn't about to open up to her vet tech and give him any kind of encouragement to take their working relationship to a more personal level. "It's been a long day. I'm fine. Thanks for asking."

Todd's eyebrows came together atop his glasses in a frown. But when she refused to elaborate, he opened a cabinet door and pulled down a bottle of disinfectant spray and paper towels. "You want me to clean up in here? I'm happy to help."

"No, I'll do it. I need to get these details into the system before I call the authorities." Plus, she needed to listen to the messages on her phone. If they were all from Aaron, she'd report them to his parole officer, Steve Kranitz. She continued typing. "Tell the front desk I'm taking a short break. I'll be right out."

"You got it." He exited into the main lobby, closing the door behind him.

Alone in the quiet for the first time that day, Hazel rolled out the stool from beneath the counter and sank onto it. She puffed out a weary breath that lifted her bangs off her forehead before she saved the information on the screen and pulled her phone from her jeans.

"Damn it." Six missed calls, all from Aaron.

And one more from a number she didn't recognize that had just come through. She tried to feel hopeful that at least it wasn't the number of the man who had called and threatened her last night. But Burke had said it was easy to buy several burner phones to prevent KCPD from tracing the calls.

Maybe it was a wrong number.

And maybe her stalker got off on finding one insidious way after another to contact her. To declare his love or frighten her or threaten her with whatever his sick agenda might be.

After pulling up her voice mail, she set the phone on the countertop. Before playing her messages, she ripped off a handful of paper towels and picked up the disinfectant spray, keeping her hands busy and pretending to divert her thoughts by cleaning as she listened.

The polite request in Aaron's first two messages turned to frustration and blew up into a curse-filled tirade by the last one. *"Don't make me fill up your voice mail with messages. Pick up the damn phone and talk to me. Or tell me where and when we can meet. We have to talk. I heard what happened to Polly's car. What if she'd been in it, Hazel? Clearly, you can't handle what's happening on your own. Screw your independence. You need me. The girls need me. I'm their father*

and I'm worried." Several beats of silence passed, and
Hazel stopped wiping down the scale cradle, thinking
the message had ended. But just when she moved to
save it as evidence for Officer Kranitz, Aaron exhaled
a noisy breath and spoke in a calmer tone. *"I blamed
you for putting me in prison. But this one could be on
me. I may have some enemies. Let me help."*

The message ended with another recitation of his
cell number and a beep. Hazel saved the message and
returned with an almost compulsive need to wipe down
every knob and surface Wade Hanson had touched. If
only she could wipe away the memories of every man
who was unhappy with her lately—every man who
might be responsible for this psychological torture of
love letters and threats and bombs.

I may have some enemies.

"You think?" Try over three hundred enemies who'd
lost their life savings and retirement funds to her greedy
ex. Or the man he'd pointed a finger at as an accomplice
during his trial in an effort to get his sentence reduced.
Hazel's testimony had put them both behind bars. And
that list of potential enemies didn't account for anyone
Aaron might have butted heads with during his fifteen-
year stint in prison.

The last message started to play, cooling Hazel's
manic energy. She stopped working and stared at the
phone on the counter, as if it was responsible for the
sudden chill in the air around her.

She heard breathing that was measured and crackling
with a slight wheeze. When her caller spoke, the voice
sounded eerily familiar. *"Ten...nine...eight... Do you*

feel the clock ticking yet?" Could Aaron have disguised his voice to the point she didn't recognize it? Had he coerced a friend into calling on his behalf? Or was there some other obsessive lunatic in her life she hadn't yet identified? *"My patience with you is running out, my beloved. Give me what I want. Or I'll take it from you."*

"Take what!" She slammed the bottle down on the counter. "What the hell do you want from me?"

A soft knock on the door reminded her that she'd raised her voice. Was there a client in the lobby, or had someone from her staff overheard her?

She punched off her cell and stashed it in her pocket as Ashley nudged her way inside the exam room. Her green eyes were narrowed with concern as she closed the door behind her. "Mom? You okay?"

"Hi, sweetie." Hazel tossed the soiled towels and put away the disinfectant, buying herself a few seconds to regain her composure before she pointed to the clipboard her daughter carried. "That my next patient?"

"Your last appointment for the day. It's a new patient." Ashley hugged the clipboard to the front of her pink scrubs. "Who was that on the phone?"

"I was listening to my messages." Hazel reached for the printout of patient information.

Instead of handing it over, Ashley tucked the clipboard behind her back. "Who left the messages? I can't tell if that's your worried face or your pissed-off face. But neither is good. I was hoping you'd be in a better mood, because I need to ask you a favor."

"What favor?"

Ashley pointed to Hazel's head. "Explain the face first."

She'd go with the lesser of two evils. Or maybe she was a fool to think either caller was less of a threat than the other. "Have you gotten any phone calls from your father?"

"From Dad? Dad called you?" Ashley shook her head. "No. Not since he first got out of prison and he begged to meet with Polly and me behind your back. That's when the judge expanded that restraining order to include us." Moving closer, she leaned her hip against the counter. "I'm not sure I'd even recognize what he sounds like anymore, unless he identified himself. What did he say?"

What was the best way to explain this honestly, without tainting her daughter's perception of her father? "He saw the news story about Polly's car and the bomb threat here. He wants to make sure you're both okay."

"He cares now? He didn't care sixteen years ago when all those people were so angry with him and our family."

"He's older. He's had a lot of time to think on what he did and what he lost." Hazel shoved her hands into the pockets of her jacket and shrugged. "He claims that prison has changed him."

"Yeah, but how? What if it just made him a smarter criminal who can't be caught now? Or do you think he really cares?"

"I can't answer that. I know he adored you both when you were little." Hazel leaned against the counter, giving Ashley's shoulder a teasing bump with her own. "I always promised that when you and Polly were of age, if you wanted a relationship with your father, I wouldn't stand in your way."

"Yeah, well, he used to love you, too." Ashley shook her head, dismissing any idea of reconciliation. "Mom, we know what he did to you. Even now that I'm old enough to understand his supposed reasons, I can't forgive him for that. He didn't know how to be a good father then, and I doubt that's a skill one learns in prison."

"So you don't want to have contact with him?" Hazel reached over to pull Ashley's ponytail from the collar of her top and smoothed it down her back. "Don't answer right away. Think about it."

"I don't need to think about it. Polly and I have discussed it more than once. We don't really know him. We don't want to. We don't want him to be a part of our lives."

"I'll talk to him, then. Or rather, I'll have my attorney talk to his." With her mood lifted, Hazel pushed away from the counter. "Now, what about this favor?"

Ashley's expression creased with a smile she could barely contain. "Well, maybe I can help your day end on a more positive note."

The smile was contagious. "I'm all for that."

"Do you need me to stay for this last appointment? Joe's coming here to take me to dinner. I'd like to change before he picks me up."

"Joe's coming here?"

"Yes. I thought you might like to check him out for yourself and see how sweet he is. After everything that happened yesterday, I thought that might ease your mind a little bit."

Hazel nodded, appreciating the thoughtful plan. "I think it might."

"Great." She handed Hazel the clipboard she'd brought in. "Here's the chart for Mr. Jingles. Looks like a standard checkup for a newly adopted pet."

Hazel scanned the printout on her new feline patient. "I think I can handle one cat without help." Ashley was already heading out the door to the lobby when Hazel stopped her. "Wait. What about Polly? Will she be on her own tonight?"

"I already talked to Sergeant Burke. He's picking her up at the hospital and taking her home. Polly's cool with that. She has to study for a test tomorrow, so she won't be going anywhere." Ashley gave her a quick hug, then practically danced out the door. "Thanks. I'll let you know as soon as Joe gets here."

"Wait. Ash?" She followed her daughter into the lobby. "When did you talk to Sergeant—"

"Excuse me? I'm Mr. Jingles's owner." A hand with polished French-tip nails was suddenly thrust toward her, stopping Hazel in her tracks.

She instinctively took the woman's hand. "Hello."

"Thank you for working me into your busy schedule, Dr. Cooper." The dark-haired woman wore a polished gray suit and held a carrier with a cat that was equally sleek and dark. "I'm Shannon Bennett."

Chapter 8

Burke checked his watch and swore. He tapped on the accelerator, pushing his speed as much as he could without turning on his siren.

He was the only one with an emergency here. If he didn't feel it like a fist to the gut every time Hazel's eyes darkened with fear or uncertainty, he wouldn't care so much about running late now that he and Gunny were off the clock. But it was nearly 5:30 p.m. And though he knew she would be the last one to leave her clinic after locking up, he'd gotten caught up in a search on the grounds at the KCI Airport that had required a team effort by KCPD and airport security to cover a large search grid after a multiple-bomb threat had been called in and a suspicious bag had been discovered in a culvert off one of the parking lots. Fortunately, the bag had ended up being an extreme case of lost luggage, and the depressed individual who'd called in the threat had been identified sitting in his car in another parking lot. He'd been apprehended and taken to a hospital. But now Burke's clothes and skin were damp with the rain, his boots were muddy and he smelled like wet dog.

But he'd promised Hazel he'd be there to protect her and her family. Knowing her independent streak, she'd walk across the parking lot and drive home alone, just as she had all those years when there'd been no one in her life to look out for her. She was a smart woman, and strong. But a stalker who knew so much about her, and so much about explosives, created dangerous circumstances that required her to be extra careful regarding her security. Hell, had he reminded her of the basic safety precautions of checking under and around her truck before even approaching it? Did she understand situational awareness? Pinpointing the location of every person in her vicinity, taking note of her surroundings and anything that seemed out of place?

Would she call him if something *did* seem out of place?

He peered through the rhythmic sweep of the windshield wipers to race through a yellow light and cross into the industrial area north of downtown where her veterinary clinic and a neighboring dog park were located. Even though he and Gunny had put in a long day, he wanted to have his partner do a sweep of Hazel's truck before she got in, just in case the perp who was terrorizing her made good on last night's threat and had escalated from blowing up her daughter's unoccupied car into a much more personal attack.

Burke eyed his cell phone in the console beside him, wondering if he should try calling her again. But since his first two messages about waiting for him had gone straight to voice mail, he focused on weaving through rush hour traffic and getting to the clinic as quickly as he could. Either she was busy, ignoring him or he was already way too late. And that was what made everything in him tighten with worry.

His blood pressure dropped a fraction when he spotted the familiar sign of her family animal clinic. He flipped on his turn signal and slowed but had to stomp on the brake as he came up behind a gray sedan that was nearly the same color as the rain. The pricey car was parked at the curb just outside the clinic parking lot. Not the safest place to park, so close to the driveway entrance. The dark-haired driver was going to get her fancy bumper clipped if she wasn't careful.

Taking a wide arc around the sedan, Burke entered the nearly empty parking lot. Relieved to see Hazel's truck, he pulled in a parking stall and shrugged into his still-wet KCPD jacket before he heard the squeal of tires against the wet payment. Climbing out, he adjusted the bill of his cap to protect his eyes from the rain and saw the taillights of the gray sedan speeding away. Maybe the police logo on the side of his truck had made the driver think twice about creating a potential traffic hazard. Or else the driver had been parked there for no good reason.

Wait a minute.

"No way." He pulled Gunny from the truck and jogged to the street. But the gray sedan had merged with traffic and disappeared. Dark-haired woman in a fancy car? She'd been wearing sunglasses, despite the gloomy weather. He hadn't seen her face, and he no longer knew what his ex-wife drove, but that couldn't have been Shannon, could it?

How could she have known he was coming here? Had she asked one of the men on his team? He was off the clock, so even Dispatch didn't know his twenty. Was she so desperate to reconnect with him that she'd hoped for a face-to-face meeting?

His hand hovered over the phone in his vest beneath his jacket while the rain drummed against the bill of his cap. No. He wouldn't give his ex the satisfaction of calling her to ask where she was, and he dropped his hand to Gunny's flank.

Maybe it hadn't been Shannon in that car at all. She'd been on his mind as an annoyance he needed to deal with ever since last night's call. He needed to sit down with her and spell out that they were never going to get back together. His heart belonged to someone else now. He'd just projected Shannon's identity onto the random brunette the way a supposed eyewitness would sometimes misidentify a suspect because their concentration had been off-line due to their emotions.

Unless… Burke planed the water off his cheeks and jaw and turned back toward the clinic door. Could Shannon have been spying on Hazel? Checking out her competition? Not that there was any possibility of a reunion, but it might be worth looking up the make of her car and, if it was a match, paying her a visit. There were already enough things standing in the way of the relationship he wanted with Hazel. The threats. Preserving a friendship. Hazel's stubborn self-protection streak. He didn't need a jealous ex thrown into the mix working against the future he envisioned for them, too.

With an urgent *"Voran,"* he guided Gunny over to Hazel's truck and ordered the dog to search.

He was stowing Gunny in the back seat of his truck after a quick towel off and a dog biscuit when the clinic doors opened. Hazel stepped out and put up a blue umbrella against the steady drone of the rain.

She scooped Cleo into her arms and handed the small dog over to the young couple who followed her out and waited beside her while she locked the door. He recognized Ashley's long blond ponytail as the two women hugged. The young dark-haired man with a tattoo snaking up his neck and a bandanna tied around the top of his head was someone new, and Burke shifted inside his boots, forcing himself to stay put, trying not to make a suspect of every man who got close to Hazel. The young man and Ashley were both wearing bulky rain pants and jackets. Burke had already spotted the motorcycle parked across the lot from his truck and suspected that Tattoo Man belonged to the bike.

Hazel shook hands with the younger man, turning as Ashley beamed a smile at Burke and waved. "Hey, Burke!"

Burke touched the brim of his cap at her enthusiastic greeting. "Hey, Ash."

In a swift move known only to escape artists and

matchmaking daughters, Ashley handed the dog back to her mother, slipped behind her and nudged Hazel forward, pulling the man with her in the opposite direction. Burke shook his head at the totally unsubtle move. At least he had one Cooper woman who was in favor of him getting together with Hazel. Ashley and the guy who was apparently her date hurried down the steps to the left of the door, where they unpacked their helmets from the storage compartment on his motorcycle.

Hazel walked down the ramp in the opposite direction at a much slower pace, meeting Burke at her truck, depositing Cleo and her purse inside before facing him. She raised her umbrella over Burke's head so that it sheltered both. "Here you are, showing up at my clinic again. Is this going to be a thing now?"

"Me keeping you safe? I think so."

She eyed his sodden, muddy appearance from hat to toe before narrowing her eyes as she frowned. "Is there a problem?"

"Long day. Turned out okay."

"But I saw you and Gunny searching my truck."

"Overdeveloped protective instincts," he joked. "Just your friendly neighborhood cop making sure you and Cleo get safely home." He thumbed over his shoulder at his truck and the weary working dog relaxing inside. "Gunny didn't hit on any explosives. I wouldn't have let you and the one-eyed fuzz ball anywhere near your truck if he had."

Finally, she smiled, a regular ol' friendly smile, as though she was glad to see him, and not overthinking or regretting the changing status of their relationship.

"Cleo and I thank you. Are you coming over for dinner?"

"Would I be welcome?"

"Me spending time with you? I think so." She gave his teasing right back, and his pulse kicked up a notch at the idea of kissing that beautiful smile.

Fortunately, he had wet clothes cooling on his skin and work that still needed to be done to temper his instinctive male reaction to sharing the intimate space beneath the umbrella with her while the rain falling around them cocooned them from the rest of the world. "I won't be there right away. After I drive Polly to her apartment, I've got a couple of leads on your case I want to follow up on."

"Leads? Like what?"

Besides checking with Justin Grant and the crime lab on the details surrounding the bomb parts mailed to Hazel, and those used to blow up Polly's car, Burke thought of the dark-haired woman in the car who had sped away. "Who was that woman who just drove off?"

Hazel glanced around the parking lot. "What woman?"

"The brunette in the BMW."

"My last client left half an hour ago. A routine check on her new cat, Mr. Jingles. She was chatty. He was fine." She nodded toward the couple climbing onto the motorcycle. "Ashley and Joe and I are the only ones here."

"Your last client wasn't Shannon Bennett, was it?"

"Yes. How did you…?" She leaned away from him, scanning the parking lot again. "Wait. *Your* Shannon?

The last name was different. I've never met her before…
I was focused on the cat, and I didn't think… Was she
checking me out? Does she think something's going
on between us?"

Hell, yeah, there was something going on between
them. Exactly what hadn't been determined yet, but he
wouldn't deny the connection between them anymore.
"It doesn't matter what she thinks. Shannon's no longer a part of my life, and I don't want her to be a part
of yours."

"She was waiting here until you came. To see if you
were going to show up." Hazel shoved her bangs off her
forehead. They were damp enough to stick up in a wild
disarray. "Is she one of those leads you're following up
on? You think a woman could be responsible for what's
happening to me?"

Burke wasn't ruling out anyone who might be a
threat to Hazel. But his ex-wife was at the bottom of his
list of suspects. "Shannon has zero access to explosives,
and she wouldn't know how to put a bomb together."

"She could have hired someone who does." Frustration was evident as she attacked her sticky bangs again.
"If she blames me for stealing you from her—"

"I've been making my own decisions about who I
want to be with for a long time now. There is no stealing. I choose."

"And you choose me."

"Damn right, I do."

"But if she's jealous, we should…"

Hazel's smile had faded. Burke wanted it back. "Forget about Shannon. Our marriage was over years ago.

I'll have a conversation with her. She won't bother you again." He wasn't giving Hazel another excuse to push aside the feelings that had finally surfaced between them. "Drive straight home to the parking garage." He pulled his keys from his pocket and stepped from beneath the umbrella. "I'll meet you at your place when I'm finished. And I'll bring dinner."

"You don't have to do that."

He strode to his truck. "I'll be there in an hour. Hour and a half, tops."

Hazel grabbed his arm to stop him, sliding the umbrella over his head again. "Jedediah—"

"Gunny's worried about Cleo. He'd like to make sure she's safe and fed and locked in for the night."

She arched a silvery-gold eyebrow. "Gunny's worried?"

This silly conversation was safer than pouring his guts out to her again the way he had last night. "If Gunny had a driver's license, he'd come over by himself. But he needs me to be his chauffeur."

"Oh, well, tell him we're in the mood for something light tonight, like a salad. It's the only way Cleo and I can justify the ice-cream sundae we intend to eat for dessert."

"With your homemade caramel sauce?" He thought of her licking that spoon again and wondered why, since a few decades had passed since he'd been a horny teenager, his body reacted so sharply, so instantly, to the thought of her licking things. Like him. *Wow.* He needed to feel the cool rain splashing in his face again. Since he'd given in to that kiss, his body seemed to have a one-track mind where Dr. Hazel Cooper was concerned. "Is there enough to share?"

"I'll make sure there is." She glanced back to her truck. "Cleo is looking forward to seeing Gunny again this evening."

"Gunny's pretty stoked about it, too."

They weren't fooling anybody here, least of all each other. Hazel reached up and brushed away the moisture pooling on his shoulders. Her fingers hooked beneath the front of his jacket to straighten his collar and settled there. All casual touches. Every one adding to the energy that hummed through him when they were close like this.

"All this innuendo is dangerous for my peace of mind," she confessed. It was reassuring to hear that, although she was fighting the chemistry they shared, she wasn't denying it. "It makes me feel like you and I are becoming *us*."

He feathered his fingers into her hair and smoothed her bangs back into place across the smooth, warm skin of her forehead. "We are, Haze. I believe in *us*. One day, you will, too. As long as we're on the journey together, I'll go as slow as you need me to."

Hazel shook her head. "That's hardly fair to you."

He cupped his hand against her cheek and jaw. "You're worth the wait."

She studied him for several silent seconds, gauging his sincerity before turning her lips into the palm of his hand and pressing a kiss there. "I want to know anything you find out."

"Will do."

Her fingers flexed inside the front of his jacket, as though she'd forgotten she was still holding on to him. He hadn't. "And thank you for taking care of Polly this evening. You score a lot of brownie points with that."

He liked brownie points. He liked the idea of redeeming them with her even better. "You raised two good people. I'm happy to help them where I can."

The motorcycle engine roared to life, diverting their attention to the opposite side of the parking lot. With the tats, the muscles and the Harley, Ashley's date looked tough. But that alone didn't make him a threat. The young man made sure Ashley had her helmet securely fastened, and he'd waited for the two women to lock up the clinic earlier. Ashley didn't seem to have any problem winding her arms around his waist as he turned his bike toward the street.

"Bye, Mom! Burke!" Ashley waved before latching onto him again and leaning into his back as he revved the motor and pulled out of the lot.

"Have fun," Hazel called after her, but they were already racing away down the street.

Burke watched Hazel wrap both hands around the base of her umbrella. Any tighter and the wood might snap. "Is that the boyfriend?"

"'Fraid so. Joe Sciarra. He's a bouncer she met at a bar." Her grip didn't relax until the couple had disappeared into the camouflage of traffic and rain. "He was actually charming and well-spoken," she admitted, "although he looks like he rides with one of those motorcycle gangs."

"Want me to run a background check on him?"

Green eyes swiveled up to his. "Can you do that? Isn't that an abuse of your position on the force?"

"Yes, and yes."

"I don't want to get you into trouble."

"One of the perks of running my own division is that I've earned enough clout to call in favors if I need to. The department will give me a little leeway if I ask for it." Since he had no idea yet who was targeting Hazel, this was a no-brainer. "There have been enough threats that I can justify getting the background on anyone suspicious in your circle of friends and acquaintances."

She considered his answer for a moment, then nodded. "Then, while you're at it, could you also run a background check on a Wade Hanson?"

"Who's that?"

"A client of mine. He's got a pretty serious grudge against women. Still, I just met him today, so he couldn't have sent all those letters."

A bad feeling twisted inside him. "Did he threaten you?"

"Not directly."

"Damn it, Haze—I told you to call—"

She splayed her fingers against his chest, quieting him with a gentle touch. "You can't stop me from doing my job. Just like I can't stop you from doing yours. I suspect him either of animal abuse or failing to report the abuse. I had to call animal control on him, and I doubt that will make him happy with me."

Burke covered her hand with his, needing the anchor of her calm strength to keep from going into protective-caveman mode and scaring her away from confiding in him. "Wade Hanson. Got it. Anything else you want to tell me?" he teased, trying to lighten his mood. He didn't expect to see the frown tighten her expression. Ah, hell. There *was* something else. "What is it?"

"Later. There are some messages on my phone I want you to listen to." Hazel fisted her fingers into the front of his jacket and stretched onto her toes to press a sweet kiss to the corner of his mouth. He treasured the gift without trying to turn it into anything more. "Go do what you need to do. Find answers for me. And tell Gunny not to be late."

Hazel suspected the low-lying areas of the city would be flooding by now with all this rain. But the intermittent downpours kept her neighbors from asking any questions as she walked Cleo inside the perimeter of the parking garage. The other residents of the building exchanged a friendly greeting or stopped to pet Cleo when they came home from work or errands. While she appreciated the security of knowing concrete and steel grating surrounded the ground level of her building, keeping threats and unwanted visitors out of her life, she didn't want them asking why she wasn't walking her dog across the street in the minipark or up a couple of blocks on the grassy area between her neighborhood and the wall that blocked the highway at the base of the hill.

Because someone keeps threatening to blow me up.

Nope, she didn't want to have to explain that one—or try to come up with a lie that would convince them that they were safe, even though she lived in the building with them.

One advantage to having a three-legged dog was that she didn't have to walk Cleo very far to get her exercise. A couple of laps around the garage was enough for Cleo to do both her businesses and clean up after her.

One *dis*advantage to having a three-legged dog was that she didn't have to walk Cleo very far to get her exercise. Security aside, Hazel felt entombed behind the garage's metal gate. Mist from the rain filtered through the steel mesh walls and made the air feel heavy. It trapped the scents of oil and dog, and the sharp, earthy smells of waterlogged foliage and mud from the landscaping outside. Although she knew it would be foolish to do so, she longed to get out into the evening air and feel the rain cool her skin and see it wash the sidewalks clean. She could feel the wind if she was out in the open, and maybe that would blow away this sense of uneasiness that left her starting at every new sound and counting the minutes until Burke showed up with dinner and that heavenly smell that was all man and uniquely his.

She needed to figure out what she was feeling and decide where she wanted her future with Burke to go. He'd been too good a friend for too long for her to give him false hope. She wouldn't be selfish and string him along just so she wouldn't lose his caring and companionship. She was a mature woman who hadn't known passion for a long time, but every fiber of her body craved his kisses and the firm, needy touches that had awakened her long-dormant desire. And no woman of any age would want to deny herself the tenderness and respect with which he treated her.

Hazel cared about Burke. She enjoyed spending time with him—eating, working, talking. They shared a devotion to animals and justice and protecting the people they cared about. She admitted a healthy lust for his toned body and grizzled jaw and teasing sense of humor.

But did she love him? Could she surrender her whole heart to him?

Because if she changed her life—if she let herself love again—she wasn't doing anything halfway. Jedediah Burke wasn't a halfway kind of man, either. And that meant it wouldn't halfway hurt if she made the wrong choice.

Although the rational part of her brain insisted on arguing the point, Hazel was beginning to think that, deep inside, she'd already made her decision. The fact that she didn't want to go back upstairs to her lonely place by herself, now that Burke and Gunny had filled up her condo with their presence, was very telling. Maybe Ashley and Polly—and Burke—were right. The only person standing in the way of a second chance at happiness was her.

And the nimrod who kept taunting her with the promise of blowing her to smithereens.

"That's one hell of a pep talk, Dr. Coop," she muttered out loud. "Cleo, what do you think I should do?"

The dog tilted her head up at the mention of her name, and Hazel reached down to scratch around the schnauzer's ears. But the need for affection lasted only a few seconds before Cleo put her nose to the ground and followed an intriguing scent around a parked car to the concrete half wall.

"Good advice," Hazel praised. "Keep yourself busy instead of worrying so much."

Hazel decided that instead of checking her watch every few minutes like a schoolgirl waiting for her first date to pick her up, she'd find something to keep herself busy and out of her head. She pulled her phone from the pocket of her jeans and called Polly.

"Hey, Mom," her younger daughter answered, clearly recognizing her number on the screen of her phone. "Checking up on me?" she teased in a breathy voice. "Or checking up on Sergeant Burke? He left here about an hour ago. Said he was stopping by the precinct office to do some research. He asked if you like taco salad. I said yes."

"He's coming over for dinner tonight to check on me."

"I kind of figured."

Based on the rhythmic cadence of Polly's voice, Hazel guessed her daughter was in the middle of a workout. "You're not out running tonight, are you?"

"No, worrywart," Polly chided with affection. "Yoga. I'm playing one of those exercise DVDs. I won't get soaked in the rain and catch a cold, and no bad guys can chase me."

Hazel followed Cleo along the wall as the small schnauzer tracked the path of whatever had piqued her interest. "Will you be all right by yourself? Do you want to come over here until Ashley gets home?"

"And be a third wheel on your date with Burke? No, thanks."

"It's not a date."

"It should be."

Hazel heaved a deep sigh that echoed Polly's tension-clearing breath. "I need to work through some things before I commit to a new relationship."

"Mom." Her daughter dragged the single word out to three syllables on three different pitches. "You've had sixteen years to work through things after Dad. You have the right to be happy. If you don't grab Burke, someone else will."

As they reached the wide mesh gate at the parking garage entrance, Cleo jerked on her leash, pulling Hazel down the ramp toward the sidewalk, insisting on tracking the scent outside. *What in the world?* Had one of the neighborhood cats sauntered past? Hazel gave a short tug on the leash. "Come on, girl. You don't want to be out in the rain, and neither do I."

"Sounds like Cleo needs your attention. I swear, you spoil that dog more than you ever did Ash or me." Hazel could hear the smile in her daughter's voice and remembered when she'd been that full of energy and certain that everything would turn out all right if she worked hard, stayed hopeful and remained loyal to the people she loved. That had been a lifetime ago, before Aaron's arrest and the divorce. Before the night she nearly died. Hazel planted her feet as Cleo jerked against the leash. When had she gotten so old and cynical? How long had surviving her life been more important than living it? Too long. She'd taught her daughters better but had reached fifty and was no longer practicing what she preached. "Mom? You still there?"

"Yes. Sorry, I got distracted." Hazel vowed to change

her life. Right now. She wasn't going to be a coward about living anymore. And if grabbing Jedediah Burke was part of that spiritual renaissance, then so be it. "You're an insightful young woman, Polly Cooper."

"Um, thanks?"

"I have to go." Her gaze followed the length of the leash down to Cleo to see what had caught the dog's attention. Hazel spotted the vague outline of something small but oddly shaped leaning against the garage gate. But the lights from inside the garage cast distorting shadows through the steel mesh, and she couldn't quite make it out. Were those little tufts of fur poking through the bottom links of the gate? Had a small animal taken refuge from the rain? "I think I've made a decision."

"Good. Talking on the phone is messing with my concentration." Polly laughed before taking another deep breath. "Call if you need anything. Good luck with Burke. Love you."

"Love you, too. Bye." Cleo was pawing at one of the tufts of fur, pulling it through the gate. Was that... a tail? "Cleo. Stop." Hazel knelt and ran her hand along the dog's back to calm the frantic thrill of discovery. "What have you found, girl?"

Whatever belonged to that striped tail wasn't moving. Shortening Cleo's leash, she tucked it beneath the sole of her boot to keep the dog away from the creature that could be ill or worse. She turned on the flashlight on her phone and shone the light through the gate. She gasped a quick inhale of compassion.

A cat.

"Oh, sweetie, what's happened to you?" The veterinarian in her quickly squelched her sympathy and she pushed to her feet. A stray must have curled up as close to shelter as it could get and breathed its last breath. Or else some coldhearted clown who shouldn't be responsible for an animal had lost a pet and dumped the creature here instead of paying for a cremation or disposing of it legally.

Hazel hurried to the pedestrian door. She would check the cat's condition for herself and make sure there was no contagious illness or even take it back to the clinic to scan for a microchip. She'd already called animal control once today. She wasn't afraid to make the owner accountable if there was one.

But Hazel froze before pushing open the locked door. Besides the cat at the vehicle entrance, there was something leaning against the bottom of the door here, too. This object had clean, straight lines instead of curves. It was covered in brown paper instead of fur.

Her vision spun with trepidation as she squatted down to inspect the oblong package that had been left just outside her secure sanctuary. She didn't need to see her name on the mailing label to know what it was, to know it was for her.

But she read it, anyway. *Hazel Cooper.* With her home address.

She shivered as the damp air penetrated her skin. She scooped Cleo up into her arms and made herself breathe, so she wouldn't pass out with fear. Or anger.

Not again. Not here.

Hazel snapped a picture of the package with her phone, then texted it to Burke's number.

He's been here. Left a package. Calling 911.

A shadow fell over Hazel, and Cleo twisted in her arms, barking as though they were under attack.

Hazel looked up at the furious noise.

And screamed.

Chapter 9

The grotesque features of the red-and-black Halloween mask framed by the hood of the man's jacket quickly took shape. But identifying the devil costume made him no less frightening than the monster that had first startled her. His eyes were recessed behind the mask, shadowed by night and impossible to identify.

Tumbling onto her butt in her haste to retreat, Hazel scrambled away, clutching the growling, barking Cleo to her chest. Even though the steel grating and coded locks kept him from reaching her, it didn't stop the man from curling one set of his black-gloved fingers through the steel links.

And breathing.

He didn't say a single word, but she could hear his breath coming in gusts and gasps, as though he was out of shape or had run up on her fast. Had he hoped she'd step outside to check on the cat? Maybe trip the bomb when she opened the door? Grab her as soon as she was on his side of the security gate? Or maybe this sicko was simply excited to see how badly he'd startled her.

She quickly got to her feet, hugging Cleo as tightly as the squirming, snarling dog allowed. "Get away from me!" she warned.

The only thing that moved was his chest, puffing in and out as he did that damn breathing. The man's dark jeans and hoodie were soaked with rain and dripping onto the sidewalk. He'd probably been standing outside for a while, no doubt watching her, and she hadn't even realized it. He'd been watching, waiting for her to be alone, waiting for her to move exactly where he wanted her before he approached. He was a dark, shapeless bulk without a human face, oozing malice and a power she didn't want him to have over her. The bottom of his mask puckered as he sucked in a deep breath, and for a moment, she thought he was going to speak. Instead, he reached into his pocket and pulled out an envelope. The dark holes of his eyes never wavered from her as he rolled the envelope into a scroll and pushed it through the grate.

Hazel watched the curled paper drop to the damp concrete in front of her.

"I'm not going to read that." It was hard to tear her gaze away from the sightless holes where his eyes should be. "Keep your damn love letters." She glanced one way toward the package, the other toward the feline corpse. "Stop bringing me these sick gifts. You need to leave me and my family alone. You're making me angry. Not afraid."

He stepped closer and she jumped back a step, making a liar of herself. Okay, so she was angry *and* afraid. But she wasn't helpless, not entirely.

It took several seconds to hear her own thoughts through the muffling drumbeat of rain, Cleo's barking and her roiling emotions. *Do something. Put him on the defensive. Fight back.*

Suddenly, she felt the phone still clasped in her hand and raised it to snap a picture of the man. He flinched at the flash and spun away for a moment. "How do you like that? I'm calling the cops. I'm sending them a picture of you."

Hazel forwarded the image to Burke's phone, then snapped another picture. And another. Not bothering to read the answering texts from Burke.

The man came back, perhaps remembering that his disguise wouldn't give him away. That he had the advantages of strength and anonymity—and possibly a bomb—on his side of the metal links that separated them.

Her phone vibrated with another response, and she finally looked down at the flurry of texts from Burke.

On my way, said one text.

The next read, Go upstairs and lock yourself in. I notified Dispatch. Help is on its way.

Get the hell away from him! read the most recent message.

Hazel retreated another step. With no gun, he

couldn't shoot her. With the gate between them, he couldn't reach her. And yet...

Her devilish suitor leaned into the grating, pushing it slightly forward with the weight of his body. He curled his gloved fingers through the links, stretching them toward her, making her feel as though he could touch her.

"Stay away from me." Hazel shook hard enough that Cleo halted her barking and nuzzled her mama's cheek. "It's okay, girl."

But it wasn't. If Hazel gave in to her imagination, the man would dematerialize and slide straight through the steel mesh to get to her.

"Give me what I want," he wheezed in a toneless whisper, finally deigning to speak.

Did she recognize that voice? It sounded like an echo of something familiar, but with its harsh rasp, she couldn't place it. Could she recognize him by his build? Smell? Anything? She hugged Cleo closer to her chest. "Who are you? What do you want from me?"

And then she saw the electronic device he held in his right hand, small enough to fit within his palm. He stroked it with his thumb. A tiny cell phone? A remote? Whatever it was, she didn't for one second believe it was anything good.

"What is that?" she demanded.

"On..." He flipped a cap off one end and pressed a button. Hazel swung her gaze over to the package, instinctively retreating. "Off..."

She flinched when he pushed the button again, expecting her world to erupt with flame and blow her into a gazillion pieces. She looked at him.

"There are innocent people in this building. You'd hurt more than you and me." She pleaded with him to remember his humanity. "Or don't you care how many people you hurt?"

His answer was an angry grunt. He charged the fence, sending a ripple of the rattling noise around the chain-link walls of the garage. "You should talk," he wheezed.

"Me? What did I do?" Hazel punched 9. "I've had enough of these games. I'm calling the police." Then 1. "Why don't you stay there and keep talking to me? Give them a chance to meet you, too." Another 1, and she hit the call button, then put the phone to her ear. "My name is Dr. Hazel Cooper. There's a man at my building. Threatening me. He has a package—I think it's a bomb. He already blew up my daughter's car." She rattled off her building address and the names of the detectives she'd been working with. "I've alerted my friend Sergeant Burke. Jedediah Burke. He runs the K-9 unit. He'll need backup." The man in the mask never moved, except to curl his black-gloved fingers into fists around the links. Not even hearing that police officers, the bomb squad and one very big, very bad K-9 cop who'd sworn to protect her were on their way could budge him.

"They'll be here any minute," Hazel warned him, repeating the dispatcher's last words. "KCPD is coming for you."

His response was to pull his fingers from the grate and slowly stroke the metal links as though he was ca-

ressing her face or her hair in some creepy pantomime
of a gentle touch.

Hazel shivered. "Stop that."

The man caressed the metal one more time before
turning the shadowed eye sockets of his mask toward
the concrete floor and the envelope he'd delivered to her.

She shook her head, refusing to do as he asked.
"What have I done that's worth killing me for? Worth
killing yourself? If you set off that bomb now, you'll
die, too. That's not much of a victory, is it?"

No answer.

"Did you kill that poor cat?"

He held up the device in his hand, pushed a button.
"On," he whispered.

As much as she wanted him to go away, Hazel realized she needed to keep him here until the police
arrived, instead of running for cover or tossing accu-
sations that might scare him away. "All right. I'll read
your note." She set Cleo down but kept the dog on a
short leash—away from the man—as she stooped down
to pick up the envelope and open it. There wasn't much
to the typewritten letter inside.

*You're going to be mine. Do you know how much
I want from you? How much I need you to give
me? Everything.*

Everything?

Not *I want you*, but he wanted something *from* her.
Hazel raised her gaze to those missing eyes as understanding dawned. These weren't love letters. They

were payback. The bombs and threats were about ret-
ribution this bastard thought she owed him. For what?
Something she had done? Some perceived slight? Could
this terror campaign be payback for something Aaron
had done in prison? Did this perv mistakenly think that
hurting her would hurt her ex-husband?

Or was this Aaron himself? After so many years
apart, would she recognize her own husband if he was
disguised like this? Was this some twisted version of
what Aaron had done to her all those years ago?

"Aaron?" She squinted through the glare of the garage lights and the shadows beyond them, trying to see
his eyes behind the mask, searching for something familiar beneath the shapeless hoodie and baggy jeans.
"Is that you? Why are you doing this?"

All he did was breathe.

Maybe this wasn't her ex. But then, Aaron hadn't
actually done the dirty work the last time he'd terrorized her, either.

"Why?" There was no answer, of course. She lurched
toward the grate, smacked it with the flat of her hand.
Cleo barked at the sharp rattling noise. When the man
jumped back from the figurative assault, it was very
telling. *That* was a lot like Aaron, too. "Coward! Show
me your face. Talk to me like a real man."

She hated the tears that stung her eyes. They were a
toxic mix of remembered shock and fear, and anger that
her life should come back to the nightmare that she'd
barely survived sixteen years ago.

"Talk to me," she pleaded in a softer tone. "I don't
understand. I'm tired of being afraid."

His chest spasmed with a rippling movement. And then she heard another sound. Laughter.

She'd admitted she was afraid of him, of his relentless torment, and that made him laugh. Hazel backed away from the mocking sound.

Big mistake, Dr. Coop. You just gave him what he wanted.

Part of what he wanted, at least. *Everything* probably involved a whole lot more than this mental anguish—like panic or torture. Or dying.

"Good," he dragged out in a toneless whisper. He pushed the button on the device in his hand and replaced the cover. *Off.* Then, with a single finger, he traced the outline of a metal link. Hazel shivered as she imagined him touching her skin with that same finger. "I'll take that as down payment on what you owe me."

She frowned. Why couldn't she recognize that voice? Or was she only imagining it sounded familiar?

She picked up Cleo, and for a split second she wished her little schnauzer was as well trained as Gunny. She'd order her dog to bite that stupid, creepily suggestive finger. She wished she had Burke's partner with her here right now to take him down and sink his teeth into him and chew that hideous mask right off his face. She wished she had Burke.

The blare of an approaching siren pulled Hazel from the violent turn of her thoughts and stiffened her spine. "You're caught."

He shook his head in a silent no. Then he picked up the package and the dead cat and backed away from the gate as swirling lights from the first official vehicle bounced off the trees across the street.

"Wait!" Hazel dashed to the pedestrian exit as the man ran down the sidewalk, disappearing into the curtain of rain and night. If KCPD didn't catch him now, he'd be free to come back and taunt her again, to hurt someone else. One of her daughters? Her neighbors? Her coworkers and patients? His threats had already escalated to the point that she was certain he intended a messy death for her. But how many innocent people did his idea of *everything* include?

She shoved open the heavy door and ran outside into the rain. "You won't get away with this!" The sirens were deafening as the first official vehicle reached her block. She halted as rain splashed her face and soaked through her clothes. Cleo huddled against her as she peered through the distorted lights of emergency vehicles and streetlamps that highlighted individual raindrops instead of what lay beyond them. She couldn't even see the corner of the building, much less the man. She took one more step, and then another, following in a hesitant pursuit. "Don't run from me now! You're not so brave without a bomb to keep me in check, are you! I want to talk to—"

A big black-and-white pickup swerved into the parking ramp in front of her, screeching to a halt on the damp pavement. Hazel jumped back from the truck that blocked her path. "No!" She dodged around the truck, trying to get eyes on her tormentor. "He's getting away."

But she ran into a wall made of man and uniform.

"Hazel!" The KCPD truck was still rocking from its

abrupt stop when Burke jumped out from behind the wheel. Leaving the engine running, he circled around the hood and locked his arm around her waist, catching her before she could dart past him. "What the hell are you doing out here?"

"Stop him!"

She shuffled in quick backward steps to stay upright as he pulled her up against the brick wall. "The only thing that kept me from going crazy imagining all the ways he could hurt you was knowing there was that cage between him and you."

She clung to a fistful of his jacket, even as she tried to slide around him. "He went that way. Around the corner. I didn't think it was safe to come out while he was still here. We need to catch—"

"It wasn't." Burke pushed his hips against hers, trapping her between him and the wall. Clearly, he wasn't letting her move away.

"Damn it, Burke." She pushed. Nothing happened. "I don't want to lose... I don't..." Her fingers slowly curled into his jacket and the vest, shirt and man underneath it. Had she never fully realized how tall and broad he was? She couldn't see anything beyond the expanse of his shoulders. And he was as immovable as the brick wall at her back. But her ebbing panic still wouldn't let her settle against him. "I don't want him to get away. He has a bomb. He'll hurt someone. He'll come back. We have to go after him."

"That's my job. Your safety is my priority." He framed her jaw between his hands, tilting her face up to study her expression, stopping any chance of her putting herself in danger. "Are you okay?"

She calmed herself in the warmth and clarity of Burke's whiskey-brown eyes before nodding. "Cleo spotted him. I was walking her around the garage. He had a dead cat he put by the gate. Like bait to lure us to him. Then I saw the package, and the dog started barking and suddenly he was…" Her arm tightened around Cleo as she remembered the devilish mask and sightless eyes. Then she felt the stroke of Burke's thumb across her lips and came back to the present. Back to a warm body and fiercely protective expression. Back to the man who felt like her future.

If she could survive the present.

Hazel eased her grip on the front on his uniform, letting her hand settle over his heart. "He was right there. As close as you and I are now, with only that grating between us. Cleo was having a fit. I backed away and tried to keep him talking, to get him to stay after I texted you."

Burke rubbed Cleo's head. "Good girl. You were protecting your mama."

Feeling his praise of her feisty little schnauzer like a comforting caress to her own frayed nerves, she turned her head toward the curled-up paper on the other side of the gate. "There's another letter."

"Did you read it?"

Hazel nodded. "I didn't want to. But I thought it would keep him here until help arrived. It's like the others—creepy and obsessive. Only… I don't think it's about love. Having him here made it feel like this is all about revenge."

"Revenge for what?"

Hazel shrugged and shook her head. "This isn't some unrequited crush like I thought it was at first. He's... angry at me. I don't know why. He wants to punish me."

Burke started to pull her into his arms, but, with a dog between them and a second and third black-and-white pulling up behind his truck, he ended up sliding his palm to the back of her neck and briefly massaging the sensitive skin at her nape instead. As he stepped back, she noticed the flashing lights of a fourth KCPD car blocking the intersection at the end of the street. Another vehicle was pulling into place at the opposite end of the block to stop traffic, while a SWAT van pulled into the parking lot across the street.

"You rallied the troops."

"We take bomb threats very seriously." He feathered his fingertips through the fringe of hair at her nape, sending a trickle of much-needed warmth through her. "I take protecting *you* very seriously."

She reached up to wind her fingers around the damp sleeve clinging to his sturdy forearm, thanking him. "I know. And I know you want to be more than just a protection detail. Part of me wants that, too. But I need you to understand the kind of baggage I come with if we pursue this relationship."

His eyes darkened with interest. "That's a conversation I want to have. But I need to be a cop right now. Later. Okay?"

"Okay."

"Sergeant Burke?" Two uniformed officers, wearing plastic ponchos and KCPD ball caps, appeared at his shoulder.

Burke blinked and the heat in his eyes had vanished. The veteran police sergeant had replaced the man she loved. He slipped his hand to the more neutral position of her shoulder and turned to the two young men. "The perp ran toward Broadway a few minutes ago. Black hoodie. Dark jeans. Halloween mask. See if you can get eyes on him but keep your distance. Chances are he's carrying a bomb."

"Yes, sir." The officers ran down the block, splitting up to cover both sides of the street.

She recognized the next cop, Justin Grant, who moved in beside Burke. His green eyes swept over her face. "Dr. Coop okay?"

Burke pushed her toward the lanky blond man before releasing his grip on her. "She stays with you. She doesn't leave your sight." He glanced down at her before giving orders to Justin. "Give your statement to Bellamy and Cartwright when they get here. Take her upstairs. I'll radio if I find anything."

Burke hesitated for a moment, tension radiating off his body, seeming uncharacteristically unsure of his next move. His reluctance to leave her to pursue the suspect reminded Hazel of the independent strength that had sustained her for more than sixteen years. She loved him for his concern but understood that the best way for him to catch her stalker and would-be bomber who could harm so many more people was to assure him she could draw on that strength and be okay without him.

She reached around Cleo to splay her hand at the center of his chest. "Go. Do your job. Gunny will have your back." She curled her fingers into the front of his jacket and stretched up to press a quick kiss to his mouth. Then she pulled away and looked up at Burke's friend. "Justin will have mine."

With his dark gaze never leaving hers, he nodded. Then he hunched his shoulders against the rain and jogged to his truck.

She heard Gunny whining with excitement as Burke grabbed the big dog's leash from the front. When he opened the back door, the Czech shepherd was dancing at the edge of his cage.

"You keep an eye on him, Gunny!" she called out.

"Come on, boy." Burke hooked up his partner and the shepherd jumped down beside him. "You got one more job in you today?" Gunny looked up at him, his tail wagging in anticipation, waiting for the command to go to work. "Gunny, *Fuss!*"

They moved off at a quick pace, following the devil man and the other two officers down the street.

Hazel watched the rainy night swallow up man and dog, trotting off to do battle with a bomb and the monster who wanted her dead.

Chapter 10

Hazel startled when she felt Justin's hand at her elbow. "The old man said to get you inside, and I do what the boss says."

"He'll be all right, won't he?" Hazel punched in the code to unlock the door to the pedestrian entrance to the parking garage. "I want him to be focused on his own safety, not me."

"This neighborhood is swarming with cops right now," Justin promised. "He's not alone in some kind of *High Noon* face-off against this guy."

"But it's so dark out there. The streetlights won't do anyone much good until the rain lets up. I didn't see him until he was practically on top of me." A fist squeezed around her heart at all the worst-case scenarios that suddenly filled her head. "A bomb and...that man... can do a lot of damage."

Justin followed her inside, locking the door behind him. "It sounds odd, but the best eyes out there are Gunny's nose. He'll smell a threat long before Burke or anyone else sees it."

"All those men and women who showed up—they aren't in Burke's chain of command, are they?" Hazel asked. "I know you're not."

Justin's grin took the edge off her concern. "I don't know anyone on the force who doesn't move when Sergeant Burke says jump. And we've been doing a lot of jumping lately."

"Because of me?"

"It's not like we don't all owe him for one favor or another. He and his dogs have saved more of our hides than we can count." Justin took off his cap and smacked it against his thigh to remove the excess water before slipping it back over his blond hair. "Besides, it's about time he found something to care about besides work and dog training. It put an end to those awkward conversations with my wife, asking me to introduce him to one of her friends because she's worried about him turning into a lonely old man. I keep telling her he's one of that rare breed of man who'd rather be alone than with the wrong woman." He winked. "I'd bet money that you're the right one."

The right one. Burke would rather be alone than with someone besides her. Something warmed deep inside Hazel, even as she shivered at the pressure that pronouncement put on her vow to remain single and protect herself from getting hurt again. Did everyone in Kansas City except for her know how long Burke had had feelings for her?

"I'm not sure I'm the best choice for him."

"He's decided what he needs. He doesn't do dumb or boring, and he doesn't do disloyal." Justin pulled a plastic evidence bag from a pocket in his jacket. "I'm sure you know how hard it is for him to trust after the hell his ex-wife put him through."

Hazel bristled at the mention of his ex. She admitted there was a tad of jealousy behind her tense reaction. Shannon Bennett had once owned Jedediah's heart. She'd been in his bed and had most likely been shielded from the nightmares the world threw at her by Burke's broad shoulders and protective instincts. He'd probably made her laugh and had shared intimate conversations and given her knee-melting kisses—all those things she could no longer deny that she wanted for herself. But mostly, she couldn't fathom how anyone would willingly hurt the good man she cared for so much.

"I know she cheated on him."

Justin snorted through his nose. "Wasn't just once. Every time he deployed, she made a new friend." Hazel's heart squeezed with anger, but Justin continued as though he was discussing the inclement weather. He knelt beside the curled letter and envelope. "A man likes to be needed, but it's also nice to know your woman can handle it if you're not there 24-7. It's probably why he likes his dogs so much. They're loyal down to the bone."

Was that how Burke saw her? As an independent woman who was also a loyal friend? With all the problems she'd had in her marriage, at least infidelity hadn't been an issue she'd gone through with Aaron. And even after everything had crashed and burned, she'd never considered being unfaithful to her vows. Of course, she hadn't been willing to trust any man enough to seek out a new relationship. Not until Jedediah Burke had walked into her vet clinic. She understood that she was the woman Burke wanted. But could she truly be the woman he needed? Did she have it in her to give him the kind of love and mutual trust that he deserved?

Thankfully, Justin switched his focus from her relationship with Burke back to the investigation. When the bomb squad officer pulled out a multiuse tool and opened a tweezers attachment to pick up the letter, Hazel pointed out that the man in the Halloween mask had worn gloves. "You won't get any prints from those."

"We'll let the lab be the judge of that." He slipped the letter and envelope into a bag and sealed it. "I want them to check for explosives residue. That can be as much of a signature in tracking down this guy as any prints." Once he towered over her again, he walked her to the elevator and pushed the call button. "Let's go."

On the way up the elevator, Justin jotted the date and location on the evidence bag. He read the message on the letter and muttered an expletive. "This guy's a piece of work. No wonder Burke has been working overtime to get a lead on him. Can you tell me anything about the package?"

Hazel absentmindedly scratched Cleo between her ears. Exhaustion was quickly claiming her now that the adrenaline spike of her stalker's visit was wearing off.

"I never saw inside it. It was shaped like a long shoe-box. Wrapped in brown paper. Addressed to me. He took it with him."

When they reached the fourth floor, Hazel set Cleo down and unlocked the door to her condo.

"Hold up." After flipping the dead bolt, Justin asked her to wait beside the door. Just as Burke had for the past two nights, the younger officer moved through each room of her apartment, checking under beds and in closets, securing every window and the fire escape exit before coming back to her at the front door. "Everything looks good. You can relax."

Right. Relax. That was still a work in progress. She was keenly aware of the difference between fatigue and feeling relaxed.

But out loud, she thanked Justin for his presence. "Thanks." She unhooked Cleo's leash, and the dog trotted into the kitchen to lap up a big drink of water. Hazel kicked off her shoes on the mat beside the door and peeled off her wet jacket before following the dog to the kitchen. She rinsed out the coffeepot and started a fresh brew before she heard Justin pulling out one of the stools behind her.

"Burke said you got pictures of the perp and the package." His tone was friendly enough, but also like Burke, he was all business when it came to the investigation. "Show me."

Hazel pulled her phone from the pocket of her jeans and set it on the island counter for him to look through. "You can't tell anything just by looking at the picture, can you?"

"You'd be surprised. The key to finding an unknown bomber is to identify his signature—the way he builds his device, the components he chooses." Justin scrolled through the pictures. "For example, how did he pick up the package when he left? Did he move slowly? Make a point of keeping it parallel to the ground?"

Hazel hugged her arms around her sticky T-shirt and realized she was soaked to the skin. That didn't help the chill she was feeling. She looked beyond Justin to the bank of windows and wondered how wet Burke and Gunny were. If they were cold. Tired. If they were facing down the devil-faced man. She'd hear an explosion, either accidentally or intentionally detonated, at this distance, even with the storm muffling the city noises outside, wouldn't she?

"He'll be okay. Gunny won't let anybody hurt him," Justin said. She dragged her focus back to him as he set his cap on the counter and continued as if she hadn't just gone to a very dark place in her head. "Now, tell me about the package itself."

"You're trying to distract me, so I don't worry about Jedediah."

He arched a golden eyebrow. "Is it working?"

"No. Still worried." She summoned a half smile to match his. "But I can multitask." The chocolatey, earthy scent of coffee filled the kitchen as she pulled down two mugs and poured them each a cup. "The man grabbed the box by one end and tucked it under his arm like a football." She replayed the memory of the man's blank eyeholes and labored breathing as he disappeared into the rain. "He ran. As fast as his huffing and puffing would let him."

Justin turned down her offer of cream and sugar and took a drink, barely giving the coffee time to cool. "Then it's not motion activated like most pipe bombs are. More likely, he set it to detonate with a cell phone where he can call in and set it off exactly when he wants. Thrill bombers often use that setup—they want to witness the destruction they cause, but from a safe distance."

A shiver crawled across Hazel's skin at the gruesome image that created. "Like an addict? Only his drug of choice is blowing things up?"

"Exactly."

She remembered the stroke of his thumb over the electronic device in her stalker's gloved hand. "Wait a minute." She picked up her phone and scrolled through the pictures before pointing one blurry image out to Justin. "It's not a great picture, but he held a device in his hand. He kept saying he was turning it on and off. I kept thinking he was going to detonate the bomb then and there."

"A kill switch."

Hazel shivered. "That sounds ominous."

"He was arming and disarming the weapon. That tells me a lot." Justin set her cell aside to text some notes into his own phone. "He might have been using a timer. Stopping the countdown to continue the conversation—or forcing you to do what he wanted." He'd wanted her to read the letter. He'd wanted her to know that he was in complete control of whether she lived or died. Hazel sank onto the stool beside Justin as he talked through his thoughts out loud. "Although starting and stopping the countdown like that would be like playing Russian roulette. A faulty disconnect or losing track of the countdown would put him right there if the bomb went off. He might have some kind of suicide scenario going on in his head—like the two of you ending together. He probably wouldn't want an audience of police officers, though, if that was the case. It would depersonalize the event too much for him. Unless it wasn't a bomb at all." He glanced down over his shoulder at her. "But another fake meant to terrorize you."

Thrill bombers? Kill switches? Suicide scenarios? This winking, easygoing man had a disturbing knowledge of explosive devices and all the ways her stalker could kill her. Not to mention the knowledge to disarm the devices himself. "Your wife must be a very brave woman, considering all the risks you take."

He nodded. "The bravest. Did you know that Emilia helped me with an undercover op when we first started dating? Of course, I accidentally forced her into it."

"Accidentally?"

His cheeks turned slightly pink. With regret? Embarrassment? A remembered heat? "My mission had gone sideways. I needed her to bail me out. She was brilliant."

While Justin told her the story of how he and his doctor wife had met in an emergency room, and a kiss to keep her from exposing his cover had led to taking down a serial bomber and eventually to marriage and starting a family, Hazel heated up soup and made sandwiches for Justin, Burke and herself. Then she changed into dry clothes and set out coffee mugs and towels for the officers who were coming up to interview her. She made a quick call to each of her daughters. Polly told her about Garrett Cho, the police officer who'd been assigned to watch their apartment. Ashley was still on her date with Joe Sciarra, who got on the phone himself to assure her that he'd keep an eye on Ash and would take her home ASAP. And though she didn't doubt that the muscular bouncer could defend himself and her older daughter, it was hard for Hazel to let either of her girls out of her sight—even knowing they were both grown, responsible young women.

Almost an hour passed before Hazel heard a knock on her door and sloshed her tepid coffee over the rim of her mug. Unlike the two detectives she'd buzzed in earlier, she'd given Burke the pass code to get into her building, so she knew he could come straight up to her condo. But still, she jumped at the unexpected sound. Justin was on his feet, his hand on the butt of his gun at his waist, crossing to the door, before Burke announced himself. "It's me, Haze. Tell Justin to let me in."

By the time Justin unlocked the door, Hazel had grabbed a clean towel and was crossing the room.

"Heads up on the muddy paw prints," Burke warned. "Gunny, *sitz*—"

"It's okay." Gunny zipped past her, leaving a trail across the hardwood floor and area rug in front of the couch as he greeted Cleo, and the two dogs sniffed and curled up together on the blanket she'd left out for the working dog. Hazel shook the towel loose and patted the moisture from Burke's face and neck. "Let him warm up and relax. Gunny's okay, right?"

"He's fine."

"And you?"

Burke carried his gear bag in one hand and held out a wilted paper sack in the other. His pants were caked with mud up to his knees and the scruff of his beard was dotted with droplets of water. "I'm afraid dinner's cold and wet. So am I."

Hazel didn't care. She tossed the towel across his shoulders and slid her arms around his waist, walking into his chest. While the dampness of his clothes seeped into hers, she aligned her body with his, tucked her head beneath his chin and squeezed him tight, saying nothing until she detected the warmth of his body and felt a deep sigh roll through his chest. She heard the double thunk of him dropping both bags and breathed her own sigh of relief when his strong arms folded around her.

"I'm drippin' on you, Doc." His voice was a husky growl against her ear.

"Just let me hold you for a minute."

"I've got no problem with that. But I'm fine, Haze." He stepped to one side, pulling her with him as Justin locked the door behind him. "Any issues here?" he asked the officer who'd been guarding her.

Justin shook his head. "The detectives took her statement. Dr. Coop let me rattle on about Emilia, the kids and me."

"You're good at talking," Burke teased. "I'm surprised you didn't put her to sleep with the way you go on sometimes."

"Would you be serious?" Hazel swatted his backside beneath his gun belt before hugging him at his waist again. "Most people run away from a bomb. You and Gunny ran right toward it. Justin was trying to keep me from freaking out."

"Freak out? Cool-in-a-Crisis Cooper?" His arms tightened around her. "Never gonna happen."

The nylon of his jacket was cold against her cheek. But where her forehead rested against the skin of his neck, she felt the strong, warm beat of his pulse. He was joking with his friend. Teasing her. All normal stuff. He was in one piece. He was okay. She was okay, too, now that she could see and feel his strength and steady demeanor for herself. As the tension that had been building inside her eased to a level much more manageable than freak-out mode, the need to be practical and stay busy seeped back in. Hazel stepped back and removed Burke's soggy cap, hanging it on the coat rack beside the door before pulling open the snaps of his jacket and pushing it off his shoulders. "He got away, didn't he?"

He waited for her to hang up his jacket before answering. "He must have had a vehicle waiting and drove off before we set up the blockade. Gunny lost his scent." Burke held himself still and let her tend him, as though he sensed how badly she needed to do something to help stop the man stalking her, even if all she could do was keep the officers working the case warm and dry. She unzipped Burke's vest and discovered the clothes underneath were just as wet. But when she unhooked his belt and lifted its heavy weight, he took it from her hands and set it on his bag beside him. Then he untucked his uniform shirt and T-shirt and took over the drying job. "Did you call the girls? Are they okay?"

Restless with nothing to do but wonder at the truth and worry, Hazel retrieved a stool from the kitchen so that Burke could sit and take off his boots. "Polly's at home. There's an Officer Cho outside her building."

"Cho's a good man." Burke tousled his brown-and-gray hair into short spikes with the towel. "The boyfriend's not there with them, is he?"

Alarm surged anew through her, and she plunked the stool down with a bang. "No. Joe and Ashley aren't home yet. Why? Did you find out something about him? Joe talked like a bodyguard—like you do sometimes. He promised to watch over her and take her home. She'll call as soon as she's there. Do you have a bad vibe about him?"

His brown eyes locked on to hers. "I've got a bad vibe about anybody I haven't personally vetted who comes in contact with the Cooper women."

Dialing her panic back a notch at his stern assertion, she knelt to untie his boots. "So nothing specific. That's good."

"Maybe not," Burke admitted. "The only Joseph Sciarra I found in the system was sixty years old. No way was the guy on that motorcycle with Ashley sixty. I was expanding my name search when you sent me that first text."

"Could Joe be a nickname?" Hazel asked, hating the idea of a man lying to her daughter more than she hated the stiff, muddy laces of Burke's boots soiling her hands.

"It's a possibility. It could also be something as innocent as him using an alias for his bouncer job. That way, unhappy customers can't track him down after hours if he had to toss them out or call the cops on them." Burke hung his vest on the hook beside his jacket. "I plan to have a conversation with him tomorrow."

"Do I need to call Ashley again?"

"And tell her what?" He pried off his boot and set it on the drip mat beside the door. "Joe can't be the man who was here talking to you because he's been with her all evening. Right?"

Of course. That made logical sense. Her stalker couldn't be in two places at the same time—and she *had* talked to Joe on Ashley's phone. Hazel nodded. She pressed her lips into a wry smile. "I'm the mom here. I shouldn't scare her more than I already have. I guess it's hard for me to trust any man right now."

His fingers cupped beneath her chin to tilt her face up to his. "Any man?"

She rolled her eyes toward the living room, where Justin was reporting the information he and Burke had gathered to another member of his team. She squeezed her fingers around Burke's wrist and smiled. "With a few notable exceptions."

"Glad I made the short list." He stroked his thumb across her lips in that ticklish caress that made things inside her curl with anticipation before releasing her. "If we don't hear from Ashley in an hour or so, telling us she's safely home with Polly and Garrett Cho, we'll call her then."

"Deal." She moved on to the next muddy boot. "What about you? The devil man didn't threaten you, did he?"

"The devil man?"

"The Halloween mask he wore. I saw it up close tonight."

"Like he needs a nickname. No. I never got eyes on him. Just that damn picture you sent me." He pulled her to her feet in front of him. His hands settled at her waist, his fingers kneading an unspoken message into the skin beneath the sweatshirt she wore. "Are you sure you're not hurt or in shock? What did he say to spook you like this?"

The man's words hadn't been as cutting as his laughter. She'd rebelled against his threats and cryptic pronouncements. But his laughter had crippled her like the blows she'd suffered the night Aaron's friend had tried to silence her. If she hadn't been a veterinarian… if she hadn't had her bag and the syringe and the tranquilizer with her…

Her attacker that night had laughed, too. Right up until he felt the needle she'd jabbed into his thigh.

The next day, when she left the hospital, she'd gone straight to the DA's office and told him she was ready to testify against her husband. She'd seen her attorney about divorce proceedings by the end of the same day.

"Haze?" Burke's callused fingers brushed the bangs across her forehead before settling beneath her chin and tilting her face up to his. "You're scaring me a little bit. Tell me what happened."

"Nothing new." She glanced over her shoulder at Justin and used his presence as an excuse to keep her humiliating secrets a little while longer. Mustering a weak smile, she slipped from his grasp. "Exhausted beyond belief, but I'm not hurt." His eyes narrowed with a question she felt too raw to answer. Instead, she smoothed his wild hair into some semblance of order and carried the wet towel to the pile beside the laundry closet off the kitchen. "The coffee's hot. Want a cup?" Not waiting for an answer, she poured him a mug. From the kitchen she heard the thud of the second boot hit the mat. "At least he took the bomb with him, right? If that's what it was."

The next thing she heard was the deep rumble of his voice beside her. "The makings of one, anyway. Gunny hit on the spot by the gate." He took the mug from her trembling hands, tested the temperature and took a long swallow of the strong black brew.

Justin strolled into the kitchen, reminding her they weren't alone. "That confirms there were explosives. I've got Dr. Coop's statement, some decent pics and a pretty good idea of the type of bomb this guy builds. I'll file the report. You good here?"

With a nod, Burke set down the coffee and walked his friend to the door. "I got this. Thanks, Justin."

The two men shook hands. "You need anything, call. Cartwright and Bellamy said they'd post a unit outside once they're done canvasing the neighborhood and taking witness statements. They've explained what to look for to the man watching your daughters' apartment, too. Dark hoodie. Halloween mask. Brown paper packages—and not the good kind."

"I owe you one." Burke opened the door.

"You owe me nothing, old man. You and that mutt have kept my team alive more than once. It's about time you let me return the favor." Justin pulled his KCPD cap over his head and tipped the brim to Hazel. "Dr. Coop."

"Thank you for everything."

The younger man winked and strode into the hallway. Burke set the dead bolt behind him and turned to face Hazel across the main room. "I need a hot shower, and Gunny needs food and rest."

In other words, he needed her to take care of herself for a few minutes. He needed her to be more than his ex-wife had ever been for him.

She summoned the dregs of her depleted strength and went to work. "I'll fix you a plate of food and take care of Gunny while you change. If you leave your clothes in the laundry basket, I can run them through the wash, too."

Instead of nodding or speaking, or any other response she might have expected, Burke strode into the kitchen, clasped her face between his hands and lowered his mouth to hers. With nothing more than his fingers in her hair and his lips moving over hers, he kissed her very, very thoroughly. Desire sparked inside her, leaping to meet his claim. Hazel rose up onto her toes, pushing her mouth into his kiss. Her lips parted, welcoming him. Her tongue darted out to meet his, and she tasted coffee and a frantic need that matched her own. She clutched at the front of his shirt, then crawled her fingers up into the damp spikes of his hair. Her hips hit the countertop as Burke's muscular thighs crowded against hers. His kiss permeated her body with a transfusion of heat. The faint desperation and sure claim of his mouth jolted through her heart. Her frayed emotions healed beneath the sweep of his tongue and the press of his body and the needy grasp of his hands.

This was what she needed. The touch of this good man. This celebration of life. Jedediah Burke erased the loneliness from her life. He shared her burdens and made her pulse race and her heart smile. He made her feel as though the emotional isolation that had protected her for so long was a mistake—that she could live more fully, love more completely in a way she hadn't allowed herself to for too many years.

But almost as resolutely as the kiss had begun, Burke pulled away with a ragged sigh. He rested his lips against her forehead for a moment, and she felt the heat of their kiss dissipating into the cool skin there.

"I needed to do that earlier," he confessed. "I was so damn scared that he was going to hurt you." He leaned back, brushing aside her bangs with his fingertips to study her expression. His chest heaved in a deep breath that showed far more control than the mewling gasps she could currently muster. "You sure you're okay?"

Where had the man learned to kiss like that? And now that she'd tasted the depths of Burke's passion, she was becoming addicted to every touch they shared. She felt weak yet energized, totally confused and absolutely right. "Is it too sappy to say I'm better now?"

He gave a slight laugh. "Then count me on the sappy side, too." But his handsome, weary expression was dead serious. "You've been acting a little weird since I got here. Did Justin say something that upset you? The detectives?"

Hazel fiddled with collar of his damp T-shirt before meeting his gaze. "I'm keeping it together for now, okay? Let's just leave it at that."

"Doc, you know you can tell me anything. About the case, that emotional baggage you mentioned earlier—anything."

"I know. I will," she promised. "But first things first." She turned him and nudged him down the hallway. "Go. Before you catch a cold. Or else I'll be worried about you all over again. And the only meds I have on hand are for canines."

When he hesitated at the bathroom doorway, she gave him another gentle push. But this time he didn't budge. "I'm not laughing, Haze. Are you sure you're okay?"

She shrugged, giving him an honest answer. "I just need a little time to myself to process…everything. My life is changing, and I need to make sure I'm making the right decisions."

"Fair enough," he answered, understanding that *he* was one of those decisions. He remembered his bag at the front door and retrieved it. "I usually take a quick shower. Do you need me to linger? Give you more time?"

She shook her head. "Take however long you need. I'll step in after I hear the water running to get your dirty clothes."

Five minutes later, with the shower running and Burke humming a sweetly tuneless song, Hazel's decision was made. She hadn't been whole before Burke strode into her life five years ago with his first K-9 partner. There was a reason she'd turned to him when she'd been afraid of those letters. A reason she worried about the dangers he faced on her behalf and to protect Kansas City. A reason she'd never considered giving her heart and her soul and her kisses to another man.

She loved Jedediah Burke, loved him with a fierce intensity that was as frightening as it was exciting.

She'd been surviving for a long, long time. But she hadn't been living. She couldn't preach to her daughters to embrace life and love hard and trust a good man if she wouldn't do the same for herself. Jedediah was her partner in every way that mattered.

Except one.

Chapter 11

Hazel tapped softly on the bathroom door and waited for Burke's invitation before pushing it open. A cloud of steamy, fragrant air filtered past as she entered the room to open the clothes hamper. As the steam rushed out of the enclosed space, she spotted Burke's bag in the corner beside the sink, his open Dopp kit sitting on the counter.

But with his damp clothes hugged to her chest, she froze, her gaze transfixed by the blurry outline of Burke's tall, muscular form through the mottled glass of the walk-in shower door. He'd stopped moving, too. He must have been rinsing his hair or easing the tightness of overworked muscles by letting the hot water sluice over his neck and shoulders. His body was arched forward, his strong arms braced against the tile wall, his head bowed into the pelting spray of water. Even though she couldn't make out a clear visual image, her brain was cataloging every detail. The sprinkles of silver in his dark brown hair. The breadth of his arms and shoulders. The graceful arch of his long back and curved buttocks. The spicy scents of soap and man, and the earthier scents of grit and sweat washing down the drain teased her nose. Something purely female clenched with a sensual awareness deep inside her. Something unexpectedly protective and faintly territorial squeezed at her heart, too.

She was a veterinarian doctor, for Pete's sake. She knew all about anatomy, both human and animal. She'd been married once a lifetime ago. But there was nothing clinical to her reaction to Burke showering in her home, nothing naive about this connection flowing like a strong current between them whenever they got close. This was how her life could be, how it should have been all along, if only she'd loved this man first.

The way she loved him now.

Burke shook his head, then shifted position behind the translucent glass, reaching for the washcloth he'd tossed over the top of the door. "Sorry about the mud. I'll clean up in here. You may have to wash those pants by themselves."

Hazel dropped the dirty clothes she held. She needed to do this. Now.

"My ex-husband… Aaron…" She inhaled a steadying breath of the tiny room's humid air to quell the terrifying memories that rose like bile in her throat.

"Sixteen years ago, Aaron paid a man to kill me. To stop me from testifying against him."

Burke's curse was pithy and succinct. Movement stopped behind the glass, although the sound of the water beating down on the tiles at his feet never ceased. "I know I promised we'd talk, but you couldn't have eased into that?"

This was already like ripping a bandage from raw skin. She'd started, and now the past was oozing out like the festering wound it was. Besides, it was easier to share the truth without Burke's dark eyes probing into hers, seeing more than anyone else ever had.

She needed to say this. She needed to say all of it. She needed Burke to know why she was such a hot mess in the relationship department. "He hired a friend of his—a man who worked for him on and off at the investment firm. Aaron used the money I'd stashed away in an account for the girls to pay him. Out in the country—I was on my way to an emergency call. A dog had been hit, left to die on the side of the road." She wanted to laugh at the prophetic analogy but had never been able to. "Maybe the dog was already dead. Maybe it never existed. Aaron took the call that night. The judge hadn't seized our house as an asset yet, so we were still living together. Separate rooms, but his lawyer said it helped Aaron's image for the press and jury to think we were still a couple, that he still had my support. He knew the DA had been talking to me."

"Aaron set you up." Burke's posture changed behind the glass, from weary like a man at the end of a long day to alert like the cop he was. He quickly rinsed off. "I want to hear all of it."

"I never saw the headlights until they were right on me. He rammed his car into mine. Rolled me into the ditch."

Burke shut off the water and reached for the towel outside the shower door.

"Because of my seat belt and air bags, I didn't die in the accident. But I was pretty shaken up, a little disoriented when I climbed out through the broken window. I knew Aaron's friend. I thought he was there to save me. That he'd stopped to help. I was so grateful. I was asking if he'd seen the dog who'd been hit. Then he smashed my head against the side of the car. He used his fists and his feet to try to finish the job."

Biting down on a string of curses, Burke stepped out of the shower, knotting the towel at his hips. "Hazel…"

When he reached for her, she took a step back, hugging her arms around her waist. He retreated to the bath mat, perhaps sensing how brittle she felt, how she'd shatter into a thousand pieces if anyone touched her right now. It was probably killing him to refrain from taking action, not to be able to fix this for her.

Instead, he raked his fingers through his wet hair. "I know there's more." His voice was tight, deep. "You're here now. Tell me how you survived."

She zeroed in on the oval pucker of his belly button, linked by a line of dark hair down to the knot on his towel. His stomach was flat, his skin beaded with moisture and flushed with a heat that radiated across the room; his muscles were taut beneath that skin. But what turned her on the most was that stellar control, that endless patience that made her feel she could share everything with him. He respected her need to fight her way through her past, to approach this relationship at the speed she needed to go. Caked with mud, dog hair and layers of protective uniform, or practically naked as the day he was born, Burke wasn't just the man she wanted—he was the man she needed.

She lifted her gaze to his whiskey-brown eyes and found them studying her just as intently as she'd expected. "Aaron's friend laughed at me. He sounded crazy. Drunk? High? I don't know. He joked about refunding the money. Said the job was too easy. He was putting me back in the car, buckling me in, telling me how he was going to set it on fire and blame my death on the accident. Once I was inside, I could reach my bag. I had a syringe with a tranquilizer already loaded. In case the dog didn't cooperate. I stabbed him with it. He passed out before I did. I called the police. I don't remember anything more until I woke up in the ambulance."

"That's the Hazel Cooper I know. You used your head and you fought back." He relaxed the fists that had clenched at his sides. "Is that when you decided to testify against your ex?"

"Murder for hire and attempted murder got Aaron a lot longer sentence than the fraud and embezzlement alone would have."

He took a step forward and she didn't bolt. "And the hit man he hired?"

"The tranquilizer I gave him must have reacted with

whatever was already in his system. The paramedics couldn't revive him."

Burke's fingers tiptoed across the top of the vanity and brushed against her elbow. Hazel didn't flinch. If anything, she shifted slightly to the left, moving her elbow into the cup of his hand. She'd just admitted that she'd killed a man—but she saw no recrimination in his eyes, felt no pity in his touch. "You weren't charged, were you?"

She shook her head. "Evidence at the scene and Aaron's money trail made it a clear case of self-defense. My testimony gave the DA the victory he wanted. It ultimately doubled Aaron's sentence."

Burke drifted a half step closer, feathering his fingertips into her bangs, brushing them off her forehead. "I've never met your ex, have I?"

Despite the gentleness of his caress, tension coiled beneath each syllable.

"I doubt it. I filed every restraining order in the book to keep him away from Ashley, Polly and me." She shrugged. "He calls me sometimes." The soothing caresses stopped. Hazel reached up to capture Burke's hand against her cheek. "I don't answer. The girls barely remember him. Polly probably wouldn't even recognize him. She was so young when he went away."

He simply nodded as if some sort of truce had been reached. "Do you think your ex is behind this terror campaign?"

"I don't know. It could be Aaron, wanting to punish me for my *betrayal*. It could be someone else he hired."

"I'll follow up on his whereabouts since his release

from prison." He stroked his thumb across her lips before pulling away. "What do you need from me right now?"

There was nowhere to retreat in the small room. And Hazel didn't want him to. "I just needed you to listen. I need you to understand why I've put you off for so many years and insisted that friendship was enough."

Lines deepened beside his eyes as he paused. "You want us to go back to being just friends?"

"No." She touched her fingertips to the worry grooves on his rugged face and willed them to relax. "I think you and I are destined to be something more. But I want you to understand that because of everything I went through, I've had a really hard time trusting men over the years. I gave my heart to a man who thought killing me was a better choice than admitting his guilt and giving us a chance to repair our fractured marriage. I trusted that we could at least have an amicable divorce and still both have a hand in raising our girls. How smart does that make me about relationships?"

She was the one drifting closer now, wanting to reassure him. She ran her fingers over the ticklish scruff of his beard, then drew them down his neck and across the jut of his shoulder.

"I know you're nothing like Aaron. But the doubts about myself have always been there. I never dealt with them because, frankly, I had a life I had to live. Children to raise, a practice to build. It's always been easier to bury my emotions than to deal with them. But you make me think about what I feel, what I want and need. I'm afraid of losing everything again. I want to be braver than I am. For you. For us. But—"

He caught her hand and raised it to his lips, pressing a warm kiss against her knuckles. "You are the bravest woman I know. You defended yourself against a man who wanted you dead. You kept your head in the face of danger. You lived your life in the way you needed to, so that you wouldn't be hurt again. And look at all the animals, all the people you've helped along the way. You have the right the live the way you need to, to choose who you want to have be a part of your life, to live—"

"I choose *you*." She took Burke's hands and placed them on either side of her waist. His fingers kneaded her skin beneath her sweatshirt but stayed resolutely where she'd put them. His nostrils flared with a ragged breath. Hazel felt the same warring need to skip the necessary words and get on with the physical connection they both craved as she braced her hands against his chest. "I want you to be a part of my life. But I'm scared I won't be any good at *us*, and I never want to hurt you."

Her thumb might have hooked around the turgid male nipple she discovered beneath the crisp curls of chest hair. His pectoral muscle might have jerked in a helpless response. But he fought for restraint until she'd said everything she wanted him to hear.

"Haze—"

"What if I can't make you happy? I know I try your patience. Why on earth would you want to be with a woman who runs hot and cold and smells like dog poop and antiseptic? Well, not all the time."

A low, guttural sound rumbled in his throat. "You

make me laugh. And I didn't do enough of that until I met you. I have more in common with you than anyone I've ever known. Except maybe Gunny."

It was her turn to laugh. "I didn't do enough of that until I met you, either."

"You have sexy hair and the sweetest mouth." His fingers dipped inside the waistband of her jeans. "And a sexy, round—"

"I've given birth to two babies." She wasn't out of shape for a woman her age, but she *was* a woman of a certain age. "I eat too many sweets, and I haven't been with a man in years. *Years*, Jedediah."

"And I'm on the stud-of-the-month calendar?"

"You should be." She framed his strong jaw between her hands and admired the contours of every well-earned line beside his eyes, the firm shape of his mouth and the angle of his nose. He wasn't perfectly handsome, but she couldn't describe him as anything other than perfectly masculine. "You'd get my vote."

He squeezed his eyes shut for several seconds before his dark lashes fluttered open and his eyes looked their fill of her face, as she'd just studied his. "Do you know how badly I want to be with you?"

Hazel nodded. Years and doubts slipped away beneath the heat in his eyes. "I *want* to be with you. Help me heal. Please."

He lost the battle a split second before she did. His hands clamped around her bottom, snapping her to him, but Hazel was already sliding her arms around his neck. She palmed the back of his prickly wet hair and tilted his mouth down to hers. Their lips clashed

like waves against a rocky shore. Tongues danced together, retreated like the ebbing tide, rushed in again.
Hazel poured her heart into every tug, every taste. She
clutched at his scalp, dug her fingers into the supple
muscles of his back.

Just like that wild ocean current, the pain rushed out
as desire swept in. Her nipples tightened and her breasts
grew heavy with the friction of Burke's chest moving
against hers. His hands slipped beneath her shirt, each
sure stroke across her skin stirring the storm building
inside her. He broke the kiss only long enough to whisk
the shirt off over her head. And then his lips were back,
grazing the tender skin along her neck, arousing eager
nerve endings with the ticklish scratch of his beard,
soothing them with the warm rasp of his tongue.

Her jeans felt rough between her legs as the pressure
built inside her. She was keenly aware of the front of
his towel tenting between them. *Too many clothes. Not
enough skin.* Had she ever felt this hot? This demanding
of a lover? This powerful? As Burke's mouth blazed a
trail over the swell of her breast, she skimmed her hands
down the length of his spine to reach the barrier of the
damp towel at his hips. She inhaled the spicy scent of
his warm skin before she nipped at the column of his
neck, eliciting a growl from his throat. "Please tell me
I haven't scared you off."

"Nope." His mouth closed, hot and wet, over the
proud tip of her breast, pulling it into his mouth through
the lace of her bra. Hazel gasped at the arrow of heat
that shot straight to the needy heart of her. "All I heard

was that you choose me. You want me. Do you have any idea how long I've been waiting to hear that?"

"About as long as I've wanted to say it?"

"I feel closer to you now than I ever have." He moved his attentions to the other breast, and she twisted against him, wanting even more. "Trust is a precious gift. And yours is hard to earn. Knowing I have it—for this—for everything—makes me want you even more."

"Jedediah…"

"Yes?"

Her hand fisted in the towel. "Too many clothes." She tugged.

He sought her mouth with his own and they laughed together as the towel landed at his feet, baring that fine, tight rump to the squeeze of her hands.

As smoothly as she'd rid him of a simple towel, he unsnapped her jeans and pushed them and her panties down over her hips. The bra went next and then he caught her behind the knee to pull her to him, rocking against her core, driving all kinds of delicious pressure into the most sensitive of places inside her. The hard length of him pressing against her told her he was just as ready as she.

"Protection?" he growled against her skin.

Hazel gasped out a curse. "I haven't been on the pill in years. Of course, I haven't needed to be. I don't know if the girls left—"

He silenced the moment of panic with a hard kiss. "Not a problem. Pants?"

"By the hamper. I haven't had a chance—"

He turned her and swatted her bottom. "I'll meet you in the bedroom."

He retrieved a condom from his wallet and joined her before she could finish pulling back the covers. Once he had sheathed himself, he lifted her onto the bed and followed her down, sliding his hips between her thighs and pushing inside her. Her body forgot how out of practice she was. She was tight for a few moments, but he held himself still until she relaxed and stretched to accommodate him. Then she was the one who reached between them and urged him to complete her. She felt more female, more alive than she had in years. She wanted this. She wanted him. Beneath Burke's hands, she felt beautiful, sexy. He coaxed her body to a peak and she crashed over, holding him in her arms and deep inside her as he crested the same wave and found his release. His guttural moan of satisfaction was as heady as any sweet nothing he could have whispered in her ear.

Sometime later, after Burke had brought her a damp washcloth and closed the door to keep the dogs from joining them, Hazel sank back onto her pillow and exhaled a deeply contented sigh. They were lying on their backs, side by side, their naked bodies still cooling from the intense lovemaking they'd shared.

Burke reached for her hand between them. "You okay?"

She laced her fingers together with his. "I'd like to say it's like riding a bicycle. But…it was never like that before. I can't feel my bones. I feel glorious." She turned her head to see him on the pillow beside hers and felt a tug of something precious and fragile in her heart. "You?"

He rolled onto his side, facing her. "You were worth the wait."

Could there be any more doubt that she loved this man? That she needed him? He was good for her ego. Good for her body. Good for her, period.

But what exactly was he getting out of this relationship besides some seriously hot benefits and...vet care for his K-9 team?

"Jedediah..."

"Dr. Cooper." When he leaned in to kiss her again, his stomach growled, saving her from asking the question she needed to. Maybe those seriously hot benefits were enough for him right now.

Laughing against his kiss, she patted his stomach. His muscles jumped beneath the simple touch, and she quickly pulled her hand away from the temptation to repeat what they'd just shared. "We'd better take care of a few other priorities."

Seizing the opportunity to end the encounter on a positive note instead of dragging the mood down with her worries again, she scrambled off the bed and opened the closet door to pull out the T-shirt and pajama pants hanging on a hook there. "We forgot dinner. We should eat before we fall asleep from exhaustion."

Avoiding the questioning look on his face, Hazel quickly dressed, adding a pair of socks and a hoodie. Burke followed more slowly, swinging his legs off his side of the bed and watching her for several seconds before striding across the hall to the bathroom. "I'll take the dogs out one more time while you heat up some food."

Nearly two hours later, Hazel was lying on the bed, curled into a ball, trying to stay warm. Even her socks and hoodie and an afghan snugged around her couldn't chase away the thoughts that chilled her whole body. She heard Burke in the doorway behind her, identifying him by the soft rustle of his jeans and that spicy clean scent that was his alone.

She wasn't sure how long he hovered there, maybe just checking on her, or maybe trying to decide if he'd be welcome to rejoin her. She'd willingly taken their relationship far beyond the friendship level this evening—it wouldn't be fair to backtrack from that closeness. Not to Burke. Not to either of them.

"I'm not asleep." Rolling over, she found him leaning against the door frame, cradling a mug of the decaf coffee she'd brewed earlier. "You don't have to watch over me 24-7."

He shook his head and came into the room. "Doesn't seem to be a habit I can break." The mattress shifted as he sat on the edge of the bed beside her. "You okay?" He set the mug on the bedside table and straightened the afghan around her. "After baring your soul—and a few other things—to me, you should be exhausted. You barely touched your dinner. And no ice cream, so I know something's wrong."

Ignoring his efforts to tuck her in, Hazel sat up to face him, hugging her knees to her chest. "Besides a stalker I can't identify who wants to blow me up?"

He didn't grin at her teasing. "Yeah. Besides that. You don't regret what happened between us, do you?"

"Other than feeling like I took advantage of your kindness?"

"Kindness?" Now he snickered a single laugh. He rested one hand on top of her knee. "I've been dreaming about making love to you for a couple of years now."

"But you kept your distance because I wanted you to."

"And then you didn't want me to. I don't think I could ever get my fill of you, Doc. But I do wonder about the timing. You've been under a lot of stress. And everything you told me—that was a major catharsis for you."

She couldn't argue that. "I needed to feel like me again for a little while. Like life is normal and people can want each other in a healthy way."

"I gather that's the healing part you wanted. But now you've had time to think." He smoothed her bangs across her forehead. "What's going on inside that head of yours? Help me understand."

Hazel captured his hand and clasped it between both of hers. It was strong and a little rough around the edges, but infinitely tender, just like the man himself. "Tonight…the devil man… He laughed at me, Jedediah. I was trying to keep him on the defensive, goad him into staying until KCPD got here. But I let it slip how scared I was, and that made him laugh. He said he'd take it as down payment on what I owe him."

His fingers flinched within her grasp, the only outward sign of his protective temper. "Like the jerk your ex hired. You said he laughed. Joked about the money.

I'll need his name, too, by the way. In case he has a surviving relative or friend who might be interested in payback."

She nodded. "He's enjoying this. He's getting off on toying with me."

"He wants to get under your skin."

"He's succeeding." Hazel pulled her hands away to hug her knees again. "I've been completely honest with you—told you some things even my daughters have never heard. I know you need me to be strong. And I'd like to think that I am. But this relentless campaign— all the memories it has dredged up—it's wearing me down. It makes me question everything I say or think or do. The last time I was afraid for my life…"

Burke gathered her in his arms, afghan and all, and pulled her onto his lap. "The last time, you didn't have me. I've got your back."

For once, she was glad his patience had run out, and Hazel snuggled in, tucking her head beneath his chin. "Like Gunny will always have yours."

He nodded. "Trust your strength, Haze. Trust mine."

She did. But if there truly was going to be a future for them, she needed to know if she could hold up her end of the bargain, and be what he needed, too. "Can you trust me just as much? I know your ex-wife… You couldn't trust her."

"No. I couldn't," he said, falling back across the bed and pulling her on top of him, keeping her close. "You're a different class of lady. She never would have been so honest with me as you've been tonight. She never trusted that I could be there for her. If she wanted comfort, entertainment, a sounding board to dump on, she'd go find it. She still does. Hell. She'll call me if her current husband can't make things right for her."

"Not everyone is cut out to be the spouse of a man or woman in uniform."

"True. Shannon was sweet and perfect and everything I wanted in a high school sweetheart. But I became a soldier. And a cop. I saw the world—the good, the bad, the weird and the stuff I wish I could forget. I grew up. I don't know that she ever will." He shifted on the bed, angling them toward the pillows. "You're an adult, Haze. An equal. You've faced more adversity than she ever had to. And you dealt with it without compromising your integrity. You found your own strength. You asked for my help, but you didn't expect to be rescued."

Hazel changed topics, suspecting he'd rather talk about something a little less personal, even though she sensed there was more to Burke's past, just as there had been more to hers. "What did Justin mean when he said you and Gunny had saved him and his team?"

He probably recognized the diversion for what it was, judging by the squeeze of her hand between them. "Usually, a K-9 unit is deployed along with the bomb squad when there's a call. We clear the building, make sure there are no secondary explosives planted in the area."

"Have you ever found secondary explosives?"

"Yes."

His simple answer probably downplayed a good deal of the danger he and Gunny had faced helping their brothers in blue and protecting the city.

"You take care of a lot of people, don't you?" she observed. "I don't want to be another burden to—"

"Do not finish that sentence." A warm, callused finger pressed against her lips. "I'm here by choice, not because it's my job. Not because of the crazy good sex we had."

"Will you stay with me?" she asked.

"I thought that was the plan." He pointed to the doorway. "I'll be right out there. Gunny's already sacked out."

"No. Will you stay *here*?" She patted the bed beside her. "To sleep. Is that asking too much of you and your patience?"

He rolled onto his side, pulling her into his chest. "Me holding you? I think I can manage."

"You smell good," she murmured on a drowsy sigh against his soft cotton T-shirt. "Justin has no business calling you *old man*. You're a man, period. Warm. Solid. One hell of a kisser…among other talents. I love touching you. You feel good."

"Do I feel safe?"

She nodded.

He pressed a kiss to her forehead. "Then close your eyes, Doc."

She did. Minutes later, physically and emotionally spent but snug in the shelter of Burke's embrace, she fell into an exhausted sleep.

Chapter 12

With his gun on the nightstand beside him, and Gunny dozing by the door, Burke finally dropped his guard long enough to fall into a deep, contented sleep. The dogs would alert him long before any threat reached him. He could use a solid seven or eight hours to re-build his stamina after burning the candle at both ends to keep an eye on Hazel, track down leads on her stalker and work his own shift duties at the training center.

And then there were the physical demands of that frantic, powerful lovemaking session with Hazel. A blissful sense of peace spilled over from his conscious thoughts and filled his dreams.

He was the only man Hazel wanted. He was certain of it. More certain than he'd ever been with his own wife all those years ago. He reveled in the knowledge that Hazel wanted him enough to demand a mutual seduction, needed him enough to trust him with her secrets. She trusted him with her body, her life. And even though he wondered if she recognized it herself, she trusted him with her heart.

An annoying buzz tried to pull him from his sweet dreams, and he shifted in his sleep. Like a man half his age, he ached to be with her again already, to feel her grasping at him, squeezing around him, calling out his name. Although the images were vague, the sensations were as real as the heat cocooning his body, opening every pore, firing up the blood coursing through his veins. He'd dreamed of Hazel before, but not as vividly as this. Laugh by laugh, conversation by conversation, he'd fallen a little more in love with Hazel Cooper every day. Now he wanted to hold on to the closeness he and the curvy vet had finally shared. He had someone in his life again after all this time. He'd waited for it to be right—he'd waited for her. Now he had more than a friend, more than a fantasy dutifully hidden away in his deepest dreams. He had a partner. He'd be safe with her. He could be who he needed to be, do what he needed to do, and never worry that she couldn't understand the call to duty that drove him. She possessed that same sense of duty—to her children, her patients. She wouldn't leave him for something easier, someone immediately available, and he wouldn't leave her. This had been his vision for so long. He knew where he wanted this relationship to go, what he wanted to ask her.

He'd take her to dinner. No, take her to the dog park. He could tie the ring to Gunny's harness and...

The incessant buzzing ruined the future he was planning with her. He opened his eyes to the darkness. As awareness rapidly pinged through his brain, Burke remembered he was in Hazel's bedroom. He was half-aroused from a soft thigh wedged between his legs, and he was suffused with heat. He didn't remember burrowing beneath the covers, and he realized now that he hadn't. Not only was Hazel snuggled in like a blanket with her omnipresent afghan, the dogs had joined them on the bed.

And a phone was ringing.

"Damn." He wasn't on duty for another thirty-two hours. Something major must be playing out somewhere in the city for an alert to reach out to off-duty personnel. He patted the back pocket of his jeans. "Where's my phone?"

Hazel was awake, too. She crawled to the nightstand on her side. "It's mine," she murmured, lifting Cleo out of the way.

Burke pushed Gunny off his feet and ordered him to the floor. "What time is it?"

"Too early for a phone call." She fumbled for her phone long enough that he reached up to turn on the lamp beside him. "Make that too late. I'm not the emergency vet on call tonight, so it must be one of my own patients... Oh, hell." She hit the answer button and sat bolt upright. "Ashley?"

"Mom!"

He heard the faint cry of panic over the phone and sat up with Hazel, instantly on alert. He braced his arm behind her back and leaned in. "Put it on speaker."

"Sweetheart, what's wrong?" Tension radiated through Hazel's body.

Ashley was panting or sobbing or both. "I need you to come get me. My car is still at the clinic. I'd call Polly, but I don't think it's safe for her to come here."

The distinct sound of glass breaking made Hazel jump. "What was that? Where are you? Are you all right?"

Men swearing and cheering in the background was not a good sign.

Burke clasped a hand over Hazel's shoulder and spoke into the phone. "Ashley, where are you? What's happening?"

"Sergeant Burke?"

No time to explain why he was on her mother's phone at one in the morning. "Answers, Ash."

Like most people, she responded to his calm, succinct tone. "Joe brought me to this biker bar—Sin City. I could tell this place was a dive even before I saw the drunk passed out at one of the tables. He said these are his friends. Only, somebody did something to someone's bike—I'm not sure what happened. This guy joked that I could pay for the damage." She squealed a split second before he heard chairs knocking over. All sure signs that a fight had broken out. "He wasn't talking about money."

Hazel shivered. "Oh, my God."

"That's when Joe punched him. Oh!" She must have dodged a falling man or flying debris. "Can you come?"

"I know the place." Burke was already out of bed, tucking in his T-shirt and reaching for his belt with his badge and gun. He wasn't taking the time to change into his uniform. "Can you get to the women's restroom and lock yourself in? Or get behind the bar and duck down? It's solid."

"The fight's in here." Ashley was breathing fast, either from physical exertion or fear. "Aren't I safer outside?"

"Not in that part of town."

Hazel had scrambled off the bed, too, circling around to keep the phone close to him while he dressed. "Where's Joe now?" she asked.

"In the parking lot maybe? That's where the argument started. It's like gangs taking sides. I came inside to report it. The bartender called the police."

"Good. They'll be there any minute. It's not far from HQ. Tell them you're a friend of mine. I'm on my way." Burke headed across the hall to the bathroom, where he'd left his bag, to retrieve socks and a pullover. Hazel was right by his side. "Can you get someplace safe?"

Ashley considered her options, then started moving. "This place is long and skinny—I don't think I can get all the way to the bathroom in the back. I'm heading behind the bar now."

A deeper, quieter voice sounded closer than the chaos at the bar. *"Come with me, miss."*

"Who's that?" Burke asked.

"I don't know…" Something crashed. There was a grunt of pain. "Oh! Stop that! Are you okay?"

"Sweetie, who are you talking to?" Hazel demanded, handing Burke his second boot to tie on.

"A man. I don't know," Ashley answered. "An old

guy who was sitting at the bar. Another guy just clocked him with his elbow taking a swing at someone else."

"Come with me." There was a scuffling sound and a choice insult for some *old man* before the noises of the fight faded.

Ashley spoke again. *"Are you okay? I have some medical training. Here. Put a towel on it. I'll get some ice."*

Then the deep, breathy voice came back within hearing range. *"I can take you somewhere. Home? A friend's house? Coffee shop? Anywhere but here, right?"* His laughter faded into a wheezing cough.

"Do not leave with anybody," Burke ordered, striding toward the front door to retrieve Gunny's harness. Hazel hurried along beside him. "I'm on my way to get you."

"We're on our way. Be safe, sweetie." Hazel disconnected the call.

Burke glanced down at her pajamas and stockinged feet. "I'm leaving in two minutes. As soon as I get Gunny geared up."

She stepped into her discarded shoes beside the door and grabbed her jacket. "No need to wait."

No way was Hazel sitting locked inside Burke's truck while he waded through this mess of drunks with leather and attitude to find her daughter. But a stern warning about not needing the distraction of keeping an eye on her when he needed to watch his own back and rescue Ashley made enough sense that she had agreed to wait just outside his truck, where she could watch everything from across the street and pace away her fears. How had her daughter gotten stuck in the middle of all this mess?

Hazel had helped with natural disaster recovery scenes that didn't have this many police cars and uniformed officers on-site. Sin City certainly lived up to its name as a bar where no one with any good sense belonged. Apparently, Joe Sciarra's argument had triggered the rivalry between two motorcycle clubs. And Ashley had been caught in the middle of it all while her soon-to-be-*ex* boyfriend, Hazel hoped, had sided with his bros instead of getting her out of the melee.

The endless days of rain had finally stopped, but the wet pavement reflected the swirling patterns of red and blue lights and piercing fog lamps from the silent police cruisers, distorting the darting figures of innocent patrons hurrying to escape the police presence and bloodied combatants trying to get in one last lick before they were lined up against the wall or ordered to the ground and handcuffed. Like wraiths sliding in and out of the darkness, officers, brawlers and bystanders alike were being shuffled to various locations—to one of the ambulances that were here to treat a variety of minor injuries, to the parking lot to drive or ride away, or to one of the waiting black-and-white police vehicles.

She huffed out a sigh of relief when Burke appeared in the doorway, with his arm around Ashley's shoulders, her daughter clutched protectively by his side. "Ashley!"

Even as she danced inside her shoes, eager to run to her daughter but mindful of Burke's warning to keep a safe distance, Hazel felt her chin angling up with pride at the sight of the crowd parting for Burke, Ashley and

Gunny. The man could sure clear a path. He oozed the sort of authority that made his coworkers respect him and the perps shy out of his way. He should have had children, she thought, sadly—he'd make a fabulous father. Protector. Father figure. Friend. Lover. And he was hers. All hers. If she was brave enough to claim him.

When she couldn't wait another second to know that her daughter was safe, and the man she loved was responsible for that gift, Hazel darted across the street. "Ashley!"

"Mom!" Her older daughter pulled away from Burke and fell into Hazel's tight hug.

"I'm so glad you're okay. *Are* you okay?" She pulled back to frame Ashley's face in her hands. Flushed cheeks, a little pale, but no sign of injury or tears.

"I'm fine, Mom." Ashley's smile confirmed that fact. "I had the daylights scared out of me. But I never was so happy to see Burke walking into that bar."

"I know the feeling." Hazel lifted her gaze to the man waiting patiently beside them. She palmed his grizzled cheek, stretched up on tiptoe and planted a firm kiss square on his mouth. "Thank you," she whispered, then kissed him again, lingering as his lips clung to hers. "Thank you."

When she sank back to her heels, heat was simmering in Burke's dark eyes and her daughter was grinning from ear to ear. "Um, what's happening here?" Ashley pointed back and forth between her and Burke. "And are you wearing your pajamas under your coat?"

"Oh, sweetie," Hazel began. "So much has happened—"

"Hold that thought." Ashley's smile vanished and heat flooded her cheeks as her gaze focused on a point beyond Burke. "I need to have a conversation."

"Whoa." When Burke reached out to stop her from charging back into the chaos, Hazel grabbed his arm and silently asked him to stay put.

She'd seen a black-haired man with too many tattoos being handcuffed and led to the back seat of a police cruiser, too. "Let her go."

"Not by herself." Burke clasped Hazel's hand and pulled her into step beside him. With a nod to the officer who initially warned Ashley to stay back, Burke stopped a few feet away, allowing the meeting with Joe Sciarra to happen, but not interfering.

Joe's left eye was bruised and puffy, and a raspberry had been scraped across his cheek. But Ashley wasn't interested in him being hurt. Hazel's girl was fired up. "They said you started the fight. You brought me here, looking to trade punches with Bigfoot over there?"

"Hey!" The overbuilt man's protest was cut short by the petite uniformed officer palming his head and guiding him into the back of her police cruiser.

Ashley waited for an answer from the man she'd been seeing. "It's nothing personal. I owed a favor and Digger needed the cash. You were fun enough to make the deal worthwhile."

"What deal? With who?" Ashley demanded.

"It was a win-win situation, baby." He winked. "You know you liked hangin' with a bad boy."

"What are you talking about? What's going on?"

Joe scanned the street and parking lot before nodding toward the guy in a baggy, long jacket and jeans sneaking down the sidewalk. "Ask *him.*"

The notion of something familiar, something off, jolted through Hazel as she watched the man with the graying blond ponytail and shaggy beard walking away. She released Burke's hand and took a step toward the man. Then another. And another. Fury blazed white-hot, clearing her thoughts, and she started running.

"Haze!" A strong hand clamped over her arm, stopping her. "What is it with you Cooper women?" Burke challenged. "I'm trying to get you away from the danger. Where are you going?"

"That man. I know him." She patted Burke's chest, willing him to see the urgency in catching up with the man before he disappeared. "At Saint Luke's Hospital. He's one of the homeless men Polly works with."

Ashley appeared beside her, studying the man as he glanced behind him and quickened his pace. "He tried to break up the fight. Help me get away. But he got hurt. He took a pretty good punch. Cut his lip and bloodied his nose. They were too out of control in there for him to do much good. But I should thank him for trying."

The man turned around and Hazel cursed. Even from a distance, through the night's distorted lights, she knew him. The man looked straight at her, then spun away, quickly disappearing into an alley. "Put Ashley in your truck."

Burke's hold tightened. "You're not following some guy down a dark alley in the middle of the night."

"Then come with me." She tugged on Burke's grip. "Aaron!"

He released her. "As in Aaron Cooper?"

"Dad?" Ashley echoed.

Burke waved an officer over to his truck and told the young man to keep an eye on Ashley. He and Gunny quickly caught up with Hazel in the alley. She halted beside a pile of trash cans and garbage bags that smelled like a used litter box. The setting was fitting for this reunion.

The man turned beneath the light from the side entrance to a neighboring building. The face was a little more weathered from sun and age, but she knew those blue eyes. Once upon a time she'd loved them. Later, they'd haunted her nightmares.

"What the hell are you doing here, Aaron?"

His shaggy appearance was a far cry from the tailored suit-and-tie up-and-comer she'd once loved. "Hazel. How's it goin', babe?"

"Don't *babe* me. This is no coincidence. What are you doing at Sin City on this particular night?"

"I was trying to save my little girl."

She rolled her eyes to the starry sky and curbed her tongue before she spoke again. "You were at the hospital with Polly, too, weren't you? Are you really homeless?"

He shrugged. "I got a place." His gaze drifted over her shoulder to the man standing behind her. "Nothing fancy like the home where we used to live."

"It was a fairy-tale facade you created, not a home. Not at the end." She might have known the truth, but she had refused to accept her marriage was a sham and her husband couldn't be trusted until the night Aaron's friend had tried to kill her. Her love and loyalty had meant nothing to him. His attempt to reminisce and claim there was a bond they still shared meant nothing to her now. "You've insinuated yourself into Polly's life, haven't you?"

"She and I are friends."

"Friends?"

"She's a kindhearted girl." He smiled. "Like you used to be."

"Does she know who you are?"

"She knows me as Russell, an Army vet who's having a hard time adjusting to life outside." She hadn't expected him to admit his deception. The old Aaron would have stuck with the lie to the very end—unless a different lie could save him. "That's not so far from the truth. I'm struggling to adjust to life away from Jeff City. Making the right friends. Finding a decent job. Not being judged."

"Why would someone judge you? A convicted felon." Sarcasm rolled out with a sharp bite that should have embarrassed her.

"Hell, Hazel, she didn't even recognize me. She doesn't remember me at all."

"You were in prison, not the military. You were there because of the choices you made. You could have done the right thing and admitted your guilt and paid back what you stole. You'd have been out a decade sooner and had a lot of years knowing your daughters."

He could justify any action that benefited himself. "If I can't be their father, then I want to know them however I can."

"By stalking them? Do you know how frightening

that is? How did you know Ashley was on a date here tonight? How did you know a fight would…" She shook her head, no longer regretting the sarcasm. "What con are you running this time?"

"I'm not hurting them. I just want to be a part of their lives."

The moment he took a step toward her, she felt a strong hand settle at the small of her back. Burke believed that she could handle this confrontation with her ex, but he was letting both her and Aaron know that he was there if she needed him. Sizing up the big man with the big dog, Aaron retreated half a step.

"Polly was easy. My parole officer put me onto Saint Luke's program to help the homeless and those who can't afford health care. I knew it was her the moment I saw her. She looks just like you when we met." He frowned. "Except for the hair. What'd you do to yours?"

Irrelevant. "And Ashley?"

He pulled back the front of his jacket and thrust his hands into his pockets. For a split second she felt tension stiffen Burke's fingers at her back. Had he expected to see a weapon? Wires attached to a bomb trigger? The tension gradually eased as Aaron continued. "I know Joe Sciarra from inside. Gave him some financial advice so he had a nest egg waiting for him when he got out."

"I'm not even going to ask if that advice was legal or not. You got a guy who owed you a favor to charm your daughter and set her up in a situation where she could have been hurt?"

"He wasn't supposed to hurt Ash. Just scare her.

Then I could come in and save the day. Make her grateful to me. I guess it got out of hand."

She wanted to walk over and slap his face for manip-
ulating their children like that. But that would involve
touching him, and that thought was about as abhor-
rent as the idea that no one she loved was safe from his
machinations. "How dare you put our daughter in danger for your selfish whims. I guess some habits you'll
never break."

"I'm sorry, babe, but your damn restraining orders
force me to be resourceful."

Hazel shook her head at the utter waste of a lifetime.
"I think of all the good things you could have done with
that brain of yours. How much you could have accomplished. If you'd used your people skills to help someone besides yourself—"

"Could've, would've, should've, huh?"

She almost felt sorry for the regret that momentarily
aged his expression. *Momentarily.*

"Look, I need to talk to you about something," he
continued. "I've been worried about you."

"I'm not your concern."

"Right. That's what New Boyfriend is for." He spared
a condescending glance up at Burke, then focused on
her again. "Then let's say I'm worried about the girls.
That's why I wanted to get close to them. I think someone is after me. You know? Fifteen years behind bars
isn't enough satisfaction for a lot of people—"

"I can't do this tonight, Aaron. I need to take care
of Ashley." She turned to walk away. She'd wanted to
confirm that Aaron had insinuated his way into their

lives again and to put him on notice that she wouldn't tolerate his games anymore. She wasn't hanging around to make nice or assuage his conscience.

"Gunny, *fuss*," Burke ordered, falling in behind her.

But Aaron had never liked her asserting herself. "This guy has shown up every place I've been. At Saint Luke's. Your clinic—"

Hazel whirled around. "You've been to my clinic?"

"I watch from the strip mall across the street sometimes. Getting a look at what I've lost. You built a nice place for yourself." He grinned smugly at Burke. "Don't worry, I keep my hundred yards away from her. You can't arrest me for parking my car in a public lot."

Aaron had been close by this whole time? "I knew someone was watching me, but I thought… You need to stop."

"I think he's following me. Or he's following the girls…" He swallowed a curse. Was he losing his temper with her? "While you're shacking up with your new boyfriend here, I've been keeping an eye on Ash and Polly. I tried to tell you something was hinky, but you won't take my calls."

"Why would I believe anything you tell me?"

His anger exploded. "I have the right to protect my own children! If you're putting them in danger—"

"That's rich, coming from you."

"Time out." Burke silenced them both. "Priorities, Haze." He moved up beside her, then edged himself closer to Aaron. "Tell me about the man you've seen following Hazel and the girls."

"I don't have to tell New Boyfriend anything. Even

if he does wear a badge. Hell, especially if he wears a badge."

"If you really want to man up and protect your children," Burke taunted, "talk to me." Hazel heard the threat in his voice. "The guy you've seen has been playing with bombs."

"Bombs?" Aaron frowned, looking honestly taken aback by the grim statement. "Polly's car? He did that?"

Burke gave a sharp nod. "He's been to the clinic and Hazel's building—with explosives and bomb parts both times. He probably knows where your daughters live, too. I need to find him before he pushes the button that could take out your entire family and a bunch of innocent bystanders."

"Bombs?" Aaron's thoughts wandered away.

"Do you know this guy?" Burke prodded.

"Not really." Aaron shrugged. "But I used to get anonymous letters in prison from some guy who said he was going to be waiting on the outside for me—to blow me up the way I blew up his life."

A chill skittered down Hazel's spine. "Oh, my God."

"Do you still have a client list of the people you cheated?" Burke asked.

When his only response was a resentful glare, Hazel answered. "It's probably in the archives at the DA's office. They were all listed as victims in the lawsuit."

Burke nodded, pulling his phone from his jeans. "It's a long shot, but let me make a few calls. I'll wake somebody up to see if the prison has any record of who sent those letters, and cross-match it with names from the DA's office. Maybe one of your clients has a job with access to explosives. At the very least, we can determine if the letters came from the same person. Here." He handed Gunny's lead to Hazel. "You know most of the commands. Use him if you need to." He gave Aaron a pointed look before he walked off a few steps to use his phone.

The moment they were superficially alone, Aaron grew defensive. "If this guy was one of my clients, he can't blame me for losing his money. There's always a risk with investments. Things happen."

Things happen. Like the man you entrusted your money to might devise a scheme to funnel all your profits into his own offshore bank account, all while selling a bill of goods that would make you want to keep paying him more money.

"You still don't understand that your actions have repercussions that affect your entire family. We're still paying the price for your greed. You may not be directly involved in what's happening to us now, but if this guy was one of your investors, you're responsible."

"The years have been good to you, babe." His wistful tone had no effect on her. "But I miss your long hair."

"It was too much work. *You* were too much work."

"I was a rich man, Hazel. The four of us would be sitting pretty right now if you'd have just kept your mouth shut." When he reached out to touch her hair, Hazel recoiled.

"Gunny?" The big dog growled beside her. Aaron wisely stepped back with hands up in surrender. *"Sitz."* The big shepherd plopped down into a sit position beside her.

"You've changed."

"You haven't." Neither had the threat surrounding her. "Please. Tell me anything you can about the man you saw. The only times I've gotten close enough to identify him, it was dark, and he was wearing a mask."

Finally, either for his daughters or for her or to avoid dealing with Gunny, Aaron nodded. "The guy I saw is about my height. More of a paunch—I did a lot of working out in prison. The loose clothes are part of my disguise." Unimpressed with his sales pitch, she rubbed the top of Gunny's head and waited for him to continue. "He's a white guy. Does manual labor, I'm guessing. Like a mechanic, maybe. He wears a uniform under that hoodie. His hands were dirty. White hair. I never got a good look at his face."

Never missing an important clue, Burke rejoined the conversation. "Anything else? Did you see what he drives?"

Aaron shook his head. "He was always on foot when I saw him." He snapped his fingers as an idea hit. "Tobacco. I've seen him spit a chaw more than once."

A chaw of tobacco. Why did that seem familiar? Did she know anyone who chewed? Was there something behind the devil man's mask she could identify?

While the wheels turned inside her head, looking for answers, Burke's hand settled at her back again. "You can walk away this time, Cooper. But if you violate your restraining order and come near any of these women again, I'll be there."

Aaron's glare was less pronounced this time. Without thanking Burke for giving him a break, Aaron turned to Hazel. "Would you talk to the girls and see if they'd be interested in getting to know me? Unless you've poisoned them against me."

"I'll ask them. No guarantees. It will be their choice. And frankly, with the lies you've been telling, you're not off to a great start. You'll have to live with whatever they decide. I won't let you hurt them again."

"Thanks." He turned and headed head down the alley toward the next cross street.

"And, Aaron?" He turned to hear her out. "If you really want a relationship with them—no games, no lies. Be patient. Be real." Like this man beside her. She clasped Burke's hand and headed out of the alley. "I want to see my daughter now."

Burke adjusted his wraparound sunglasses on the bridge of his nose as he drove back into the city after spending several hours at the K-9 training center. It felt prophetic to feel the sun warming his skin through the windshield again. After so many days of one rainstorm after another, the October sun felt more like the beginning of a new page in his life instead of the last hurrah of summer.

It had been a long night with little sleep, but he felt energized by anticipation rather than fatigued. His life was changing, and he was ready for it. His patience with Hazel had paid off. They were a thing now—in a relationship. And once he figured out who was behind all the threats and put the crud behind bars, he intended to make that relationship permanent. He ignored his goofy grin reflected in the mirror. There were some things even his patience couldn't wait for.

After leaving the Sin City bar in KCPD's capable hands, they'd driven straight to Ashley and Polly's apartment, where the three Cooper women shared a laughing, tearful "yell me everything that happened" reunion that included several warm hugs for him and thank-you bites of cheese for Gunny. At his insistence, to streamline their security and for their mother's peace of mind, Ashley and Polly packed up their bags, and he loaded them into his truck. Although he was a little amazed at the toiletries-to-clothing ratio each young woman stuffed into her small suitcase, like their mother, they'd been quick and efficient. Then he'd dismissed Officer Cho and driven them all back to Hazel's condo, where she served the girls hot chocolate, encouraged them to talk as late as they wanted to and succinctly announced that he would be sleeping in her room. With her. If the girls had any objections to those arrangements, they could talk about it in the morning.

He didn't know whether to laugh or be nervous when breakfast that morning had been eerily quiet.

Garrett Cho had stopped by to pick up Polly and drive her to class at Saint Luke's, and Burke struggled with an unfamiliar urge to take the younger man aside and find out more about his background and his interest in Polly. Then he'd driven Hazel and Ashley to work, and gone to his office at the K-9 training center to follow up on last night's phone calls regarding the leads they'd gotten from Hazel's ex. Some of the leads were paying off as Detectives Bellamy and Cartwright ran down the short list of potential suspects from the list of Aaron Cooper's swindle victims. If any of those names connected to explosives, and crossed paths with Hazel's world, then chances were they had their man. Besides, the Cooper women were babying Gunny enough that he wanted to run the dog through his paces to make sure he remembered he was a trained police officer and not a spoiled house pet.

His time with Hazel and her daughters was crazy, chaotic and full of love. It was the life he wanted. He glanced at the dog panting behind him in the rearview mirror. "You okay with that, partner? You know you're still my number one guy, right?"

Gunny whined in response to being talked to. Burke decided to interpret the dog's excitement as an agreement. But his own smile quickly faded as his phone on the dash lit up with a call from his ex, Shannon. Better deal with this issue, too, if he wanted that life with Hazel.

He punched the answer button and immediately put it on speaker. "Sergeant Burke here."

"You know it's me, Jed." Her sultry voice held a little of that poor-me, damsel-in-distress tone. "Is this a good time to talk?"

With her? Never. But there were some things they needed to settle, once and for all. "I know you went to see Dr. Cooper. Were you checking out the competition?" He flicked his signal to shift into the passing lane. "FYI? There is no competition."

"So you two are serious about each other?"

"Yes."

Judging by that huff of breath, it wasn't the answer she wanted to hear. "Do you love her?"

"I do."

"You and I can never…?"

"No." His answer was gentle but as firm as he could make it. "Go home, Shannon. Talk to Bill and work things out. He loves you."

Discussion done, as far as he was concerned. He disconnected the call and breathed a sigh of relief. He was one step closer to the future he wanted.

He was cruising to a stop when his radio flared to life. "Delta K-9 one, please respond." The dispatcher relayed a call to bomb squad personnel summoning him to a Bravo Tango at a Front Street address.

Bravo Tango.

Bomb threat.

Burke swore. He turned on the siren and lights and stomped on the accelerator. He barely heard the dispatcher's apology about calling him in on his day off, or her explanation about the other bomb detection dog being out on another call. He punched in Hazel's number on the phone. It went straight to voice mail.

He picked up his radio. "Delta K-9 one—10-4." He answered that he was responding to the call and raced through the red light.

He knew that address.

Hazel's clinic.

Chapter 13

"What the hell are you still doing in here?"

Six feet plus of angry Jedediah Burke coming through the swinging door of her operating room, armed and dressed in full protective gear, was a scary thing to behold.

Hazel already knew the clock was ticking; she didn't need him startling her like that. "I'm working as fast as I can. I was in the middle of surgery. I had to at least close her up before I could move her." She tied off another suture in the abdomen of the skinny cattle dog mix. "I told everyone to leave and put Todd in charge of evacuating all the animals."

"Nobody's here but you and that dog. Part of our sweep means getting all personnel off the premises before we even search for explosives." He and Gunny circled to the opposite side of the table. "What can I do to help?"

"Get out of my light, for one." She waved him back a step and concentrated on finishing up as quickly, if not as thoroughly, as she normally did. He glanced around the small surgery room, then put Gunny to work searching, making sure this room, at least, hadn't been rigged to explode. "Is it as bad as those sirens out there make it sound?"

"This area's clear," Burke replied, though it didn't help her feel relieved. "How much longer?"

"Todd and I were in the middle of this operation when Ashley told me a client found a brown paper package in the men's room." The picture Ashley had shown her had looked frighteningly familiar. "It's just like the one the devil man had."

"There's another one at the front door. Gunny hit on it."

Her hand shook and she nearly dropped her needle. "There's more than one?"

He moved in beside her, resting his hand on her shoulder. "Easy, Doc. You got this. But work a little faster."

Gunny suddenly jumped to his feet, his sharp ears pricked toward the door. When Burke pushed the door open slightly to check out the canine alarm, she heard the snuffling and whining, too. "Do I hear a dog in the back? Where's Todd?"

"KCPD's set up a perimeter. Nobody is allowed back in the building."

"We have to get him." He gave her a pointed look.

One. More. Stitch. "I can't leave my patients…" When she saw that he was about to argue, she shook her head. "You wouldn't leave Gunny behind."

He gave her a curt nod. "I'll get whoever is in the kennel. Finish up."

Moments later, he was back with Shadow, the big Lab, in his arms. "We're all clear. Let's go."

Hazel frowned, remembering something important about the dog on the operating table. Athena had perked up with a little food and fluids, and was fit enough to be spayed.

"What is it?"

"Tobacco."

"What?"

Hazel shook off the unfinished thought. This wasn't the time to be solving mysteries. "Nothing. Go. I just have to give her an injection to wake her up. I'll be right behind you."

"Make sure you are."

He pushed through the swinging steel door. Seconds later, she heard the back door opening and closing. She gave the injection, made sure she had a heartbeat and breath sounds, then disconnected the dog from the oxygen mask and IV. The back door closed again. Burke wouldn't let her be at risk for very long. She wrapped a blanket around the groggy canine and lifted her in her arms. "We're coming."

It took a split second for the odd sound to register. The door hadn't opened and closed a second time.

Someone had locked it.

But she was already pushing through the swinging metal door out of the surgery room. "Burke?"

She pulled up short.

The devil man.

"Ticktock, Dr. Coop." He held up a triggering device, like the one he'd showed her that night outside her building, and laughed. His thumb rested on the button. "Is it on or off? How long do we have?"

She shrank back against the metal door. "How did you get in here?"

"There are lots of places to hide away in all these little rooms. I just had to be patient." The man in the grotesque mask breathed heavily with excitement as he reached inside a different pocket and pulled out another trigger. He pressed that one. "On."

There was no countdown this time. The floor rocked beneath Hazel's feet and she stumbled as a deafening boom exploded at the front of the building. Some light debris from the ceiling floated down like snow, but more alarming were the pings and instant dents of a dozen tiny missiles hitting the other side of the metal door. That door had probably just saved her life. If she'd still been in the surgery room…

She pushed away from the wall where she'd fallen. "Are you crazy?"

Perhaps not the right thing to say. The devil man took a menacing step toward her and pulled out a third trigger to replace the one he'd just used to blow up the front of her building. He fisted it in front of her face and jammed the button with his thumb. "On! Now I'm finally getting what I want."

A heavy fist pounded on the exit door behind him. "Hazel!"

"Burke!"

"I'm not interested in company, Dr. Coop." The devil man opened the storage cabinet beside the back door and tossed piles of blankets and towels onto the floor so that she could see the bomb behind them.

"Get away from the building!" she warned, afraid that explosive was the one ticking now. "He's put a bomb by the back door!"

She heard cursing and running. The smells of sulfur and ash drifting through from the front of the clinic stung her nostrils.

She smelled something else, too.

Tobacco.

I've seen him spit a chaw more than once.

The disjointed pieces from so many sources finally fell into place. Hazel hugged the dog sleeping in her arms a little tighter and squared off against the man who'd made her life hell for too many long months. "Take off the mask, Wade."

He grunted, as if surprised to be recognized.

"Are you afraid to do this face-to-face? Afraid to show me the truth?"

He tapped one of the triggers. "Off." Then he pushed back his hood and tugged the plastic mask over his head. He grinned at her with his stained teeth. "Doesn't matter if you figured it out. I will destroy you. Just like your husband destroyed me."

"Can I at least get this dog to safety?"

"It's a stupid dog." He picked up the trigger again

and frowned, as if he couldn't remember the sequence of the countdown.

Hazel did. But she wasn't going to tell him he'd turned the countdown off. The trigger in the other hand meant another device was already ticking toward detonation. "How can you care so little about life?" she asked, hoping to distract him from turning on the device again.

"Because I don't have one." The distraction didn't last for long. He pressed the button. "On. Aaron Cooper stole all my money. My life savings. My future. I lost my house, my truck. My friends called me an idiot for falling for his lies. I drank too much and finally lost a good job. I've been working on a road crew. I'm a trained engineer, and I've been working on a stinking road crew. That's where I found that dog you're holding."

"But your wife—"

"She left me. Earlier this year." Probably about the time the letters had started arriving. "She said she finally had enough of me being a loser."

"So you picked up the stray and blamed her, so the authorities would investigate her."

"Yeah. Sweet little bonus—causing her grief. If she'd been loyal to me, I might not have had to go to such drastic measures. But mostly I just needed a way to get to you. So I grabbed Athena and brought her in."

Because he couldn't get to Aaron. Maybe because no amount of punishment or atonement could make up for a ruined life.

"And the explosives? You picked them up on your job, too?"

"Where's your husband, Dr. Coop? Why isn't he rotting in prison? Why isn't he dead? Where's my justice?"

"Aaron is not my husband. You're hurting the wrong person."

Her words didn't seem to be reaching him. She couldn't hear Burke outside anymore. She could barely hear her own thoughts over the fear pounding through her pulse. Wade had blocked her path to escape. He'd probably rigged this entire building to blow.

She *did* have a life. She had a career she loved. Two beautiful daughters. She hadn't told Jedediah that she loved him. "How many bombs are there?"

"I've left a present for you every time I came to your clinic, whenever I visited that scrawny dog. I'm gonna bring this place to the ground." He leaned in, running his tongue along his yellowed teeth. His eyes were rheumy with a serious lack of sleep—or madness. "You wanna see 'em?"

She backed away, glancing all around her, wondering if there was any safe place inside the clinic where she could barricade herself from the next explosion. "I believe you."

"Off." He laughed again, enjoying her distress. "Isn't it fun not knowing how many seconds you have left to live? It's kind of like not knowing how long you have until the next part of your life implodes." He took a step toward her, backing her down the hallway. "And the police have kindly cordoned off the area so it's just you and me and a countdown." Another step. Was he pushing her toward something? Trapping her? "Your husband destroyed my life. Now I get to do the same to him. I want to destroy *everything*." He raised the trigger and clicked it. "On."

She heard the shattering noise of breaking glass from somewhere in the damaged part of the building. Hazel spun around.

"Gunny! *Fuss!*"

A streak of black and brown rushed past her. She nearly cried out with relief because she knew Burke wouldn't be far behind.

With a vicious snarl, Gunny leaped, chomping down on Wade Hanson's upstretched arm and swinging his legs around to pull the man down to the floor. Gunny twisted, his powerful jaws never losing their grip on the man's arm.

Wade was screaming as Burke stormed in.

"Gunny! *Aus!*" Burke gave the command for the dog to stop biting and ordered him back to his side. He pushed Hazel and Athena behind him and leveled his gun between both hands at the man on the floor. "Stay down!" While Hanson writhed on the floor, cradling his arm and complaining about stupid dogs and sharp teeth, Burke cuffed him and explained his miraculous appearance. "He locked the back door. I couldn't get in. When the front of the building blew, I thought the worst."

Hazel appreciated his fear, but there was no time to talk. "There are more bombs. He had two triggers in his hands. I don't know what they're attached to, but he said they're counting down."

"Then we're getting out of here." He hauled Wade to his feet and shouldered open the back door, shouting to the cops outside. "K-9 officer coming out! Gunny! *Fuss!*"

Running ahead, Gunny led the way to the fenced yard behind the building. Hazel hurried out next, carrying Athena.

Hanson laughed, even as Burke dragged him to safety. "Time's up."

Hazel spun around. "Burke!"

A wall of black protective gear snapped around her body and pushed her to the ground. Her clinic erupted with three thunderous booms. A storm of fire shot high into the air, while debris rained down on the mud and grass all around them.

It was nighttime again by the time Justin Grant, his bomb disposal team and the KCFD let Hazel back onto the premises again.

So much destruction. So much anger.

She and Burke had been treated for minor injuries and released while Wade Hanson was handcuffed to his hospital bed, being read his rights and the long list of charges leveled against him. She herself had cleaned and put a couple of stitches in a cut Gunny had suffered from flying shrapnel, while Todd had seen to Athena's recovery. All their patients had either been sent home or were being boarded at another animal hospital.

With the girls safely ensconced back at the condo, and Burke at precinct headquarters helping Justin fill out paperwork on the case, Hazel had returned to the clinic. Or what was left of it. Between the explosions, fire and all the water from KCFD's fire hoses, there was little left but the concrete slab and the frame of the kennel's back wall.

Sorting through the rubble for anything salvageable, Hazel was surprised that she didn't feel sad. She spotted a metal stool and waded through a puddle of standing water to set it upright. After drying the top with the sleeve of her jacket, she sat, scanning the place she had built all those years ago despite Aaron's wishes to the contrary.

She was happy—no, intensely relieved—that no one had gotten seriously hurt, not even one of her precious patients. This clinic represented her old life. And it had been razed to the ground. She would rebuild. With a more open floor plan with fewer places for crazed bombers with a vendetta to hide. She could upgrade the technology of the facility. She'd come back, stronger than ever.

When Gunny trotted up to her, she petted the dog and smiled. "Free health care for the rest of your life, young man. All the treats and toys you want, too."

"You're making my dog fat."

Hazel stood and smiled at the deep voice that sounded so tired, so sexy. "Did you finish up at work?"

Burke nodded. Somewhere along the way, he'd showered and changed into a clean uniform. "We found all the bombs. Justin and his team neutralized them."

"You mean Gunny found them all," she teased.

"I mean this is finally over." Burke pushed aside a mangled examination table and joined her beside the stool. "Hanson has been arrested. Your ex is on notice and shouldn't cause you or the girls any more trouble."

"I wonder if Aaron will be called as a material witness by the DA's office. That would be an ironic twist. We'll see if anyone rams a car into him to keep him from testifying."

Burke chuckled. "You've got a wicked sense of humor, woman."

She rested a hand against his chest and smiled up at him. "What I've got is hope."

"Yeah?"

"You are the bravest man I know. The most loyal. The most caring. You put your heart on the line with me. Even when you didn't know how I felt yet."

His hands settled at her waist. "I knew how you felt, Doc. You just had to realize it."

She lost the smile, wanting him to understand how serious she was. "I love you, Jedediah Burke. I don't want to waste another day of my life believing that being safe is the same as being happy. I can have both. I deserve both. I'm safe with you. I always have been. I needed to break some old habits and finally believe it. And, God knows, you make me happy."

"You gonna marry me, then?" he asked. "I've been patient for a long time."

Nodding, she wound her arms around his neck and pulled him to her for a kiss. "You were worth the wait."

* * * * *

Danica Winters is a multiple-award-winning, bestselling author who writes books that grip readers with their ability to drive emotion through suspense and occasionally a touch of magic. When she's not working, she can be found in the wilds of Montana, testing her patience while she tries to hone her skills at various crafts—quilting, pottery and painting are not her areas of expertise. She believes the cup is neither half-full nor half-empty, but it better be filled with wine. Visit her website at authordanicawinters.com.

Visit the Author Profile page
at Harlequin.com for more titles.

K-9 RECOVERY

Danica Winters

To the men and women in blue
who serve our great nation.
Thank you and your families for your sacrifices.

Acknowledgments

This book would not have been possible without a great team of people, including my editors who had to patiently wait on my broken butt. Don't worry, I'm fine now—just very appreciative for kind people in a world where chaos is the order of the day.

I'd also like to extend special thanks to Detective Sergeant Ryan Prather of the Missoula Sheriff's Department, who walked me through handgun training and building clearing; the K-9 unit from the Gallatin County Sheriff's Department, who showed me exactly how amazing well-trained K-9s are; and last to the cutest EOD rottweiler on the planet—Daisy—and her kind handler, Troy Kechely.

A great deal of research has gone into this and every book I write, so any errors are solely my fault, and I apologize in advance for any perceived mistakes. This author is far from perfect but loves to create stories that will always keep you, my readers, turning the page.

Thank you for reading.

Chapter 1

Love was a language everyone spoke, but few were fluent. Elle was definitely one of those who struggled.

It wasn't the concept of love that she found difficult to embrace—a union of souls so enmeshed that nothing and no one could come between them. At least, that was what the fairy tales that had been spoon-fed to her as a child and adolescent had told her. Perhaps it was these insipid stories that had set her up for failure in the relationship department. According to those stories, love was built on a foundation of ball gowns, champagne and whispers of forever, while reality peppered her with missed dates, drunken late-night phone calls and broken promises. As far as she could tell, love was all a lie.

The three-year-old girl standing before her was just another reminder of the consequences to the innocent when lies and love went too far.

"Ms. Elle?" she said, her voice high and pleading, though she had asked no real question.

"What is it, Lily babe?" Elle smiled down at the little blonde whose hands were covered with the remnants of cotton candy and pocket lint. She reached into her purse and pulled out a packet of baby wipes.

She was really starting to get this whole caretaker thing down.

"No," Lily said, pouting as she put her hands behind her back and stuffed her cherubic cheeks into the shoulder of her jacket.

Or maybe Elle wasn't doing quite as well as she thought.

"Just a quick wipe and then you can head back out to the swings. Okay?"

"I want juice." Lily smiled, her eyes big and bright. It reminded Elle of her dog, Daisy.

She put the wipes back and handed her a box of apple juice from her bag. "Only one, okay?"

Lily didn't say anything as she took the juice box, walked over to the sandbox and plopped down, already chatting with a new friend.

She had just been worked over by a toddler. *Damn.*

Before long, and after a series of carefully constructed arguments on Lily's side, they found themselves headed back to the Clark house. They walked up the steps to the front door of the colonial-style home, a throwback to the type of residence built by people who'd come to the wilderness of Montana to make their fortunes—and succeeded. The house was hardly the only sign of generational wealth. Everything, down to the three-year-old's shoes, wing tips she would likely only wear once, spoke of what old money could buy.

When Elle had been three, she had been running barefoot through the sands of Liberia while her parents were taking contracts and acting as spooks for the United States government. Though they had been gone for several years now, she missed them.

The door swung open before they even reached it, and Catherine stepped out. She sent Elle a composed smile, the woman's trademark—a look of benevolence and influence all wrapped into one.

"She was perfect, as per usual," Elle said, watching as Lily slipped behind her mother's legs and disappeared into the belly of the house without so much as a backward wave. "Bye, little one!" she called after Lily.

It was a good thing she wasn't a sensitive soul or the little girl's apathy at her leaving would have broken her heart. Actually, it did hurt a little, but she would never let it show.

Catherine looked after her daughter but didn't say anything as the girl shuffled up the stairs.

Watching Lily's toddling steps up made Elle's skin prickle. She couldn't believe Catherine was letting the girl ascend to the second floor without a helping hand. One little slip, one poorly planted foot and Lily could have been lost to them all—and that girl was a gift. Everywhere she went she left the glitter of laughter.

"Do you want me to help her up to her room?" Elle said, stepping into the parlor.

"No," Catherine said, waving her off.

In the living room to her left, there was a group of

men standing around and talking. They were all wearing suits and ties, except one, who was dressed in khakis and had a stinking cigar wedged into the corner of his mouth and a tumbler of scotch in his hand. The men looked like models for a fraternity's alum party or a political gathering.

"Thank you for taking her. It is appreciated." Catherine reached over for her purse, like she was going to pay Elle as if she was nothing more than a teenage babysitter.

She stopped her with a wave of her hand. "No, ma'am, please don't."

"I know I pay your company, but you need a tip at the very least."

She wasn't an hourly charge kind of woman, and the only reason she had agreed to take this security position was because she was the most temperate of the Spades. The boys would have handled the little girl like she was an egg, especially given the fact that Lily's father was a senator.

Elle couldn't give two shakes who the girl's parents were, except right now, when she was forced to face the fact that Catherine's focus was on her friends and not on her baby. Elle hadn't even seen the senator since she had taken the security position three months ago.

She had to reserve her judgments about the family. Her interactions were limited to drop-offs, pickups and little else. Catherine had made a point of not letting her interact with Lily when she was around.

Catherine stuffed a $100 bill into her hand. Part of her wanted to throw it on the ground and tell her to screw off, but instead she slipped it into her pocket. As she did, Catherine closed the door in her face.

It was no wonder the woman's daughter wasn't the kind for long goodbyes.

Maybe she didn't have to reserve judgments after all—Catherine was a brat.

That would make it easier to say goodbye when this security detail came to an end. But it was going to be tough to say goodbye to Lily.

As she walked to her truck, she took one long look back at the house. Lily was sitting in her bedroom window looking out. When she spotted her, the little girl waved.

Yes, saying goodbye would be hard.

As she got into her truck, she sighed and then rolled out toward the ranch. The miles drifted by as she forced herself to think about something other than the little girl. Tonight, she was supposed to have Daisy work with members of the local sheriff's department, who had graciously offered up their Search and Rescue and training warehouse as well as give assistance in running hides.

Daisy had come so far in just a couple of years; from a crazy little rottweiler puppy, she had turned into a dog that was capable of finding a castaway shoe in a rainstorm from a half mile away. She wasn't perfect—there would always be off days—but she was better than even Elle could have hoped.

When she made it home to the Widow Maker Ranch, Daisy was waiting for her at her little cabin. Her nubby black tail whipped back and forth violently as Elle walked in. The dog spun in excited circles, prancing, her face as close to a human smile as it could get.

Yes, she loved that dog. So had Lily, until her mother had put a stop to her bringing Daisy onto the property—even when only in her vehicle.

Loading Daisy and the gear up into the truck, she made her way over to the training warehouse. They hadn't worked there before; mostly she had worked with the K-9 units from the city police department, so this would be a fun, new experience.

Arriving, she found a tall, brooding sheriff's officer standing beside the bay doors. He was doing something on his phone, and he looked put out that he was standing in the icy near dark of the late winter night. Most people she worked with forgot any apprehensions the moment they saw Daisy. She was beautiful, with her gleaming black coat and buckskin-colored face and paws, and a blaze mark on her chest. And she loved everyone.

The man looked up from his phone, and his eyes flashed bright green in the thin light. He was stocky, and he wore a knit cap. When he gazed at her, he smiled for a split second, but as quickly as the sexy smile came, it disappeared and was replaced with what she assumed was a trademark scowl.

"You were supposed to be here ten minutes ago." He stuffed his phone away.

She wasn't late, she was never late, and the accusation made her hackles raise. She wanted to growl back at him and tell him to look at his watch, but she resisted the urge. They were here at the sheriff's invitation. Clearly this man wasn't here of his own volition.

"There must have been a miscommunication. Sorry about that." She was careful not to put the apology on herself or her mistake. If anything, he should be apologizing for the lack of a professional and warm welcome.

He said something under his breath.

It was a good thing he was handsome and she wanted this hour to train with Daisy, or she would have told him to pound sand then and there. She hated not having the upper hand. If he was sexist, too…she would be out of here in no time. Daisy could train somewhere else.

"If you like, I can come back another time." When someone else wanted to work with her and Daisy.

He sighed, the sound resigned. "We're both here."

She flipped her keys in her hand, thinking about how easy it would be to get in her truck and start the engine.

"Look," she said, her frustration finally threatening to come to a full boil, "if you don't want to do this, it's okay. I can promise you that I'm trustworthy and Daisy and I can use the training warehouse without supervision. You can just unlock the door and go. I will lock up when we're done. No big deal," she said, giving him the out he appeared to want.

His whole body shifted, like he suddenly must have realized how he was coming off to her. "No, no. As one of the search and rescue coordinators, I'm more than happy to help." He turned to the door and entered the code. The garage door ground open, exposing the interior of the building.

One side of the warehouse kept a variety of trucks, rafts, snowmobiles and mobile command units marked with the Missoula County Search and Rescue badge.

The other half of the warehouse had been set up to look like a makeshift house.

She led Daisy out of the back seat of the truck and clicked her onto her lead. He had his back turned to them and didn't seem to notice the dog.

It was silly, but Elle was a bit crestfallen. No one ignored Daisy's beautiful face. She was always the star of the show. How dare he snub her baby dog?

Today really wasn't having any pity on her ego.

She followed behind him as he walked into the makeshift rooms built around the facility, making the interior of the warehouse look like something out of a movie set.

"We were just using this place for room clearing today," he said, pointing at a spent flash-bang on the floor in the staged living room. "I was going to clean up but decided to wait until you were done."

She nodded. "The more scents, the better. I like to make it hard on her."

He smiled, a *real* full-toothed smile, and he finally looked down at Daisy. "May I touch her?"

Finally, they were getting somewhere.

"Sure," she said, looking at the nameplate on his chest. "Sergeant Anders."

He glanced up at her and looked surprised before connecting the dots with how she would have known his name. "Sorry about being a little short with you," he said, bending the knee to Daisy and petting her.

The animal leaned into him, her bulletproof vest pressing against his. They made quite the pair.

Daisy's butt jiggled as she tried to wag her tail. "She likes you."

At least one of them did. If nothing else, Daisy's endorsement of the man was something to like him for.

"I'm a huge dog guy—it's why I offered to stay behind and help you out."

He had *offered*?

"Well, I appreciate your helping me." She felt suddenly embarrassed that she had taken an instant disliking to him. Maybe she really was too fast to judge.

She would need to focus on her self-improvement for a while.

"What do you need me to do?" he asked, motioning around the place.

She reached into her tactical bag and took out a Ziploc. "This bait has a scent on it. I'll take Daisy outside and make her wait. Then I'm going to need you to take this out of the bag and plant the cloth somewhere in the facility. I don't want to touch it. She knows what I smell like and can use that."

He threw his head back with a laugh. "We'd hate for her to cheat."

"She is smarter than I am sometimes." She smiled.

He looked at her as he stood up, studying her. "I find that hard to believe. The handler is just as important as the dog in K-9 work."

She pushed the bait into his hands and moved to step out the side door before he could read anything on her face. "I'll wait out here."

She felt something in her chest shift as she walked away from him. Was he hitting on her? Or was she just seeing something that wasn't there because she had been without a man for too long?

Yeah, there was nothing there. She had just witnessed a mirage in the desert of her love life. All she needed was to go on a date with a man, leave in the morning and forget about feelings. Relationships were for people who had the time and patience to deal with them; she had better things to do.

She shifted her weight, like she was readjusting her nonexistent, feelings-proof vest.

"Daisy, you are not a good influence," she said, scratching behind the dog's ears as Daisy looked up at her and gave her a doggie grin. "Like I said. You know what you did, didn't you? You're devious."

Daisy wiggled. "If you want a man in our lives, we can get you a cute dog to run with. Don't you dare look at me and get any kind of silly ideas."

Chapter 2

What a long damned day. He loved training with the special response team, or SRT, but going from 6:00 a.m. until 6:00 p.m. had drained him. When he'd agreed to take care of the K-9 handler, he'd had no idea it was going to be a woman. As soon as she had stepped out of that truck, he'd hated his decision to volunteer even more.

She was way too good-looking, with her long brunette hair pulled back into a loose ponytail and her skintight tactical pants. Looking at her, and the way she moved, he instantly wondered if this woman was here to train or to flirt. He had a history with women who fell in the latter category. He'd met his ex when she had signed up for a ride-along. Things had seemed normal during the ride, but the next day the texting had started, and quicker than he realized, he was in it deep.

Amber had been great—things had been easy between them—but that had led to most of their problems. She would bow to anything he wanted, with no counterpoints, no opinions of her own and always acquiescence. He had needed a woman who challenged him.

Breaking up with her had been murder. She was nice enough and there was no concrete moment that had torn them apart after two years. It just was...*time*.

She hadn't taken it well and had begged him to stay. He had been tempted to give in—she wasn't a bad girlfriend in any way—but if he was honest, he didn't want to settle for happy enough. He wanted more than that in his life. He wanted a woman who made his heart race when she walked into the room. It sounded stupid, but he wanted a woman who could speak to his soul even in moments when he knew he was wrong and then she could make him right.

But what he was looking for, what he needed, wasn't something he would ever find.

He'd damned well given up looking. And until he figured out what he really wanted, something that made some sense, he wasn't about to jump into a relationship again. He didn't want to hurt anyone because he didn't know what he needed—he was a better man than that, or at least he would have liked to think he was.

Grant walked around the facility, running scent for Elle and her dog before planting the T-shirt behind a cushion on the floral-patterned couch in the makeshift den. There was probably a better place to hide the smelly thing, but it would have to work. The quicker the dog found what it was looking for and the quicker the beautiful woman and her cute dog were gone, the better.

As he walked back, he reminded himself not to look her in the eyes. If he did, if the little niggle of excitement he felt upon seeing her was truly going to be some kind of feeling, staring into her eyes wasn't going to help. Better to avoid trouble than to walk headfirst into it.

She looked up as he opened the door leading outside. Blue. Her eyes weren't just plain old blue; rather, they were the color of the sky on a summer day—crystal clear and bright, full of spirit.

Damn it. Error. Major error.

"Did you plant the shirt somewhere?" she asked, the question sounding as awkward as he felt.

He nodded. "What else you need me to do?" He squirmed as he stood there, holding the heavy metal door open for her.

"If you want to watch, you can follow us through. But I've got it all from here, or rather... Daisy does," she said, sending him a sexy smile.

Daisy looked up at her, like she realized they were talking about her, and her entire body vibrated with joy. It was as if the dog knew what was going to come and was loving her job. If only everyone on his teams loved their jobs the same way this dog seemed to.

He watched as the woman gave the dog a command in what sounded like Russian.

Though he had worked with K-9 units during SWAT calls, this was one of the few times he had a chance to see what it took to teach the dogs he often saw in action.

He walked behind them as she followed the dog.

She wove back and forth, locating the scent. It struck him how different the dog looked from the bouncing, wiggling beast Daisy had been outside to this focused task-driven animal that was now working the room in front of him.

It was impressive.

"I thought most K-9s were German shepherds?"

"Most are, or Belgian Malinois." She didn't look away from Daisy as they worked. "Rotties are somewhat rare in the SRT game, but more common in search and rescue. They are a breed with a peppered track record in the court of public opinion, but they are having a resurgence in popularity."

He heard the words she was saying, but all he could focus on was the sound of her voice and the way her words were flecked with an accent he couldn't quite put his finger on. She sounded like she was from somewhere farther north, but it wasn't quite Canadian. There was also the twang and hard *A* sounds of the Midwest. Where had she grown up?

Maybe she was a corn-fed girl out of Iowa. Hard raised and strong as hell. It would definitely explain how she had gotten into such a male-dominated field. However, maybe he was wrong—there were more and more women getting into search and rescue, and they were all better for it. The next commander was likely even going to be a woman, Melody Warner. She was as badass as they came in SAR. She could pull together a swift-water rigging quicker and better than any man he knew.

His phone buzzed, and he ignored it, though he knew it was likely something to do with work.

"How did you get involved with rottweilers?" he asked, trying to ignore the pull to answer his work phone—it should have been priority number one, but all he could focus on was her and this place and how she smelled like floral perfumes and rubber dog toys.

"My best friend runs Big Sky Rottweiler Rescue. They focus on rehoming rotts who have been surrendered or abandoned to shelters." She rushed after Daisy, who was pulling hard on the leather lead as they made their way down the hall. "Daisy came to me after living in a cage for over a year."

He looked at the beautiful, healthy dog who was sniffing the ground like it held all the answers.

His phone buzzed again, an angry bee just looking to lance his flesh. "Excuse me for a minute." He lifted a finger, knowing she would go about her business though all he wanted her to do was stay by his side and continue his time with her. Being here, watching her work and just learning the steps was the break he needed from his day.

And yet, life called.

"Hello?" he asked, turning away for a moment and walking toward the main door.

"You're working with Elle Spade right now, correct?" He instinctively glanced in her direction as the sheriff spoke.

"Yeah, why?"

"Tell her that there has been an incident…involving one Lily Clark and her family." The sheriff paused, clearing his throat. "I have also approved your volunteer SAR team to act on this one."

"What are you talking about? What happened?" And why would he be asked to tell Elle about it? He was having a hard time pulling the real meaning together behind the sheriff's cryptic instructions.

"A three-year-old girl, Lily Clark, and her mother, Catherine, have gone missing. It looks as though there was some kind of altercation inside the residence, but the team is still sorting through everything. I have yet to get the full report from the crime scene." Grant heard the clink of ice in a glass, but he wouldn't dare ask the sheriff if he had been drinking—such questions only led to lies or trouble. "We aren't sure what happened to the mother, but we have reason to believe the little girl slipped out of her house and may be lost in the national forest service land that abuts their property. Both are, as of yet, unaccounted for."

"I'll pull together my team, and we will head out there as soon as possible."

"Sooner than that. I need you out there now. Go grab Elle and get in your truck. Head straight there and let your team take care of everything else. If you need me to call in one of the coordinators to help, I can."

That wasn't procedure, and he couldn't make sense of why the sheriff would be pushing him like this when he damned well knew that everything SAR did was done as quickly and safely as possible—not only for those they were sent to rescue or recover but also for all members of the unit.

"Yeah, call in Commander Warner. She is the best team leader we've got. But can I ask why the push?"

The sheriff sighed. "Lily Clark isn't just an average

kid. She is United States Senator Dean Clark's daughter. If we don't get that girl back…" The sheriff trailed off.

He didn't need to explain that the senator controlled much of their funding—or lack thereof. If a senator turned against them, they would be limited to nothing more than donations and fundraising events.

Basically, if they failed…so did their program.

As awful as that might be, though, it didn't compare to the situation at hand—a missing girl, probably frightened beyond imagining.

"I'll be there as quickly as I can. Text me the address. You make the call to Warner. Get her up to speed. Out." He hung up his phone, remembering that he hadn't even asked the sheriff why he was supposed to tell Elle about the girl's disappearance. Hell, it was probably so she could bring the dog.

He ran down the hall. "Hey, Elle, SAR got a call!"

She stepped out of the makeshift den, Daisy holding a rubber ball in her mouth and wiggling while Elle pushed the T-shirt he'd hidden back into the Ziploc bag. "Do whatever you need to. I can lock up here. Seriously, and thank you for letting us train with you."

His face puckered. "Actually, the sheriff just called personally. He knew you were here and asked that you go with me on this one."

"Really? Why?" She cocked her head, an oddly canine mannerism, but it fit the woman.

"Do you know the Clarks?" he asked, his stomach clenching, though he wasn't sure exactly why. "Lily and Catherine?"

She stared at him, unmoving and unblinking, as

though her world had just come crashing down. Daisy stopped moving and looked up at Elle like she could feel the change in the energy around the woman just as abruptly as he did. The dog sank to the floor, laying her head on Elle's feet and letting the ball fall from her mouth and roll haphazardly over the concrete.

"What happened to her?" Elle asked, her voice sounding breathless as all the color drained from her features.

It was strange, but he could understand the dog's sudden need to touch her, to comfort her in the only way possible. And yet he barely knew this woman or why this news would affect her so dramatically. "Something has happened up at their place, some kind of altercation."

"What kind of *altercation*?" She spat the word.

"I can't tell you." He moved to touch her, but she jerked away. "Are you going to be okay?"

She rushed past him, bumping hard against him like she had somehow forgotten he was there even though he had been speaking to her.

Daisy ran behind her as they sprinted outside.

As he stood there, he could make out the sound of her truck revving to life and her tires squealing on the asphalt. As quickly as the woman nosed her way into his life, she had sprinted out of it—and he was far more confused than ever. In a matter of minutes, he'd gone from safely contained and tired from a long day, to geared up and having his and his team's asses on the chopping block…and it seemed highly likely it was all because of her and secrets he was yet to discover.

Chapter 3

The entire ride back to the Clarks', Elle couldn't think of anything except Lily. She'd only been missing a matter of hours, and already things had gone haywire. She should never have left the little girl.

Hopefully the altercation Grant had alluded to was nothing more than a fistfight, nothing involving weapons. She should have asked Grant more questions. If only she had been thinking. That was always one of her biggest and most profound faults—emotions and actions first, questions later. It wasn't a recipe for success in her personal or professional life.

She grabbed her phone. She could call him. But as she looked at the screen, she realized she didn't have his number. *Damn it.*

No doubt, if she had been able to talk to him, he

would be unlikely to give her much. He'd been pretty vague with providing any sort of details, and when it came to law enforcement and anyone in special operations, she had learned long ago that when they kept silent, it was for a reason.

That silence was always chilling.

Her mind went to all the dark places as she sped down the road. Lily had to be okay. Catherine could fend for herself—well, so long as the altercation was as minor as she hoped. Yet why would the sheriff ask for her to come if it was something inconsequential?

Perhaps it was so she could act as a witness. Or maybe they needed her there to help Lily calm down. Maybe the little girl was asking for her.

She smiled faintly at the thought. Of course, that was probably it. Otherwise the sheriff would probably not even know Elle existed.

Then again, Grant had first told her that *SAR had a call*. That meant search and rescue teams were involved. Which meant that one or both of the Clark ladies were missing. It was probably Lily. Maybe Lily was just playing, hiding away in some closet in the house and Catherine couldn't find her.

Yes, this was probably all blown out of proportion and Elle was just jumping to the darkness out of habit— she and her military contracting teams had spent far too many nights planted in the tumultuous and dangerous world of war-ravaged countries.

Her mind drifted to Afghanistan. They had been running an operation for the military-contracted agency, or MCA, she'd been working for at the time, taking her dog into the mud houses and working to clear them of explosives. In the Pashtun region, none of the dwellings were for single families. Rather, extended family groups crowded into them, and they normally held between twelve and twenty people. Most of the residents hated dogs and Americans and, with her having both strikes against her, she was never a welcome sight—not to mention she was a woman working in an area heavy with Taliban forces.

On her last trip, she had been operating in a building that had already had one IED detonation in the courtyard. When she'd arrived on scene, the team before her had pulled out all the remaining living members of the family. The complex had taken on an eerie, disquieting feel that spoke of the horror that had filled it only hours before her arrival.

It wasn't the first time she had been to a place like that, where the acrid scent of spent explosives still mixed with the tang of freshly spilled blood and lingered in the air like a eulogy, yet when she got to the courtyard, she hadn't been prepared for the scene that had unfolded.

She had to work through a number of bodies, most so thoroughly peppered with shrapnel that if it weren't for their clothes, it would have been hard to tell if they were women or men. There was a small crater where the initial blast had happened. There, at the edge, was a well-worn pair of children's Adidas sneakers. One was tipped on its side, as if the kid who had been wearing them had been blown out of them.

She later learned that, according to eyewitnesses,

the child had picked up the bomb and had been playing with it when it detonated.

She'd been shipped out later that week and had never
been happier to get out of a country.

It had taken her a long time after her feet had arrived
on American soil for her soul to come home, as well.
No matter how many debriefings or offers to speak to
chaplains happened, she would never again go to sleep
without the image of those shoes popping into the front
of her mind.

Ever since that day, she'd been on a mission to be on
the front line when it came to children and her job. Most
would have backed away, put distance between themselves and the possible horrors that would hurt them the
most, but not her. It was odd, but seeing those horrors
made her want to do everything in her power to never
have those tragedies or hellscapes happen again—and
therefore witnessed by anyone else.

She could be the whipping girl so others wouldn't
have to endure the same traumas.

Trauma. Her past. All of it was swirling into her
mind and masking the reality of her present. She
couldn't let that happen. Not now. Not when Lily was
likely in trouble.

Maybe it was the trauma that scared her the most,
nothing more than the ghosts of the past haunting the
present. More than likely, Lily was probably just being
Lily and hiding in the house somewhere, she reminded
herself. Maybe her father had called in the cavalry when
really only patience and steadiness were all that were
needed.

Maybe this was nothing more than the senator pulling strings in order to bring the media to their knees at his beck and call—attention to him and his family, especially in their time of need, would likely be helpful in any sort of political campaign. Hell, he was known for pandering to the media.

If this was some kind of political move, she was going to have to quit the job on the spot. Then again, she couldn't leave Lily alone and unsupervised with two such toxic people.

As she crested the top of the hill, she turned down the driveway that led to the Clarks'. The place was lit up with a collection of red and blue lights. The image made her stomach drop. In the evening shadows, the lights reflected off the snow and made it look like some sort of scene out of a murder documentary.

Murder.

No.

There was no way Lily could be dead.

Yet the scene made it clear that this situation was far more serious than what she had been hoping to find.

As she pulled up the driveway, her thoughts moved to the men who had been standing around in the living room like frat boys when she had been here earlier.

Was she here because of something they did? It wouldn't have surprised her if things had escalated into a full-blown altercation with that kind of crowd. When there was a room full of self-important and power-hungry men drinking and smoking cigars, no doubt they would have been trying to one-up each other. They were probably playing at the hierarchy of asshats.

For now, she just needed to get the information she required and go to work in helping Lily. She couldn't go down the road of what-ifs and hows. She was here to help, first and foremost. The rest of the professionals on-site could help her make sense of everything else. It was the reason they had teams. And, in her case, she not only had the crew that was already swarming around the house, but her family, as well.

Whatever the police couldn't handle—or were limited in what they could legally do—her family and teams at STEALTH could step in and take care of. It was one of the best things about her job and family. She was always surrounded by badasses. In fact, some could have even said she was one, but if she was, it was because of her dog. If she had to pick the biggest badass in her family, the title would have to go to her sister, Kendra.

She parked, got out of her truck and walked to the back door to check on Daisy. Grant pulled in behind her, a sour expression on his face. As he exited his truck, the look on his face deepened. "Don't you think you were driving a little fast?" From the tone of his voice, she would have thought he was kidding, but from his expression he was clearly annoyed.

"If Lily is in trouble, there's no speed limit in the world that's going to keep me from getting to her." She gave Daisy a scratch behind the ears as the dog stared at her and attempted to make sense of everything that was happening.

"So, you do know this girl?" Grant asked. "I mean, I assumed you did…given the fact you ran away from me like your ass was on fire. But you could have at least let me give you the lay of the land before you tore out."

She huffed. He wasn't wrong. "Yes, I know Lily. I was hired as her guard by her family. I only left here a few hours ago." She clicked Daisy's lead onto her collar, readying her for whatever their next steps may be. "What's happened to her?"

His sour, annoyed expression was quickly replaced with one of a pained empathy. "From what I was able to glean on the ride over, the mother and her child have gone missing. They initially believed the little girl may have slipped out of the house sometime after you left... but the scene's—"

"Lily didn't sneak out of the house," she said, interrupting him. "Lily isn't that kind of girl." Her thoughts came in a mad dash.

"I know, but—"

"If anyone is at fault here, it isn't Lily. Her parents are..." She glanced up at the front door of the house. The senator was nowhere to be seen. "They are not as *attentive* to Lily as parents should be. In fact, I'm surprised they didn't have a nanny on staff. They should have."

Catherine and Dean hadn't been especially forthcoming with why they had hired Elle and her team to watch over Lily, but if they thought there was enough of a security threat that they needed to call in private VIP teams, then obviously there was something going on.

She should have pushed for more answers before taking this job. She should have gotten all the details. And yet, they had been vague. In a world of shadows, she hadn't found it surprising at the time. Maybe it had been their hubris or hers, but as long as she was around, she hadn't been overly concerned that anything bad would happen to Lily. But that had been on the condition that she was around. This had happened after her watch had ended. She should have been adamant about making sure that Lily had around-the-clock coverage. Or at least that they had boots on the ground outside the house.

She looked at Grant. He'd crossed his arms over his chest and was looking down at his feet, and she realized that she had once again spoken over him. When would she just start listening instead of pushing her way through life?

"Sorry. So, both Catherine and Lily are missing?" Elle asked, more focused on the child than the mother. At least Catherine could look out for herself.

He nodded. "No one knows where they went, but there was a sign of a struggle inside the residence. A table is broken and, from what the deputy on the inside said, there were shots fired within the house, and a gun registered to Catherine was found under a sofa. It was a .38 Special, and they believe it is the same caliber as that which left the holes in the walls."

"So you believe Catherine was shooting at someone?"

Grant shrugged. "Hard to say how this played out as of now. We are pretty early on in our investigation. You know how these things have a way of distorting under first impressions."

He spoke to her as though someone had filled him in on some key details of her life, but she couldn't imagine who or when. She had always been insistent about keeping herself to herself, but then again, this was Montana.

"One of the neighbors said they saw you leaving the house this afternoon," he continued. "It is believed you were one of the last people in or out of the house."

"What? No. I wasn't the last one here by any means. There were quite a few men in the living room, socializing with Mrs. Clark, when I left. But, wait..."

He didn't call her here to help in the search. No. He'd called her here because she was one of their possible suspects.

"Am I a suspect in their disappearance?" she asked.

If she had been the lead working this case, she would have been her first stop, too. And it had been one hell of a play for Grant to bring her right to this place and put her on the spot, when, in fact, he was really questioning her. She had fallen for his game hook, line and sinker.

But she wasn't afraid—she had nothing to hide.

"I didn't say anything of the sort," he said. "However, what time did you leave here?" Grant asked, careful to phrase his questions in a way that if she hadn't been aware she was being interrogated, she wouldn't have picked up on it.

"I left about thirty minutes before I met up with you." She scowled. "I know what you're thinking, but I'm telling you right now that if there was anything or any information I could give you about this little girl's disappearance, I'd be the first to do it."

Grant twitched. "You're always two steps ahead, aren't you?"

"I just live in this world, one of law enforcement and carefully constructed realities."

He chuckled. "I do appreciate that we have the ability to speak the same language on this." He seemed to relax, whatever suspicions he held about her momentarily falling to the wayside.

He was trying to play her again, to make her feel comfortable around him in an attempt to get more information. Little did he know, she was a master at that stupid game. However, it was odd and uncomfortable for her to be sitting on the receiving end.

"Do your guys know how long they've been missing? Who called this in?"

He leaned against the front of her truck. Daisy whined at her, and she stroked her head.

"Again, I don't have all the details, but I think it was a neighbor who reported hearing gunshots."

"Any blood?" She clicked off Daisy's lead and closed the back door of the truck, leaving the dog safely tucked inside. "Did your guys look everywhere for Lily? That girl won't just answer to anyone. If she's hiding in there, she's probably not going to come out for anyone other than someone she knows." She took a step toward the house.

"Stop," Grant said, putting his hands up to keep her from advancing. "I know what you are thinking, but you can't just barge into that house and start yelling for Lily. This is potentially an active crime scene. Whatever we do, we have to be careful. We have to follow procedure, at least as much as we can."

Her hands were balled into tight fists, almost like her

body wanted to strike out and take down anything and anyone who stood between her and Lily's safety—or lack thereof—even if that someone was the sergeant.

She tried to control her impulses to run into the house and flip open every cabinet and overturn every drawer in her search for Lily, but it was a struggle. Daisy whined from the back seat, and when Elle glanced over at her, Daisy barked.

I know. I screwed up, Daisy, she thought. *I never should have left today. I knew something wasn't right. I effing knew it.*

Daisy's nose pressed on the glass, and she whined again.

She should have trusted her gut and not left when she had seen the men in the house alone with Catherine. She should have taken Lily and gone somewhere…anywhere. And yet, she hadn't listened to the little voice, and now her ward and her mother were missing.

She thought about Gavin de Becker's *The Gift of Fear*. Like so many other self-help and self-defense–themed books, it spoke of a person's intuition being their greatest weapon in their defense arsenal. There was nothing more effective to defer crime and injuries than to avoid situations that put a person at risk. Yet the only person who had avoided anything was Elle—she had wanted to avoid a confrontation with Catherine, and in the end…

Her boss was nowhere to be found.

One confrontation and she could have saved a woman and a child from disappearing.

Elle had avoided conflict and walked them straight into danger.

Maybe she needed to read that book again. Then again, she didn't need a book to tell her to be afraid. She knew all too much about that on her own.

"Would you mind taking me through the house? I won't touch anything, but if we are going to look for Lily, I'm going to need to know where we are going to have to start." *And whether or not she is still alive.*

"Why don't we leave Daisy for now? I want to do a quick walk-through and then, if you feel it necessary, we can have her do a sweep. Okay?" Grant asked, giving her a pinched, pleading look.

She opened the back door and clicked Daisy's lead in place and then helped her step out of the back. "Dog goes. In a case like this, I can promise you that she is likely to pull more information than we ever could. Humans are always at the dumb end of the lead."

Chapter 4

The house still smelled like it had when she left, a strange mix of whiskey, expensive women's perfume and cigar smoke. Now, however, beneath the familiar odors was the distinct scent that came with the police—disinfectant, sweat, leather and gun powder.

She lifted her shirt, taking a quick sniff to see which world she smelled of after being in the training warehouse, but all she could smell was this morning's shower, fresh air and Daisy.

Careful to slip under the tape, she walked into the foyer and glanced into the living room. The various law officers were in other parts of the house now, so the room was empty. "When I left, Catherine was here with a group of about eight men." Daisy sat down beside her, leaning against her, her body tight and ready for action.

"Do you happen to know the identity of any of those men? Or what they were doing here?" Sergeant Anders asked.

She shook her head. "This family has a lot of foot traffic in and out of the place. It's why I normally take Lily out of the house when she is under my care. It is easier to control the variables."

"Are you saying that the type of people who came through this place weren't who you would call reliable and safe?" he asked, reaching for his pocket like he wanted to take notes, but then he stopped and dropped his hands back down to his sides.

"It's not that they were drugged-out meth heads, or people who you would look at and think they were dangerous—actually, far from it. These people weren't the kind to keep themselves in bad company. Their lives were completely taken up by their image and the public's opinion of that image. Especially right now, as the senator is up for reelection and is behind in the polls."

She looked at the spot where she had last seen the stranger in khakis who had been smoking the cigar. Aside from the broken side table and three bullet holes in the wall to her right, nothing was out of place. If anything, it was too clean. Had someone staged this?

Grant bent over slightly and pointed toward the couch. "Right there, see the gun?" He pointed in the direction he was looking.

She crouched down. There, on the floor under the couch, was the .38 Special. She didn't recognize the gun, but she hadn't even been aware that Catherine owned a gun, let alone kept it at the ready.

"This room is ridiculously clean," Grant said, standing up. "Do the Clarks hire a cleaning staff?"

The question seemed kind of out of place, but she assumed he must have been thinking the same about the lack of detritus and debris in what they had been told was the site of an altercation that may or may not have led to Lily and Catherine going missing.

"Yes, but they only come in once a week," she said.

"Did Mrs. Clark always keep house in such a way?"

She stood up and chuckled. "Everything about the Clarks was always picture-perfect. I agree that this isn't much to work with for investigators, but... Who knows?" She shrugged, trying to dispel some of her nerves. "This whole thing may not be as bad as we first assumed. Did your people try and call Catherine? Dean?"

Grant gave her a look that would have crumbled a lesser woman. "Yes, we tried to contact Catherine and Dean. Dean is unavailable. We have the Washington, DC, police department looking for him in order to notify him about what has happened. And Catherine's phone was found in the backyard—its screen was cracked, but we have bagged it for evidence and our teams will see if they can pull any information." He started to walk again, and she followed after, Daisy close at her heels.

"Were you and Mrs. Clark close?" Grant asked, looking over at her with a sidelong glance.

She shook her head as they made their way toward the back of the house. "Hardly. I'm nothing more than an employee. In fact, today she tried to give me a hundred-dollar tip. It was her way of reminding me that

I'm nothing to Lily other than paid help—not a friend, not a parent and definitely not someone irreplaceable."

Grant reached up and touched her shoulder, the motion far too real and sympathetic than she was prepared for. He didn't need to say he was sorry; she could see it on him, and she didn't like it.

"It's okay. Sometimes it is good to be reminded to keep a little emotional distance from your work. And, regardless of how much I enjoyed Lily, I needed to keep in mind that the care of her was a job." Yet, even talking about what the girl *shouldn't* have meant to her made her ache with concern.

"Do you feel like you failed at that job?" he asked, almost as though he could read her truths on her features.

A lump formed in her throat, and she knew if she spoke, her voice would crack with pain. She simply shrugged.

"No matter what, Elle, you didn't fail this girl. You did exactly what you were paid to do during your working hours."

Had she? Her gaze moved to the travertine floor and the beige-and-gray speckling of its glistening surface; in her few months here she had never noticed the way it flowed like water.

He sighed. "I can see you are just like me. When you're off the clock, you struggle to leave the job at the doorstep. I know what that's like. And I know what you're likely struggling with. But you can't do this to yourself."

"My guilt will subside when I know that Lily is safe—and her mother."

He opened his mouth and then shut it, but she knew

what he was going to say…that they both needed to be prepared for any possible outcomes.

As they walked by the stairs, she pointed in the direction of the living quarters. "Do you want me to show you Lily's room? Maybe there is something there." Really, though, she was just hoping that as soon as she stepped into the room, Lily would come bounding out from inside her closet or from under her bed; she loved to play hide-and-seek.

Even as she considered it, she could feel in her gut that such a thing wasn't going to happen. Lily wasn't in this house. There were at least twenty different law enforcement personnel circulating through the residence, taking pictures and documenting the scene. Several were talking on their phones, and their voices mixed into an odd cacophony of stoic babble and garbled calls from dispatch on handsets.

He started up the stairs, and she stepped around him, leading him down the long white-carpeted hallway toward the girl's bedroom. "I could never understand why anyone in their right mind would have carpet this color when they have children. Since I've been here, they've already had to replace the carpet in Lily's bedroom once after she spilled a glass of grape juice—organic, of course."

He smirked. "I can't profess to understand or comprehend the thought processes of the extremely wealthy."

"It's wasteful." As she spoke, she realized that she had completely unleashed all of the opinions and judgments she had been withholding. Yet, with the sergeant, it may not have been the wisest of choices.

She needed to shut up. All he needed to know were facts that would help them locate Lily and Catherine. Everything else was frivolous.

The window where she had last seen Lily was open, and the cold winter air crept through the little girl's bedroom. It sent a chill down Elle's back, but she wasn't sure if it was because of the cold or the fear of what the window being open could have meant.

By the window, on the corner of the ledge, was a Barbie doll, her hair half-shorn and the other colored pink with Magic Marker. If Catherine had seen such a doll, it would have been pitched in the garbage and replaced with a new doll, hair intact.

"Lily was sitting there," she said, pointing at the ledge. "She waved at me when I left, then I came to see you."

"After Catherine gave you the tip?" Grant asked.

She gave him the side-eye.

"I'm just making sure that I'm tracking all of this correctly."

"Yes, after Catherine slipped me the money. I still have it." She reached down toward her pocket, but he waved her off. "Why do I get the feeling you are struggling to trust me?"

"I don't rush into anything, especially trusting people I just met—even in law enforcement. Don't be offended. It's not a reflection on you."

Was that this guy's way of telling her he was all kinds of screwed up? He'd hardly be the first LEO she'd met with a chip on his shoulder and a need for therapy. In fact, it was so normal, that she was forced to wonder if it was a chicken-or-the-egg kind of conundrum. On the other hand, perhaps the same could be said of her.

Beside the bed she spotted the wing-tip shoes, the ones with the black around the tops, that Lily had been wearing when she'd left. They were askew, pitched exactly where the little girl must have taken them off. No other shoes were missing, making her wonder what Lily was wearing. She couldn't have been out of the house. Not in this weather, not without shoes.

Then again, that was assuming she had been taken out willingly. If that little girl was out there in the cold, whoever had her would have hell to pay. *If* someone had her.

Grant's handset crackled to life. "Officer 466, we have blood. Requesting backup." He recognized Deputy Terrill's voice.

Pressing the button on his handset, he leaned into the mic. "Ten-four, location?"

"Four sixty-six, we've located it just outside the property line to the south," Deputy Terrill said.

Grant glanced over at Elle, whose eyes were wide and filled with fear. Blood was never a positive sign, but at least they had something to help them find the missing Clarks. Yet, he couldn't help but wonder if including Elle on this one was going to be too much for the woman. "Elle, if you don't want to come with me, you don't have to. You are welcome to stick around here with one of the other officers and help them look around the house and see if you can pull more evidence."

Elle shook her head violently. "There's no way I'm

not going to be involved on this. But let me get Daisy ready. She knows Lily's scent." She patted the dog's head.

He smiled. She was right. This dog was probably their best bet in tracking down the woman and child. "Go for it. I'll meet you around back." Her jaw was set, and where there had once been fear in her eyes, the look was now replaced with rage. He could understand it. "Again, Elle, if you change your mind about going along, all you have to do is let me know—we can get another handler in here. Sometimes when we're too close to a case, it can take a lot out of us."

"It's far harder on me knowing that Lily and Catherine are out there somewhere, possibly hurt, and I'm doing nothing about it. There's not a chance in hell I'm going to change my mind."

Elle and her dog walked out of the bedroom, but she looked back one more time as if she hoped that she would spot the little girl hiding somewhere in a corner or behind a drape, when they both knew all too well what the likely outcome was in a case like this.

He waited a few minutes, looking for anything out of place—a hair band, blood spatter, even an empty glass. But the only thing that seemed slightly out of place was the little girl's shoes. Clearly Lily had been in a hurry when she'd removed them. Just from the way they were strewn on the floor, he could almost tell the child's personality—it was the only part of the room that really spoke of the little girl and not her mother.

Elle had made a point of telling him that the family

was definitely the kind who would keep everything in line. Which made him wonder exactly how the Clarks had found themselves in this kind of predicament. Then again, sometimes when people held on too tight, it was because they were the ones who had the most to fear if they lost control. He knew a little bit about that—he always felt as if he was one hairbreadth away from disaster, both in his personal life and his professional one.

As he made his way out of Lily's bedroom, he walked past the master bedroom. From inside, he could hear a few officers talking about the senator in colorful language. As their sergeant, he should have stuck his head into the room and reminded the team that it was more than possible that one of them had their cameras rolling and everything they were saying was likely being recorded, but he didn't bother. They had already been warned they were always being monitored. At this point, if they wanted to talk smack about the senator, he wasn't going to be the one who put his ass on the line to stop them.

Then again, crap always rolled downhill, and if he didn't speak up, this could well end up with him standing at attention in the chief's office and taking a tongue-lashing for not keeping his team in line during a high-priority call.

He opened the door without announcing his presence. The three officers standing near the end of the bed glanced up at him with guilty looks, and the deputy on the left put his hand up in a slight wave. "How's it going, Sarge? You find anything?"

The deputy next to him had a slight redness to his cheeks. They all knew they had been caught.

"I'm sure I don't need to tell you how important this case could be for our department. I recommend you guys get your asses in gear and do everything in our power to find these missing females and all while not running our mouths." He pointed at the camera that he had attached to his vest.

All nodded, reminding him of three little monkeys—no see, no hear, no speak. He didn't care if they had to tap the message on the floor to one another, just so long as they fully understood that it was truly all their asses on the line here.

If they didn't get the Clarks back into their custody quick, fast and in a hurry, the media would blow this all up and they would be the ones taking the most flak. No doubt, as team leader, he would be made out to be a Barney Fife—some bumbling cop from a bygone era who didn't always know his ass from his elbow.

Yeah, he couldn't run the risk of those girls being gone for any more time than absolutely necessary.

Without so much as a backhanded wave, he rushed out of the bedroom and downstairs, nearly jogging as he made it outside.

A group of team members was standing outside the white vinyl fence, the kind that looked beautiful but was brittle and prone to shattering in the cold. The snow was deeper in the back of the house, and it crunched under his feet as he was careful to walk in areas not taped off. Perpetrators' footprints could be on the ground.

Deputy Terrill looked over at him and gave him a tip of the head in acknowledgment as he said something to the other two officers he was standing with.

Daisy popped out from around the side of the house, her nose already to the ground as she wove back and forth, working over the scene. Her black tail stood at attention as she moved toward him and Elle came into view.

He stood watching the dog move right and left, huffing as she took in the cold winter air and picked apart the medley of odors that must have been peppering it. He'd always heard a dog's sense of smell was at least a thousand times keener than a human's, which meant Daisy could probably pick up everything that had happened in the house today…all the people who had walked through its doors and even the cars they had driven in. Hell, she probably could make out the scent of the discarded fast-food wrappers and chewed gum that were in the garbage bags inside the people's cars.

Having that kind of ability to make out scents was an incredible superpower, but what made it even more incredible was that these dogs and their handlers had also managed to create a system of communication through training that enabled them to understand what the other was looking for and when it was found. He had seen the K-9 units work before. He'd even been asked to take a bite during training—and he would only do that once. He had tremendous respect for the human-animal bonds that allowed these teams to do their jobs effectively.

Elle finally looked up from Daisy as the dog slowed. He met her gaze, and there was an intensity in her eyes that made it clear she was just as on-task as the dog. Yet, as he looked at her, he couldn't manage the same level of professionalism—all he could think about was the brunette hair that had fallen free of her messy bun and was cascading down her neck. She had a slender neck that curved delicately into the arch of her shoulder. The notch at the base of her throat was exposed, and sitting at its center was a diamond on a gold chain.

The place where her necklace rested looked soft, kissably soft. If he kissed her there, was she the kind of woman who would tip her head back and moan, or was she the type to pull in a breath and tighten in anticipation? If he had to guess, she held her breath. She didn't seem like the kind of woman who would melt easily under a man's touch.

The thought of another man touching her made the hairs on the back of his neck rise.

He turned away from them, forcing himself to work. This wasn't the time. Actually, it was never going to be a good time to think about her the way he was thinking about her and all the things he would like to do to her body.

"Sergeant Anders, over here," Terrill said, motioning toward something on the ground.

He made his way over to Terrill as Daisy worked a weaving path across the backyard. He didn't know what scent Elle had put her on, but from the way the dog moved, he couldn't help but wonder if it was some small, skittish mammal—the scent path moved like a rabbit.

Careful to keep in the trail the officers had already created in the snow, he slipped between the rails of the fence and came to a stop beside Terrill. "What's going on? You found blood?"

Terrill pointed at the ground a few feet out from where the men stood. There, the snow had been trampled down and there was a mess of small footprints. It looked as though someone had lain in the snow and rolled around, but it was hard to tell the size of the individual—even if it was an adult or a child. Yet, at the edge of the compressed snow was a splatter of blood. The holes the warm blood had created in the snow were dime sized, and if the holes hadn't been edged in the pinkish-red stain, it would have been almost impossible to see. It definitely wasn't a quantity of blood that would mean whomever it had belonged to was close to death, but that was the only good news.

Daisy whined from behind him, and he turned and watched as she slipped under the fence and moved toward them. She pulled on her lead, the muscles in her shoulders pressing out hard as she tried to force Elle to come where she wanted her. Elle stopped, holding Daisy back.

"Sidet," Elle commanded in Russian.

Daisy dropped to her haunches, sitting. There was no moment of hesitation, no pause between command and obedient action.

When he'd been a kid, they'd had a chocolate Lab. The dog, Duke, would only listen to him when and if it was beneficial to the dog. He couldn't even begin to imagine how much these two must have worked and trained to get to the perfection of that simple command.

She was definitely capable of a level of dedication that he envied. He had always thought himself good at his job, but the officers under his command weren't nearly as well trained.

Maybe he needed to start giving them treats and praise.

He smirked, but it disappeared as he noticed the terror in Elle's eyes as she looked at the droplets of blood in the snow.

"Can you tell us whose blood that is?" he asked, afraid that he knew the answer before he had even asked the question.

She chewed on her bottom lip for a quick second. "I had Daisy on Lily's scent, but that doesn't necessarily mean that blood belongs to her. If there was someone out here with her, it could be theirs," she said, but he could hear the feeble hope in her tone.

Elle stepped around the bloodstain and moved toward the timber. He followed a few feet behind her, letting her and the dog do their work. There were two sets of tracks in the snow, what looked like a man's and a woman's. Their footfalls were wide apart, as if they had been running.

She stopped after about twenty yards and turned to him. "Look."

The footsteps in the snow appeared to grow closer, like the man and woman had slowed down and then come to a full stop. Where they had stopped was another set of small footprints—complete with toe marks. At the center of one of the child's footprints was a pink smudge, as though she had blood on her barefooted step.

Lily was in far more danger than either of them had assumed.

Chapter 5

The wind had kicked up as the sun was touching the tips of the mountains to the west; snow was fluttering down, and with each passing minute it seemed to be coming down faster in plump, wet flakes. If they didn't work quickly, soon the easy trail would be obscured and they would have to rely solely on Daisy's nose.

She tried to quell her disgust as she looked at the marks in the snow where Lily had been dragging her bare feet.

Who in their right mind would have brought a three-year-old out into the cold and then made her walk barefooted in the snow?

When she found the kidnapper, she would personally make sure they hiked twice as far without their goddamned shoes—and that was *if* Lily was okay. If she was hurt, or if her little feet were frostbitten, there would be more than hell to pay.

Is there something worse than hell? She paused at the thought but followed Daisy as the dog moved ahead.

All she knew was that anyone who hurt Lily would suffer pain at her hands that would be real and unbearable. It was more than possible that she would be the one who ended up in jail, but if she got justice for Lily, it would be worth it.

Her jaw ached as she jogged with Daisy, and she realized that she had been gritting her teeth, though for how long, she didn't know.

There was another long drag mark in the snow where it appeared as though Lily had literally stopped walking and had been pulled ahead.

That a girl. At least her friend was putting up a fight.

Since she had been taking care of Lily, she had been spending time having the kiddo do simple exercises—jumping jacks and push-ups, squats and lunges. At the time, Elle had been using the exercise as something to do to keep Lily busy, but now she was glad she had helped the girl gain strength. Though, never in her wildest dreams had she thought the child would need the stamina and strength they had been working to build for surviving the elements.

Thankfully, she hadn't spotted any more blood in the snow. If it was Lily who had been bleeding, she was going to survive…probably.

If only she had some kind of idea why they were out here, what had made them disappear into the woods.

Was the man with them keeping guard, or had he taken them? Were they running or being forced to run?

Her mind went wild with a million different theories, playing them out from start to finish. Though it was good for her to be prepared and to try to make sense of what had happened, she wasn't a detective; she was merely a private security contractor, and she couldn't rush to any conclusions. If she assumed anything, it could adversely affect their tracking and Grant's team's investigation. Well, *her* opinions and assumptions wouldn't affect them, or at least she didn't think they would; they seemed like a team that had their roles and expectations dialed in.

She could make out the sounds of his footfalls crunching in the snow beside her, and she glanced over at him. The red light on Grant's body camera was on, indicating he was recording everything they were doing. *Good.*

If they missed anything, or if something unexpected happened, he would have a record of it. Maybe they could find things after the fact when they were back in their warm offices and reviewing the recordings. Though, if she had her way, there would be no need. She wouldn't be stopping her search until Lily was safely back in her care and out of harm's way.

The mountain grew steeper and, as the sun slipped behind the peaks and cast them in the cold, wintery shade of impending night, the trail they had been following became harder and harder to see. As she wove around a bend in what must have been a game trail under the snow, the footsteps they'd been following disappeared. For a moment, she stopped and waited for Grant to catch up. He was saying something into his handset, and as he stopped beside her, he struggled to catch his breath.

She would have assumed a sergeant would be in better shape—he must have spent his entire adult life getting to the position he was in within the department. Yet he probably was more of a paper pusher than a boots-on-the-ground kind of guy. It was one of the benefits from moving up in any organization—manual labor grew lighter while mental fortitude became more pivotal.

"You okay?" he asked, letting out a long breath as though he was forcing his body to fall back in line with his hard-edged spirit.

She nodded. "The trail just disappeared."

He looked down at the ground, seeming to notice it for the first time in at least a mile. "You're right." He glanced up at the sky, and a fat snowflake landed on his cheek. As he looked back toward her, she watched as the flake disappeared into nothing more than a droplet of water, which he wiped away with the back of his hand.

Even in the gray, she could see his cheeks were cherry red from the cold and exertion. She considered slowing down for him, allowing him time to recover, but there was no time for rest. Not when it came to Lily. They had to go.

"Hasn't Daisy been leading us, not you?" he asked.

She shook her head. "Yeah, but no. We've mostly been just following the tracks. The problem with snow and cold is that in this kind of weather, especially with the wind, the scents she uses to track can disappear pretty rapidly. The wind alone can really make the odors drift off course. That being said, I'll put her on this, but if they got off this trail, it could really slow down our progress."

He gave a dip of the head, and though she thought he would have been secretly relieved to slow down, he looked as frustrated as she felt. "We won't stop, Elle, I promise. I will do everything and put every resource I can behind finding Lily." His handset crackled, and she could make out a woman's voice but couldn't hear what she was saying. A thin smile moved over his lips and he looked up at her. "Search and rescue is on the ground. They just arrived at the house."

She glanced down at her watch. They had been on the trail now for a little under an hour. At the pace they had been moving, that made them just less than three miles from where Lily had last been seen.

"They are putting together their plan, but for now it sounds like they are going to bring up their four-wheelers, then send hikers out to catch up with us, maybe even get Two Bear helicopter to fly them in, but they are still working on that. I let them know we are still running tracks, but that the tracks may have given out."

A thin wave of relief washed over her. At the very least, they wouldn't be the only two on the mountain searching.

She gave Daisy her command, and the dog got on scent. Daisy pulled at the leather lead, glad to finally be back in control of the situation. The rocks under the slick pack of snow made travel slippery as they moved higher and deeper into the timber. The snow went from a few inches deep to now nearly touching her ankles over her hiking boots.

Hopefully when the trio had made it to this point in the trail, Lily was no longer being forced to hike without her shoes. She could imagine Lily now; she'd never been one for long walks, and especially not any that involved her being scared and uncomfortable. Lily had to have been crying the moment she had left the house, and by this point she was probably exhausted and in an overwhelmed flurry of hiccups and sobs.

Elle's chest ached as she thought of Lily and how scared she must have been.

Lily, baby girl, it's going to be okay. She sent up a silent prayer to the universe. Hopefully Lily knew that she was going to come out here looking for her, that she would never let her get hurt… And yet, hadn't she done just that?

She tried to swallow back the guilt that welled in her throat. Guilt would do nothing to make things better; all it would do was obscure her focus on the goal of getting Lily back and into safety.

Daisy pulled harder as they moved up a switchback.

The world was almost pitch-black, and between the falling snow and the enveloping timber, she couldn't even make out light from the stars. Luckily, the city lights from below were reflecting off the clouds and giving her just enough illumination to find her next step.

Lily would have hated this. She hated the dark. On the rare occasions she had been there to put Lily to bed, Lily had always asked for a night-light and for Elle to promise to stand in her room until she had fallen asleep.

The first night had taken two hours, three bedtime stories and nearly one million glasses of water and trips
to the restroom.

She smiled at the memory and how it brought with it
the faint scent of baby powder and new dolls.

Lily would be okay. She had to be okay. *I'm coming
for you, baby.*

She sped up.

Maybe the trio had stopped for the night. If they were
out here on their own volition, they would have likely
called it a night and put down a place for a camp—
along with a fire to keep them warm. If they were kid-
napped, if the perpetrator wanted to keep them alive
and relatively unscathed, he would have needed to let
them rest soon.

Which meant all they had to do to catch up with the
trio was keep pushing forward.

The wind pressed against her cheeks, blowing down
hard from the top of the mountain. Elle pulled in a long
breath, hoping to catch the tarry scent of burning pine
and a campfire, but she couldn't smell anything but the
biting scent of ice.

Without a fire it was unlikely that anyone could survive a night out here, not at the mercy of the elements.
Without shoes and drained from miles of hiking, Lily
would be especially at risk. She didn't have the body
mass or the gear to be out here like she was for any extended period of time, let alone the night hours when
the temperature was expected to drop at least another
twenty degrees.

Daisy paused.

"What is it, Daisy? *Poshli*." She took a step, urging the dog forward.

Instead, Daisy sat down and looked up the mountain, signaling.

"What did you find, girl?" She walked to Daisy and searched the ground; she couldn't see anything, and she was forced to flip on the light on her cell phone to illuminate the ground. There, barely poking up from the snow, was a purple mitten.

Lily's mitten.

The lump returned to her throat. Not only did Lily not have shoes, but now she was missing a glove.

Why hadn't they stopped to pick up her glove?

They must have been moving fast. Catherine wasn't the best mother Elle had ever seen, but she was hardly the worst. She had seen terrorists use children in ways that she would have never thought of or expected, but Catherine wasn't the type who would just let her daughter freeze. Catherine loved her.

Elle had to assume she would fight for her daughter. Perhaps that was where the blood they had found had come from. Perhaps it was Catherine's. If she had been in the mother's shoes, she would have fought tooth and nail until they were safe.

Then again, from the trail they had followed so far, there hadn't been any more areas where it looked as though there had been an altercation—at least not when they could make out the tracks in the snow. Did that mean that Catherine had just gone along with the man? Had she allowed herself to be pliable? Or had the man been threatening them? Or was Catherine out here for some purpose that they didn't yet understand?

Grant stopped beside her, taking pictures with his cell phone and noting the mitten for the camera.

The wind washed through the timber, making the branches rub against each other and creating an eerie melody from nature's cello. The sound made chills run down her spine.

It's nothing. I can't be afraid. There's no time for fear. Not for myself.

Clearly, she had watched too many horror flicks, but she couldn't let them seep into this search.

Grant slipped on a pair of nitrile gloves and took out a plastic bag from his pocket. Ever so meticulously, he leaned down and picked up the mitten and glided it into the bag, careful to keep it as pristine as he could, no doubt in an effort to protect any evidence they acquired should they need to take this to court or be judged for their actions later.

They both stared at the glove for a long moment. There was a faint red stain on the seam near the fingertips of the mitten, almost as if Lily had touched a wound with the edge of her glove.

"Does it seem odd to you that they would have remembered to bring her gloves but not boots?" Grant asked.

"If I know anything from my experience with kids, it's that they can never find their shoes when you're in a hurry." There was a wisp of a smile at the corners of her lips, but it was overtaken by the gravity of the moment.

She pointed the light of her phone up the mountain.

It was hard to tell how far they were from the peak, or how much farther they would go from here. How far could Lily have gone if she was bloodied and cold?

Not much farther.

"I bet that blood isn't from her. It's probably Catherine's," she said, her voice sounding hollow and dampened by the snowy world around them.

Grant frowned, shrugging. He turned on the light of his phone and illuminated the bagged glove as if doing so would give him the answers they were seeking. "It's possible. But hell, anything is." He clamped his mouth shut like he was refusing to say another damned word on the subject, always the cop. There was nothing they were better at than being unflappable.

She both loved and hated that calm in the face of chaos. Why couldn't he just say what he thought, what he feared? Then again, she had enough fears and imagined outcomes; if he laid his upon her, she wasn't sure she was strong enough to bear the weight.

Why couldn't she be stronger?

Hopefully Lily was proving to be far more formidable. Lily's smiling face floated to the front of her mind, making tears well in her eyes.

The wind rustled through the pines, hard and faster, and there was the drop of snow from branches, the sound reminiscent of footfalls. Just like the answers, even the forest was attempting to run away from them.

There was a thud and a crack of a branch, and she shined her light in the direction of the sound. She wasn't entirely sure whether or not it was more snow falling or something else, maybe an animal. This time of year, bears were in hibernation, but it could've been something large like an elk or even possibly a mountain lion.

Wouldn't that be crazy, them coming up the mountain looking for the missing Clarks and their possible kidnapper and then she and Grant falling victim to another kind of predator? The darkness in her heart made her laugh at the sick humor.

She looked at Daisy, but the dog was sniffing the ground around where they'd found the mitten and seemed oblivious to the noise coming from the woods. Daisy was good, but just like her, the dog had a habit of being almost myopic when it came to the task at hand.

She moved the beam of her light right to left, and as she was about to look away, she made out the unmistakable glow of two eyes from her peripheral vision. Instinctively, she stepped closer to Daisy and in front of Grant as though she was his shield. She moved the light in the direction of the eyes, but as she did, they disappeared into the thick stand of timber. Though she searched the area where she thought the animal had gone, she didn't see it again.

Daisy wasn't the only animal who seemed to be drawn to Lily—or rather, the scent of blood.

If the scavengers were starting to descend, she and Grant were likely walking into something far more sinister than simply two missing people.

Her stomach roiled at the thought.

She looked to the place where they had found the glove and then up at Grant. She thought about telling him of the eyes in the darkness, but she held back. There were plenty of things to be frightened of, but eyes star-

ing out of the darkness seemed like the most innocuous
of the dangers they faced. Whatever animal had been
staring at them had been skittish. It was likely more
curious than anything else.

Like people, there were different kinds of predators—those who preyed upon weakness and were op-
portunistic killers, almost scavengers in their selection
of their weak quarry, and then there were those predators who sought more challenging prey in order to test
their killing abilities. The animal in the woods was
likely more the scavenger type and less the stalker...
Or perhaps it was situationally dependent. Perhaps the
predator in the woods was seeking an easy meal because of the spent blood and wouldn't waste its energy
stalking them.

"You okay?" Grant asked. He put his hand on the
side of her waist, and the action was so unexpected that
she allowed his hand to remain.

She didn't like to be touched.

"Yeah, just thought I saw something, but it was nothing." It was strange how she wanted to protect this man.
Instead of stepping away, she wanted to reach out, to
shield him.

Or maybe it wasn't about the man at all. Maybe she
was just acting this way in an effort to protect herself
from feeling more fear. But now wasn't the time for
some deep introspection; no, this was the time for Lily.

He motioned up the hill. "Do you see that up there?"

She had no idea what he was talking about. "What?"

He pointed his finger more vehemently as if his simple action would clarify the entire situation for her. "Up

there, see that line in the snow? There, under the tree." He shined the beam of his flashlight near the base of a large fir tree.

She finally spotted what appeared to be a drag mark in the snow. Though they were at least a dozen yards from the spot, it appeared to be the approximate width of a body.

Carefully, they picked their way straight up the hillside, moving through deadfall. There was the snap of sticks and the crunch of the snow as they slowly struggled upward. It was steep, and as they neared the tree, Grant grunted. She glanced in his direction in time to watch him slip, then catch and right himself.

If that mark in the snow was a drag mark, how could anyone move a body through this? They could barely walk through it on their own even without a three-year-old.

When she was growing up, her father had taught her to hunt. When he wasn't jetting around the world and taking down bad guys for the US government, he had taken her and her siblings out into the woods. They had spent time every fall and early winter in the woods, tracking and learning the patterns of animals. Her father had always told her it was so they could be more in touch with nature, but as she grew older, she realized it was just as much about human nature as it was about flora and fauna.

One of the things that her father had drilled into her was that when animals and humans were injured, they would look for areas of cover. Most animals would run downhill toward water sources—creek beds and rivers.

If water wasn't close by or if they were significantly injured, they would seek shelter from trees.

As she stopped to catch her breath, she realized that what they were looking at wasn't likely to be a drag mark from someone being pulled up the hill, but it was more likely whoever had been hiding had slid down. They were, simply put, injured prey hiding from the predator. Little had they known, but predators and scavengers were everywhere around them.

Daisy whined, pulling hard at the lead and nosing in the direction of the tree.

"I know, Daisy." She tried to control her heavy breathing; until now she hadn't realized how much the hike had taken out of her. "Hello?" she called, hoping that if there was someone at the base of the tree, someone they couldn't yet see, that they would call out an answer...anything, even a grunt that could act as a sign of life.

Grant was a few steps ahead of her and stopped as she called out, but there was nothing, only the cascading sounds of the winter wind. Somehow, the world around them felt colder.

Ascending the last few yards, in the thin light she could make out the edge of a bench beneath the tree, a flattened area that sometimes naturally occurred under large, aged trees thanks to years of deadfall accumulation, which then became alcoves.

She silently prayed she was wrong, that her years of wilderness training were making her jump to the wrong conclusions. For all she knew, the animal they had run into below had made a kill and was actually watching them to make sure they didn't find its quarry.

Goose bumps rose on her skin.

It was strange how a person's sixth sense could pique and the mind could usher it away with a million different reasons to not pay it heed. Yet, when it came down to the critical moment, it was usually the sixth sense that would be proven right.

Daisy leaped up and over the edge of the bench and immediately sat down, indicating something. Grant stood beside her, holding out his hand and helping Elle up the last step so she could be beside the dog.

The bench under the tree was larger than she had thought it would have been—it was approximately as wide as the widest point of the tree's canopy, and as she stepped up, the dead limbs of the tree tore at her hair and scraped against her cheeks, forcing her to push the limbs away. It was really no wonder animals would have chosen this alcove to tuck in and away from the world.

Grant grunted as he stepped up. She held back the branches so he could move beside her without being ripped to shreds by the gnarled fingers of the protective sentry. The dry twig in her hand snapped, the sound making her jump.

"You're okay," Grant whispered, as though he was just as at odds with the fear in his gut as she was. His hand found its way to her waist again, and this time instead of merely allowing his touch, she moved into it ever so slightly.

"I'm fine," she lied.

He moved the beam of his flashlight in the direction

of the base of the tree, but there were so many branches that he was forced to crouch down. As he moved, he sucked in a breath.

She dropped to her knees in the snow and dirt beside him. There, slumped against the gray bark, was a woman. Her hands were palm up in her lap. She listed to the right, and her face and shoulder were pressed into the brackish moss and bark. Her face was down, but thanks to the bottled, platinum-blond color of her hair, Elle knew she was staring at Catherine.

She glanced at Catherine's fingers. The tips were purple, but her skin was the gray-white that only came with death.

Chapter 6

The Two Bear helo touched down at the top of the mountain just short of midnight on one of the longest days of Grant's life. He had thought he had been in good shape, but apparently a six-plus-mile hike straight up the face of a mountain wasn't something his body was adequately prepared for. He waited as the coroner stepped out of the helicopter, followed by a few more members of the search and rescue team.

The members of the team who had come up from the bottom of the mountain had finally caught up with them, and those volunteers were now in a holding pattern, sitting and resting while they waited for the helo team.

The commander, Melody, stepped out and made her way toward him, holding her head and crouching down to protect herself from the rotor's wash. "Any new information?" she called over the noise of the blades.

He shook his head and motioned for her to follow him toward the rest of their waiting team. The helicopter took off, dipping its nose as it turned and descended back down toward the valley and the city at its heart.

Part of him wished he was on the bird, having completed the task and having found Lily and the man who was still at large. Unfortunately, he had fallen short.

The coroner followed in Melody's wake, looking down at his phone like he was deep into reading something on the screen. As they stopped, the coroner bumped into her. "Whoa, sorry," he said, finally looking up. "How long has it been since you found the deceased?"

Well, at least he wasn't one for screwing around.

"It's been about two hours."

"And you said she was limp when you found her? No signs of rigor mortis setting in?" The coroner made a note on his phone.

"We only touched her to try and get a pulse, but her neck was soft to the touch."

The coroner nodded. He was all about getting straight to the point. If only Grant had more people in his life who ran on that kind of a timeline. Elle was just starting a campfire as he glanced over at her. As if feeling his gaze, she looked at him. Their eyes connected for a moment, and he could see that hers were red and tired.

She needed to get off this mountain, or at the very least take a rest and then start fresh in the morning. Yet he was sure that no matter what he said to her, or how hard he tried to convince her, there was nothing he could do to pull her away from this. She wasn't going to stop until Lily was safe.

Unfortunately, their trail had run dry. No matter how much Daisy had sniffed and searched, it seemed as if where Catherine's body had been found was also the last place there had been any active scent. They had spent at least an hour while they had waited for the teams, looking for any leads. Nothing. It was almost as if Lily and the presumed man had disappeared the moment Catherine died.

As the flames took hold and enveloped the logs in the fire, Elle made her way over to them. Melody and the SAR team who had just arrived sat down next to the four already around the fire, and they all started talking, something about maps and directions. A few were checking their radios and getting ready for the dog and pony show.

The coroner looked up from his notes. "From the temperature out here currently and from what information you have given me, I think it is fair to assume that our victim has been dead for no more than four to six hours based on the primary indicators. The cold has kept her from going into full rigor mortis, but I would expect, given her glycogen output hiking up the hill, if my math is correct, the victim will probably start having the onset of rigor mortis within the next hour. But first I must see the vic."

He wasn't sure what to make of the information. Did that mean that the coroner wanted to get her off the mountain before she was completely immobilized?

"Can you take me to her?" the coroner asked, holding on to the strap of the satchel that was crossed over his chest.

Elle looked at him, asking for an invitation though she said nothing aloud. "Yeah," Grant said, "Elle, why don't you join us?"

She gave him a tip of the head in thanks, but the coroner gave her a quick side-eye before sighing and shrugging her presence off.

"Let's go," the coroner said, pointing vaguely downhill. "It is colder than the backside of the moon up here, and I have a hot cup of coffee with my name on it sitting in my living room."

Was that the sand in this man's craw? That he was having to come out to the woods in the cold in the middle of the night in order to retrieve a body?

He had met the deputy coroner a few times—he worked in the same office, but the deputy coroner was on the other side and they rarely shared more than a few words socially. Now, he wasn't too upset that his time had been limited with the officer. They were definitely cut from different cloth. When he'd been acting as coroner a few years ago, he was always jonesing to go on a call—not that he wished anyone an ill fate—he just found the work fascinating. It was a small thing, helping the dead find rest. Yet it brought solace to the victims' families, and someone had to do it.

If Grant hadn't become a cop, he wouldn't have minded going to work as a medical examiner. He always loved working through a good mystery, and nothing was more confusing than people—though the living were far more confusing than the dead.

Elle led the way down the hill, taking the broken trail until they were standing just above the ledge and the tree where Catherine could be found.

The coroner looked over his shoulder at him, like he found it a nuisance that he was going to have to crawl down over the ledge and onto the bench to get to the deceased woman. Yep, this coroner would need some more hours on this job. It was a great learning opportunity, but it seemed as though the kid was not quite realizing that just yet. Until he did, Grant would make sure to make a few calls when he got back to the office.

Grant and Elle climbed down onto the bench, carefully working around the limbs of the tree until they once again found themselves face-to-face—well, rather face to *head*—with Catherine. The coroner took a series of photographs, making sure that they were holding up lights to help illuminate the scene.

The coroner clicked his tongue a few times before reaching into his satchel and taking out a pair of nitrile gloves. He set to work taking more pictures and then going over the body. He took measurements of the scene, documenting everything in his phone before finally touching Catherine's head. He moved her chin up and peered under her neck. There, beneath the base of her chin, was a large abrasion. "Hmm."

He took another picture and made a note.

The coroner's movements were slow, methodical as he started at the top of the woman's body and worked his way down. He unzipped her jacket. Her white silk blouse was stained deep crimson red, some areas so dark that it was almost black with blood. At the center of the blackness were slits in the cloth and the flesh beneath.

Grant sucked in a breath.

"Yep," the coroner said, sounding unsurprised, "looks like we have found the most likely cause of death. Looks like we have at least ten or fifteen puncture wounds here, but the medical examiner will have to open her up for the official count—and the weapon used, but from what I can see… I'd guess it was a large fixed-blade knife. There are some wide, deep punctures here." He moved back a bit of the woman's stained shirt to expose what looked like a two-inch-long stab wound.

As he moved the shirt slightly, Elle let out a thin wheezing sound, making Grant turn.

Tears were streaming down her face, and Daisy was licking her hand. He hadn't been thinking. If he had been, he would have never put her in the position to watch her former employer being poked and prodded.

He wrapped his arm around her shoulder and led her away. Whatever the coroner found, he could tell them later. For now, Grant needed get her the hell out of there.

Elle's body was rigid under his arm, but she didn't resist as he led her away. Daisy followed in their footsteps, watching warily as her mistress slowly picked her way back up the hill. It took twenty minutes to climb to the top of the mountain, where the SAR team had moved out, leaving the campfire gently flickering in the darkness. To the north, he could make out the thin lights of their flashlights as they started to make their way over to the other side of the mountain saddle.

As he stood with Elle in the thin firelight, watching the beams of flashlights bounce around and move between the smattering of trees at the top of the mountain, he couldn't help but feel the futility in their situation. If their kidnapper was capable of such a brutal murder, one with possibly dozens of stab wounds, they had to be angry. And when a killer was so filled with rage, there was no telling what they might do—and not even a child would be considered out of bounds when it came to murder.

Chapter 7

Elle didn't know when she fell asleep—she sure as hell hadn't meant to, not with everything happening. Yet, at some point when she had been sitting beside the fire wrapped in Grant's warm embrace with Daisy on her feet, she must have succumbed to her exhaustion. As she woke, she looked out at the fire. During the night, someone must have kept it fed, as it was in full roar, a trio of large blackened logs at its heart.

She was lying on a bed of pine boughs, and there was a thin Mylar blanket over her. It surprised her that she had been sleeping so hard that someone could have moved her in such a way, but at the same time, exhaustion had that effect on her. Honestly, she couldn't recall a time she had been more physically or emotionally drained.

She had been in some real pits of hell before—her thoughts drifted back to the empty pair of shoes at the bomb site—but even then, she had struggled to find sleep. During that time in her life, she had turned to sleeping pills and vodka. Her body never allowed her to sleep like she had last night.

There was the crunch of footsteps in the snow behind her, and she considered pretending she was still asleep. Yet, no matter how much she wanted to hide from the reality that she was confronted with, Lily depended on her.

She turned. Grant was standing with his back to her, looking out at the sun as it peeked over the top of the mountains to the east. Daisy was seated on the ground beside him, and he was scratching behind her ears. Of course, Daisy would be amenable to a good-looking man who wanted to give her attention. And yet, Elle couldn't help but be a little bit jealous that the dog had given herself so freely over to the man.

"Where is everyone?" she asked, sitting up.

"After you fell asleep, I helped the coroner bag Catherine's remains. Two Bear dropped the line from the helo, and we got her on board." He took out his phone and peered down at the screen. "Catherine's remains were transported to the medical examiner's office, where they are already performing an autopsy. They found hair samples on her body, and they have started performing DNA analysis in hope we can find the identity of the murderer."

She nodded, wishing she was slightly more awake so she could make sense of everything that Grant was trying to tell her without the fuzziness of having just woken. "I'm sorry I fell asleep. You should've woken me. I could've been out there helping you guys." She was suddenly embarrassed that he had witnessed her inability to keep pace with what the situation required. "Where's the SAR team? Have they found anything, any idea as to Lily's location? Has there been a ransom call?"

He looked down at his hands as he scratched Daisy's head slightly more vigorously. "No calls. Yet. They have started working their way down the mountain. This morning, actually about an hour ago, on the other side of the mountain saddle, they found evidence that a helicopter had been on-site."

"Another helicopter, as in one besides Two Bear?" She was confused.

"When Two Bear airlifted the SAR team out, we talked to them, and they said they hadn't been in that specific area—we are thinking someone picked up Lily and her kidnapper before you and I made it to Catherine."

"How do they know it was Lily?" She heard the frantic note in her voice.

"They found a child's tracks near the pickup site. They were covered by last night's snowfall. Lily is gone, airlifted out. If nothing else, at least we know she is still alive and didn't have to spend the night on the mountain."

Thank goodness. "Is there any way we can track her helicopter? There has to be some kind of flight record, right?"

"I have my teams working on that, but whoever this kidnapper is, they have resources that up until now we weren't aware of."

She put her hands over her face and rubbed at her temples. "We were so close. We had a chance to save her..."

He put his hands up in surrender. "It's okay, we will find her. She's relatively unharmed. She's going to be okay."

"You can't tell me any of that." She stood up, the motion so fast that her head swam. She reached out, but there was nothing to support her and Grant rushed to her side. "I don't believe you." She tried to pull away from his touch, but her body was unsteady and he gripped her harder to keep her from falling.

"You need to sit down for a minute. You're probably really dehydrated after yesterday. Did you even drink any water?" He reached behind him and grabbed a water bottle that had been clipped to his utility belt. He opened up the lid with a squeak and handed it over.

Though she was upset, she allowed him to help her to sit and took the water. She hadn't realized how thirsty she was until the ice-cold liquid hit her parched lips. She closed the bottle and handed it back to him with a nod. Logically she knew she wasn't angry with the man who was trying his very best to help her, yet all she wanted to do was snarl and bite at him. Why did he have to be so perfect, having everything she needed before she even knew she needed it—all while looking sexy?

She took another swig of water and reached up to touch her hair, forgetting she was wearing a knit cap.

Her hair poked out from under the edge of the hat above her ears, and she could instantly envision what a mess she must have looked like. Running her fingers over her cheek, she could feel the indentations made by the pine boughs; there was even a small pine needle stuck to the side of her cheek, and she had to scratch to free it from her skin.

Though, what did it really matter what she looked like right now?

The fact she cared about that at all concerned her more than her actual appearance. She wasn't one to get too wrapped up in vanity, but when she was, under these circumstances, it made her wonder what she wasn't admitting to herself when it came to her feelings toward Grant. His hand was on her shoulder, and she found herself enjoying the warmth of his touch.

He barely knew her, and he had gone out of his way last night to make sure that she was comfortable and warm. Taking care of her in her moment of greatest weakness. Did that mean that he also felt something, or did it just fall under the scope of him being the nearly picture-perfect hero he seemed to be?

No. She almost shook her head. *If he is perfect, we would have Lily back in our custody. She would have never had the time to get away.*

As quickly as the angry thoughts came to her, she batted them away. It wasn't Grant's fault she had allowed the little girl to fall into the wrong hands. This was all her fault…everything could be pinned down to her and her error in judgments.

"What's the matter? Are you okay? Do you need

anything?" Grant asked, sitting down on the ground beside her.

Daisy trotted over and gave her a quick lick to the face as if she, too, could tell that Elle was struggling. She wrapped her arm around the dog's neck, and Daisy perched against her, nuzzling her snout under Elle's chin and snuggling in as she hugged her. "I love you, angel," she whispered into the dog's fur.

There was nothing like a dog's touch to calm the most turbulent storms in the soul. Hopefully Lily had an animal with her, something that she could touch that would help her stay calm—that was, if she was still alive.

A sob threatened to escape from her throat, but she tried to bite it back. She was too slow, and the sound rattled from her, far too loud.

Grant's hand moved to her knee, and he put his other arm around her, surrounding her with his stupidly perfect body. Didn't he realize that he was making this all so much worse by being kind? If he would just stop helping her, she could control some of the weakness and stonewall it with her normal aplomb and resolve. What was it about this man that made her break down and actually *feel*?

His thumb gently stroked her inner thigh, and she felt what little control she still had drift from her. Didn't he realize what he was doing to her? He was going to make her totally melt down. There would be tears. No woman in the world wanted to wake up and just go straight to fear and crying over the things that were outside her control.

There was only one way she was going to get out of this moment by not breaking down and just crying in front of him again. She had to do it if she wanted to save what little pride she had left.

Before she had a chance to reconsider her impulsive thought, she leaned over and pushed her lips to his. He hadn't been ready, but neither was she, and his lips were pulled into a thin smile, making it so she kissed the cool slickness of his teeth.

What was I thinking? Gah, I can be so stupid sometimes.

Embarrassment filled her and she started to move, but before she could pull away, he took her face in his hands and closed his mouth and kissed her back. The tip of his tongue darted out, and he moved it gently against her bottom lip; she followed, tasting the lingering sweetness of his gum and the bite of the cold mountain air. He caressed her cheeks with his thumbs, and his lips slowed, moving her starved, hurried action into a sultry, deep kiss. It was like he could read her mind, follow her thoughts…thoughts and desires she didn't even know she had…and yet that he could satisfy.

If she hadn't gone through so many emotions, she would have called this her very best first kiss. What if this was her last first kiss?

What if she had screwed up her best first kiss by stealing it in the wrong moment but with the right man?

Worse, what if she had just had her first and last kiss with Grant? What if he was once again just trying to save her feelings by doing what he thought she wanted him to do and once they got back down into the valley

and back to their lives, he would let her down grace-
fully? What if none of this was real? Or what if he was
only kissing her because she was kissing him—was it
just some kiss of opportunity?

As his tongue flicked against hers, she tried to force
herself back in the moment, to stop thinking about all
the things that were flipping through her mind. Daisy
plopped down on her foot and let out a long sigh. The
sound made her smile, and as she did, Grant let his
hands move from her face and he sat back.

"Was my kiss that bad?"

"What?" she asked, finally opening her eyes and
looking at him. "No…that's not it." He had the best
eyes—they were green around the outsides and brown
in the middle, and in the thin morning light they even
picked up bits of gray and purple from the sky.

His eyes, just like the man to which they belonged,
were perfect. They were everything, every color…he
was the embodiment of all the things she wanted to see
and feel, and damn it if he didn't make every part of
her body spark with want. But she couldn't have him.

She stood up, carefully away from Daisy, and Grant
moved to reach for her, but she noted how he stopped
himself. Maybe he realized they were wrong, too.
Maybe he had seen her kiss for what she had intended
it to be—a stopgap in the moment, anything to make
her stop feeling. And then…well, and then it screwed
everything up.

She turned her back to him, afraid if she looked
into that perfect face and those perfect eyes she would
sink back down to the ground and beg for him to take

her into his arms. Closing her eyes, she reached up and touched the place on her lip where his tongue had brushed against her. It was still wet from their kiss, and she gently licked the residue.

She tasted like him, and she wished she could keep that flavor on her lips forever—it could be the one part of him that she could keep. The rest of him, she had to let go. Not only was she far too big of a dumpster fire to think having a relationship was a good idea, but she needed to get Lily back and make sure that she would still have a job with STEALTH after this major screwup.

"Elle, you don't need to run away from me."

Oh yes, she did. But unless she and Daisy were about to jog down a damned mountain by themselves, there weren't a whole lot of places she could run to.

"I'm not running away." *Not a lie.* "I just…" *Can't get caught up in falling for someone right now, or ever.* "I don't want to…"

"It's okay," he said, sounding dejected. "You don't need to tell me that you think it was a mistake to kiss me. You're hardly the first woman to kiss and run."

Now that sounded like a story from his past that she wanted to hear, but if she stopped and asked him about it, he might get the wrong idea.

"What is wrong with women?" he countered.

Every hair on the back of her neck stood up. "What in the hell is that supposed to mean?"

His face fell, and he gave her an apologetic stare; he looked like Lily did when she knew she had said something she wasn't supposed to and had been overheard.

Unlike Lily, she couldn't send Grant to the corner for a timeout and a moment to reflect on his mistake.

"I… I don't mean you… I just meant…"

"You most certainly did mean me," she seethed. "Have you men ever stopped to think that maybe it isn't the women who *have something wrong* with them? Have you ever considered that maybe it's men and their failure to actually talk to women? Maybe if you could actually take a moment and express yourself carefully and with accurate language, maybe we could work together?"

"Whoa," he said, sitting back like she had just thrown mud at him. "I… I'm sorry."

She turned to the fire and kicked a pile of snow atop the flames; the logs sizzled as the ice hit them and instantly evaporated into the dry air. She kicked again and again as Grant tried to talk to her, but she blocked him out with the manic kicking and her heaving breaths as she fought the fire, choking it out.

As she worked herself down off the edge of anger, she realized her mistake. Grant hadn't meant to be misogynistic, not the now not-quite-as-perfect specimen of man. He had definitely misspoken, but he wasn't guilty of the things that she had called him out for being.

Just like his statement about kissing and running, it was easy to tell that her own baggage had come back to be hauled out and strewn into the open.

"Elle," he whispered her name, begging, "please listen to me."

Exhausted by her fury, she took a deep breath and released it into the steam rising from the fire. Finally, she turned but said nothing as she looked at him. She didn't know what she wanted him to say to her, or what she should say to him. If anything, she should have apologized for her outburst. She was embarrassed by her overreaction, but at the same time, she had found something cathartic in the meltdown. Maybe Lily and her toddler tantrums had worn off on her, but if they had, there was something to be said for their efficacy in bringing her back to an internal stasis.

She dropped her hands to her sides, releasing the tension from her shoulders as she finally met his pleading gaze. "I'm listening," she said plaintively.

He reached up and took her hands in his, squeezing them. "I think you are so beautiful. I kissed you because I wanted to kiss you. And damn it, if you'd let me, I'd kiss you again—"

"But," she said, interrupting. It was only what he said after the *but* that would really matter. Those words would be the ones he truly meant, the ones that weren't said to assuage the pain but instead would do the tearing.

"*But* you aren't in a good place right now."

She opened her mouth to speak, or perhaps it was from the shock of his words. Did he mean that she was too big of a mess to give love to? Or did he mean that he thought she would never be in a place where they could be together?

Well, if he felt even remotely close to either of those things, she didn't need him. Her anger threatened to boil back up thanks to the salt he had thrown.

She closed her mouth. Maybe he wasn't wrong; she

had already admitted to herself that she was a dumpster fire right now. But how dare he actually call her out for it?

Could she really be upset with him for saying what she had clearly been unable to hide?

No. She couldn't be. It wasn't his fault for the way she was feeling. It was only hers.

All she could really do was try to find the stasis she had thought she had brought into her life only moments before. It sucked, feeling this unbalanced. If only there was some simple fix—if only his kiss could have been that for her.

Though it had led to nothing more than a few extra hurt feelings, at least she had tried. For a moment, he had given her an escape from her thoughts, but it was her responsibility to set things right.

She squeezed his hands as she closed her eyes, taking in the smell of the campfire and the world around them.

He was a sweet man. He was trying to do the right thing. No matter how badly she wanted to push him away and tell him he was wrong in his assessment of her, she couldn't deny the nearly perfect man hadn't missed the mark.

He stood up and let go of her hands so he could wrap his arms around her. He pulled her into his embrace and held her there. She went rigid for a moment, at odds with all the feelings and thoughts inside her, but as his breath caressed her cheek and warmed her, she fell into the rhythm of him. She wished he wasn't wearing a heavy coat so she could hear his heart. It was strange how listening to another person's heartbeat could bring calm. More than calm—she couldn't help but wonder if that in this instance listening to his heartbeat would also bring some semblance of love.

She needed to press herself away at the mere consideration or fluttering of the word *love* from within her. That was the real fire. That word, that sensation, had the power to burn down everything, including the feeble foundation of self-control she was teetering upon.

"You're okay." He whispered the words into her hair, but as he spoke, she could hear the thumping of a helicopter moving toward them in the distance.

As relieved as she was to hear the chopper coming, she couldn't help feeling disappointment, as well. She needed this moment, one only his embrace could provide.

Chapter 8

His father had always told him that the key to a good life was to live for today and prepare for tomorrow. It had been two days since he had spoken to Elle, and he couldn't help the feeling that if he had heeded his father's advice, his life could have been going in an entirely different direction. If only he had given in to more than just her kiss, if only he had told her that he wanted her...all of her.

Sure, they didn't need to act on it, but if he had just told her all the things that had been roiling inside him at least she could have known, and he could have been free from going over the what-ifs.

He'd had no excuse to contact her, which made it worse. The case wasn't moving, and the trail seemed cold. No ransom calls had come in. No new information. He knew there were others in DC working it—with a US senator involved, FBI and Secret Service were in the mix—but they weren't sharing information in anything approaching a fulsome way. No one on his team had even been able to get to the senator for an interview. Two days after his wife's murder and daughter's disappearance.

Luckily, it was only in his downtime, the hours after he came home and was standing in the shower, that his mind had been allowed to wander to that night spent on the mountain beside Elle. She had been so sexy, lying there in the campfire light, the oranges and reds picking up the bits of copper in her dark locks and making them shimmer in the night.

He couldn't think of any other woman who'd stayed in his mind that way, where he remembered those kinds of details about her. It made him almost feel bad. He had been with his ex-girlfriend for two years. He had loved her, but he could barely even remember the feel of her hair in his fingers or the color of it in the moonlight. Yet he had spent one night with Elle—probably one of the hardest nights she had ever experienced—and he couldn't get the thoughts of her out of his mind.

Had he really ever loved his ex like he had thought he had? Or were time and absence making those little details, the ones he was noticing about Elle, disappear from his memory? He hoped it was time, because every woman he professed to love deserved to be loved with as much energy and feeling as he could muster. What was love if not given in its entirety?

Any man worth his weight should give his woman

every ounce of himself. It was why he couldn't understand cheating. While he could understand the ability to love more than one person in life, he couldn't understand how a person could have enough love to give two people everything they had at the same time. It was impossible. And if a person wasn't giving all of their love to the person they were with, and had the capacity to spill the same romantic love out to others, then they had to have been with the wrong person.

That was what had happened with his ex. He hadn't cheated, but he found that he could suddenly look at other women and think about wanting them. In that moment, he had known his relationship with her was over. She was a good woman, a lawyer, but he couldn't be with anyone whom he couldn't give himself fully to. She deserved better, a love that would keep them both up at night. And he loved her enough to give that to her, even if that meant it was another man who gave her all she deserved.

It had hurt to let her go, even more when he explained that he didn't think he was enough for her, and she hadn't wanted to accept his rationale. Yet, in the end they had gone their separate ways as friends. She had married a doctor a year later, and Grant couldn't have been happier for her.

Sometimes, like now, he found he was jealous of her ability to move on and find the right man for her while he was still single, but he was happy for her. She deserved the best things in life, and if life wasn't ready to bring him the same grace of happiness...well, he had to just accept the things it did have to offer.

As he turned off the shower and stepped out and started drying off, his thoughts moved back to Elle. Was she the one he was supposed to have in his life? Was that why every thought he had came back to her? Or was it that he was addicted to her because in that moment on the hillside he got to be her knight in shining armor?

He nearly groaned at the thought. He did not just think that.

Yep. There had to be something wrong with him. Maybe he needed to just have a few more minutes alone in the shower in order to clear his mind. Yeah, that could have been it.

She wasn't interested in him. If she had been, she would have called him by now. As it was, he was surprised she hadn't called him to check in on the case. Two days was a hell of a long time when there was a little girl missing.

So far, they had managed to track down the helicopter that had picked up the man and Lily. It had come from the Neptune airfield and was owned by a private party who was hard to track. It was registered to an LLC out of Nevada called NightGens, and when he had tried to call the company it was registered to, he had only come to voice mails and dead ends. Even their address was just some lawyer's office in Las Vegas, and that fellow had been close-mouthed, not even willing to admit he handled the business. Grant had reached out to LVPD, and they'd done him a solid by scoping out the airfield only to come up empty. It had looked abandoned.

Whoever owned that helicopter must have loved their

anonymity, or else the person who had hired them had known they needed a company and a team that could keep them from being found. Either way, it made his investigation and search for the little girl that much harder.

Luckily, Deputy Terrill had taken the lead on Lily's disappearance and had been putting boots on the ground when Grant was off shift. His phone had been pinging nonstop with updates from the teams, but so far everyone had been coming up empty-handed.

The little girl's father, Dean Clark, was set to return to the state today, and Grant would be at the airport waiting to pick him up the minute his plane touched down. The senator had been informed of his wife's death and his daughter's disappearance but had been playing on the stage in Washington, DC, and some office assistant had informed him Senator Clark was working with federal authorities and would talk to him when he returned.

Grant had a hard time not being angry with the man. In this day and age, when information availability was nearly immediate, he couldn't believe that the senator hadn't bothered to check in with the law enforcement who'd first been on the scene. Then, there was nothing about this case that hadn't been a goat rope. If things started to go smoothly and things just easily clicked into place, Grant wasn't sure if he would have trusted it.

From what Grant had been told, the senator hadn't received the news well, which was to be expected. One of the members of the team who had been tasked with tracking him down had managed to talk to the agent who'd first given Clark the news. The senator had actually begun to cry. It was the man's one saving grace in being nearly inaccessible.

In an investigation with a wife and child involved, normally the first suspect on any list for a disappearance or death was the spouse. They were usually the ones with the motive and opportunity. However, from the limited number of interviews they had been doing with household staff and neighbors, including the one who had reported the crime, the senator and his wife appeared to be the picture-perfect couple.

He had even been able to pull the phone records for both Catherine and Dean, and neither had seemed to have any dastardly texts or phone calls from lovers. Really, on paper, they were just as picturesque as everyone had touted them to be. Then again, Elle had made a point of telling him how everything would be exactly that way with this family.

No one on his teams had yet to figure out who the other people had been in the house the day of the kidnapping, the ones Elle had seen. They'd reached out to neighbors, friends, business associates. And fingerprints had been smudged or nonexistent. If those men had been involved, they were smart enough to wipe things down.

After putting on his shoes and grabbing his phone, Grant headed out to his department-issued truck. His phone pinged, and he considered not looking at it while he got settled into his driver's seat.

But it could be Elle. He couldn't gain control of the thought, and if he was honest with himself, it was the only thought he had every time his phone had gone off since he had left her.

She had almost run away from him when they had come down from the mountain. Unfortunately, he had been forced to go in and write up his report about what had happened up there and then give it to the oncoming teams. He had told her to call him and given her his card, but...yeah, nothing.

Maybe she had lost his card. Maybe she'd left it in her pants pocket and then washed it, making it into the little crispy white ball of paper that he so often found when doing his own laundry.

He took out his phone and looked down at the screen. It was another of the deputies who had been on last night. Apparently, they'd had just about as much luck as he and his team had in tracking down any leads.

If they didn't find something soon, anything that could point to Lily's location, he feared that the little girl would get lost to the system. Sure, no one would ever just say they would stop looking, but the everyday grind of what they did, answering calls and serving warrants, had a way of pulling attention away from the crimes that he truly wished he could solve.

If he never found Lily, he would never forgive himself. Elle would never forgive him. From the look on her face when he had told her about Lily going missing from the mountain, he couldn't help but feel like she was already blaming him for not having found her. If only they had hiked faster, if he hadn't slowed them down, maybe they would have made it to Catherine before she had been murdered... And if they hadn't focused so much on Catherine's body, maybe they could have made it to Lily before she had been swept off the mountain.

There had to be answers, something he was missing.

For now, though, he had to call Elle. He had to know she was okay. Hopefully she was doing better than the last time he had seen her. She had been such a mess; her emotions were all over the map and all he could do was be there. It hadn't been enough. Not when all he wanted to do was set things right and be the hero whom she had so desperately needed and yet he had been unable to become.

He had let her down.

He pulled her information up on his computer and found her phone number. Hopefully she wouldn't be too freaked out that he was taking the lead and calling her first. If she was, he would play it off like he was doing his job and nothing more. Hell, he *was* just doing his job by making sure that she was home and well cared for. He could even pull the Daisy card and ask about how the pup was doing; a hike like that could be hard on a dog.

He punched in her number, and after the third ring he was just about to hang up when he heard the distinct click of her picking up the call. "Hello?" she asked. Her voice sounded tired.

Hopefully she had been taking care of herself.

"Hey, Ms. Spade? This is Sergeant Anders from the Missoula County Sheriff's Office. How are you doing today?" What was wrong with him? Why did he go into full professional mode even though all he wanted to do was be himself and ask her all about herself?

It was no wonder she hadn't reached out to him.

"Hello, Sergeant," she said, but she sounded slightly confused. "I'm doing...okay."

He read into the silence of her answer—no doubt she was worried about Lily. How could he have been so stupid as to ask her how she was doing—she wouldn't be all right.

"Did you find her?" she asked, fear flecking her voice.

Of course that would be why she would think he was calling. The pit in his stomach deepened. For once, he wished he could be the hero. "Unfortunately, no. I was calling to check in on you."

There was a prolonged silence, so long that for a moment he wondered if the call had been dropped. He was going to say her name, but then he heard her breath.

"Like I said, I'm okay." She cleared her throat. "But what has happened...it shouldn't matter how I'm feeling. The only thing that matters to me is Lily. If you want me to be okay, I need her to be found and be safe."

He felt like he was on the stand in the courtroom, every action he took or would take being called into question. If he was in her shoes, though, he would be just as adamant about what needed to be done...and if anything, if things weren't being handled as he wanted them to be, he'd be taking matters into his own hands.

Given who her family was, he had to wonder if she was doing the same. Yet he wasn't sure how he could bring it up. She and her crew weren't the normal armchair quarterbacks; they knew what they were doing and had resources that even he and the department didn't have—on top of it all, they didn't have to adhere to the same set of rules and standards that he and his teams did. STEALTH group had lateral freedoms that he envied. It was really no wonder that when it came to international matters, one of the best weapons the government had was military contractors.

From what he knew about their group and others like it, they worked under the UN and had some immunity and leeway others didn't.

"Elle, about your team and your family…" he started.

"What about us?"

"Have you guys made any progress on the case, gotten anything my teams haven't?" He didn't even bother to ask her *if* they were working on this.

She gave a thin chuckle. "I don't know everything your team has pulled, but we have been running into roadblocks. You find the LLC, the one that owns the helo and airport?"

"Is that why you haven't called me? You didn't need me to get answers?" And did she not miss him at all? He tried to make it sound cute, his insecurities, by giving a little laugh, but even to his own ears it sounded false.

She mustn't have been thinking about him like he had been thinking about her. If she had, there wasn't a chance she had gone this long without reaching out. He had waited as long as he humanly could.

"I was actually planning on calling you later today. I was hoping you had gotten farther ahead." There was a tension in her voice that he wanted to assume was her own attraction and pull to him, one that matched his own. "Do you want to meet up today? There are a few things that I wanted to look into, and I was hoping you could give me some of the findings, if there are any, about Catherine's autopsy."

Though he was more than aware he shouldn't have been excited about seeing her and discussing the dead and missing, he couldn't help himself. He would take every second he could get with Elle, even if it wasn't in date form.

"Sure, they are supposed to be wrapping things up and getting the last toxicology findings today. I'll give the medical examiner a call and see if I can pull the full reports. In the meantime, I'm heading to my office. Meet me there."

When he arrived at the courthouse and headed up the stairs to headquarters, she was already standing outside the nondescript door that led to the back offices. It made him wonder if she had been inside his world before. Most people didn't know anything about his department or their sanctum aside from it being on the third floor. It constantly surprised him how well his world of law enforcement was masked from the public eye just by being hidden in plain sight.

When she saw him walking up the steps, she smiled, and it was so real that it hit her eyes. He loved that smile, the way it lit her up even though their lives were dark and heavy. Did he have the same lightness? With all the things he had witnessed and been a part of— the lives that had ended in his hands and the worlds he had watched collapse—it wouldn't have surprised him if that part of him had died.

"Hi," she said, giving him a small wave.

He swallowed, trying to keep control of the emotions that were working through him. "Hey. No Daisy today?"

She shook her head as he walked by her and keyed in the code to open the office door.

"She is back at the ranch, hanging with the pack."

"The ranch?" he asked.

Elle nodded as he opened the door and motioned for her to walk ahead.

"Yeah, my team stays at the group's headquarters at the Widow Maker. They have quite a spread, and each year it is getting bigger." She slipped by him as she spoke, and he couldn't help but look at how her black, firehouse-cloth pants hugged her curves.

She did have some great curves. From the lines on her ass, she liked bikini-style underwear. Probably red. No. Blue. She seemed like the kind of woman who wanted relaxed, easygoing lovemaking. In his limited experience, it was the women who wore red panties who were the wild things and those who leaned more toward blue who were more of his speed.

He couldn't look away from the way her hips swayed as they made their way down the hall toward his office until she turned around and looked at him. He jerked, hoping she didn't notice him looking at her like he had been. She didn't need to think he was some kind of pervert. He wasn't like many of the other cops, guys who were all about their dicks. Sure, he could pull any number of women, but he didn't want just anyone. He was looking for a whole lot more than just sex.

She said something about the case, bringing his

thoughts back to work and he turned away and pretended to read a flyer someone had tacked to the corkboard until he could regain his composure.

"Did you hear me?" she asked, walking back to stand beside him.

"No, what?" He shook his foot ever so slightly.

"Were you able to get the toxicology reports you told me about?" she asked.

Sure his body was not going to give his thoughts away, he turned back to her. "I haven't gotten a chance to look yet. We just got done with our report." He motioned down the hall. "My office is this way. If you're going to ride with me today, I need you to fill out some forms. And to be honest, it's been so long since I've had a rider with me—I assume you'd want to tag along on the case—that I don't even know where the forms are. It may take me a minute to get everything together for you."

He actually couldn't remember the last time he'd had someone outside law enforcement ride with him. It had to have been when he was working patrol, but that had been almost three years ago.

She blushed. "I'm glad you thought enough of me to want to let me join you, then. I thought that what we were doing…it was something you did. You know, joint task force–style."

He gave her a half grin. She wasn't wrong—he did work with a variety of people, but normally they didn't hang out while doing their jobs. "I do work with others, but working with private contracting groups is a new one for me. Trained with you guys before at the Special

Operations Association for the state, but that's about it. We don't often cross paths." He walked into his office and she followed behind. "Feel free to take a seat."

She cleared her throat, like she was trying to dispel some of her nervous energy, or that could have just been his wishful thinking.

Landing on his email, he found the latest from the medical examiner. Clicking on the file, he opened up the complete autopsy reports. "Yep. Looks like we got everything back on Catherine," he said, looking over at Elle. "And, by the way, just to cover our bases...whatever I tell you, it needs to stay between us."

She frowned. "That shouldn't be a problem, just so long as I can let my team in as well—at least, if need requires. Will that be okay?"

"As this is an open investigation, I'm afraid there may be things that I can't tell you. But what I do tell you, you can give to your team...if need requires."

She nodded, but from the tight expression on her face, he could tell that she was slightly annoyed that he couldn't just give her all the answers. He wished he could, if it would make things easier on her. Yet, in his world, there were too many prying eyes and ears and few people he could trust. If something got leaked about this case, something that he had told her, and the kidnapper got off on a murder charge because of Grant's misstep, he wouldn't be able to forgive himself.

Though he was certain that Elle wouldn't do anything or say anything to intentionally cause problems, it was the littlest cracks in a case that could cause them to crumble or implode. And there were few things worse than watching a person he knew was guilty walk for a crime they had committed.

And that was *if* they got their hands on the person or people responsible for Catherine's death and Lily's disappearance. Right now, it was one hell of an *if*, and it just kept getting more precariously unattainable with every passing hour.

He clicked open the file and stared at the pictures the ME had sent over. Catherine's body was exposed. In the woods, he could tell she had been stabbed repeatedly. Yet, seeing her cleaned up and naked, the savagery took on a whole new level. There wasn't any part of her that hadn't been touched by a blade. Whoever had come after her had even sliced at the back of her ankle.

Had they been trying to cut her so she couldn't run away? Had she been trying to run?

From the multitude of wounds, the killer had to have been full of rage—as he had first assumed. Yet who could have been this angry with the woman?

He looked at the picture of Catherine on her side, her back exposed. She had at least fifteen stab wounds to her torso, one just where her kidney was located and another over her heart. Either of them would have been enough to end her life.

One thing most people didn't realize was how slowly a person died. There were only four things that could instantly end a person—a stabbing wasn't one of them. Which meant that, for at least a few moments, Catherine had to have known what was happening to her and that she was likely experiencing her last moments.

The thought made a chill run over his skin.

Maybe she had been fighting, and that was what had caused the rage. It made sense. She had been off the trail when they found her. Maybe she had broken free and the attacker had tried to catch her, cut her Achilles tendon to slow her down. Maybe she had run and hidden under the tree, but the killer knew she wasn't long for the world. That order of events, that made sense... finally. He had an answer as to how she had ended up where they had found her.

He clicked on the picture of Catherine's arms. On the back of the forearms were the bruises and slashes consistent with defensive wounds. She had been fighting.

Good for her.

It was a strange relief to know that this woman hadn't gone down easily. She hadn't won, but she hadn't just given up, either. There was an incredible amount of bravery in her end, one that he appreciated. If only her fight could have been enough, at least enough for them to have found her before she passed.

Unfortunately, he hadn't made it to her in time.

And that, that inability to save everyone who needed his help, was one of the hardest parts of his job.

"Are you okay?" Elle asked, and he realized she was staring at him. He had no idea how long she had been watching.

He pinched his lips. "Yeah. I'm fine. From the looks of things, Catherine fought hard."

Elle sent him a tired smile. "That doesn't surprise me. I just hope that we can work fast enough that her daughter doesn't have to."

He nodded, unable to look her in the eyes. Scanning

the document, he paused as he spotted something in the section about Catherine's clothing. There, it read:

Blood located on upper arm of gray coat. Two-square-inch sample removed and analyzed. Using a precipitin test, it was found blood was human. Blood was type O pos. Deceased was found to be AB positive. As such, blood was not that of the deceased. Further DNA testing is required. Sample sent to state crime lab in Billings.

He wasn't sure whether or not he could give the information to Elle. On one hand, it was intriguing; clearly there were multiple people injured. But what if the injured party wasn't the attacker, but was Lily?

Such information could set Elle over the edge.

"Do you happen to know Lily's blood type?" he asked.

Elle frowned. "No, why?"

"Just curious." He could probably get his hands on that information by the end of the day. At the very least, perhaps he could find out if the other blood was the same type. If it wasn't, they could still hang on to the hopes that the little girl was still alive.

Chapter 9

She couldn't handle sitting there in his office and doing nothing. Elle had never been one for inaction, and ever since she had gotten off the mountain, she had been working on finding Lily. Her boss at STEALTH, Zoey Martin, had put all their tech gurus on task, running drones, LIDAR and every other thing they could to scour the mountain. Then she had them go over every flight record in hopes that they could track down the child.

Unfortunately, even with all of the professionals on their team and their abundant resources, they had come up empty-handed and Elle had ended up sitting here, as hobbled by the sheriff's department and the crime lab's response time as she was by her team's lack of information.

Grant's face was stoic, but she noticed him read something and then move in closer to the screen, making her wonder if he was having a hard time seeing something and needed readers or if he was just focusing hard on something she couldn't see. He was too young for readers, so he had to be focusing. Was it to do with Lily's blood type?

After he had asked her about it, everything in him had seemed to shift. It was like watching Daisy. When she was looking for a scent, she would weave right and left, working the area. Yet when she picked it up, her whole body shifted; she went rigid and the weaving stopped.

Just by watching him read, she could see his weaving had stopped. Grant had picked up a scent.

Unfortunately, he had made it clear that he was only going to give her information on a need-to-know basis. She wished he would trust her and open up, but at the same time she could completely understand the nature of his job. His inability to give her information wasn't really about her, or any of her failings. There were parts of her job that she wouldn't have shared with him, either. Yet it didn't change the fact that it sucked. Lily's life was on the line, and here they were having to play the game of politics and secrets.

She sent a text to Zoey. If anyone could get their hands on Lily's blood type, it was Zoey. She could probably either personally hack a hospital's records system or have one of her team members do it before they even left the office. What that woman could do with a computer was impressive.

In fact, she could probably get into Grant's computer right now. Sure, law enforcement and the courthouse likely had several layers of cybersecurity, but that didn't make them impenetrable. As quickly as the option came to mind, she brushed it away. Whatever was in that report, she would come to learn it on her own. Zoey didn't need to get into more trouble than absolutely necessary.

In fact, she had an idea, and better, she wouldn't have to call in the big guns.

"How do you feel about HIPAA guidelines?" she asked, giving Grant a mischievous grin.

He scowled, but the action was sexy and only partially judgmental. "Why?"

"How badly do we need to know Lily's blood type? Is it critical or just a curiosity?" She silently begged for it to be the latter, just some potentially inconsequential detail that had only a minor bearing on their case.

A pain filled his eyes and moved straight into her core. "It could be pretty important."

She nodded, looking away from him out of fear that if she continued to meet his gaze, what little control she had over her fluxing emotions would collapse. "Then I'm on it."

She picked up her phone and pulled up the email Catherine had first sent her when she had agreed to take on Lily's security detail. There, she found the numbers and information she was looking for. She dialed the pediatrician's office, and a secretary answered. The woman sounded cloying and chipper, at odds with every part of Elle's current existence.

"Hi, Mary," she said, regurgitating the woman's

name in the same chipper tone in hopes it would soften the woman up to the ask she was about to make. "My name is Catherine Clark, and I'm calling about my daughter, Lily Clark."

"Hello, Mrs. Clark, so great to hear from you. How can I help? Is Lily doing okay?"

Grant's eyes were wide with surprise, and her mischievous grin widened into a dark smile. Sometimes the best part of living in small communities was the inherent trust that came with it; fortunately for them today it could be used to their benefit—hopefully.

"Lily is just fine," she lied. "I was just filling out some paperwork for an upcoming summer camp, and I was wondering if you could provide me with some information I have missing from my records. Would you be able to do that?"

"Hmm." The secretary paused, as if she was considering what information she was willing to give. "What kind of info do you need?"

"First, we would need her vaccination records," she lied, trying to think of what reasonable things a camp would need in order to sell her real ask. "Also, it looks like they have a question about blood type, as well. Would that be on record?"

The woman tapped away on a keyboard in the background. "Can you give me her date of birth?"

Elle rattled it off, thanking the real Mrs. Clark for being the ever-so-uptight mother—at least when it came to hiring the help—and also thanking law enforcement for not yet releasing the information about the murder and kidnapping to the media. Otherwise, Mary wouldn't be dealing with her.

"If you like I'd be more than happy to email this information over to you," the secretary said.

"That would be great," she said, giving the woman her encrypted email address that she used for STEALTH. "By chance, did we have her typed and crossed?"

"Yep," the woman said, "looks like she is O positive. Don't worry, I will go ahead and attach those results to the email, as well."

Elle smiled as she thanked the woman and hung up the phone. She looked over at Grant, her smile so wide that it was actually starting to pinch at her cheeks. "It is amazing what a mom can accomplish in five minutes. I don't know if you are aware, but being a mom may actually be kind of magic."

He nodded, but there was something wrong about him. Her smile disappeared.

"What's wrong, Grant?" She slipped her phone back into her purse.

"She's O positive?" he asked, a strange pleading tone to his voice almost as if he was hoping that he had heard the secretary wrong.

"Yeah, why?" There was a long pause, and with each passing second, her body clenched harder and harder, threatening to collapse in upon itself. What wasn't he telling her? What did he know? "You have to tell me what is going on here, Grant. You can't leave me in the dark."

He looked up at her, and she could have sworn there

were tears in the corners of his eyes, but as quickly as she noticed them, he blinked them back. "The examiner found some blood on Catherine's sleeve. Blood that didn't match. It came back as O positive." His voice thinned as he spoke, becoming almost unintelligible.

She swallowed, hard. Lily had been injured...

Elle slumped back into the chair as the news flooded through her senses. She brought her hands to her mouth, chewing on the edge of her fingernail.

Lily was out there, hurt somewhere. She was sitting here and doing nothing. Yet, what could they do? Who could they talk to that would know anything, that could lead them to her?

Futility. This was pure hell.

Grant moved to come closer to her, like he wanted to somehow take back the words he had said to her, but the findings weren't something he could control. This wasn't his fault. None of this was his fault—it was all hers. She put her hand up to stop him from moving closer, and he sat back down in his chair across the desk from her.

He looked dejected. Had he needed to be consoled just as she did? Or was his need to comfort her for her alone?

Right now, it didn't matter. Nothing mattered but getting Lily back.

"Grant," she said, her voice hoarse from the silence and stress.

"Hmm?" he asked, watching her.

"I can't just sit here and hope to find answers."

He nodded, sadness marking his features. "I know.

But there are only so many doors we can knock on to get answers. This case, it's proving to be far more complex than what we had initially assumed it would be, especially with federal law enforcement involved. It's been hard getting anyone to answer our calls in DC, let alone share much beyond what we already know. According to the feds, the senator has had the usual string of death threats, and he'll share those with us when we see him. I hope you know I have been stopping at nothing to get Lily home."

He grabbed some papers as they spit out of the printer and handed them over to her, waivers for her to ride along. She signed them and slid them across his desk. "Can you print out the autopsy findings, too?"

His eyes darkened, and he shook his head. "I can answer questions and give you information, but that could get me into some hot water."

She sighed, but she couldn't pretend that she didn't understand the whys and hows of his thinking. "Fair. But what else did they find? Is there anything? Did they ever manage to get into her phone?"

"iPhones are known for being ridiculously hard to get into without a password. I was hoping that when we meet up with Senator Clark he would give us that." As he spoke, he glanced down at his watch. He picked up her signed forms and stuffed them into the basket on his desk. "In fact, we need to head his way."

She didn't want to stay here and be helpless, but she didn't really want to go and question the senator, either. The good news was that he probably wouldn't even know who she was, as they'd never met each other in person, but that wouldn't stop the growing dislike she held for the man.

How could it have taken him so long to get back to the state when his *daughter* was missing? She would have taken advantage of every possible resource—hell, she *had been already*, to help Lily.

Grant stood up and pulled on his jacket. "His plane, if it's on time, should be arriving in fifteen minutes."

"Do you really think he is going to freely give us information? And you know whatever he has to say, it will be nothing but lies." She felt the fire on her tongue as she spoke.

Grant glanced over at her, his eyes widening. "I take it you don't like Dean Clark?"

She shrugged. "I don't like him or his political ads, but in reality, I don't even know him. He is never with his daughter. In the months I have been working there, I have not once actually seen him in person, let alone heard Lily talk about him. I honestly couldn't tell you one time that she said the word *Daddy*."

He checked his utility belt and then stepped toward the door, motioning for her to walk ahead of him. "That's interesting. You ever have any idea why he is so distant?"

"From the family or from Lily?" she asked, walking into the hall as he closed up and locked the office behind them.

"Both, either… I'm curious. I don't have any kids, but if they didn't talk about me, I would take it pretty hard. I would like to think most men want their children to love them." They made their way out as they spoke.

"Not all men want to be fathers, and I think it's fair to assume he is one only because then he can pull constituents from the suburbs. If he is anything like Catherine, you know what he is focused on—and it most certainly isn't actually being the person he pretends to be." As she spoke, all of her secret and pent-up feelings about the family came boiling to the surface.

In fact, she hadn't even realized she had been thinking such things, and yet there they all were coming out of her mouth like she had opened up some kind of fire hose full of unspoken opinions.

Grant was silent as they made their way outside and to his truck. He opened up the door for her, and as she climbed in, she couldn't help feeling as though she had perhaps said too much and had come off as something and someone she wasn't. She didn't hate Dean or even wish him ill; she just couldn't understand him.

As Grant closed the door and walked around the other side, she watched him move. His coat was stretched tight over his shoulders, and for the first time she noticed how wide they were and how his body was the perfect V-shape of a man who worked out. He stopped and picked something up, and as he moved, she couldn't help but stare at his round ass. That ass. Damn. He must have been the master of squats.

The animalistic part of her brain, the part she wished she could control, made her wonder how it would feel to have him in between her legs. She could almost feel his ass in her hands as he made a few of her wilder fantasies come true.

Maybe it was the tension of the case that turned her

thoughts to carnal pleasures and away from the grimness of reality.

What would it be like to feel his breath mix with hers? To have him whispering all the things he wanted to do to her in her ear?

She shifted in the seat, trying not to let her thoughts reach her body but already knowing that there were some things—just like her thoughts about Grant—that she could not control.

It had been incredible just to kiss that man. Yet things had gone all kinds of wrong when they had. It was up in the air as to what would happen if they were ever to try again, but damn if she didn't want to.

She licked her lips as he got in, and she sucked at her bottom lip before letting it pop out of her mouth as she gave him one more sidelong glance. He started to look over at her, and she quickly glanced away. He didn't need to know the thoughts she was experiencing about him right at this moment. If he did…well, she didn't want to know where it would lead. At least not yet, not right now.

Maybe if they finally found Lily and put Catherine's killer behind bars, then she could focus on getting back into the dating world. Her loneliness could have been the driving force behind everything she was feeling when it came to Grant.

There were a million reasons they couldn't be together. First and foremost, that they worked together—but that wouldn't be a permanent thing. And well, for all intents and purposes, she didn't really *know* him. She wasn't the kind of woman, or at least she didn't think she was the kind, who fell head over heels for a man after having just met him. She was far too methodical for that kind of nonsense. Then again, Daisy had approved, and that spoke volumes about what kind of man he was.

"Lily is going to be okay. It's all going to be okay," he said, looking as though he wanted to reach over and touch her once again.

He kept doing that. "Why don't you want to touch me?" she asked, looking down at his hand.

He balled his fingers into a fist and then extended them toward her. "I want to. Believe me, I *really* want to touch you, but I have to be careful. In my job, if we lay hands on someone, those folks are going to jail."

She tilted her head back as she laughed. "Well, then don't touch me. I have shit to do."

Now he was the one laughing, and she ate up the rich, baritone sound of him cutting up. That would be an amazing way to spend a day, in his arms and listening to that sound.

She reached over and extended her hand to him, palm up. "If you promise not to arrest me, I think we can try this thing."

He slipped his hand into hers, pulling their palms tight. It felt secure there in his grasp, and the image of him bending over and all the things she wanted him to do to her body flashed through her mind.

"I'm glad you wanted to touch me again. I was afraid that I had scared you away." He smiled at her.

That smile…she wasn't sure which part of him she liked best. His eyes pulled her into their medley of colors and lines, but then he spoke. Even his voice...oh, his voice.

"You are something special, Ms. Spade." He lifted her hands and gave her a soft kiss to the back of her knuckles.

Her legs tightened together, giving away all the places her body was responding to his lips on her skin. She didn't know what to say to him. Did she compliment him back, or would it be too forced and inauthentic? But she couldn't just say nothing—maybe she should say thank you, but if she did that, would she seem like a narcissist?

"Thank you," she said, smiling at him. Self-love and knowing her self-worth wasn't narcissism, it was power. And damn it, she wasn't a doormat.

It felt strange and wonderful to claim her power and go against so many of the life lessons that had been thrust down her throat as she had grown up. Her mother had been a powerhouse and her father had been supportive of having a wild child as a daughter, but it was ridiculous how the world worked to stuff a woman in the submissive patriarchal box. If a woman didn't cook for her man, she was lazy. If she liked sex, she was a whore who must have been with hundreds of men. And if she could see the power in herself, the fire within her, she was a stuck-up brat.

His smile widened. "It's nice to hear a woman accept a compliment for once."

She forced herself to look over at him instead of coyly looking down at her hands. "Well, I appreciate you telling me what you are thinking and feeling. Seriously, it is amazing what two people can accomplish if they actually just say what they are thinking and feeling to one another—at least in the way they can."

His grip loosened. "I'm sorry about that. That I can't give you everything you want in the investigation."

Crap.

"That's not what I meant, not at all. I just meant in life." She squeezed his hands in hopes it would reassure him. She wanted to explain it more, to tell him all the things she was thinking and how she wasn't the kind to be intentionally rude or cruel, but they were pulling up to the terminals.

"It's fine," he said, letting go of her and putting the truck into Park. "I'm just glad I get to touch you, at least once in a while."

She felt the heat rising into her cheeks, but she wasn't sure what had caused it, his sweetness or the thought of his skin pressed against her again.

How could this hard-edged, stoic man who had intimidated her when they first met be such a soft-hearted guy when they were alone? He was full of contradictions, but damned if she didn't have a growing need for what he was offering.

Like a true gentleman, he came around and helped her out of his truck. She cleared her throat as she tried her damnedest to stay cool. It was possible that his being a gentleman was a result of his job, and likely a habit of cuffing and stuffing. The thought made her giggle lightly.

"What are you laughing about?" he asked, closing the door behind her.

"Nothing." *And everything.* How had she found herself holding hands with a man she could have sworn was hotter than the surface of the sun?

If he knew all the things she had done and seen, she had a feeling he would accept her for them. And yet, the thought of being with someone in their field—door kicking, so to speak—made her somewhat uncomfortable. Could two people in their world really work? She could be a bit manic about her job, and she had a feeling he could, too.

He hadn't even called her for two days after their night in the woods. That had to mean something, didn't it?

The doors at the front of the terminal opened, and a good-looking man with graying hair at his temples came sauntering out in a barely mussed Armani suit.

Though she had never met the man, she would have known Dean Clark anywhere. She had seen his picture over the fireplace every morning since she had started this job, and his photo ran in campaign ads. And damned if he didn't look exactly like the oil painting of him and his family.

As though he could feel her staring at him, he glanced over at her and their eyes met. In the cold steel blue of his, she could see she may have finally found answers.

Chapter 10

Senator Clark was exactly the man Grant would have expected him to be after having watched him on the news over the years. He'd once heard gossip that the senator had opposed a Veterans Affairs funding bill for a new hospital, but then when the bill passed and funding was granted, he made sure to show up on the day they broke ground—nothing like a photo op at the expense of truth.

The senator swept back his pomaded hair as he spoke to a woman who was beaming up at him when they walked out of the terminal together. He smiled, and Grant wasn't sure he had ever seen a more lustful, flirtatious gaze on any woman. If only the woman knew the truth—that the man she was talking to had come back to Montana because his wife had been murdered.

If anything, at least the senator had just moved himself firmly into the number one position on Grant's list of suspects.

Grant gritted his teeth but smiled as he made his way over to the man. "Senator Clark, I'm Sergeant Anders. We spoke on the phone." He normally would have extended his hand in a show of respect to those he was working with, but he had a hard time acting congenial when the senator had been so damned hard to get in touch with.

The senator kissed the woman on the cheek and slipped something into her purse as he bade her farewell, then he finally turned to Grant. "Hello, Anders. I thought we were going to meet at my hotel?"

His hackles rose and he started to say something, but the man cut him off.

"Regardless, I do appreciate just getting this all taken care of as quickly and as efficiently as we can. I need to get Lily back and find justice for my wife," the man said, a look of concern finally flickering over his features.

Grant wondered if his reaction was nothing more than a staged response and a canned script. He hated to have hope this man was genuinely concerned for his wife and child.

"I'm glad you feel that way, sir," he said. "If you wouldn't mind, perhaps we can find a quiet corner in the airport and we can chat." He motioned back inside.

The man was wheeling a small carry-on bag, and as Grant spoke, he looked down at it as if he was put out that he would have to be seen dragging around a suitcase for any amount of extra time. "Do you mind if I put this in my vehicle?"

He wasn't sure that he could trust the senator to come back, so instead of merely letting him go, he motioned toward Elle. "Sure thing. I could certainly stretch my legs, as well. Nothing quite like sitting in a truck or behind a desk and making phone calls all day." He tried to sound jovial, nonescalatory in any way.

Dean looked over at him and smiled, but it was just as fake as the man it belonged to.

Insincere people, especially those like politicians who used phony concern as a campaign tactic, were hard to read. It made getting information incredibly challenging—and this case would be no exception. The honey and the wax would be inseparable.

Elle walked closer and looked to him. As she did, he realized the senator and Elle didn't actually know one another. How could the man not even know whom he had hired to take care of his child?

"Senator, this is Elle Spade. She is the woman who was hired to help protect your family." As he spoke, Grant nearly bit off his tongue as he realized what he had said and the unintentional burn his words may have left. "She works for STEALTH."

The senator stopped and looked her up and down, like he was taking her all in before choosing his words. If only Grant had taken the same time. He mouthed "I'm sorry" to Elle, but she just shrugged. Her simple action only made him feel that much worse. Of course she was probably beating herself up for what had happened, and then he had gone ahead and made it all that much worse.

"I'm sorry about what has happened, Senator Clark. Please know that I offer my most sincere condolences. Your wife was a remarkable woman," Elle said, bowing her head in sympathy. "I would have never left your home that day if I had known what was going to take place after I had gone."

The senator put his hand on Elle's shoulder, and she tensed under the man's grip. Though the action looked as if it was meant to ease her guilt, there was something insincere about the gesture. Or perhaps Grant was just picking up on what he wanted to see. He didn't like the senator, but that didn't necessarily mean that at his core the man was a monster—or at least more of a monster than any other human being.

Grant's mind wandered to all the things he had seen on the job and the saintlike people who turned out to be the greatest monsters of all and the dangerous-looking biker types who went out of their way to work with law enforcement to stop crimes from happening. Assumptions could be obstacles when it came to finding the truth.

"Thank you, Ms. Spade." The senator squeezed her shoulder. "Know that I don't hold you or your team responsible for what has happened. This was my own mistake. I wish I had told Catherine she required twenty-four-hour protection."

Elle looked even more surprised than Grant felt. The man couldn't have been this kind or understanding. Yet, there he was. Was Grant wrong about him?

Grant watched the senator's features, hoping to read any kind of details the man might give away in his body language. "Why *did* you hire protection?"

"I had been receiving threats. The Secret Service was aware and offered to protect my wife as well as myself, but she refused. She found my job and all these things, safety hazards included, to be invasive." The senator started walking again.

Elle nodded as she walked beside the senator. "She had mentioned that to me on occasion."

The senator gave a thin smile, but it quickly disappeared. "Catherine has always been a stubborn woman. No amount of my talking could convince her to take these threats seriously. She wasn't naive, but she really felt that by living in Montana we would be kept away from the big-city dangers."

Grant nodded. "Do you have a record of any of these threats? Any you think are more credible than others?"

Senator Clark took out his phone as they walked. "What's your email address? I can send you exactly what I sent the Secret Service. I'm surprised they haven't shared it with your team."

Grant wasn't surprised. Federal agencies often had communications and turf issues. It would have been nice if the senator had greased the skids on that.

He handed the man his card. "You can send the information here."

"Great. Just give me a moment." The senator didn't even slow down as he typed away on his phone. "There you go, will be to you in a moment."

They came to the long-term parking, and Grant

stopped walking. "I'll wait here for you while you put your bag away." He lifted his phone slightly.

"I'll be right back. I'm happy to give you as much time as you need to go over all the details. However, I do have some other meetings this evening." He glanced down at his watch. "Actually, I have one with the local media outlets starting in just an hour, and I was hoping to clean up before I met them."

"Sir, I mean this in the most professional way, but I would like to think that should I need you to answer questions about your wife's murder and your daughter's disappearance, I will take priority."

The senator smirked. "Oh, they are my number one priority. They always have been and Lily always will be. However…my job doesn't stop because of events in my personal life. This state and the people within it depend on me and my delegation. I must be able to perform to my greatest abilities. I may only be in this job a few more months before the election is over, and I have people breathing down my neck to make certain things happen."

"People who would use your wife and your family's safety as a card to get you to do what they wanted?"

"Perhaps this is me being as naive as my wife, but when it comes to my world, there are certain things that good, moral people won't do. As you will see in that email, the people who have threatened me are not the kind of people you would call *upstanding*. These are folks who have issues." The senator twisted his bag, clearly annoyed at being held back from being able to do exactly as he wanted.

"Hmm," Grant said, but Elle was giving him the side-eye and he didn't have a clue what it meant. "Let me look things over."

The senator dipped his head in acknowledgment. "I'm parked not far from here."

As he walked away, the only sounds were of the fellow travelers who were chatting away in the parking lots mixed with the scraping sound of plastic suitcase wheels as they ground against the pavement. Oh, he knew that sound entirely too well.

Elle stood beside him as he pulled up the senator's email. "You watch him, make sure he doesn't get lost."

She nodded.

"Did you know about the death threats?" he asked.

"Catherine didn't mention them, but I assumed there had to be something going on—why else would they have called STEALTH? We aren't cheap, and we don't take contracts for people who don't have legitimate safety concerns." Her head was on a swivel, as she must have been monitoring the senator.

He scrolled through the email, which read as though it had been drafted by a lawyer even though it had been sent from the senator's personal account. In the email, he mentioned three possible threats, and with each person of interest he had provided a picture and evidence of the direct threats. One was an audio recording of a voice mail left on the senator's personal phone by a man who called himself Jazz Garner.

He wished he was in his truck so he could listen to the audio and run the names through the database, but it would have to wait.

The next was an email sent by one Philip Crenshaw. He was wearing desert tac gear and a shemagh wrapped around his neck. There was a gun in his hands, but he wasn't displaying a flag or patches on his gear. He was standing next to a mud house, similar to those Grant had seen in pictures of the Middle East. If he had to guess, the guy looked like a contractor. But what contractor would send a senator a death threat? They weren't the kind to threaten, they were the kinds to kill—with no one being the wiser.

Strange.

He pulled up the email. The spelling was poor and the grammar was worse, but the message was clear— if Senator Clark didn't vote for the bill SB 102, there would be hell to pay. Grant had heard of the bill, but he couldn't recall what it was about.

Regardless, he wasn't sure why this had been deemed a credible threat. Yeah, the guy looked intimidating, but without seeing the man's picture it wasn't an email that would have made the hair rise on his arms.

The last threat was from one Steve Rubbick. Another email. In this one, the man had cited neo-Nazi propaganda before writing, "...you and your wife will feel my wrath. I will cut you down like the sheep you are and mutilate your corpse while I make her watch..."

The man went into details, listing things he planned to do to Catherine that made Grant's skin crawl. This man had put time, thought and rage into his threat. Grant could understand why the senator would have taken note. The only thing that wasn't listed was where the man intended to kill them or the senator's home ad-

dress. Either the man hadn't known it or perhaps his letter was nothing more than a rant by a madman.

More than the details or even the diatribe of whys,
it was the rage that drew Grant's ire the most. Catherine had been stabbed more than seventy-three times
in total. That kind of overkill was something that was
only done in a heightened stage of emotional turmoil.

With murderers he had interviewed in the past, when
they committed homicides like this, they talked about
going into an almost trancelike state. They found pleasure in the method, pulling the trigger and focusing on
the muscles in their fingers and the smell of the spent
gunpowder, or when stabbing, they found a rhythm in
their motion and lusted after the sensation of the point
piercing the skin, slicing through muscle and glancing off bone.

"Anything?" Elle asked.

"Definitely some things to go off." He pulled the
picture of the contractor on his phone. "How long have
you been active in the contracting world?"

She shrugged as she stared out into the parking lot.
"I dunno, more than five years now, why?"

"One of our possible suspects is a contractor, or was
one." Asking her if she knew this guy was like asking
someone from New York if they knew another New
Yorker; the chances were almost nil. Yet, he had to
check. He lifted his phone for her to see. "Do you recognize this guy?"

Elle reached over for his phone, not letting her watch
on the senator down. She glanced at the photograph
on his phone. Her gaze flicked over the image and she

looked up, but a second later she looked back at it and stared.

"So, you do know him?" he asked, surprised.

"I didn't know he was a contractor." She frowned. "But he is one of the guys who was with Catherine the day she was killed."

Holy shit.

It couldn't have been that easy. No way. Yet, these stars aligned. Finally, they had gotten their break. They would have gotten it earlier if the senator had bothered to work with the locals.

She flipped to the next photo on Grant's phone. Elle's breath caught in her throat. This man in the photo collage from the senator had also been standing in Catherine's living room the day she had disappeared. The photo of the third man, who was identified as Jazz, was the only one of the group she didn't recognize.

The contractor, Philip, was the man she'd seen smoking a cigar. She closed her eyes, trying to recreate the last image she could recall of the living room and where the men had been standing when she'd last seen them. Steve had been across the room with the group of men, but she couldn't recall what he had been wearing or if he had said anything to her.

There was the sound of footsteps approaching in the distance, and she looked up and watched as the senator returned. He had a smile on his face and gave them a small wave. "The email help at all?" he asked.

Grant returned the man's smile and gave him a stiff nod. "Interesting. We will definitely look into things."

He reached into his pocket and withdrew Catherine's cell phone; it was bagged and tagged for evidence. "I was actually hoping you could help me with one more thing before I hit you with too many questions. Do you know the passcode for your wife's mobile device?"

The senator reached up and ran his hand over his neck, unintentionally covering his weak point. He was stressed. Daisy would do the same thing—cower and cover her neck—if she was upset or concerned for her safety. It was an instinctual move, and Elle had even caught herself doing it sometimes. Yet the senator doing it in this moment struck her as odd. Why would opening up his wife's phone make him uncomfortable?

"I don't know if I can get you in, but I guess I could try." He held out his hand. "You think there's anything on there that could help point you in the right direction, as far as possible suspects go?"

"Don't take it out of the bag." Grant handed the phone over. "As you well know, we're just trying to put some pieces together here. We are trying our hardest to get to the bottom of this case and find justice for your wife as well as locate Lily."

Taking the phone, the senator tapped in a series of numbers. He opened it on his third try and, as it opened, he chuckled and handed the phone back to Grant. "The code is 062510. I'm sorry. I thought the feds already gave this to you."

"What is that?"

"Our wedding anniversary." The senator smiled. "Catherine was always a wonderful wife." As he spoke, his voice cracked with emotion.

Grant nodded. "From everything I've heard about your wife from the witnesses we all have interviewed, it sounds as though you were a very lucky man. I am sorry for your loss."

The senator nodded, clearing his throat. "You guys have anything on Lily yet? The last I'd heard your teams hadn't managed to locate anything that could point us in her direction. Is that still true?"

Elle twitched.

Grant put his phone away and rested his hands on his utility belt, masking his badge. "Unfortunately, we are still struggling to find where she could be located. Again, we are looking."

The senator's eyes darkened, and she could tell he was angry. For the first time, she liked the man. But it had taken talking about Lily before she had seen any genuine emotion.

"Would Lily have known any of the men that were referenced in your email?"

The senator balked. "No, what would make you ask that?"

This time, she wasn't sure if the reaction was real. "I was just wondering if you know of anyone who she would have felt comfortable going with. For a while, on the trail, we found her tracks. She had been walking side by side with her kidnapper for almost a mile."

The senator closed his eyes, and his head dropped low. He ran his hands over his face as they stood there in the cold. When he lifted his head, there were tears in his eyes. "You of all people have to know that I've been a shitty father when it came to Lily. I haven't been with her nearly enough. The truth is, I didn't know you—and I should have. If I tell you I know who was coming and going in her life, that would be a lie. And that, that is something I'm not proud of."

She wouldn't have expected those words to come out of the senator's mouth in a thousand years. He was a seasoned politician, and even for a person in that role, the level of candor and humility in his words stunned her.

Grant nodded, and he also seemed to appear to soften to the man. "Senator, we have all made mistakes in our lives. And as much as I wish you could give me the right answers to our questions, I prefer the honest ones."

The senator dabbed at the corner of his eye, collecting himself. "Do you know when they will be releasing my wife's body? I was hoping to take care of her funeral arrangements while I'm in Montana."

"The medical examiner has filed their reports, but there are a few more tests before everything is finalized. However, I think that you can now claim her remains at any time."

"I will let the funeral home know," he said. "In the meantime, if we are done here, I need to see the rest of my family and take care of some business. If you need to ask me more questions, or if things arise that need my attention, please do not hesitate to reach out."

Elle was sure Grant had more questions for the man, and he had to be as put out by his dismissal of them as she was, but Grant didn't say anything.

The senator turned to her and extended his hand. "And I want to say thank you. I appreciate you coming out and working with the local law enforcement in helping to find my daughter. I didn't fail to notice that you are going above and beyond the call of duty."

She appreciated the flattery. "You are welcome, sir. And I promise I won't stop looking for Lily until I have her in my arms."

"I'm sure that is true." The senator gave her a double pat to her shoulder. "Good evening, and again. Thank you both." He turned and walked away, leaving them standing there at the entrance of the lot.

If she had to explain the situation to someone who hadn't been there, she would have had to admit they had just been worked over by the senator. He was definitely a power player in the world of communication. The old adage of "could sell ketchup Popsicles to a woman in a white dress" came to mind.

They watched him pull out of the lot and make his way to the toll booth before Grant finally turned to her. "What do you make of that?"

She shook her head. "I think that if he's who we need to talk to in order to get answers, then this investigation is going to take a while."

Chapter 11

Grant tapped away on his computer inside the truck. Elle had gone quiet, but he couldn't tell if it was because she was relieved or upset. She was softhearted, and surely the senator had thrown her for a loop, yet she wasn't giving her thoughts away.

If anything, she looked *okay*. Maybe the senator's words had helped to mollify the guilt she must have been feeling about Lily falling to the family's enemies.

Grant opened the audio file. The sound was poor and the man who was speaking was slurring as he spewed hate for the senator. He didn't mention Catherine.

"Do you want me to look through Catherine's phone?" Elle asked, finally breaking the silence between them. "Maybe I can pull something."

He reached into his pocket and handed it over to her. "Have at it."

They had gotten a warrant after they had sent a preservation letter to request that the phone company save the data from the phone as well as from the senator's, but so far, he hadn't received the device's text message and call history. With it open, they might not have to wait for the company to get on the ball.

She tapped in the unlock code and flipped through the screens while he turned back to his computer.

He started by running Jazz through the database. The man came up known, but clean. Next, he turned to the contractor, Philip. Nothing came up when he typed the man's name in the database. As a contractor, the man might be using a false name, Grant thought. He ran the name as an alias, but no matter how deeply he searched, he couldn't even pull this guy's driver's license or known address.

His thoughts moved to Elle. Was she the same way? Was her name even Elle? What if she was working under an alias and just couldn't tell him? If she was, so was the rest of her family. The Spades were well-known in the small, local law enforcement community. They and the rest of the STEALTH group were always more than willing to lend a hand or get information when they were in a pinch.

Yet that didn't make what he knew about her any more real or accurate than what he knew about the senator. The realization bothered him, deeply. At the same time, he couldn't condemn her or judge her because of her lifestyle. There were innumerable details that he couldn't give her about himself. Besides, what was really in a name or background information...even in a past? He liked the woman who sat beside him, the woman who wasn't afraid to show her emotions, who worked harder than most people he knew and lived to make the world a better place.

He sat there thinking about everything as he stared at the screen and pretended to read through the list of ongoing and open calls coming from dispatch. "Elle," he said, finally unable to hold back any longer, "do you use an alias?"

She jerked as she looked up from Catherine's phone. "Huh?"

"Is your name really Elle?" He felt sheepish for even asking.

She chuckled. "You finally going to ask? I was wondering if you would."

He shrugged.

"Yes, my name really is Elle. But when I'm not home, I work under any number of names depending on where in the world I will be. Why?"

He was secretly thankful she had trusted him enough to give him her real name.

"The guy you recognized, do you think he's working an alias right now?" Grant lifted the phone so she could look at the man again.

"If he is on a contract right now, he probably is using a false name." Elle paused for a moment. "And if he was working under an alias, it makes me think he is definitely the man that we should be looking for."

Grant nodded, but he hadn't needed her to point him in the man's direction; he was already there. He typed in the next suspect's name and waited as the computer

ground through the data. Several different Steve Rub-
bicks popped up; they were a variety of ages rang-
ing from eighteen to eighty-four. From the picture, he
guessed the guy they were looking for had to be in his
late thirties to early forties. Three off the list fit the
demographic.

He clicked on the second one, and the man who
popped up was a ringer. Same dark eyes and cleft chin.
According to arrest records, the man had been locked
up for a PFMA, or partner/family member assault, five
years ago. Since then, he'd been free of trouble, but in
his booking photo there was a swastika tattooed at the
base of his throat.

According to his arrest record, his last known address was just outside city limits.

"I have a hit." Grant smiled. "Buckle up. Let's take
a ride out to Steve's place. See if we can find him."

Elle buckled her seat belt, but she barely looked up
from the phone. It surprised him that she wasn't more
excited, but even he was feeling like this very well could
be an ill-fated run. The man had been at the right place
at the right time to fall well within their list of suspects,
but he seemed like the kind who wasn't about to just
roll over and give them the information they wanted. If
anything, he looked entirely antigovernment in the way
he sneered back from his booking photo.

How had such a man ever even stood in the same
room as the senator's wife? STEALTH had been tasked
with personal security for Lily, but apparently they
didn't have any active roles in monitoring who came
and went from the property. And if Catherine wasn't

taking the death threats seriously, it definitely made sense that she wouldn't have pushed the security team for that kind of vetting.

It all came back to being from a sparsely populated and isolated state. Around here, there was an inherent trust. And that naive trust had come back to bite the Clarks squarely in the ass. On the heels of his thoughts was his pity for Elle. What a mess she had found herself in—the scandal would undoubtedly mark her career if the public ever caught word of what had led up to Catherine's death and Lily's disappearance.

Even though STEALTH wasn't responsible for the breech, they would be the ones who would find themselves being scrutinized by the court of public opinion. Luckily, the news hadn't really broken too wide. The only thing he'd seen mentioned was that the sheriff's department was investigating a possible homicide. No word of Lily.

But when and if it came out that a senator's wife had been murdered, it was possible that all hell would break loose. He would be getting calls from every Tom, Dick and Harry who would swear they saw something and knew all the answers. And then there would be the mix of people who wanted to both commend or condemn him and his fellow officers for the work they did. It was an understatement to say his hands would be full.

"Do you have any idea what the men were doing with Catherine? Anything at all?" he asked as they drove toward Steve's place.

Elle shook her head. "I have no idea. Besides myself, Catherine was the only woman there and I thought that was strange, but I didn't pay it too much mind given the nature of her husband's job."

"But you didn't hear anything?"

She nibbled at the inside of her cheek. "They were just acting like frat boys, laughing and joking. I don't remember anything that was said, but I would assume that based on how they acted with one another, they likely knew one another fairly well."

"Do you think the men worked together? That they could all be contractors or in the same crew?"

She nodded. "Maybe, but before any are hired, they have to go through a rigorous background check. This Steve guy isn't someone STEALTH would ever consider hiring, not given his radical leanings—that kind of person makes for a hell of a liability."

"I thought you all lived above the law? No offense intended," he added, but she didn't give any indication that she had taken it as anything more than a legitimate question.

"No one is above the law, not even us." She sent him a knowing smile. "Though we do get to run with a looser set of guidelines."

He could imagine, but he'd also seen innumerable headlines about black ops crews that had run afoul of the law—and changed their names and continued on taking care of the business that would always keep them employed. The only people or organizations he had actually heard of being shuttered were the ones who actually did hire people like Steve—the wild cards who got lost in the bloodlust.

If this guy was a contractor by trade and not merely

some radical, then they very well could have been walking into a hornet's nest. This guy looked like the kind who would be solidly antigovernment and loaded for bear. He probably was the kind who had a target range in his basement and a bug-out tunnel coming out of a panic room.

Grant had no doubt that if he looked up the man's ATF records, he would find a list of gun serial numbers that would make any revolutionary proud. And that was what the man had bought legally. Who knew how many guns and incendiary devices he had bought from gun shows and out of the back of people's cars? Gun trades were a common thing in all rural communities, but in Montana it was well-known that a person could buy or trade for an unregistered gun within the hour if they felt the need.

In most cases, those kinds of trades and purchases weren't something to be overconcerned about; it was just like any other flea market or garage sale purchase. See a need, fill a need kind of thing. Yet, when it came to radicals, they were the reason that it was frowned upon. In all of his years in law enforcement, there were only a small number of cases in which they had solved a homicide by using a gun's serial number. Most of the time, serial numbers were only used to return stolen guns to their original owners.

As they drove up to the house, there were signs on the trees along Steve's dirt driveway that read Trespassers Will Be Shot in dripping red spray paint on plywood.

"Nothing like feeling welcome," Elle said with a dry laugh.

"It may not be a bad idea for you to stay in the car while I introduce myself to this guy."

Her mouth pinched closed.

"I just want you to be safe. You're only a rider. If you were on duty, I'm sure that you would be more than capable of dealing with this guy," he added, trying to tiptoe around her.

Her scowl disappeared, and he was pretty sure he had even seen her dip her head slightly, as if she was thinking, *damn right*. She was something. He liked that she was soft and hard, lace and leather. He had always wanted a woman like that, one who had the power to take control and face the enemy, and who knew she was a badass who could save herself—but one who still occasionally needed saving.

Right now, she didn't need to be saved, but he could still give her some level of protection against the unknown and potentially dangerous.

The road leading to the house was scattered with potholes and cobbles that made the truck bounce and jump, working his suspension. Why was it that all these societal outliers couldn't take care of their property? Or was it some kind of thing that they wanted to slow any intruder's advance to their front door? In this case, he would have believed the man capable of that kind of thinking. If he was watching them on a closed-circuit camera, then he was probably already grabbing his mags and getting himself ready for a shootout.

Luckily, Grant's pickup wasn't easily identifiable as a

police vehicle. It wasn't until a person was up close and personal that they could see the light bar in the windshield that really gave it away. To the layman, it was just another truck, but to this guy… Grant was glad to be locked and loaded.

They came around a bend in the driveway, and the small, boxy house came into view. The place had a corrugated steel roof that was covered in a red patina of rust. The sides of the house were covered with rotting gray wooden siding a few feet up from the ground and then above was torn and faded plastic construction wrap. One of the front windows had been broken, and instead of fixing the glass, the occupants had covered the broken seams with silvery duct tape.

The driveway obviously wasn't some plan to slow; rather, it appeared as though it was neglected out of hardship—just like the rest of the place.

The state of the place was a bit of a shock. Some military contractors made more than $100,000 a year. There were a lot of things a person could do with that kind of money. This man's property didn't give off the scent of prosperity in any way. Maybe he wasn't a contractor after all. Then again, it was also a known thing that when it came to contractors, many had the attitude "earn it to burn it," and that could certainly have been the case here.

It would be smart to look bedraggled from the outside if a person was keeping a gun warehouse behind the walls. Robberies could happen anywhere, but most criminals who were after large hauls weren't going to target a place like this. Then, that could have been thanks to the spray-painted signs, as well.

If he had been on patrol, this would have been one call he would have loved to take. With something like this, at a place that put off the don't-screw-with-me vibe, it was always because there was something interesting and usually dangerous to find.

"I don't feel good about this. Did you let dispatch know that we were heading out here?" Elle asked, running her hands over her hair.

"Don't worry. We will be just fine. Dispatch knows where we are. And you know what to do and how to do it if anything unexpected goes down." He tried to sound unconcerned but wasn't sure he had sold it.

Not to mention the fact that he hadn't actually told dispatch where they would be located. This had been a last-minute, seat-of-the-pants decision to come out here, but dispatch could find him via his phone if they needed to. His phone, just like everyone else's in America, could be tracked with little more than a few clicks of a button.

He pulled the truck to a stop and, with a quick check of his utility belt, stepped out.

"Don't go in the house," she said, still on guard.

The last thing he would do was enter that house, unless things went sideways. "Don't worry, babe, this will be okay."

Though there was no way he could promise anything other than that the future was unknown, she appeared to relax a tiny bit.

He closed his door behind him and looked back at

her one more time before he walked up the steps and knocked on the front door. There weren't any visible cameras, but there easily could have been pinhole cameras carefully placed out of sight.

Grant could hear footsteps coming from inside the house. His heart picked up its pace, and he could feel a thin layer of sweat forming on his lower back, but he couldn't allow his central nervous system to kick in right now. He was the one who had to be in control, even in the midst of an adrenaline jolt.

He tensed to listen, hoping that from somewhere inside he would hear the pitter-patter of small footfalls and Lily's little voice calling out to him. Good God, it would feel so good to get this case buttoned up, and then he could think about all the things he wanted to do to Elle.

Beneath the *bomp, bomp* of an adult's footfalls was a strange pattering *click, click, click*.

He had to have been losing his mind or willing things into existence. There was no way in the world that just because he had been hoping to hear Lily's footfalls at that exact moment that he actually was, but then again, fact could be stranger than fiction.

"Hello?" he called, putting his hand on his sidearm.

"I'll be there in a goddamned minute. Hold your goddamned horses. I'm just putting on my pants." A man's voice, raspy and tired, sounded from inside.

The man could take all the time he needed; the last thing that Grant wanted to see was some guy's tally-wacker wiggling about while he asked him some questions. Unless it was like Pinocchio and grew any time he told a lie.

That was terrible.

Yet, he found himself chuckling. At the same time, he couldn't help the little voice in his head that wondered if that man wasn't actually in there putting pants on, but was instead loading a gun and getting ready to shoot him. A push of adrenaline ran through him, making his hands tremble ever so slightly. He squeezed them into tight balls, willing them to come back to fully being under his control.

Control. He breathed out as he knocked on the door again.

This time instead of the man yelling at him, the door flung open. He gripped his pistol, hard. At knee level, a black-and-white goat wearing a hand-knitted purple sweater with a large yellow *A* on it came bounding outside. It bleated at him, and he was sure it was as close to an expletive as a goat could muster.

He had seen some strange shit, but this was a new one. When he looked back, a man was standing in the doorway and smirking out at him. "What in the hell do ya want?" the man asked, spitting on the ground beside Grant's black boot.

Any hopes of getting this on the right foot were now shot.

He paused, taking in the man who was leaning against the door frame and sneering at him. He was balding, with a comb-over, fortysomething, and wore a torn flannel shirt. His hands were beat-up and his knuckles were bruised, but they seemed right at home on the fellow.

"Are you Steve Rubbick?" Grant asked, ever so

slightly angling so he was sure that the other man could see the badge attached to his utility belt.

The man's gaze flittered downward to his tin star, and the smirk disappeared. "What the hell do you want?"

"My name is Sergeant Anders from the Missoula County Sheriff's Office, and I was just hoping to ask you a few questions. Nothing too major," he said, trying to put the man a little more at ease.

The man bristled. "We don't need no law out here. You ain't welcome."

He wasn't sure what the man meant by "out here"—they were hardly off the grid, being only a few minutes outside the city, but he didn't dare press that issue. "I can understand you not wanting to talk to me today. I get that you weren't expecting this kind of visit during your day." He spoke unassumingly, trying his best to mirror the man and his speech. "I know when I get a day off from work, the last thing I wanna do is deal with all kinds of nonsense."

The man chuffed. "That ain't no shit." He leaned his body more against the frame, putting his hands over his chest.

At least he wasn't coming at him armed and ready for a showdown. "That's a nice little goat you got there. What's its name?"

The man smiled. He had all his teeth, but as he smiled his neck muscles shifted and exposed the tattoo at the base of his throat. Dollars for doughnuts, the goat's name was Adolf.

"He's Arnie and he's a real dumbass, and yeah, I'm

Steve." He didn't extend his hand, but some of the steeliness that he had greeted Grant with had melted off. "That dumbass loves to eat all my goddamned flowers in the spring. Last year, I spent a buncha money on petunias at the store and he ate every damned one of 'em. He's lucky he ain't goat burger."

It was working; the man was letting his guard down and he wasn't even really aware he was doing it. This was one of Grant's favorite aspects of his job—figuring out how to relate to people to get them to open up. People, by and large, were creatures of habit. They ran by a system of social mores and cues that dictated their behaviors until drugs, alcohol or stress affected their judgment.

"I ain't owned a goat. I bet they're a lot of work." He smiled at the man, the action easy and coated with the proverbial butter. "I was always more of a dog person, myself."

The man laughed. "Oh, dogs are good, man. I always had 'em around as a kid, but goats… They the best watchdogs I ever owned. Ain't no one gonna sneak up on me at night with ol' Arnie around."

This just kept getting stranger and stranger, but he wasn't sure he wanted to dig a whole lot more into the man's way of thinking, or else it might dirty his boots. He could empathize all day with odd thinking, but he had to remain objective in order to get this job done.

"I can't imagine who would be sneaking up on you. You got one nice little spread here."

The man puffed up with pride. "I worked real hard getting this place together. I worked for every dime I ever earned, and there ain't no one that is gonna think they're gonna step foot on here and take it away from me."

Though he didn't completely understand the man's ramblings, Grant got the general idea he didn't want to be screwed with. "I bet. What kind of work you do?"

"A little of this and that. I'm telling you, I worked harder than an ugly stripper for each and every dime."

He didn't doubt that for a minute; money was hard to come by for those who weren't born into it in this state. "You look like the security type. You workin' at the mall?" he asked, playing dumb.

The man huffed, clearly a bit put out by his assumption. "Damn, man, what kind of weekend Rambo do you think I am?" He snickered. "I just got back from spending the last six months overseas."

"Overseas, huh? So you've not been around here long? Know anyone named Clark? A girl named Lily?"

The man's eyes narrowed. "Clark's a pretty common name, and like I said, I ain't been back home long. Had a gig in the sandbox."

So, he was likely a contractor. But somehow it just didn't jibe. This man wasn't like any of the other contractors he had ever met. He was more like something out of an FBI video about who not to trust.

"What were you doing over there?" He leaned back a bit, flashing his badge like it had the same effect as truth serum.

The man glanced down, his eyes drawn by his reflexive action. "Well, I ain't supposed to be talkin' about it, but I've been cleaning up a few governmental messes here and there. You know, taking care of business that needs seein' to. That kind of thing."

"You've been contracting for the government, eh?"

The man beamed like he couldn't have been prouder if he had won a gold medal at the dumbass Olympics.

"Which outfit you work for?" Grant asked, giving the man an attaboy bump to the shoulder. "That's some cool shit right there. I got a couple of buddies who have spent some time over there in the sandbox, doing that kind of thing. Good money in it."

The man couldn't have puffed up any bigger or else the buttons on his shirt would have popped open. "Yeah, real good money. But ain't no picnic. You gotta be tough. I seen shit over there…man, there just ain't nothing like it." He stared off into space like he was picking up some memory, likely one that had the power to keep him up at night. That, or he was thinking of a woman. Either way, this man wasn't sleeping anytime soon.

As Rubbick spoke, Grant couldn't help but notice that he had carefully maneuvered around his pressing question. He was probably used to not giving answers, which was something Grant knew a little about himself.

"Who's the woman ya got out there?" the man asked, waving his hand in the general direction of his truck. "She a rider?"

He was a bit surprised Rubbick didn't at least recognize Elle if this was the same person who had been at the Clarks' house. Then, she had said that they had only briefly seen one another, and it was as she had been making her way out of the house. It was more than possible that she had just been a blip on Steve's radar.

"She is a friend of mine," Grant said, trying to sound relaxed and as if her presence was just a normal thing. "I know you can't tell me a whole lot, thanks to the NDAs in your life, but I need to get a few answers to my questions in order to cross you off my list in a murder investigation. You tell me the crew you're working with, and I'd be more than happy to give your boss a call and get you approvals to talk."

The man's eyes narrowed as though he was studying Grant for signs of weakness, but he wasn't about to find any that Steve hadn't already inadvertently pointed out.

"Me and my brother, we're with STEALTH. They are out of Montana here."

The blood drained from his face and Grant had to put his hand against the house and pretend to lean in order to keep himself from swaying. The man had to be screwing with him. "Excuse me, you and your brother work for STEALTH? What's your brother's name?"

"My brother goes by Ace." The man nodded, sending him a crooked smile. "And yeah, STEALTH's a great crew."

He swallowed back the frog in his throat and tried to keep his gaze from skirting over to Elle. He didn't think the STEALTH crew was large enough to have members, especially in the same town, who didn't know each other. So, one of them had to have been lying to him, but who was it, Elle or this man?

"How long you guys been with that group?"

The man tapped his chin. "I guess it's been about a year now."

"Hmm." He couldn't remember how long Elle had been working with them, but he assumed she had been there for a long time. Maybe he had assumed incorrectly.

Or maybe they were both working for STEALTH but were intentionally kept away from one another and used as a system of checks and balances by their superiors. He'd heard of other organizations, the military usually, that used counterspies as a way to keep their troops accountable and from swaying in the wrong directions.

All the possible explanations he could come up with seemed unlikely, but for the life of him he couldn't wrap his head around everything the man's admission had just done to complicate his case—and Grant and Elle's burgeoning relationship.

Chapter 12

When Grant came back to the truck, he was oddly quiet. His eyes were shadowy, and he avoided meeting her gaze as he got in and buckled up. She wanted to ask him what was wrong, but she doubted Grant would tell her.

He slammed the door shut and rolled out of the driveway and onto the main road without a word.

"How did it go?" she asked, already somewhat knowing the answer, but not sure what else to say in order to alleviate the tension which was reverberating around inside the cab of the pickup.

"Fine." He scowled.

Oh shit.

She hated that word. *Fine* could mean a million different things—from calling out a hot woman on Venice

Boulevard all the way to being the last word spoken at the end of a relationship.

In this moment, she had a feeling it was the end of something, and she hated the word even more.

"Did he admit to being at the Clarks' place the day Lily disappeared?"

"No." His jaw was set into a hard line.

"Did he know anything about Lily's current whereabouts?" She tried to unlock his jaw with another question.

He shook his head.

She chewed on the inside of her cheek, trying to think of a way to stop whatever it was that was happening between them. What could Steve have said that would have upset Grant like this? Grant hadn't arrested him, so that had to mean that he didn't believe, or at least couldn't prove, the man had anything to do with the crimes.

"Where are we going now?" she asked, hoping what he needed most was just a change of focus and then they could get back to being where they had been with one another before he had gone up to that damned house.

"I'm going to take you to your place. What's your address?" His words were short and hard, and they hit her like stones.

The air in her lungs escaped her as his words struck her. "I… You…" She motioned back toward the man's place. "What in the hell happened back there? We were doing good. We were a team, and now you come in here and act like I'm your enemy."

He let out a long sigh, and it reminded her of Daisy

when she was trying to relieve her body of stress. It was funny how people liked to pretend they weren't animals. In all actuality, Daisy was a far better soul than either of them could ever hope to be. All Daisy cared about was loving and pleasing her, through her work and through her play. There were no complications, no games—only love.

"I'm sorry. I didn't mean to be an ass with you. Not my intention. I'm just… I guess I'm trying to sort through some new information. That's all." He put his hand out, palm side up and open and closed his hand like he wanted to hold her hand.

Was that where they were now? Could she hold his hand? Five seconds before he had been furious. Did he think he could just give her his hand and everything between them would go back to being all good?

She couldn't help herself. There were all kinds of pains that could be healed with the complexity that came with a lover's touch. Not that he was her lover— not yet, anyway. And even if his touch didn't fix the weirdness that had come between them, at the very least she wouldn't feel quite as alone. They could navigate this as long as they were in it together, no matter what the world had in store for them.

She slipped her hand into his, and he wrapped his fingers around hers. His hand was so much bigger than hers that he nearly encompassed her completely. She liked that feeling of solidity that came with being touched by a man who was so much bigger than her; he made her feel as if he could protect her from almost anything.

"I know you don't want to tell me what happened, but I hope you know that I'm here if you need anything— even just someone to listen and help you sort through your thoughts."

He twitched as he looked over at her. There was something in the way he stared at her that made her feel as if he was trying to read her for secrets and lies. The warmth and sense of protection in his touch began to dissipate and be replaced with the bitterness of distrust. She tried to swallow back the flavor of it from her mouth, but it lingered on her lips.

He finally looked away. "Where are you staying?"

She tried to pull her hand back, but his grip tightened ever so slightly. "Why do you want to get rid of me?" she asked, trying to say the words lightly when all she really wanted to do was yell at him to just open up and tell her exactly what it was that was bothering him so much about her. "Why won't you tell me anything about your conversation? Did he tell you something about Lily? Something bad?" This wasn't merely new information—this had to be something to do with them. She could feel it. It couldn't be about Lily.

He let go of her hand. "Seriously, it's not about Lily. He…he didn't have anything valuable to give us. There hasn't been anything you've lied to me about, is there?"

"What?" she asked, frowning. "No, why? Did the guy tell you something, something that is making you question me?"

He stared out at the road like it was all he could focus on, but he wasn't blinking. She had hit on something.

"He did, didn't he?" she continued. "What did he tell you?"

"I just need to talk to your bosses. That's all." Finally, he let go of her hand, as though he was getting as frustrated as she was.

"Why? Please, Grant, talk to me." It felt weak having to beg him like she was, but she was out of ideas.

He ran his hand down the back of his neck and pulled his truck over to the side of the road.

What terrible thing had Steve told him that it required Grant to pull over in order to talk to her about it? She had seen cops talk on the phone, text and work on their computer, all while driving. She couldn't imagine anything that would have made him respond as he was.

"How long have you been working with your team?"

"The Shadow team or STEALTH?"

He shrugged. "Both."

She looked up and to the left as she tried to pull numbers from her memory. "My family and I have been working together, in some facet or another, for the last ten years. We are the only members of the Shadow team right now. As for STEALTH, we've been working for them for a couple of years. Why?"

"Do you know everyone who is employed with them?" he asked, staring over at her as he clenched the steering wheel.

"I know most, but they have contractors that work for them all over the world." She wasn't sure what he was getting after.

"Ah," he said, and his grip loosened on the steering wheel. "So, it's possible that there could be someone working out of here that you didn't know." He huffed. "I gotta say I'm relieved. I thought for sure that you would know everyone working here."

"I do. Or at least I think I do," she said, as what he was implicitly telling her sank in. "Wait, did Steve say he works for STEALTH?"

"Both him and his brother… Ace." He nodded. "I have to wonder if he was trying to screw with me." He chuckled and ran his fingers through his hair. "Not gonna lie, I'm not quite sure what the hell was going on back there. He threw me. I was worried you were hiding something from me. Something that could have screwed this investigation."

A pit formed in her stomach. She wasn't intentionally keeping anything from him, but that didn't mean anything. There could be any number of things he could have needed to know that she had at her fingertips and yet he was just failing to ask.

"I'm not going to hold anything back from you, Grant. I told you, you can trust me."

A smile finally flickered over his features. "You don't know how much that means to me. Seriously. I have to admit, it freaked me out…the thought of you keeping something like that intentionally from me. I guess, without meaning to, I have come to trust you without you ever telling me it was okay. I felt a bit like a fool."

She smiled back. "There are only a few people in this world that I would say I trust with my life, but you are one of them. I feel lucky to have met you." She looked down at her hands, wishing she was still touching him. "But I have to say, you freaked me out, too. I want you to know that whatever you are thinking, just ask. I can't stand the thought of you thinking I'm something I'm not. And sure, I have a lot of secrets and I have made more mistakes and done things others would judge me for, but I don't want to ever have to hide anything from you."

She wanted him to be hers and for her to be his. She didn't know if he wanted the same, but if she didn't put herself out there and take advantage of these quiet and raw moments that seemed so scarce between them, she would regret it later.

"Why didn't you call me after the night in the woods?" he asked, and she couldn't ignore the faint hurt that flecked his voice.

She pressed her palms together as she tried to find the words. "I… I didn't know how to handle that—you. I just was such a mess. And to be completely honest with you, my team and I had been working hard to locate Lily."

"If you had found her, would you have even called me? Or would your team leaders have made the phone call to the department?" There was a note of insecurity in his words, and it made her chest ache.

"I would have called you. I just… I was a mess."

"But you aren't now?" he asked.

Though she was aware he was just trying to feel her out and measure what she was feeling toward him, she couldn't help but be a little hurt. "I know we've only just started hanging out. But being with you—" she paused, finding her words "—actually, just being *near* you is incredible. You drive me wild. I never, in my wildest dreams, imagined that I would kiss a man in the middle of a job."

He laughed.

"You can laugh all you want," she said, sending him a little smirk, "but I'm serious. I'm normally all business when I'm working. Especially when I have Daisy with me. And with Lily and Catherine, I needed to give them my solid focus, but up there on the mountain, sitting with you… I don't know how to explain it."

"But it felt *right*?" he asked, finishing her thought.

"Yes. *Right*." She smiled as he reached over and took her hand. He drew their entwined hands to his lips and gave her knuckles a kiss. "But it's something more than that. I just can't even—"

"I know exactly what you mean," he said, pulling his truck back on the road.

She wasn't sure that he did, but she was glad they were at least on the same page, a page that could serve as the first of many in building their full story together.

"If you want to talk to Zoey, I'm sure she would be happy to answer any questions you have," Elle said, glad to take some of the pressure off the emotions she and Grant were feeling and trying to navigate together.

She had never completely understood why love had to be so hard. In the history of her relationships, love had never been easy. She had felt love before, but it was something that was so fleeting in her life. If anything, love was a weakness. And maybe that was why she didn't want to talk about it, why they both wanted to push it away and simply focus on the task at hand.

But if they were going to make a go of this thing between them and try and strive for a real relationship, then they needed to talk about the feelings and the weaknesses that came with them. Yet she wasn't sure either of them was ready for that kind of thing. Like they had said, they had only known each other for a short time. In those limited days, love and lust had one hell of a way of looking like each other's identical twins.

After okaying exposing the location of their headquarters to him with Zoey, she pointed Grant in the direction of the Widow Maker Ranch. Sarge, the beloved black gelding who lived at the ranch, was running along the fence line as they made their way to the main house.

Zoey's office was offset from the house in a separate building not far from the stables. In the distance were a series of cabins and row houses. Leading to them was a dirt road, and at the end of it was a flatbed full of trusses, as if they were planning on building yet more cabins or houses.

"I live back there," she said, pointing to the cabin that sat second from the end closest to them. "It's a two-bedroom with one bath, but it fits me perfectly. I was just glad to have my own cabin. A couple of my siblings have chosen to take rooms in the house instead of private cabins." She didn't know why she was telling him all the superfluous details, but she would do anything to make things comfortable between them.

She had no idea why she was feeling so nervous with him—even with their hands intertwined and the acknowledgment that there were mutual feelings between them, she couldn't make her nerves recede. Part of her wondered if it was because of the lingering feeling of his lips on her skin and how badly she wished to feel them again.

"Zoey is probably over there," she said, pointing at the office. "That's our main headquarters. It's where we take reports and have our meetings."

Grant nodded. "But not everyone who works with STEALTH is allowed to be present?"

She shrugged. "No. The main team leaders are normally at most meetings, but folks like me—the grunts—are normally kept out. AJ or Zoey are normally the ones I get my information from."

He nodded and seemed far more at ease.

They parked and made their way over to the ranch's main office. The enormous room was newly constructed and still had the smell of fresh lumber, and it mixed with the ozone smell of the electronics that filled the main area. Zoey was sitting at the far end of the office and swiveled around in her chair as they walked inside. Her hair was purple today, and she had a fresh black tattoo on her neck. "Hey, guys, how's it going?"

Elle smiled. She'd always liked her boss; Zoey was the kind of woman who would not only take no crap from anyone, but she would also make sure that she protected all those around her. If Elle had a choice, she would be just like her when she grew up.

She chuckled at the thought.

"Sorry to bug you," Elle said. "This is Sergeant Grant Anders. He works over at the sheriff's office, and he is helping with the Clark case."

"Ah, I see." The small smile on Zoey's face disappeared, and she searched Elle's face like she was wondering what she had told Grant.

"He has some questions for you."

"Nice to meet you, Mrs.—"

Zoey stood up and stuck out her hand. "Just call me Zoey. I'm not about the patriarchal crap. I may be married and a mom, but no one owns me. My husband and I are partners."

Grant shook her proffered hand. "Nice to meet you. I appreciate you seeing me."

She crossed her arms over her chest, and as she moved, Elle could make out new ink on the top of her breasts, as well. The woman was so cool. Elle had never been one for getting tattoos, but Zoey had her questioning her stalemate on skin art.

"Most of the surveillance team is out for the day, but I should be able to get whatever it is you need," Zoey said, motioning vaguely at the computer screens lining the walls.

"That's great. Right now, though, we were just out talking to one of the men Elle pointed out from the Clarks' place before Catherine disappeared." He glanced over at Elle. "He mentioned that he was working for STEALTH."

Zoey nodded, turning away and making her way back to her workstation at the far end of the windowless room. "What did you say his name was?"

"Steve Rubbick. You heard of him?"

"Hmm. I don't know that name, but you know how it is. These guys could be working under any number of names." Zoey kept her face turned away from them as she tapped away on the computer. "What did he look like?" Finally, she glanced over her shoulder at them.

From the blank expression on Zoey's face, Elle would have said that Zoey was telling the truth about not knowing the man.

"He looks a bit like an extremist. Swastika right here on his neck," Grant said, pointing to the base of his throat.

"Ah," Zoey said. "Well, I don't have to search shit, then. While you can see I'm a fan of ink, I'm not about to hire anyone with gang tats or who are of a questionable moral character." She turned to face them. "I'm proud to say that we only hire contractors who have exceeded our standards and perform at a high ethical level both personally and professionally. We don't want to hire folks we have to monitor."

"Do you know a Philip Crenshaw?" Elle asked, thinking about the frat boy.

"I don't know the name. You have a picture?" Zoey asked.

Grant pulled up a picture of the man from his phone and showed it to Zoey. Zoey choked out a thin laugh. "Yeah, now him…him, I know. He tried to get hired on with us. I handled his interview process. Couldn't have recalled his name, though."

"But he doesn't work for you, I take it?" Grant asked.

Zoey pointed at him. "He had the credentials, but that man was a wild card. He'd had some things in his past that ran a little too far into the legal and ethical gray. I wasn't there and couldn't say if he was right or wrong in making the decisions he did in the heat of the moment, but let's just say I wouldn't have been pleased if he was working for us."

"Do you know where we could locate him?" Grant asked. "I couldn't pull anything up about his last known whereabouts."

"I can see what I can find on him. I will probably have to use the facial recognition software. It may take me a while," Zoey said, pointing at the screens. "You guys have a few hours to burn?"

Elle wasn't sure about what Grant had on his docket, but she hated the thought of not actively searching for Lily. Yet there was little they could physically do without more information—info that was at the mercy of Zoey's tech skills.

"We can hang out for a bit." Grant nodded.

Elle smiled. "I'll just text you their pictures. Maybe you can see if you can pull up anything on Philip."

Grant looked over at Elle. "In the meantime, I'd love to take a look around your place."

That was the last thing she had expected Grant to say, and she could feel her cheeks burning at the thought of being alone with him in her house. At the same time, he hadn't said anything even slightly suggestive.

"Uh, yeah. I'd be happy to show you," Elle said, walking toward the office door with Grant following close behind her.

As they made their way outside, Zoey let out a belly laugh. "You guys have fun. I'll text when I find something. I won't come knocking."

Elle's face burned. Yeah, Zoey definitely worked

on a whole different wavelength than she did; she was far bolder.

Their feet crunched on the frozen snow as they made their way across the parking area and toward the row houses. Her arm brushed against her pocket, and she felt the familiar bump of a phone and realized she still had Catherine's cell phone. "Wait." She pulled the phone out of her pocket and showed it to Grant, then held up her finger, motioning for him to wait for her there. "I'll bet she can make something out of this. I'll be right back."

Though she had started to go through the phone, she had found little usable information. The woman had a million contacts and got more texts and phone calls than a retail pharmacy. Elle had gone through what she could in the time she'd had, but given just the volume of information held in the iPhone, it could have taken her days to find anything—let alone anything that would point them toward the killer or Lily.

Zoey was already tapping away when she made her way back into the office. "'Sup? You guys done already? Girl, you work fast." She sent Elle a devious smile.

"We aren't that kind of friends," Elle said, but the burn returned to her cheeks. Just because they weren't those kinds of friends yet didn't mean that she didn't want to see him naked and underneath her.

"Yeah, right." Zoey laughed. "You do know I'm in intelligence, right? Even if I wasn't, I can see the way the two of you look at each other. Remind me not to put you into an undercover role. You can't lie for shit."

"You've put me in all kinds of undercover roles. I did great." She stuck her tongue out at Zoey.

"True as that may be, you can't lie to me about that man," Zoey teased. "Is there something you needed?"

"I forgot," she said with a nod, holding up the bagged phone for Zoey to see. "Here's Catherine's phone. I wrote the unlock code there on the bag." She handed over the phone, pointing at the numbers scrawled in black Sharpie.

"Sweet. I can definitely use this." Zoey gave her a wide smile. "In the meantime, seriously, go and have some fun."

Zoey stood up and shooed her out of the office, but as Elle took one more look back at the computers, she saw Philip's face staring out at her from the screen. His eyes were dark and brooding, far from the jovial man she had last seen smoking a cigar while laughing with Catherine. The man staring out at her looked like a true, cold-blooded killer.

Chapter 13

The little cabin was even smaller on the inside than it appeared on the outside, and Grant could understand why several of Elle's siblings had chosen to take rooms in the main house over these tiny dwellings. It was smart of the STEALTH company to keep their contractors on-site, especially given the nature of their work and the security risks.

Elle's hands were trembling as she pressed the numbers and unlocked the door. He wanted to tell her not to be nervous, that he didn't have anything less than completely honorable intentions on his mind. Yet he was as nervous as she was, and, well, the rest would have been a lie. He had wanted to press her down and make love to her from the moment their hands had touched. But he wouldn't pressure her for anything. If she wanted to be with him, she could lead the show.

Then, she didn't really seem like an aggressive kind of woman. He doubted she would take the lead and make the first moves.

She opened the door and flipped on the lights as Daisy came barreling down the hallway toward them. "Daisy girl!" she said, clearly as happy to see the dog as the dog was to see her.

Daisy dropped down and rolled over in front of them, her tail wagging so hard that her whole entire butt moved right and left on the vinyl flooring. Elle squatted down and loved on the animal as he chuckled. There was nothing sexier than a woman playing with and loving on her dog.

Daisy stood up and finally seemed to notice him; she lunged toward him and rubbed herself around his legs, almost catlike in her excitement. He was slightly taken aback by the dog's warm reaction to his being there, but they had spent a night together taking care of Elle. "Hi, Daisy," he said, squatting down and giving the dog a vigorous scratch behind the ears. "I missed ya, pupper dog."

He caught Elle smiling out of the corner of his eye.

Daisy gave him a big, slobbering kiss to the side of his cheek. Daisy's breath smelled like dog food.

"Oh," Elle said, covering her mouth with her hands. "She's not much of a licker. Sorry about that. If it makes you feel better, she is the ranch dog who is the least addicted to eating horse manure."

"I'm glad." He laughed, but as Elle must have realized what she said, her face turned crimson.

"I, uh…" She ran her hand down the back of her neck

and looked toward the main living area. "Obviously, I don't have people out to my place very often. I'm sorry if it's a mess. In fact, I can't say that anyone other than my family has been here." She cringed as she looked at her couch, where a basket full of folded laundry sat ready to be put away.

"Your place is cleaner than mine," he said. "I get two days off a week, and I have to say that I don't really enjoy spending my downtime doing chores. I can't even tell you the last time I mopped a floor. Don't feel bad."

"With Daisy around, if I didn't mop the place, it would be covered in muddy paw prints." She let Daisy outside. The dog bounded away, and Elle looked about, making sure she was safe, then closed the door. "She should be good outside for a little while. She sticks around. Want a drink or something?" She rushed away from him toward the kitchen, as if being close to him was making her even more nervous than she had first seemed when they arrived.

He followed her toward the kitchen. "I'd take some water, but I can get it." He wasn't sure who was more on edge, her or him. It was as if all the feelings he'd been having for her had culminated into this single moment and he couldn't quite sift through them all.

He walked to the small cabinet by the sink and grabbed a glass out of the cupboard, but before he could fill it with water, he turned around toward her and put the glass down on the counter. "Are you sure you are okay with my being here? We could just go back to my truck or—"

She moved toward him and threw her arms around

his neck, and her lips pressed against his. For a second, he couldn't quite make sense of what was happening, but then he wrapped his arms around her and pulled her body against his as he kissed her back. She nibbled at his lower lip, and her tongue flicked against his.

He hadn't pegged her as the dominant type, but he had never been more excited to be wrong. She leaned into him, and though he couldn't tell, it felt like she was even lifting her leg as she tiptoed to kiss him. He slid his hands down from her back and took her ass into his hands. It felt even better in his palms than he thought it would. She had to work out, but not so much that there wasn't the softness that he loved on a woman.

She was the perfect combination of soft and toned, feminine but strong.

He laced his lips down her neck, and her breath caressed his skin in a moan. His body awakened at the sound. He could listen to that sound, the weak moan of a woman in want, forever. His lips found the base of her throat, and he traced his tongue along the hard edges of the little V-shape. She sucked in her breath and held it.

He stopped, taking a moment to look at her. Her eyes were the color of the sky in the middle of a storm, promising a temporary break for the sunshine. "You are so damned beautiful. You know that, don't you?"

She tried to avoid his gaze, but he drew her back with his finger until she was staring at him again. "Don't look away. You don't need to. I want to look at you, all of you." Her gaze drifted to his chest, but he didn't know exactly what she was thinking. "If you're not ready for this, or if you are rethinking things with me, don't worry, you can tell me. We can stop this right here and now. We can just go back to being friends."

Elle reached up and took his hands in hers and finally looked up into his eyes. "No. That's not it. I want you. I want this. I want to do things with you that I've never done with anyone else. I just…"

"You don't feel it?"

She frowned. "What? No."

"Then what is bothering you?" He kissed her hands but kept looking into her eyes.

"I haven't had sex in a long time. I just don't want to be bad." Her hand tensed in his.

He started to laugh but checked himself as she began to pull away. "No, don't go. I didn't mean to laugh. You surprised me, that's all. I thought you didn't want me—I didn't even think you could possibly be feeling insecure about anything. You are the most beautiful woman I've ever known."

"You don't need to lie to me. I know I'm not ugly or anything, but I'm hardly anything special." She looked away again.

He leaned in close and whispered into her ear, "You are something incredibly special to me." He kissed the top of her ear ever so gently. "And I am not concerned about how you are in bed. I think that as long as we are together and we talk, we can be amazing together. You just have to talk to me. Okay?"

She looked up at him and smiled, and there was a new light in her eyes. "It's funny, you telling me that, when that's all I've wanted from you from the very beginning."

"We both have a lot to learn. I will never be perfect—"

"And you know I'm not," she said, giggling.

"You are much closer than I am, but regardless, we can be imperfect together." He kissed her forehead and ran his hands through her hair, pushing it behind her ears and cupping her face. "Well, you can be perfect and I can try to keep up." He kissed her lips gently. "And I promise I will try to talk to you, to tell you what I'm thinking."

She reached up and unbuttoned the top of his shirt. "Right now, all I'm thinking about is how badly I've wanted you."

He smiled wildly. "What do you want me to do to you?"

She looked at him with wide eyes, leaning back in mock surprise. A cute smirk took over her lips. "Take off your shirt." She let go of him and stepped back.

He felt silly, but Elle telling him what to do was so damned sexy, he could have eaten it all up. "As you command," he said, slipping the buttons clear of the holes and leaving his shirt open and loose.

"All the way off," she said.

"Elle." He whispered her name in surprise as he slipped his shirt off his shoulders and let it drop to the floor. He reached for her, but she stepped back playfully.

"What?" she asked, giving him an innocent look. "Vest, too."

He peeled the Velcro straps open and pulled the vest over his head. Then he stripped off the white T-shirt that he always wore underneath.

She sucked in a breath as she watched him, making him smile. That was one hell of a reaction, a reaction he would never get enough of hearing.

"I thought you were feeling out of practice?" he teased.

"That doesn't keep me from knowing exactly what and how I want it. It just means I've had plenty of time to think of all the ways I want to be pleased."

He pressed hard against his zipper. There was just something so sexy about a woman who could talk openly and honestly about sex. If they could say what their hearts desired, then they were probably more than happy to do all the things they wanted to do with their body, as well. And that, that freedom, was something he had always found a great quality in a lover.

She may have been out of practice, but he had no doubts that she was going to be the greatest lover he had ever been with. Then, he had to be grateful for any woman who wanted to give him the gift of allowing him to enter her body.

The thought of slipping inside her, slowly...so slowly...and watching her face made him feel as if he was going to drip.

"Now what do you want me to do?" he asked, opening his arms and exposing his naked chest to her.

She stepped closer and ran her fingers over the tattoo on his left pec. "What was this for?" she asked, tracing the edges of the black bear paw.

Her fingertips moved slowly along the paw; in their tenderness it reminded him of the pain and reasons he'd chosen to get the tattoo. "One of my best friends was

killed in the line of duty. He was shot while performing a routine traffic stop that turned ugly. I got it in his
memory, over my heart—I never want to forget that in
my world, every day is a gift."

She moved in closer, pressing her body hard against
him. "That is beautiful and so true." Her hands slipped
down his chest, running over the lines of his stomach
and toward his utility belt.

He reached down and unclicked his belt, carefully
taking it off so it didn't bump against her. There was
nothing worse than dropping that heavy-ass thing on a
toe. He threw it on the couch behind them. Before turning back, he glanced at the front windows and made
sure the drapes were pulled closed. The last thing they
needed was someone walking by and peeking in on
what he hoped was about to happen. He needed to protect her privacy as much as he did his own.

"We should take this to the bedroom." He reached
for her hand, and she nodded, leading him down the
short hallway.

The place was simple, two bedrooms and a bathroom, kitchen and a living area. For his life it would
have been perfect. He had to imagine it was for hers,
as well.

She slipped the door closed behind them and clicked
on a bedside lamp, casting her purple bedroom in a
thin light that made everything in the room seem like
something out of a burlesque club. He hadn't imagined
her bedroom being anything like it was, though he had
to admit he had never thought of anything in her bedroom besides her.

There were black satin sheets on her bed, and just like the woman they belonged to, they whispered of fantasies so close to being realized that he was forced to reach down and unzip his pants.

"Take them off," she said, motioning to his pants.

He slid the zipper all the way down and then let them fall to the floor, exposing his gray boxer briefs. She smiled as she glanced at his package, and her expression made his heart leap with joy as he took pride in knowing she liked what he had to offer.

Yet she had no idea. If there was one thing he prided himself on, it was knowing how to please a woman. There was nothing that he would rather do than bring the woman he was with pleasure. He'd heard about men being selfish lovers, only caring about getting theirs, but what was the point of such behavior? He would get his, that wasn't a question, so why not take joy in the journey of pleasure that two people could experience together?

He'd never understand a woman who stayed with a man who wouldn't try to make sure she enjoyed herself to the fullest. If he wasn't selfless in the bedroom, what made a woman think he would try to make her happy outside the bedroom?

"Where is your mind right now?" she asked, looking up at him with an inquisitive look on her face.

He smiled. "I was thinking about all the ways I want to pleasure you." Reaching over to her, he slipped his hands under the edges of her shirt and slowly pulled it up and over her head, exposing her hot-pink lace bra.

He felt stupid for thinking she was a blue underwear kind of girl when she stood there wearing this.

If he wasn't already hard enough to cut glass, the sight of her luscious curves would have done it. If he wasn't careful, he was going to have to apologize for losing control.

"It's your turn." He motioned to her pants.

Instead of listening, she turned to her phone and clicked a few buttons. As impatient as he was for things to continue, he was glad for the reprieve. Chris Stapleton started to play from a Bluetooth speaker she had set up in the corner of the room. This was a girl who knew how to set a mood.

With the beat of the music, she unbuttoned her pants and slipped them down her thighs, pulled them off and threw them on the footboard of her bed. She was wearing hot-pink panties that matched her bra. He'd once heard that if a woman was wearing matching underwear, then they had chosen to have sex when they'd gotten dressed that day. Had she known this was going to happen all along, that they were going to find themselves in a position to share their bodies?

The thought alone turned him on, and in combination with her standing in front of him...*damn.*

A growl rippled from his throat, and he pulled her into his body. He wanted to rip those panties off her with his teeth and then gently kiss every part of her body that the lace had touched.

She gasped as his mouth found her throat, and he cupped her breast in one hand and the small of her back with the other. Every part of her was about to become his.

"Tell me you want me, Elle." He sounded raspy as he spoke her name, and she shivered under his touch.

"Grant, I've wanted you…since the first time we met." She was breathless with want.

"I know that's not true, but I appreciate it anyways," he said with a slight laugh. "I was a dick when we first met, and I'm sorry. But I'm glad you saw past that… that you were patient with me while I found my way to you." He kissed the lace at the top of her bra, taking in the soft scent of flowers on her skin. "To here. To now." He pushed the lace away, exposing her nipple and pulling it into his mouth.

She threw her head back and arched her back as he sucked. He popped it out of his mouth and licked the sensitive nub, then rubbed it gently with his thumb as if thanking it for allowing him the honor of tasting her.

She gasped as he repeated himself on her other side.

He moved his hand between her legs, over her panties, and traced her wet, round mounds until he found what he was looking for. Dropping down to his knees, he pulled off her panties, not wanting to destroy his new favorite article of clothing—one he hoped to see again in the future.

He lifted her leg over his shoulder and pulled her into his wide-open mouth. He grabbed her, holding her upright even though her body threatened to collapse. He licked her like she was a Popsicle, not just some damned little lollipop. He wanted her all in his mouth and he wouldn't stop until she was either dripping down his chin or begging for something else.

He was her plaything, and they were both going to love every second of it.

Her body moved in tandem with his tongue, rolling and pressing, pulling and sucking. It could have been minutes or hours, he had no idea. He was lost in her.

"Grant…" She moaned his name as he felt her clench around his tongue and gasp. "Oh my…" She moved, and he didn't miss a beat as she fell back against the wall and gave herself fully to her release.

She panted his name as she pulled him up to his feet. "You…are fantastic," she whispered, taking his lips and licking herself from them.

Reaching down, she slipped him inside her, and as she did, he knew that without a single doubt, he had found the woman and the place that could be his forever.

Chapter 14

She was shocked Zoey hadn't texted or come and knocked on her door by now; she was normally super quick at pulling information from a multitude of sources even when on her own. Elle looked down at her watch. It was getting late.

The last thing Elle wanted to do was to move from her place on Grant's chest to pick up her phone and send Zoey a text, but now that she could think about something other than him, she needed to refocus on their case.

Lily was still missing, and Elle had to believe she was alive somewhere, just waiting for them to find her. Maybe Zoey had come up with something by now.

With a groan, she moved off his chest, and he finally looked up. "Where are you going?" he asked, touching her back as she sat up.

"Have you heard from anyone?" she asked, nudging her chin in the direction of his phone that was hanging haphazardly out of the back pocket of his pants. "I can't believe we actually got to be alone for this long. Normally one of our phones is going off." She frowned. Was something happening, something that was keeping everyone so busy that they had forgotten to inform them? Her anxiety rose.

He sat up, grabbing his phone as she did the same. "All I have is the regular thing—texts from my guys at the department and a few emails. Nothing to do with the case. You?"

She picked up her phone, and it vibrated in her hand. There was a text from Zoey.

Shit. What did we miss?

If something had happened while they had been making love and their temporary reprieve from reality had affected their case and finding Lily, she wasn't sure she would forgive herself—even though the sex with Grant had been absolutely breathtaking.

Zoey's text was vague, nothing more than Give me a call.

Did that mean she had found nothing? That all the information they had given her had proven to be of little use and they were really going to be starting from square one once again?

They shouldn't have waited. They shouldn't have taken any downtime. Why did the needs of their bodies, to feel one another, have to be so extreme?

She glanced over at Grant, who was leaning back in the bed and had one hand under his head against the headboard. His tattoo was stretched over his pec and she found herself staring at him again, wondering how she had gotten so lucky to find him in her bed.

If she wasn't careful, and if she didn't have such a personal connection to the case at hand, she could have easily found herself falling back into those arms and going for several more rounds. She could have made love to him every day for the rest of her life, if the fates would allow.

Yet she couldn't help but worry that now he had been with her, he was going to wake up from whatever lust trance she had managed to cast on him and realize he was out of her league.

She was an empowered woman in a male-dominated field, and logically she knew that what she felt was non-sensical, but she couldn't help the dark voice in the back of her mind that told her she wasn't enough for Grant. Unfortunately, this wasn't the first time she had felt this way around a man. The last time, she had tried to make the guy happy, telling him what he wanted to hear at the expense of being herself and living her truth. In the end, she had morphed into someone she had thought he wanted instead of her authentic self, the one he had said he had once loved.

She couldn't overthink this if she wanted to keep Grant. Well, if he wanted to keep her.

Running her hands over her face, she tried to wipe away the thoughts that were haunting her. She stood up and put on her clothes, slipping her phone into her pocket. She was almost afraid to face Grant in the event he would see she was already starting to feel insecure.

Though she was sure she could feel safe with him, and as soon as he pulled her back into his arms she would feel right at home, she feared it. To fall in love, to be her authentic self with this man was to make herself truly vulnerable. And any time she had ever been vulnerable with a man—well, with anyone, really—she ended up hurting.

Until she was sure he was worth suffering for, completely, she needed to protect her heart. And she wouldn't protect it by giving herself to him again, or by giving away any more of her power in what relationship they did have.

"I'll take by you getting dressed that Zoey must have texted you?" he asked, making her realize she had never really answered his question and had just had an entire fight with him without ever saying a word.

Or was it a fight? Maybe it was just her being self-conscious.

If he took her in his arms and kissed away all the feelings she was having right now, he was the one—the man she could love, the man who could read her body and just solve all of her problems.

"She wants to see us." He picked up his clothes and started to get dressed, too.

She'd hoped for a sign, maybe something in neon, that suggested they had a future together—she would have liked for him to be her forever—but she shrugged off the sentiment. She wasn't a teen crushing on her idol. There was work to do.

Making her way out to the kitchen, she grabbed a

bottle of water and a second one for Grant, putting his on the counter while she waited.

Hoping for a sign might have been too much to ask for, but there had to be something that told her he was the one…something he did or said that could prove he wanted her for something besides her body and that thing that had happened between them hadn't occurred just because it had been a possibility. She just needed some kind of solid proof that this was *real* and not just another lover—as much for herself as for him.

Her phone rang, and she pulled it from her pocket. It was Zoey. "Hello?"

She was met with the muffled sound of a phone being moved around and Zoey yelling things in the background. Though she wasn't sure what she was listening to, Zoey's voice made her blood run cold as she screamed for help.

The line went dead.

"Grant!" She dropped her water bottle.

He came running down the hall, his shoes untied. "What? Are you okay?"

"We have to go." She grabbed her coat and slipped her gun into her waistband as she moved outside.

He followed behind her as he readjusted his utility belt. "What's going on?"

"Zoey needs us." She motioned her chin in the direction of the office.

He tied his shoe and quickly caught up to her as she sprinted toward headquarters. There weren't any cars she didn't recognize in the ranch's parking lot, but that didn't mean anything. This ranch had been infiltrated by enemies before. It had happened before she was hired, but there was still talk about it to this day—normally after a night centered around campfires and whiskey, like the former attacks were some kind of horror story that were used to scare them at night.

It worked.

She shoved open the door to the office, and it slammed against the wall behind it. She expected to find Zoey midswing in some kind of fistfight. Instead, Daisy was on the ground wrestling with a stray dog Elle didn't recognize. The stray was bloodied and its ear was half hanging on, and as it jumped up to its feet, it snarled at her as though it was going to attack.

"Daisy!" Elle screamed, watching as her dog lunged, taking down the dark brown mutt-looking dog.

She wasn't upset with her dog, but she was afraid. Daisy was her baby. Nothing could happen to her baby. And yet, there was nothing she could do.

The dogs tore at each other, ripping with the teeth and diving for each other's throats. Daisy seemed to be winning, standing over the dog and having it pinned down to the ground between her front legs. But the brown dog broke free and grabbed Daisy's front leg and swept it out from underneath her, dropping her to the ground and taking the top.

Elle's throat threatened to close as she watched the dog tear away at Daisy's fur, throwing black hair every which way around the office.

She looked up at Zoey, who was standing there, looking as at a loss as Elle felt. What had happened that had caused the fight? Then, what did it matter? All that mattered was that Daisy came away from this unharmed. She couldn't stand the thought of losing her baby.

Just like everything else that had gone wrong, this was her fault, too. She had been so stupid. She should have been focusing on her case instead of taking Grant to her bed. If she had just kept her head in her work, Daisy wouldn't have found herself in the position she was.

It was no wonder Elle couldn't keep Lily safe when she couldn't even keep her own dog from being hurt.

What would have ever possessed Zoey or the Clarks to ever entrust her with a damned child?

"Daisy, come!" she yelled, hoping the dog could hear her over the melee, but Daisy only looked at her with the white-eyed stress eyes of a dog in trouble.

She had to do something. There was no way she could stand here any longer and just watch as her dog was hurt.

Picking up an office chair, she jabbed at the snarling stray, pressing against it with the wheels until the dog unlatched from Daisy's throat. Elle's fingers pressed into the coarse carpet-like fabric as she lunged, using the chair like it was a door-breaching ram.

"Get out of here, dog!" she screamed.

Grant held open the door as she pushed at it with the chair until the brown dog stepped outside, its hackles raised and its teeth bared. When it realized it was no longer cornered in the office and had found its way back outside, the dog looked around wildly and took off in the direction of the mountains.

"What happened? How'd the fight start?" She turned on Zoey.

Zoey shook her head. "I think Daisy was trying to defend me, but I don't know. The dog just showed up and there was a snarl and..." She trailed off.

Daisy laid her head down on the ground and whimpered, and Elle ran over, sliding on her knees on the tile floor as she neared the animal. "Are you okay, baby? Mama is here," she said, careful to reach down and touch the dog gently in case she was still scared.

Daisy looked up at her with a sad, pained expression. "Let me look you over, honey. I promise I won't hurt you. I just need to check that everything is okay."

She looked back over her shoulder at Grant as she touched Daisy's shoulder. "You need to go find the other dog. Make sure it's okay. And it'll have to be tested for rabies."

He nodded, but he didn't look nearly as worried or upset as she did, and the thought irritated her. "And hurry about it. If that dog is hurt and heading to the mountains, we may never find it again if you don't move fast. I don't want to have any other lives on my hands." She spat the words, feeling the hurt in them but not allowing it to register.

Though she wasn't looking, she could feel the unspoken conversation that was happening between Zoey and Grant right over her head, and it pissed her off even more. She had every right to be angry—at the situation, at her choices and at the fact she had once again fallen short.

She was so goddamned tired of not being enough

and of doing something for herself for once and instantly having to pay the price in a pound of her best friend's flesh.

She leaned into Daisy and put her forehead against the dog. "I'm so sorry, honey. I've got you, Daisy. I shouldn't have left you outside. I'm so, so sorry."

The dog leaned in and gave her a sweet lick to the side of the face, like she was accepting the apology, even though Elle was nowhere near deserving of the dog's mercy.

That, this bond between her and Daisy, was what true love was. Pain and misery, injury and assault, and then forgiveness and love beyond all that agony. It was seeing a being at its worst and in its most vulnerable state and yet staying by their side.

It was endless faithfulness. No matter what.

No man, not even Grant, could offer her the same love as Daisy.

She had been a fool to be so selfish. Never again.

There was a growing pool of blood around Daisy's neck and chest. It stained the white tile floor, and Elle tried not to panic. Ever so gently, she ran her hands down the dog's body over the lumps and welts caused by the dog's bites and then around her thoracic area until her fingers felt the warm, wet tear just below her throat and at the front edge of her right shoulder.

"Baby..." she cooed, tears welling in her eyes and forcing her to blink them back. "Zoey, grab me some towels."

Zoey ran past her and headed toward the bathroom, coming out with a stack of hand towels and a roll of pink vet wrap. "Will this work?" she asked, handing it all over to her.

"Just press that towel right here, keep your pressure." Elle stood up and ran toward the back room where they kept all of their tactical gear in case they needed to bug out.

She pulled open her locker, exposing her black tactical bag, and pulled out a QuikClot kit she kept in it all the time in case of emergencies. She didn't know if the clotting agents would work on her dog, but she couldn't think of a reason they wouldn't. And, at the very least, it would slow the bleeding enough that she could hopefully get Daisy to the vet's office.

Elle made her way out to the main office and ripped open the kit. Zoey moved back, and she pressed the pad to the dog's exposed muscle. Daisy whimpered, trying to lick at the wound and pull off the gauze, but Elle kept her from getting to the pad. "Hold the pad there for a second," she said, motioning for Zoey to take over.

"It's going to be okay," she said to Daisy, repeating it over and over while she made sure the dressing stayed on the wound by wrapping it in the pink vet wrap.

From the look of the wound, it wasn't too bad as long as they got the bleeding stopped. After that, she would just need stitches and time to heal. Hopefully.

Elle pulled a shirt off the hook by the door and slipped it over the dog's head and covered up the wound and the dressing. "That's my good dog, Daisy. Mama has got you."

She stood up and, lifting with her knees, picked

the rottweiler up. She held her against her chest as she looked over at Zoey. "Grab the door, will you?"

Zoey rushed by, holding open the office door and then jogging ahead of Elle to open up the back door of one of the ranch trucks. She put down a blanket and then helped lift Daisy inside. The dog's eyes were still wide, but now it appeared as if it was more the pain and most of the adrenaline had started to wear off.

Zoey ran back to the office and quickly locked up; when she came back, she was carrying the truck's keys.

Daisy let out a long, breathy moan and laid her head down on the blanket and gave Elle one more look before closing her eyes. The look made Elle's stomach pitch. Daisy was going to be all right. She had made her pup a promise, a promise she intended on keeping no matter what.

Clicking the back door shut gently, she made her way around to the passenger's side of the truck and moved to get inside. She looked toward the mountain, and as she did, she caught a movement out of the corner of her eye. Walking out of the woods, carrying the brown dog, was Grant. He'd wrapped the dog in a blanket, but it was looking up at him like he was some kind of hero.

She ran toward his truck and flung open the doors as he approached, carrying the other pup. Though she was upset about what had happened, it was terrible to ever see an animal in distress. "Is she okay?" Elle asked, motioning toward the dog as Grant moved to set her in the back.

"She is banged up, needs a few stitches. How's Daisy?" He ran his hand down the dog's head and

scratched her gently behind the ears. The dog was panting but otherwise seemed to have fared better.

"Same, but seems to be hurting." She looked back
over at Zoey. "We are heading to the vet's office. Follow us over." She started to jog back to the ranch truck
but stopped and looked back at Grant. Her heart pulled
her back to him, but if forced to choose, she couldn't
leave Daisy alone. Not again.

"Grant?" she called, and he looked in her direction.
"Thank you. I appreciate you finding the dog. You're
a good man." She gave him a sweet, delicate smile and
a tip of the head.

It had been a long time since she'd been around a
man who wasn't on the Shadow team who could actually be trusted. It hurt her deeply to turn away from
him and go to the ranch truck, to her waiting boss and
her dog, but she knew she had to focus on the sure
things in her life, and they included Daisy, Zoey and
the STEALTH team. When she allowed herself to get
distracted, she let them all down.

Chapter 15

With the dogs back in surgery at the after-hours emergency vet clinic, Grant was left standing in the waiting room with Zoey and Elle. He had a sinking feeling that Elle felt this was partially his fault, that if they had been focusing on the things they had been hired to focus on, that none of this would have happened to her dog. He couldn't blame her.

Though he didn't own an animal, he understood the bond that came with owning one. He and his dog Duke had been inseparable until Grant had gone off to college. Duke crossed the rainbow bridge when he was away, and when he'd come home, it had never again felt the same. A part of him had gone over that bridge with his best friend.

If Elle was feeling even a small percentage of that

same kind of pain, it was crazy to him that she was even allowing him to stand in the same room with her. The lady at the desk disappeared into the back, and Zoey finally turned to them. "This is probably going to take a while."

Elle nodded, and as he looked at her, he noticed how tired she looked. It wasn't just the kind of tired that was in the eyes. Instead, it appeared as though it was all the way down in her bones. He wanted to hold her and comfort her, but here in front of her boss seemed like one hell of a piss-poor place. She needed to keep it together in front of her boss, at least as much as she could, given the circumstances, and if he pulled her into his embrace, he had a feeling he would have to take her back to bed and hold her until her tears ran dry.

"I know you don't want to leave Daisy," Zoey said, looking down at her hands and then flipping her purple hair back and out of her face. "Did you ever get my text?"

Elle nodded.

"Did you manage to pull something?" Grant asked, hoping for the best.

Zoey pushed her hands over her chest and looked around as though making sure that they were alone and couldn't be overheard. "I had a phone call. It wasn't *great*."

His heart rate spiked. "What is that supposed to mean?"

Zoey looked over at Elle and then at him. "Senator Clark called me not long after you left my office." She cleared her throat like trying to remove the discomfort that was reverberating between them. "He made it clear that he will be pursuing a lawsuit against our group for negligence in the death of his wife and disappearance of his daughter. He is going to try and ruin us."

Holy shit.

Elle opened her mouth then closed it several times, and a single tear slowly escaped her eye and trembled down her cheek. "I… I'm so sorry." Elle sounded choked, like Zoey's statement was gripping her throat and threatening to kill the last parts of her soul that had, up until now, remained unscathed.

This was all his doing. Clark hadn't been gunning for Elle until they had pulled him off the woman admirer outside the airport. He should have known better than to publicly embarrass the senator, especially in front of a woman he might have been trying to get into his bed. The man was a narcissist, and while Grant was sure that he was hurting after his wife's death and the loss of his daughter, for a man like the senator, the worst kind of pain was always going to be the pain to his ego. He was nothing if he wasn't being pedestaled and revered—especially by the opposite sex.

"He is just looking for someone to blame," Grant said.

Elle looked at him, and there were more tears in her eyes. He could tell there were a million things she wanted to say, but in her current broken state he would take this on for her. If this was the only way he could show how much he cared about her, how much he secretly *loved* her, he was going to protect her. He was her man, even if only in his heart and only until the end of this case. She needed him, though she would never say it aloud.

"I know you're right," Zoey said, careful to avert her gaze from Elle in what he assumed was an attempt to allow Elle a moment to collect herself and keep her dignity intact.

He always hated losing his edge in front of a superior officer. That kind of thing had the power to kill a career, or at least throw a major hurdle in front of advancement. Maybe it was different for women, he didn't know, but he didn't think it would be good for her, either.

He stepped in front of Elle, shielding her with his body even though he was sure that Zoey cared for her. There was a bond between the two women, he could see it in the way they treated one another. No doubt, it was a saving grace in their line of work. It probably even provided them with some additional level of protection, to have a fellow woman at her side, but that didn't mean that weakness would be perceived as anything other than just that. And in teams like theirs, weaknesses could bring harm.

Elle exhaled, and he could feel her move behind him like she was brushing the tear from her face and shaking off the display of emotions. She stepped out and took her place beside him. "So, if you know it is just misplaced anger and this really isn't my fault—"

Zoey stopped her with a raise of her hand. "Whoa. I didn't say it wasn't our fault."

"You mean *my* fault," Elle said.

Zoey looked away. "All I'm saying is that things could have gone differently. There were definitely some aspects of our handling of our security duties that could have been better. Perhaps better communication from both sides of the desk would have stopped this from ever happening. Regardless, we are going to walk away from this incident with a large black eye and an even larger hit to our bankroll."

"Don't worry about your bankroll," Grant said. "I'm sure that we will make things right here. We will get Lily back and find whoever was responsible for Catherine's death."

"Even if you do, I don't know if that is going to stop the senator from gunning for us," Zoey said. "And as such, I can only do one thing to protect our company. It's something I don't want to do, Elle. Especially not here and now, but my hands are tied…at least until and *if* you guys can get the senator off our ass. Elle, I need you off the team."

Elle nodded. He expected her to cry, but instead her jaw was set and anger sparked in her eyes. She pushed past Zoey and made her way outside.

"What in the hell, Zoey?" he growled. "You don't move against your team members when they need you the most. She did her goddamned job, she did exactly what she was told and now you are taking this out on her? You are wrong right now in how you are handling this, and I think you know it. She was already hurting, and you just took her out at the knees."

Zoey started to say something, but he didn't want to hear it.

"I have been a part of this investigation from day one, and let me tell you, from everything I can see, she isn't the one in STEALTH who was the problem." He looked her up and down and then, without waiting for her to speak, he charged out of the office.

Elle was sitting in his pickup staring out through the passenger-side window and into space. He had no idea how he was going to fix this. Even if he could, he wasn't sure that the damage to her career would be repairable. While STEALTH would likely recover, it was doubtful that Elle could say the same.

He still just couldn't believe that Zoey would have moved against one of her own like this, but going against a senator could be deadly if she and her team weren't careful. It was one of those situations in which it was live by the sword, die by the sword. They had chosen to work with vipers, now they would have to take the teeth.

Unfortunately, the teeth had pierced the neck of the mother of the child she had promised to protect.

As he got in and they hit the road, there was an impenetrable silence between them. He didn't know if he should tell her he was sorry or unleash a diatribe about how stupid her boss was, so he remained quiet. She and Zoey had been friends, but that probably only made what had just happened that much worse. She had been wounded by someone she trusted.

Her phone pinged, and he looked over and saw a text from Zoey flash over the screen. "What does she want?" he asked.

"I'm sure it's not to apologize and beg me to come back. And even if it was…" Elle sighed as she clicked the message off without reading it.

Grant touched her knee. "If you don't like your job, if you want to follow another path in life, you have my support. I will do whatever you need to help you out."

She chuffed. "I have no idea what to do right now. I don't have any damned answers. If you didn't notice, my entire life just came crashing down. The last thing I want or need is some guy who is only going to make things worse."

Was that what he had become, just *some guy*?

He wanted to argue with her, to tell her what she had just done to him and to his feelings. He wanted to tell her how all he wanted to do was be the man she needed and not like the men in her past who must have let her down. He loved her. But she mustn't have felt the same way.

In that case, he just needed to button his feelings up and cinch them down. He wasn't a fan of self-inflicted pain, and that's what he'd be doing to himself if he kept after her when it was clear she was dismissing him.

Though he was more than aware she was likely striking at him out of her own pain, he hadn't been prepared.

Yet, what did it matter? He had his answer as to her feelings toward him one way or another. At least it was a solid, unwavering rejection. A clear rejection was far better than half-assed feelings and empty promises.

"Stop," Elle said, touching his hand on her knee as she stared down at her phone. "Pull over."

"What?" he said, jerking the wheel to the right and pulling the truck to the side of the road. "Are you okay?" he asked, forgetting he was hurt and angry at the mere thought that she needed him.

"I'm okay," she said, not really paying his question any mind. "Zoey said that she just managed to find another phone that was linked to the Clarks. She sent me the phone number, but said she is going to have her people dig into it, as well. Hoping to get the phone records as soon as she can."

He smiled; information like that was right in his wheelhouse. Opening up the computer that sat atop the truck's middle-seat console, he started it up. "What's the number?"

She rattled it off as he typed it into NexTx, a cellular tracking program used by law enforcement. He laughed wildly as the phone pinged. "You are going to love this," he said, turning the computer for her to see it.

"What am I looking at?"

"Right now, the phone is located near the Blackfoot River, just down I-90. Twenty minutes ago, it was moving. And five hours before that, it was in Mineral County."

"So what?" She frowned. "There is nothing tying it to our case other than the fact it is a phone on the Clarks' account. For all we know, they had given one of their other employees a work phone."

He couldn't deny that she might be right. There were any number of reasons a senator and his wife would have needed a phone, but that didn't squash the feeling in his stomach that they had just stumbled on something; whether it would prove to be helpful or hurtful was up to time to tell, but at least it brought them something they needed most—hope in the time of darkness.

Chapter 16

Elle looked down at her phone, half hoping that Zoey would send her another text and tell her that she was sorry, but she knew that it would never come. Even if Zoey was wrong, she wasn't the kind to apologize—ever.

Unlike her, Zoey was unflappable. She could stare into the fire and let the world burn down around her without ever blinking, even if she wasn't the one who threw the match.

Though she was incredibly angry, she couldn't hold a grudge against Zoey. Her boss had taken her on and allowed her to pursue her passion for K-9 work without even the tiniest of pressure to rush her dog's training. If anything, Zoey had been incredibly understanding about the kind of work she did and the benefit it was for the team. The only real mistake Zoey had made was allowing her to be assigned to the care of a senator's child.

It was Elle's failure that had brought them here; Zoey was right. And she had been justified, actually *forced*, into letting her go. If Elle had been thrust into Zoey's position, she probably would have made the same choice.

The road zipped by them as they drove down the interstate in the direction of the Blackfoot River, where Grant had gotten the ping on the phone. He kept looking over at the computer, checking to make sure that the phone's location was relatively unchanging.

She couldn't believe his reaction to this minor piece of evidence. It was like he saw this as their saving grace, when there was no saving anyone here. Her career was over, her dog was hurt and they were on the rocks. And Lily was still missing. If this wasn't a last-ditch effort on his part to save... *Wait, what is he trying to save?*

She glanced over at him, and there were storm clouds in his green eyes. His brow was furrowed, and even without reading his mind, she could tell that he was on a mission. In a strange way, it lightened some of the heaviness in her heart. Her life had unraveled into one huge heaping mess, one she couldn't bring another person into out of the knowledge she would never be able to give them everything they deserved, but to know he was trying to help her took some of the pain away.

There was nothing he could do to make it all better, or take back what had happened to Daisy, but he was doing *something*. That said something about him. She had lost count of the people in her life who had made her promises only to find out they were as empty as the hearts of the people who had made them.

He was different, she could give him that. And, if her heart would have been capable, she could have loved him for it—maybe in another life.

Grant put his hand out, palm up, like he wanted her to reach over and take it. Though she wanted to, it would mean things she wasn't sure she wanted to promise. She was hurt, angry and emotionally compromised right now. And hadn't he been the one to tell her that was enough of a reason—being emotionally compromised, that was—not to get involved?

She pretended not to notice his extended hand, like it wasn't some kind of elephant in the pickup. Her fingers twitched like they wanted to come over and take his even without her mind agreeing to the plan. While she held no doubts about wanting him, he was just her type—hot, dominant, strong, and she'd be lying if she didn't say she loved how he protected her.

She liked to think she was tough, as she was more than capable of getting herself out of physically perilous situations, but when it came to the emotional ones, sometimes it was damn hard to be a woman.

"Elle." He said her name like it was a secret on his tongue, and the sound made her skin spark with yearning.

"Hmm," she said, trying to still seem the tiniest bit aloof.

"It's okay for you to hold my hand."

She looked over at him, and warmth rose into her face. Why did she always have that reaction when it came to him? She'd never thought of herself as much of a blusher, but when he talked to her like that and in that tone of voice, she melted.

"I…" she started, but she didn't know exactly how to express to him everything that she was feeling. "I… I don't want to be hurt anymore, Grant."

"No matter what happens, with any of it, I will keep you as safe as I can. I won't promise that you won't get hurt in this life, but I can promise you that I will do everything in my power to make sure that I'm not the one doing the hurting."

He didn't move his hand, and she stared down at his fingers. She wanted to believe him and give herself over to his beautiful words, but there was so much pain in her heart.

She sighed, and her hands trembled in her lap. After a moment, she reached over and slipped her fingers between his. He couldn't take away the pain and guilt she was feeling, but at least she could have one positive thing in her life. And maybe doing this wasn't the smartest thing, getting involved when she wasn't at her best, but if she waited for a *right time*—a time that she was completely ready and at ease—she damned well could have been waiting forever. Her emotions and her life were always in flux. That was what life was, one fight rolling in on the shirttails of the one before.

She deserved something good in her life, and she would figure out how to do this love thing right—that was, if this was going to be a serious thing between them.

Did she ask him? Did he ask her for monogamy? She hadn't had a real boyfriend in so long that she couldn't quite remember how things had been made official with her last. In fact, maybe they hadn't been official—he'd been more than happy to step out of their relationship to sate some needs he later told her she hadn't been filling.

Why did she have to think about that right now? When things were starting to turn and go right? She needed to focus on Grant. Only on Grant. And just like earlier, she needed to be here with him. Beautiful, sexy things happened when she gave herself to him.

The thought of him between her legs made her shift in her seat. If she closed her eyes, she could still feel the last place his mouth had been on her. If only she could keep that feeling forever. But maybe that was just the afterglow speaking, all of this…the confusion and the weird feeling that was entirely too close to love. Love was perilous, at best.

But damn it if she didn't think she loved him. There was just something about being close to him. She loved to watch his mouth form words and the way his green eyes brightened when he spoke about things he enjoyed or memories from his past.

His thumb fluttered over her skin, and she closed her eyes for a moment, just taking in the full sensation that was his touch. Even her hand fit perfectly in his; how was that possible?

They got off the interstate and took a frontage road in the direction of the last ping off the phone. According to the tracking program, the phone was stationary and hadn't moved for the last thirty minutes.

"What are we going to do after this? Do you think we can pull anything else from the flight records? Maybe we should go see Steve again." She tried to swallow back the anxiety that was rising within her.

He squeezed her hand, the simple action more effective to control her anxiety than anything she could have done. "If this doesn't pan out to be anything, don't worry. We will get Lily back. And, I told you…as for your job…you have plenty of options. If you can't stay at the ranch, I will help you find an apartment or whatever. You don't have to leave Montana."

She hadn't even thought about all the ramifications of losing her job with STEALTH yet. Of course, she couldn't stay at the ranch—that was headquarters for a group she no longer worked with. Zoey hadn't mentioned anything, but she had been trying to let her down gently—which was somewhat out of character for her. Zoey was far more the kind to have a spreadsheet and an exit survey to give people upon their firing.

She had been fired.

Her breath stuck in her chest, and her hands started shaking. She had no job, her dog was possibly going to have long-term damage regardless of what the vet said and now she couldn't breathe.

Grant glanced over at her and frowned as he looked at her complexion. "Babe, take a breath. In. Out. In and out." He breathed a few times like the problem was that she had forgotten how, not that her body was trembling on the precipice of a full anxiety attack.

"Don't freak out." He paused his breathing exercise. "What can I do to help you?" He started to pull the truck over, but she waved him off.

"No," she said, trying to mimic the Lamaze-style breathing. "Don't stop."

He smiled at her like he was deciding whether or not to say what was just on the tip of his tongue.

"What?" She inhaled.

"The last time you said *don't stop* was at your cabin," he said, giggling as he blushed. It was crazy to see him act in a way she had been chastising herself for, and him looking absolutely sexy while doing it.

A giggle escaped her as she exhaled. It felt strange, like with the giggle she was finding her center again.

He laughed harder, but she didn't know if it was at her or the situation or what, and she began laughing harder, too. She laughed until tears started to form at the corners of her eyes. It didn't make sense and maybe this was some kind of mania or magic, but she could feel the craziness that had overwhelmed her seep out with every laugh. Her heart lightened as her tears fell. Maybe this laughter was the catharsis her soul needed, especially since it was brought on by and hand in hand with Grant.

He was changing her life. He was willing to pick her up when she was at her lowest. He hadn't said he cared, but he had to have cared for her. Maybe he couldn't make all of her problems disappear, but he could damned well make things lighter.

The computer flashed, and Grant pulled his hand away so he could navigate the screen while also driving. "The phone is here," he said, looking around like there would be some kind of sign pointing directly to the device.

She let her giggles go dry and ran her hands over her face, wiping away the remnants of stress. Her life would be okay. She had a friend, even more than a friend, in Grant. She could see things lasting for a long time if they would make whatever it was they were doing official, but even if they remained only between-the-sheets friends, then she would have to be satisfied.

Until the future came, all she had to do was help the little girl who needed her the most. She wouldn't give up on her, no matter what.

Grant pulled the pickup onto the side road where the program had dropped the last ping for the phone's location. The road was a fishing access point, and there were several brown-and-white signs marking the spot, one with a drawing of a fish on a line, another with the image of a boat. She'd driven by many of these signs while in Montana, but she couldn't say that she had ever actually driven into one before. They came to a stop at a large roundabout parking area with a boat launch.

The river was flowing, but ice pocked the edges and a white mini-berg floated past them. It was odd to think anything the senator owned would be at a place like this.

Elle picked up her phone. "I need to know if Zoey managed to get the phone records for the number. And check to see if she found anything on Philip." She tapped the message and hit Send, not listening to the voices in her head that told her she had no business reaching out to her ex-boss. Zoey would help them if she could; they were friends.

As she waited for a reply, Elle gazed around the parking area. There were a few trucks parked tailgate into the spot in true Montana man style. What was it about men here that made them all want to prove to the world how good they were at driving a truck? Her smile returned.

In the farthest corner of the lot, away from all the trucks, was a crossover. It was muddy, and its wheel wells were caked in the muddy brown ice brought on after hours of interstate driving in winter conditions.

"There," she said, pointing at the car.

"Good a place to start looking as any," he said, smiling over at her. "Good eye."

He parked next to the red Subaru, and she got out and walked over beside the car. There was no one inside, and from the lack of ice over the engine on the hood, it was clear it had been recently driven. Inside the car was a collection of fast-food wrappers, one from Sonic—a chain that didn't have restaurants anywhere close. Either the driver had been all over the west and had just gotten back, or they were terrible at cleaning up their mess.

She glanced at the car's license plates; it was from Montana and started with a four—the number for Missoula County. Snapping a picture, she texted the plate to Zoey, as well.

Grant turned away and started to type the license plate number into his computer in the truck.

She stepped around the back of the car. In the back seat was a small booster seat. Her heart jumped. Had Lily been in this seat?

She bit back the thought. There was nothing to indicate that this search for the phone actually had anything to do with Lily. If anything, it was just one more possible lead they had to work through only to be left empty-handed. Her hopes were running away with her reality.

"You're not going to believe this," Grant said. "That car is registered to one Philip Rubbick."

Her phone vibrated with a message from Zoey almost at the same time as Grant spoke. Looking at the message, Elle's mouth dropped open. "Zoey says Philip 'Ace' Crenshaw is the owner of NightGens LLC. He hid his ownership under a bunch of other names of businesses, so it was hard to find."

"The company that owned the helicopter?"

"One and the same." She lifted the phone in her hand so he could see the text Zoey had sent them.

He smiled, his eyes filled with hope and excitement. "That means that it's likely Philip 'Ace' Crenshaw and Philip Rubbick are one and the same—Steve's brother."

"Holy crap." Had they finally pieced the puzzle edges together? She put her arms on the windowsill of the truck as she tried to pull together and make sense of everything she and Grant had just learned. "If Steve was working for this other crew, why would he have said he worked with STEALTH?"

"Smart move on his part, really. He sent us on a dead lead. In the meantime, while we were chasing our tails, he got to talk to his brother and tell him that we were getting closer." Grant scratched at the stubble on his chin. "I can't believe I screwed it up. I even noticed the marks on Steve's hands."

"What?" she asked, frowning.

"When someone stabs another person, especially when enraged, they often cut and damage their own hands. And Steve…well, his hands were mangled. But, to be honest, they matched the rest of him. Like I said, he threw me off my game. I should have paid more attention," he grumbled.

"That's not your fault. Now that we have some answers, we will just get your people to go pick him up."

He wasn't done whipping himself. "I can't believe I never asked Steve if he knew Philip. It didn't even cross my mind that they would be related. I didn't go deep enough. Maybe if I had, we wouldn't have gone on a wild goose chase and Daisy wouldn't have gotten hurt."

"None of that was your doing." She put her hand on his arm, trying to return some of the comfort that he had brought her. "Besides, we did have some *fun* while we were waiting. I have to believe that everything happens for a reason. And we could have looked into a million things deeper and not found answers. Don't be so hard on yourself."

He put his hand on hers and intertwined their fingers. He leaned down and kissed her knuckles ever so gently. "First, I have a feeling that regardless of what would have happened, we would have had some *fun* together. It just wouldn't have been the same."

"Does that mean you still regret it?" She lifted a brow in warning that he should take a minute to think long and hard before answering.

He chuckled. "I regret nothing when it comes to you, and us." He turned her hand over and kissed her open palm. "From the ugliest moments, we can build beautiful futures."

She didn't move. Futures? Did that mean he thought this was going somewhere? They were going to be fly-by-night, or fly-by-the-case, lovers? She loved the thought.

"We…" She pulled her hand back and patted the windowsill. "We probably need to focus."

He looked slightly crestfallen, and she immediately felt guilty for her response.

"I mean, I'm glad you don't regret anything," she said, tilting her head and sending him a gentle smile. "I most certainly don't, because there is something between us. I don't know what it is, but there's something I've never felt before. It's like you and I *fit*."

The look of hurt left his eyes, and his smile returned. "I hope that's not just the kiss talking."

"What kiss?"

"This one," he said. Taking her face in both of his hands, he pulled them together.

She leaned into the cold steel of the dirty truck, not caring about the mud that would be all over her clothes or the way the cold, wet road grime was threatening to pull all the heat from her body. All she cared about was the way his tongue worked over the edge of her lip and flicked at the tip of her own. She pulled his lower lip into her mouth and gently sucked on it. She could never kiss this man enough. His lips were like sugar, addictive in all their sweetness.

He ran his thumbs over her face, gently caressing her skin as their kiss slowed. He leaned back, searching her eyes, and the look in his gaze made her heart shift in her chest—almost as if the entire beast had moved locations in her chest, forward and closer to him.

She took his hands in hers and, removing them from her face, she kissed his open palm. "You are incredible."

"And so are you," he said, his voice husky.

"Let's find this phone. Maybe it has something about Lily on it. Then we can focus on what we are going to do about us," she said, though right now she knew exactly what she wanted to do with him and his body.

"Yes," he said, rolling up the truck's window and turning off the ignition before getting out.

She took the moment to readjust the holster inside the waistband of her pants. She always hated sitting in a car with them, but at least her gun was small and could go unnoticed and unseen.

"You warm enough?" he asked, grabbing a pair of gloves from his door and slipping them on. "You need some gloves?" He motioned to the cubby in the door where another pair of large men's gloves rested.

"No, thanks," she said, aware that her hands would be freezing if they were outside for any long period of time. She stuffed her hands in her coat pockets. "Hopefully we will be moving enough to stay warm and we will make quick work of getting this phone into our custody."

She looked over at the car. "Do you think it's in there?" she asked, pointing at the window.

He shrugged. "If it is, there's nothing we can do without getting a warrant to do a search."

"Did you check the phone's location again? Does it tell you exactly where we can find it?"

He pinched his lips closed. "Unfortunately, it's not pinpoint accurate. That being said, it's going to be close. I'm thinking within five hundred yards of the pin, give or take some."

"Do you think you should call in some more deputies? Maybe they can help us look over the area?"

He took out his phone. "I'll text a couple of them. If they're not busy, they can join us."

She totally understood. "Maybe they're bored and would like to pursue a lead with us."

He laughed. "They might be. There weren't many open calls." He pointed toward his computer inside the pickup. He zipped up his jacket and pulled on his gloves. "On days like these, where there aren't a lot of calls, I used to look for things like this to do. There are times when I miss being on patrol instead of mostly sitting behind a desk and filling out reports, but I don't miss the slow days."

He reached down and took her hand in his.

"Right now, I could use some slower days." Their footfalls crunched in the snow.

"I hear you there, but for what it's worth, I'm glad all this brought me to you."

"I would have preferred different circumstances, maybe meeting you at a bar or something." She leaned into him, touching his arm as they followed the footsteps that led from the car and toward a hiking trail. The snow cover was patchy, with swaths that had thawed and refrozen and areas where the powder had completely receded and patches of cottonwood leaves littered the ground.

The single set of footprints that had led from the mess of footprints around the car soon disappeared and was consumed by the forest. Though they had a lead here, a solid lead to someone who very well could have known what happened to Catherine and Lily, something about the situation still felt strange, *off* in a way that Elle couldn't quite put her finger on.

They walked slowly, searching the edges of the trails for any signs of a discarded cell phone. If Steve had told Philip that they had gotten on their scents, it was more than possible that Philip had discarded the car and the cell phone at this access. It was doubtful that they were actually going to find Philip, but they would do the best they could with the information they had.

The world smelled of biting cold, tall drying sweet grasses, rotting leaf litter, all mixed into the swirling odor of clean river water. Walking around a gentle bend in the trail, they came to the river.

A man was sitting on the bank, his head down and his knees up. His arms were outstretched, palms together. He looked at odds with the world in only a black sweatshirt and jeans. She couldn't see his face, but there were touches of gray in the brunette hair at his temples. His neck had a long scratch on the back that was still bleeding.

"Hey," Grant said, calling out to the man.

The man jerked, and he looked up. His gaze moved from Grant to Elle. His eyes widened as Philip recognized her. "What in the hell are you doing here?"

Philip reached behind his back and moved his hand under his sweatshirt to a bulge that Elle knew all too well was a gun. She hoped she was wrong; she hoped she didn't have to do what she had been trained to do in a situation like this, but as he moved the cloth of his sweatshirt back, she saw the exposed black grip and the butt end of a Glock.

Her hand dropped to her own gun, and in one swift movement she cleared her shirt, drew the weapon, aimed and fired. It all happened fast. A single motion. As the round left the gun, she saw the spray of black gunpowder. She'd never noticed that before with this gun. Was it a dirty round? What kind of ammo had she been using? It was whatever STEALTH had provided. They wouldn't have used dirty rounds.

And then she realized she needed to come back to the moment. She couldn't stop shooting until the threat was completely neutralized.

When a person was shot, they didn't stop. Inertia and adrenaline could keep a person moving even if they received a fatal wound. Philip was proving to be the kind of target that she had trained for. She let her finger move forward on the trigger, letting it click to reset, and then she pulled slowly again. It was almost a surprise as the second round left the barrel. She wasn't sure where she had hit Philip, but she had been aiming at center mass. In training, she was normally never more than a few centimeters off at this kind of range.

She'd definitely hit him, but Philip pulled his gun. He took aim and she fired again, but as her finger pulled on the trigger, Grant rushed at her from her left and pushed her out of the way, his gun in hand. Shots rang out, but she wasn't entirely sure who had done the shooting.

Her Sig Sauer kicked out the hot brass, and it skittered beside her as her shoulder hit the ground.

Blood. There was so much blood.

Chapter 17

The ground was red around Philip where blood seeped deeper into the snow, melting it and diluting the blood further. The man had dropped the gun in his hand when he had collapsed, his muscles going limp in death. The side of his face was pressed into the ground, and his hands were opened at his sides.

Elle was lying on her back in the snow, and he could make out the sounds of her erratic, amped breathing. He knew that feeling well thanks to the many fights he'd been in while working patrol. That adrenaline hit affected everything.

At her side was a patch of red blood. She'd been hit. He'd been too slow to help her.

It shouldn't have gone anything like this.

"Are you okay?" Grant asked. "Where does it hurt?"

She was running her hands over her body, as though even she wasn't sure where the bullet had torn through her. She had been hit—there was no question about the blood that was pooling around her.

He wished this had all played out differently. If he had been paying attention to what he should have been paying attention to, Elle would have never gotten hurt.

"Is he down?" She pointed in the direction of Philip.

Grant stepped over to him and pressed his fingers against his neck, searching for the pulse. He found nothing. "He's gone."

"That was not at all how I wanted that to go down," she said.

She moved to sit up, but as she did, he could tell the world swam around her and she was forced to lie back down in the snow. "I already called dispatch. The troops should be here soon. But it's a bit of a drive for EMS to get here, so we're going to have to keep you calm and your blood pressure low. I need to take care of that wound. Stop the bleeding." He pointed to her midsection. "Open your coat and lift up your shirt."

She moved to wave him off, but as she did, she grimaced in pain. Her adrenaline must have been starting to decrease and allowing the pain to set in. "I'm fine. Really," she said, though he already knew better.

"Do you have to be stubborn right now?"

"Do you always have to try and get me naked?" she teased, closing her eyes as she laughed.

He squatted down beside her and started to help unzip her jacket. The bullet had pierced through the jacket's shell and the goose down, red with blood, was poking out.

If only he had reacted quicker, he would have been the one to take the hit instead of her. At least she had been able to draw down on the target; she definitely moved faster than both him and the other man.

It was easy to see she had spent thousands of hours training for a moment like that. Hell, from her reaction alone, he doubted that this was her first time in a life-threatening situation. Later, he'd have to ask her about it.

No doubt, somewhere in her contracting past, there were literal skeletons. He didn't judge her for any of it, but he didn't envy her, either. Being in a situation like this, where a life was taken and more lives were still at risk, left long-term scars. And he didn't mean the scars that would be left by any physical wounds.

"I am going to open up your shirt. Is that okay?"

She nodded. "I think I'm okay. It hurts but I'm going to make it."

She was talking to him, which was a good sign, but he had to see the damage for himself. He gently lifted up the hem of her shirt. On the left side of her abdomen was a dime-size hole. "I'm going to roll you slightly. Just tell me if I need to stop. Okay?"

She bit her lip but nodded.

As he moved her, he spotted a larger exit wound on her back where the bullet had passed through her body.

He was surprised, given the velocity in the range of the round, it hadn't hit him, as well. In a single shot, Philip could have had them both.

"The good news is it looks like it went straight through. Hopefully it didn't hit any major organs, but from where it's located, I think it's important that you don't move and we try to keep you as still as possible." He laid her back down, flat. Gently, he lowered her T-shirt and zipped her coat back up, trying to keep her as warm as he could.

"How did the bleeding look?"

"Actually, it looked pretty clean. The bleeding appears to just be oozing, but make sure to hold some pressure on the wound." He stood up.

"What are you doing?" she asked, putting her hands to her abdomen and pressing.

"I'm going to go grab my medical kit. I'll be right back. Don't move." There was a lump in his throat as he jogged back to his pickup and grabbed his red first aid kit. He could at least stop the bleeding and get her stabilized and ready for the EMS teams when they arrived.

Yet he couldn't help the nauseating feeling that he was the one who was responsible for all this happening. It had been his brilliant idea to come out to the middle of the woods, nowhere near emergency care, and then he'd ended up getting her shot.

If he had only reacted faster. Pulled the second he saw Philip's hand moving toward the gun. But he hadn't been completely sure that the man was going for a gun. They hadn't provoked him, but Grant should have known the shape under the man's sweatshirt. He'd seen it a million times before, but his hope had run away with his good sense.

He had promised himself and Elle that he would protect her, and now she was lying out there bleeding into the snow after having taken down a man. And for what? They hadn't found Lily, and Philip had pulled the trigger before they got any answers.

Her shooting had solidly been in self-defense and every jury would side with her, especially with him as her witness, but they would still have to sit through endless rounds of questioning and he would have to sit through IA questions and hearings before being cleared. This was going to take so much out of both of them, and all because he had chosen to go on a wild goose chase.

No. He had just been doing his job to the best of his abilities. He was making choices based on the information they had been able to accumulate up to this point. Sometimes bad things happened, and in this case, inexcusably terrible things, but there was no going back and fixing his mistakes. He couldn't focus on that right now; instead, he needed to focus on helping Elle in the only ways he could.

As he made his way back to Elle, he found she had moved and was now sitting up next to Philip. She was still gripping her side. In her hand was a black phone he didn't recognize. She was tapping away with one finger, and for a moment he wondered if that was in fact the cell phone they had been looking for. But if it was, how had she found it?

"Elle, why are you sitting up?" he asked, looking at her back where the blood had stained her jacket and was oozing freely from the hole.

She shook her head, ignoring his reprimand. "I found his phone."

"Philip's? Where?"

She shrugged as she looked back over her shoulder

at him and gave him a guilty smile. "Well, it was ringing from his pocket."

"You and I both know you had no business disturbing the crime scene," he said, walking over to her and opening up his first aid kit.

He hated to admit it, but if he had been in her shoes, he would have probably done the same damned thing—procedure or not.

"Business or not, I think you'd be interested to hear that it was Steve on the other end of the line."

He stopped and stared at her. "Did you answer it?"

She nodded. "The number came up as restricted, and when I answered the guy Steve started talking. He said something about Lily, and then, 'The senator changed his mind. He wants us to keep her safe.' When I didn't say anything, I think he got suspicious and he hung up."

"But you never spoke?" Grant asked, worried now that if Steve knew they were on the receiving end of that phone call, they could have found themselves in more danger than they were already in.

"No." She shook her head. "He didn't know I was there, I promise."

"But he must know something was up with Philip." His entire body clenched. "And if they were talking about the senator, they must be on his payroll. It's going to be hard to prove in court, if we ever get them there and get Lily back, but I think the senator may have a whole lot more to do with his wife's death than he alluded to."

"No kidding," she said, clicking on the phone screen, but it had locked.

Grant sat down beside her in the snow. "Here, let me get this QuikClot on you. I don't want you losing any more blood. I can't lose you."

She stopped working on the phone and looked over at him with a gaze he hadn't seen her give him before. He could have expected hate, disgust or even disappointment after the situation he had gotten them into and the pain he had caused her, but instead she looked at him with what appeared to be *love*. Those eyes—those beautiful almond-shaped blue eyes—when she gave him that look, he was surprised the snow around them didn't melt.

"Lift your shirt. Let me take care of you."

She put down the phone and pulled up her jacket and her shirt, exposing the exit wound as he slipped on a pair of gloves. He packed the wound and taped down the gauze, then moved around to her front and repeated the treatment. The entire time, he could feel her staring at him, but he wasn't sure why and he wasn't sure he wanted to ask. If he asked and the look in her eyes wasn't love, it would hurt. And he was already hurting because of the mistakes he had made when it came to her.

As he put down the last piece of tape, he finally looked up at her as he took off his nitrile gloves and slipped them into his pocket to throw away later.

"Grant," she said, her voice soft.

"Hmm?" His fingers moved over the tape one more time as if he was checking to make sure that it was firmly adhered, but in truth all he wanted to do was keep touching her. He needed to touch her skin, to know she was okay, to know she was going to make it through this.

"Thank you," she said, touching his face gently with her fingertips.

"No. I'm so, so sorry." His voice cracked with all his feelings, feelings he couldn't make heads or tails of right now. "This happened because of me. If I'd just gotten the drop on him first. Or if we hadn't walked up from behind him… Hell, maybe I should have just tried to take him down before he drew down on us. I screwed up, Elle, and you are hurt because of me."

She shook her head. "I don't care about a stupid bullet wound. I'm telling you now, I've seen things like this happen before—this kind of wound—and I will be all right. If anything, at least I will have a cool story to tell at the bars on a Friday night," she teased. "But really, this wasn't your fault. From day one, actually from the day I put my hand on my first pistol, I knew this could happen. I knew the risks. I made the choices."

"But I put you in front of the round that hit you."

"Technically, you did try to push me out of the way. If you hadn't, I would probably be in an entirely different situation right now. So, really, you saved my life." She ran her thumb over his cheek as she looked into his eyes. "I owe you my life, Grant."

He was left speechless. All he could do was touch her hand with his and kiss her open palm. He pressed his face into her palm.

"We need to focus, Grant. I can't have you feeling bad. Seriously, we need to focus on Lily. When we get back, we can focus on us."

Though she was making a good point, he didn't want to move out of her hand. He pulled back. "Yeah, Lily."

He ran his hands through his hair and down over the back of his neck as he stood up and away from her.

"Do you think Philip did something to her?" She pointed to the scratch on Philip's neck. "Do you think that was why he was sitting here, by the river?" Her gaze moved to Philip's dead body and then out to the icy water.

A little girl couldn't survive water like that even when it wasn't ice cold and whispering of hypothermia. Only a monster would have killed a little girl, but monsters were one thing he was used to dealing with—and though Elle had been strong through this shooting, if Lily was lying out on the riverbank somewhere, that could break anyone.

"I'm sure she's okay." Grant looked around like he would suddenly see the little girl just standing on the riverbank, silently watching them and grateful that they had finally found her. Yeah, right, like they could get that lucky.

He looked over at Philip's body. There had been a car seat in the Subaru. It was possible that Lily could have been around here, but maybe he had dropped her off with someone else—maybe Steve had told him to ditch her and run. There were any number of possible scenarios that could have played out before they came upon this man.

But maybe there was something on the body that could help them find the girl. Something, anything, was better than nothing at all—and though he hated the thought, they needed to have answers even if those answers meant Lily was dead.

Chapter 18

Elle tried not to focus on the pain in her side. She had told Grant she was going to be fine, that she wasn't hurting too bad, but the pain threatened to burn through her like a hot iron. She'd heard it burned when a person had been shot, but she had never expected this kind of intensity. She could only imagine what it must feel like to have a baby; if it was anything like this, she would be adopting.

Parents didn't have to be blood relatives of a child. If Senator Clark had anything to do with his wife's death and his daughter's disappearance like they had come to assume, then it only proved the point that guidance and love determined parentage more than biology. She could provide those things to a kid. She wouldn't even adopt a baby—rather, she would adopt an older kiddo.

She wanted to bring a child into her life that had no one, nowhere to go and had felt abandoned by the world.

If Lily was found safe and alive, she silently made a promise to the ether that she would follow through and adopt a kid someday. She would give them more love and guidance than even she had received. If she was hoping and praying to the ether, she added in a prayer for Daisy to be healthy, too.

She also added a plea for Grant to be hers. This time, thinking about him and their future didn't feel like such an outrageous dream.

Maybe it was too much to ask for it all, but she didn't care.

Picking up the black phone she'd taken from the dead man, she reached over for Philip's thumb so she could open up the device. However, as she moved to touch him, she noticed a tuft of hair. There, under his pointer and middle fingers, was a clump of fine blond hair. It was the same color as Lily's.

Her heart fluttered in her chest. What did that hair mean? "Grant," she said, "look." She pointed at Philip's hand. "That's Lily's hair."

"Are you sure?" Grant asked, moving beside the body and taking his phone out and snapping a picture of the hand holding the wispy blond locks.

The hair was dry. Did that mean she hadn't been in the water or that he had been holding the hair in his hand long enough for it to dry after he had committed murder?

"She has to be around here," Elle said, standing up. "We have to find her."

"Elle, you aren't in any kind of shape to go search for Lily. If she is out here, our team is on their way. We can start our search as soon as they get here."

She put her hand on the cottonwood tree next to her, steadying herself as she got up and on her feet. "And what if she is out there in the water somewhere? Wet and hurt? Do you think she can really wait? It's cold and she is likely alone. She has to be so scared."

He looked down at Philip and then back up at her. "If you promise not to go anywhere—"

"I'm not making any promises to that effect, Grant. So you can either help me look for her or you can get out of my way. We are so close to her. I have to find her. I have to know she is okay."

Grant shook his head. "I'm not going to let you put yourself in more danger. For all we know, you could be bleeding internally. You know I want to find Lily, too. Finding her has been the major driving force behind this entire case. But let's say she is deceased. You risking your life is not only dangerous, but it's downright illogical."

She knew he made sense and that his admonition was coming from a good place, but she wasn't about to sit here and do nothing when the child she loved more than herself was possibly hurt somewhere near. "I'm telling you, Grant, if she is out here and relatively unharmed, she is not going to answer or come near anyone she doesn't know or trust."

Grant ran his hands over his face in frustration, but he had to have known he wasn't going to get anywhere in this fight. There would be no stopping her, not now.

"You know kids. She is probably terrified right now. And they always make everything their fault. That means she likely feels everything that has happened to her up to this point is because of some mistake she made. What if she thinks she is going to get in trouble? Can you even begin to imagine how scared she is right now? She has been through so much." Her voice cracked. "I can't. I can't sit by and do nothing."

Grant sighed like he understood and empathized with what she was saying but still didn't agree.

She loved him for the way he wanted to protect her and keep her safe, but this wasn't about her. This was about someone else she loved, someone she had promised to protect and someone she had let down. This was about an innocent, sweet child.

"I know you want to do the right thing by everyone here. It's what makes you the man you are—the good man, the man I have come to love—but I have to find Lily." She paused. "If only we had Daisy."

"How about I call in the other K-9 teams? We can get them on this." He smiled. "And wait…did you just say you *loved* me?"

She wasn't sure if the faintness she was feeling was because of her admission or because of blood loss, but she found she needed to press her shoulder against the tree so it could support more of her weight. She sent Grant a sexy half smile. "Loving you is easy to do. You are the perfect combination of all the things I have been looking for in a partner. I never thought I'd meet anyone like you, and then you just appeared in my life."

He blushed and looked away.

Shit. She hadn't meant to admit her love for him. Not here. Not yet. And then there he was, not saying it in return. He didn't love her. He was going to run away.

She pushed herself off the tree, not giving him another second to come up with something to say instead of "I love you, too."

As she walked toward the river and away from him, she wasn't sure what hurt worse, the bullet wound or the pain in having her love rebuffed.

"Elle, stop. Wait," he called from behind her.

Yeah, right. The last thing she wanted to do right now was look him in the eyes. She had just made a hard situation impossibly harder. And there was no reeling back in the words she had let fall from her lips. She couldn't believe her own stupidity.

She knew better.

She had always vowed to never tell a man she loved him before he told her. And there she went breaking her own rules for a man who didn't even feel the same way.

What an idiot.

If she wasn't going to die from her wound, she was certainly going to die from embarrassment. She started walking down the riverbank, downstream.

"Elle, please stop," he said, only steps behind her.

She shook her head, afraid that if she opened her mouth to speak, all the pain she was feeling would come spilling out and she would say more things that she would regret.

"Don't be like that, Elle. You just caught me off guard. I didn't expect you to—"

"Lily!" she yelled, cutting him off. She didn't want

to hear his excuses. There was only one acceptable response to someone telling a person they loved another. He started to make a sound. "Lily!" she called again.

If Elle could have run away, she would have, but her feet slipped on the icy river rocks and every step she made was deliberate to keep from sliding and falling. She didn't need Grant having to rescue her again.

Thankfully, the third time he tried to talk to her and she called out Lily's name, her adolescent stonewalling took effect and he stopped trying. She felt stupid for treating this situation—a situation she had caused—like this, but she couldn't think of another way to make things less awkward. It just was what it was at this point, and she had no one else to blame than herself. She had read the feelings between her and Grant incorrectly.

As they walked, the only sound became the gurgle and rushing sounds of the river, their footsteps clattering on the cobbles, and the occasional call of magpies and ravens in the distance. Her ego was definitely feeling more pain than her side, and it threatened to bring her to her knees.

It was fine, though. After they got through this investigation, she could go back to being by herself. She could find another job, and if nothing else she could train dogs at some chain store or something. The last thing she wanted to do was go back into contracting work, going overseas and watching as hellish crimes happened to the most innocent people. Though, admittedly, she didn't have to go overseas to find those kinds of monsters.

To her right, she heard the sounds of whimpering.

The sound was soft and mewing, and Elle stopped walking in hopes it wasn't just in her imagination.

"Ms. Elle?" Lily's voice broke through the pain filling Elle's soul.

"Lily? Lily, is that you?" she called, her voice taking on a manic, relieved tone.

Tucked into the hollowed-out center of a cottonwood, barely visible in the distance, was Lily. She was wearing a dark blue coat and white boots, and she waved a dirt-covered gloved hand.

Tears sprang from Elle's eyes and poured down her cheeks as she forgot about her own pain and rushed toward the little girl. She stepped over downed trees and pushed through the brush, and as she grew closer Lily stood up and started to run toward her. Lily extended her arms, throwing them around Elle's legs as they found one another.

As she pulled her up and into her embrace, Elle wasn't sure who was crying harder or was more relieved.

Chapter 19

The hospital staff had been incredibly kind in allowing Lily and Elle to stay together in the emergency room. In all reality, even if they had tried to pull them apart, Grant was sure that neither would have allowed it. Even during the ride in the ambulance, the two ladies had been inseparable, according to the EMS workers.

After Elle had told him she loved him, all he could think about was her, and if Lily hadn't called out to them, he was sure that he wouldn't have seen her hiding away in the tree. Elle had been right, and as much as he had hated the idea of her striking out into the woods to find the girl, it was because of her that Lily had been found.

He made his way toward their room and knocked on the door frame. Elle was lying down in the hospital bed, Lily's head on her chest. Lily's eyes were closed, and from the steady rise and fall of the little girl's back, he could tell she was fast asleep.

Elle looked up at him as he made his way inside. There was hurt in her eyes, but he doubted it had anything to do with her side. Whatever she had been feeling from that had likely been fixed with some kind of meds by now, which meant the pain in her eyes was one he had put there.

"How are you two doing?" he asked.

She nodded. "Lily is all good. They checked her out, and aside from a few bruises and a missing patch of hair, she seems to be not too worse for the wear. The only thing they want me to watch are her feet. Her little toes were pretty cut up after walking barefoot in the snow when Steve took her from the house."

"Is that what she said had happened?"

Elle nodded. "She won't tell me what happened with her mother, but I'm hoping it is because she didn't see her mother's death. I didn't press her too hard about details. I'm sure when she is feeling a little better, we can talk more, and I'm sure she'll be assigned a counselor. I just wanted her to feel safe and secure for now." Elle paused. "The hospital asked if they should contact the senator."

"What did you tell them?"

"She is a minor, and he is her parent. They were put into a tough situation." She paused. "I told them we needed to wait to hear from you. You are in charge of this investigation."

"I appreciate that." He smiled, stepping closer to her

and putting his hands on the rail of her bed. "I think we can make that work. I'll call my teams in and we can arrest the senator in the parking lot—away from Lily. They have already taken Steve into custody. He didn't put up a fight, and he has been happy to talk."

"That's surprising." She chuckled gently, as though she wanted to keep her movement to a minimum in order to not disturb the sleeping child.

"Yeah," Grant said, smiling. "The only thing he was worried about was the stupid goat. He made sure that it was taken to the neighbor's house before he left. Sounds like he is going to give up everything—including the senator. He already told my team all about the senator hiring him and his brother—and how the senator was going to try and pin everything on them thanks to the falsified death threats."

"No doubt the senator has lawyered up by now," Elle said, rolling her eyes.

He felt exactly the same way. "I'm sure he has."

"Did Steve tell your team why the senator hired them? Was it his intention to kill the girls?" Elle whispered.

"I think he wanted his wife out of the way—they were having problems, she had even contacted a divorce attorney—but I don't know about Lily. From what Steve said, with the election coming up, Dean Clark was hoping to pull sympathy votes thanks to his wife's death. He'd already hired a publicist to handle the press and manipulate the public's opinion of him."

"So, he was planning on killing two birds? Using his wife's death to avoid public scrutiny and also to gain votes? He was pandering to the public's sympathies to win?"

"Are you really surprised? What won't a seasoned politician do to make people bend to their whims?"

"You have a point." Elle nodded. "If it turns out that he was planning on having Lily murdered, too, what do you think will happen to the senator?"

"Regardless of what he had intended, we will arrest him for a murder-for-hire plot, but what else the district attorney will go for is up to her—I'm hoping homicide gets added to his charges. The good news is that, no matter how good a lawyer he has, he will be going to prison. And if they prove that he was also planning on killing his daughter, then I'm sure he will likely never leave that prison."

"And what will happen to Lily? Where does she go from here?" She hugged Lily tighter.

He sighed, knowing it was unlikely she was going to like the answer. "She will go into the care of CPS for now while they try to contact the next of kin. If they agree to take her, then they will be her legal acting guardians."

She nibbled on her lip. "I would ask that they go to Catherine's side."

He nodded. "I'll make sure to recommend that to protective services."

"I know that they have a large, distinguished family, so I'm sure they will take her, but I would love it if I could come and see her once in a while."

He reached over and brushed a strand of her brunette hair out of her face and pushed it gently behind her ear.

"You saved this little girl's life. She is alive because of your quick actions and unwavering efforts to find her. I'm sure that no one would have a problem with you seeing her. You are her hero."

She smiled and tears welled in her eyes.

"Elle, you're *my* hero." He smiled. "And I hope you know I love you."

She reached over and took his hand in hers. "You don't have to say that if you don't really mean it. It's okay. You don't owe me that."

"Elle, you know I say what I mean. And I may be slow to know my own feelings, but there is no question in my heart about how I feel about you. I *love* you. I know we haven't been together for all that long, but I can't wait to see where things go. And, as cheesy as this might sound, I can see being with you forever."

"I love you, too, Grant." She smiled, and a tear trembled at the corner of her eye. "And I can see loving you always. You are the man I've been searching for."

He leaned in and gently kissed her lips. "And you are the woman I can't imagine spending a moment without."

There was the sound of clicking, like toenails on tile, and then there was a knock on the door. Grant stood up.

Standing in the doorway looking at them, wiggling manically, was Daisy. She wore an inflatable tube-shaped blue collar, and the effect made him chuckle. The dog didn't seem to notice; she only had eyes for Elle. If anything, he could understand the dog's need to be near her.

"I hope we're not interrupting," Zoey said, smiling. "But someone needed her mom. She's been whining ever since we left the vet's office."

Elle smiled widely. "Oh, Zoey, thank you so much. Is she doing okay?"

Zoey nodded. "She has a few stitches and will have to wear the inflatable collar for a while to make sure she doesn't get at her stitches, but she will be fine."

"What about the other dog?" Grant asked. "If she doesn't have anyone, I have a buddy who has been looking. We can get her a home."

"That would be perfect." Zoey smiled. "And speaking of home, Elle, you are welcome to come back to our team whenever you and Daisy are ready." Zoey let go of the dog's lead.

Daisy was a black dart as she charged past him and jumped into the bed beside Elle. She lay down and started licking Elle's face wildly, nudging Lily awake.

Lily opened her eyes and smiled at Daisy. Just when Grant had thought there was no sweeter sound than hearing Elle say, "I love you," Lily started to giggle. He had never experienced a moment more pure or entirely perfect, and in the sound, he knew he had found his future.

* * * * *